ANITA FAULKNER writes warm and witty romcoms from her upcycled bureau near the Cotswolds. Described by her agent Kate Nash as 'a sparkling new voice', Anita loves dreaming up quirky characters and extremely awkward dates. Her debut novel A Colourful Country Escape (remembered for those naughty peacocks) was shortlisted for two Romantic Novelists' Association awards. It was followed by The Gingerbread Café – which is too delicious to be missed. Anita is thrilled to share that her third romantic comedy novel, You Had Me at Pumpkin Patch, will be published by HQ Digital this August. It's packed with the same warmth and wit – and a whole lot of pumpkin antics.

When Anita's not scribbling notes for her next story, she's busy coaching other writers, running her friendly fiction writers' membership, Writers' Dream House, and getting excited about books in her Facebook group, Chick Lit and Prosecco. If you're a fan of books and stories, Anita would love to stay in touch! Come and join her mailing list for backstage news, the best offers and her exclusive monthly LOVE letters… https://bit.ly/anitafaulknerhotnews

YOU HAD ME AT PUMPKIN PATCH

ANITA FAULKNER

ONE PLACE. MANY STORIES

HQ
An imprint of HarperCollinsPublishers Ltd
1 London Bridge Street
London SE1 9GF

www.harpercollins.co.uk

HarperCollinsPublishers
Macken House, 39/40 Mayor Street Upper,
Dublin 1, D01 C9W8, Ireland
This edition 2025

1

First published in Great Britain by HQ,
an imprint of HarperCollinsPublishers Ltd 2025

Copyright © Anita Faulkner 2025

Anita Faulkner asserts the moral right to be identified as the author of this work. A catalogue record for this book is available from the British Library.

ISBN: 9780008781613

This novel is entirely a work of fiction. The names, characters and incidents portrayed in it are the work of the author's imagination. Any resemblance to actual persons, living or dead, events or localities is entirely coincidental.

All rights reserved. No part of this publication may be reproduced, stored in a retrieval system, or transmitted, in any form or by any means, electronic, mechanical, photocopying, recording or otherwise, without the prior permission of the publishers.

Without limiting the author's and publisher's exclusive rights, any unauthorised use of this publication to train generative artificial intelligence (AI) technologies is expressly prohibited. HarperCollins also exercise their rights under Article 4(3) of the Digital Single Market Directive 2019/790 and expressly reserve this publication from the text and data mining exception.

Printed and bound in the UK using 100% Renewable
Electricity by CPI Group (UK) Ltd

To Neil and Luca –

the two pumpkins who make my patch complete.

1

It was one of those crisp autumn days where surely *nothing* could go wrong.

'So you caught him googling *what*?'

Rosie winced at the sound of her friend Vix's voice, blasting through her phone's earbuds. Well, perhaps one thing *had* put her off her honey nut cornflakes earlier, but she wasn't going to let that ruin a lovely morning. Because this was the first day of her favourite season.

Rosie looked around, breathing it all in. It was brisk enough to wrap up snugly, even though the sun was sparkling. Gold and amber leaves fell like confetti, dancing around her as she crunched along the tree-lined street, past tall Regency buildings with balconies worthy of love scenes. She'd even treated herself to a warm cup of pumpkin-spiced latte, topped with ...

'Earth to Rosie.'

Rosie winced.

'Your voice trailed off and I missed the last bit. Then you went suspiciously quiet. Is everything all right with you and Cassius?'

She hadn't gone quiet. Had she? On second thoughts, it would be infinitely better if she didn't say *that* out loud anyway.

'I was *juuuuust* . . . admiring the particularly pleasant foliage.'

What perfectly decent people Google-stalked when they were bored was their business. Rosie herself looked up all sorts of weird things when she was researching her romance novels, even if her efforts had amounted to no more than a pile of cutting publisher rejections, because the romantic bits were *oddly lacking*.

Vix sighed. 'I'm sensing you don't want to talk about it. *Again.* Just promise me you'll keep your head out of the clouds, OK? I love that you often live in imaginary worlds. But please stay vigilant.'

'Mmm hmm,' Rosie promised, through a slurp of nutmeg and cinnamon deliciousness. Vix was starting to sound like her mum. *Stop daydreaming, Rosie.* Didn't they realise daydreams were the best place to be?

Rosie wriggled her way out of the doomed phone conversation.

Her oldest friend was wonderful, but sometimes it was handy that she lived seven hundred and ninety-eight miles away. Friends tended to ask a whole lot of questions about things she didn't like poking around at. Like her back catalogue of eye-wateringly unfortunate relationships, which had no bearing on her present one with Cassius. It was no wonder she often preferred fictional friendships.

Anyway, she had work to do.

Lifting her chin, Rosie kicked onwards through the leaves, steeling herself for another morning at KJ Marketing where she worked as a content writer, creating articles and newsletters on the enthralling topic of dental health. It wasn't exactly her dream job, but she'd dropped by the bakery to grab swirly, orange-iced cupcakes, so at least she could enjoy the small rebellion of risking tooth decay as she mulled over the perfect description of fillings.

Rosie took a deep breath and pushed through the door of the dingy office. She was one of the early birds, as always. It wasn't actually her turn to sort the cakes this week, but the others always forgot, and there was no way stingy Kelvin would let them out before lunchtime. He timed them to the second and she was pretty sure he'd ration toilet roll if it wouldn't start a riot. Rosie shivered at the thought as she made her way to the main office.

'Rooooosie Featherstone.'

The hair on the back of her neck stood up as she heard Kelvin call her name. He tended to have that effect on people. Or maybe it was the use of her surname, which for various reasons, often embarrassed her.

'Yes,' she replied, as patiently as she could. Couldn't he even let her take her coat off? She put the latte and cupcakes down on her desk, yanked her already droopy ponytail, and mustered a smile.

'You've got lippy on your teeth,' he said, squinting at her mouth.

'Thanks for the self-grooming tips,' she mumbled into her hand. He was too self-absorbed to notice when anyone was being sarcastic, which with his wonky goatee and kipper breath, she definitely was.

'I'm not here to sort your life out. That would be a job, wouldn't it!' He laughed at his own attempt at a joke and tried to play-slap her on the arm.

Rosie sighed, her patience waning. Her life wasn't exactly where she'd expected it to be by her fourth decade, but she had somewhere to live and a steady job, and her current boyfriend hadn't been on *Crimewatch*. She was positively winning next to Kelvin.

'So . . . you called me?'

'Oh yeah, that. You're fired.'

Rosie froze, midway through shrugging off her coat. 'Whaaa . . . *what*?' She'd worked there diligently for ten years and had never broken a rule. She didn't nick the notepads or steal her colleagues' oat milk, and she definitely wasn't the sort who photocopied her backside for giggles. 'I'm sorry, what? What have I done?' Why was the room spinning? She reached out to try and grab something, but her hands were failing her.

'Ah, nothing really.' Kelvin tried another jovial slap on the arm. Rosie staggered backwards and landed in her chair, which made a tragic, fake leathery farting noise. She didn't have the energy to wince. 'You're not fired, as such. I just don't need you anymore. I'll make you redundant, or whatever. I've got a robot to replace you.'

Rosie's eyes darted, as though C-3PO might amble out of the kitchen looking all productive, and presumably not having a gale-force-nine emotional breakdown like she was about to. Maybe droids didn't moan about making the coffee either.

'Not an actual robot, you numpty. You know. A chatbot. Artificial Intelligence. AI. I can type a few words into this new Kimberkoo Chat software, and it will write anything I want, at the speed of lightning. Amazing, hey? The words just appear on my screen like witchcraft, and it doesn't cost me a penny.' He grabbed a wadge of papers from the top of a creaky filing cabinet and slapped them on the desk with a flourish. 'Just look at this article it wrote on the future of gum disease. It would have taken you hours to put this together, and you probably would have ballsed it up.'

Her throat tightened. *Ballsed it up?* She was good at writing.

Wasn't she? She snatched up the papers that he'd plonked on the desk like Exhibit A in the surprise takedown of Rosie Featherstone. Her eyes motored through the first half a page. 'But it sounds . . . like a robot.' She had to admit, it wasn't *terrible*. And it was hard to write about gum disease and make it sound bubbly. But somehow, the thought of a computer program taking over from real people – impassioned, creative writers – gobbled at her insides.

How was this even happening?

'When I write something, it's like a gift,' she heard herself saying. 'From my heart to the reader's. An expression of my soul.'

Kelvin screwed up his face. 'It's about periodontitis. What's that got to do with anyone's soul? I always did think you were a bit strange.'

Rosie gripped the sides of her chair and pushed herself to standing. 'I am *not* bloody strange! And it's disingenuous, isn't it? Pretending it's written by humans and that it's heartfelt, authentic, honest. But really, it's just something puked out by a computer program. How is that right?'

'Like I said, it's just perio . . .'

'But where does it stop? Next, you'll get it to write your nan's birthday card, or impassioned words to loved ones, or your wedding speech, if anyone ever agrees to marry you.'

'Yep, it can do all of those things and more. They've got it writing novels, you know. I bet it could write those romance books you always drool over.' He nodded to the stash of well-loved paperbacks on the shelf behind her desk, which often kept her company on a quiet lunchtime, when she wanted to escape from the world.

Rosie's gasp could have emptied the room of air. *Writing novels?* That robot-worshipping stink bag. 'Love stories should be written by *people*. Laptops can't love. They don't know what it feels like.'

'Big expert on it, are you?' He tilted his head.

From his crooked smile and dustbin teeth, she wouldn't mind betting he was an expert on gum disease. But she wasn't rude enough to say that. She pursed her lips.

Kelvin held up his hands. 'Don't shoot the messenger. Technology is better at some things than us. Artificially intelligent software taking over from mediocre writers is the future. Get over it. Go and find something you're *actually* good at. Make yourself irreplaceable, as Beyoncé would say. Like me.'

The words caught her in the breastbone like the sharp jab of a knife. Words had power – especially when they came from the mouths of mean people. Goodness knew whether *software* should be left in charge of them.

'Anyway, I'd usually get my money's worth and make you work your notice. But Kimberkoo Chat is quicker and better, and it doesn't use up all my pumpkin spice or try and tart up my office with autumn-leaf bunting. You can take that crap with you, by the way.'

The painful words twisted a little deeper, even if the look on his annoying face suggested he thought he was doing her a favour.

'And let's face it, you always were a bit of a spare part. I mean, you're welcome to stick around and do the cleaning, or something. The bogs are in a right old state. And I think we've run out of loo roll . . .'

Spare part? Bog roll? Rosie felt her jaw clench. She was not hanging around for any more of his verbal bottom trots. Kelvin was probably breaking all sorts of employment laws, and she was sure she had rights. But just then, she had no desire to stick around or fight to spend another excruciating minute there. He could shove his stupid job where the toilet brush didn't shine.

She charged around her desk, scooping up her precious romance novels, and the bits and bobs she'd brought in to make the place look loved, piling them into her oversized handbag. Then with only the tiniest pang of guilt, she grabbed back her cakes, because she absolutely needed them. He could keep her cold latte.

'I'm actually not bad at writing,' she huffed over her shoulder as she marched towards the door. At that moment she wasn't quite sure she believed it, but she wasn't admitting that to a bad boss in a sweaty tracksuit. 'And I won't be outdone by a robot.'

Rosie stomped through the creaking doors of KJ Marketing and out onto the street, acutely aware that she *had* in fact been outdone by a robot, or whatever the hell Kimberkoo Chat was.

The autumn chill hit her in the face in a way that hadn't bothered her just minutes before. Tears were stinging her eyes, and she could barely make sense of her thoughts – but somehow, her body took over. One foot in front of the other, faster and faster until she knew she was on her way back to the flat. Her hands tore at the cupcake box, splitting it open and shoving one into her mouth to soften the blow. She didn't care that icing was smearing around her cheeks or that she was blubbering like a two-year-old over ten wasted years, working for someone who thought she was distinctly average and would replace her in a heartbeat. She just had to get home.

Home to the safety of Cassius, who'd be quietly working at his desk, but ready to jump up and give her a big, compassionate, human-sized hug. What she wouldn't give for one of those. Because some things could not be done better by a robot.

2

Rosie was chomping her way through her fourth cupcake by the time she realised that iced treats *probably* weren't the answer. But nobody could blame a girl for trying.

The cold air continued to sting her face. With her nose running and her mind racing, not even the rich colours of autumn had a hope of calming her. She was giving herself a pep talk about *not* being a crummy 'spare part', when she turned the corner of the road they called home.

It was Cassius's flat and had always been too flashy for her taste. It was all white and glass with too much stainless steel like somebody was about to perform an autopsy, and she'd probably never get used to everything being voice-activated. But Cassius was gorgeous in a techy-nerd kind of way, with his slightly wonky glasses and the way he got excited about the latest new digital thingamabob. And he was sweet with her. He hadn't batted an eyelid when she'd introduced colourful throw cushions, and that robot vacuum cleaner he'd bought her was super handy, even if it wasn't the most romantic of gestures.

But despite not being her choice of living space, their flat on

Cybourne Road had been a sanctuary compared to the Regency townhouse where she'd lived with her family since her sort-of once fiancé James had died. Living with the Featherstones had been like existing in a Cheltenham version of *Made in Chelsea*, with her mum Farrah and half-sister Flick casting themselves as party-girl socialites. As much as she loved them, next to those two Rosie had always felt like a gnarly pumpkin at a ball.

Rosie battled with her key in the lock of the flat's main front door, which had never seemed to like her. '*Here*,' Cassius would usually say, leaning in to help her and managing first time. She gave a tiny smile through her mouthful of crumbs. She just needed that hug and a day of sobbing on the couch watching reruns of *Murder, She Wrote*. She'd always wanted a typewriter like Jessica Fletcher, and at least *somebody* would never employ Artificial Intelligence to write her words.

The lock finally gave in, and Rosie shoved the door open. Maybe she'd have time to call the maintenance person, now she didn't have a job to go to. Although Cassius would probably suggest replacing it with something eyeball-activated. She exhaled, feeling the weight of the morning's shock still heavy on her chest. Her role at KJ Marketing hadn't been the best of jobs, but it had been *hers*. One of the few constant, stable things in her life, for ten whole years. It had seen her through her grief with losing James in that horrific, unexplained cactus accident seven years ago. Working for Kelvin had never exactly been dreamy, but having her role ripped out from under her had come as a huge, earth-wobbling shock. Maybe she was suffering with some bizarre version of Stockholm syndrome.

As Rosie stood under the ultra-bright false lights of the communal hallway unravelling her scarf, she wondered if she'd even manage to get another job as a writer if Artificial Intelligence was the future. Surely there would be far fewer positions and a lot more competition. *Mediocre*, Kelvin had called her. Another sting of tears hit the backs of her eyes.

Thirty-six years old, living in her boyfriend's flat with a door that didn't want to let her in, no job, no prospects, and her only ever hope at getting married had been squashed by a giant prickly pear. Was that really the size of it? She sucked in a jagged breath and wiped the cake icing from her cheek. No. She still had Cassius, and their relationship was promising. He wasn't wanted in four countries like the ex who'd popped up on *Crimewatch* for impersonating a lollipop lady, nor did he have a penchant for stuffing toy dogs with stolen knickers, like Dingo Dave. She and Cassius had a happy future ahead of them, and as far as work was concerned, she'd sort something out. She was like a piece of toast that always landed butter side up. Well, at least after a few attempts, and a bit of picking off carpet fluff.

She navigated the lift, trying to ignore the irritating voice of robot lady, who seemed to be stuck on a '*doors closing*' loop. 'Perhaps when one door closes, another one opens,' Rosie told the tinny voice. Yes, today could only get better, couldn't it? Once she stopped trying to make friends with the lift computer, that was.

Rosie reached the front door of their flat, which Cassius had set up with swipe-card entry, even though her sister had once managed to get in with her Black Amex, and Rosie's Boots store card would sometimes do the trick. She swiped herself in and stepped into the hallway, which was dark compared to the brightness of the communal parts. Perhaps Cassius had popped out.

'Ouch.' Rosie looked down to see she'd stubbed her toe on a gigantic cardboard box in the hallway. How hadn't she noticed it? Well, it hadn't been there that morning. Had it? Rosie put down her bag and squinted at the packing label. It was addressed to Cassius, and he'd opened it already. Probably the latest bit of tech from somewhere or other. The way her day was panning out, at least the box was big enough for her to hide in.

Rosie wasn't in the mood to negotiate lighting with the voice-activated thing that Cassius called Serena. Serena might only be a piece of smart technology, but she did not like Rosie and had a canny way of delivering the exact opposite of whatever Rosie wanted. So she kicked off her boots and paced towards the bedroom to hang her coat.

'Need anything, Zoe?' Serena chimed sweetly from the speaker in the corner. Who was Zoe? Probably another of 'smart' Serena's jokes.

'A break from annoying robots trying to take over my life?' Rosie whispered, because there was no point in infuriating her.

As she reached the bedroom door, Rosie stopped. What were those unexpected sounds, emanating from inside? Another of Serena's not-so-funny capers? Serena could definitely play romantic music, even if Rosie had never heard *that* tune before. Could she replicate Cassius's voice too? And what was that odd grunting, interspersed with a cat-like whimpering? Cassius wouldn't even let her have a cat.

Rosie put her ear to the door, her heart beginning to beat hard in her ribcage. Was she about to inadvertently burst in on a grunty cat burglar who liked stealing stuff to the sound of the saxophone? She grabbed a steel vase from a nearby shelf. It would be a handy defence if they tried to attack her.

The dodgy cat noise came again, but louder this time. Like it was . . . excited? But the swoony sax music kept drowning it out.

Hang on. Wasn't Cassius quite partial to a bit of woodwind? Was he in there doing something reckless with the neighbour's moggy? Rosie gasped. That would be one thousand times worse than *Crimewatch* guy. Cassius would never do that. Every part of her wanted to run for her life, but she had to prove to herself that she was thinking nonsense – and she really did need to put her coat away.

And then Vix's words from earlier that morning came back to her. *'Please stay vigilant.'*

What were her vigilant eyes about to see?

Rosie took a deep breath, steadied herself, and barged the door open, clinging to the sturdy vase with one shaking hand.

'Aaaaaaaah!'

Rosie wasn't quite sure who was screaming. Maybe it was all of them. All of them being herself, Cassius . . . and whoever the hell was lying across their bed unclothed with her legs in the air, as though she was riding an upside-down bicycle.

Was it a *who*? Or was it a *what*?

Rosie screamed again, feeling like she was on the world's most horrific fairground ride, and she was desperate to make it stop. The metal vase fell from her hand, crashing down onto her toes. Pain seared upwards. The vase bounced across the wooden floor, in near slow motion, each landing making a deafening crack. Naked Cassius rushed towards her, looking more scrawny and awkward than she'd ever seen him. She jumped backwards, pushing her hands out to keep him at bay and praying her fingers didn't touch anything hairy.

All that commotion, yet upside-down cycling *woman* hadn't flinched. She simply lay there, emitting the strange sexy cat noise, and groaning *'Cassssssiuuuus'* like he was taking her to dizzy feline heights when clearly, he wasn't.

'What are you doing here?' Cassius tried to usher Rosie out of the bedroom, as if there was absolutely nothing odd to see.

'What am *I* doing here? What about *that*?!' Rosie pointed behind him.

The thing whimpered again.

'Deactivate, Zoe.'

So that was who Zoe was. Well, Serena was quick at learning names when she wanted to be.

'You gave it a name?' Rosie hissed. She could only assume it wasn't human, as much as its naked pink body had been crafted to look freakishly person-like. *The thing* had arms, legs and remarkably good boobs, now she came to gawp at it. It had a much better figure than Rosie had ever managed and was obviously good at staying in uncomfortable poses. Maybe it could write goddamned novels too.

It was abundantly clear that when she'd spotted Cassius internet searching sexy robots over his breakfast bagels, that hadn't been the first time – and he hadn't stopped at window shopping. To think she'd naively believed he was just curious about the latest technology. And with what he'd been doing with his purchase, there was little chance of a refund.

Zoe made a robotic deactivating sound, pulling Rosie back to this terrifying version of the present.

'What I'm doing here,' Rosie continued, 'is coming back to hide from life, because stingy Kelvin has replaced me with a robot. Much like my appalling *ex*-boyfriend.'

They were standing in the doorway of the bedroom, trying not to look at the unfortunate tableau inside.

'A robot?' Cassius scratched his head. 'A robot writer?'

'Not a physical robot, you computer-shagging buffoon. One of those Artificial Intelligence things. A *chatbot*. Presumably it's better at stringing words together than your new cat-whimpering girlfriend.'

'Ahh, a chatbot. They're not really robots at all. AI is *software*, not . . .' His voice trailed off, as though acutely aware that the next part was ill-fitting for the situation. He covered his groin.

'Hardware,' Rosie finished, with a weighty sigh.

And with that, she marched into the room, pulled a holdall

from under the bed, and began throwing essentials into it as fast as her arms would allow her, trying her best to ignore robot woman and her particularly supple limbs. It seemed Rosie was a '*spare part*' even in her own bedroom. Perhaps her crappy boss had been right. She was easily replaceable, like some kind of minor character in the story of her own life. Didn't everyone deserve a chance at playing the heroine?

'Can't really blame me,' she heard Cassius grumbling, somewhere behind her. 'You're still clinging to the fantasy of that dead James bloke. At least Zoe has a bit more life in her than him.'

'You bloody loser,' Rosie yelled as she slung her bag over her shoulder and left the room. If she'd ever compared him to James, she'd been right to conclude that Cassius would never measure up.

When she reached the hallway, she spied the huge box again and felt her heart plummet. So that was what the *special delivery* was all about. How had she seen this woman-sized box and not put two and two together? Was her head actually in the clouds? She gave the robot's empty box a swift hip barge, because that seemed like the best revenge she was going to get. A small collection of envelopes that she hadn't noticed before fell off the box and floated to the floor. The day's post. She pulled out anything with her name on it, only half-registering the bright orange envelope with the handwritten address that on any normal day would have stood out like a big sore thumb. But today was not a normal day. She shoved the mail into her pocket.

It was time to get out of there. Rosie had no idea where she was going, but one thing was clear. She needed to get as far away from civilisation and disrobed robots as her clapped-out Citroën would carry her. Which probably wouldn't be far enough.

3

'Come on, Doll. Surely you can get us a bit further away than *this*?'

Rosie wanted to scream and cry and kick things like she was a very cross donkey, even though she had not been brought up to use nice boots as weaponry. Her eyes had just witnessed things that no respectable sensory organs should ever have to see, and yet another relationship had disappeared down the slippery slope to doom, because she'd opted to ignore the blindingly obvious. And all her hopeless car wanted to do in support was conk out.

Thanks. A. *Bunch*.

Rosie unfolded her body from the vehicle, her unsavoury mutterings making the cold air foggy. She'd only made it about fifteen miles into the countryside before her car had all but said *'You're on your own, love'* before coming to a spluttering stop.

She knew it was hopeless trying to bargain with her little old banger. She'd only bought the ancient green Citroën Dolly to clash with the pristine white Range Rovers that her mum and sister proudly parked outside the townhouse she used to share with them and her comparatively sweet stepdad, Giles. Her mum had called it *that dreadful green gooseberry*, which had made Rosie's inner rebel sing. Childish, but true. And who wanted to be a grown-up?

Rosie tried to give the car a shove from behind, although she knew it was pointless. You needed two people for a jump-start, and it seemed Rosie was now a one-person show. Her heart sank, which she'd come to realise was actually a thing. It had felt heavy since she'd been drop-kicked from her job, then had been forced to flee from her android-bonking boyfriend, dragging her emergency belongings and huffing obscenities that would have made a pirate blush.

How was this happening to her? And what the hell was she going to do?

She'd spent the drive yelling angry song lyrics at her windscreen and trying to erase the horrific images from her mind, but it was likely they'd be etched there for all eternity. Even lying on her latex back with her legs in the air, Zoe was doing a better job of winning at life than Rosie was.

She shook her head to dislodge the awful scene, because what was the point in taunting herself? Now she was here. Wherever *here* was.

Rosie pulled her coat tighter against the unseasonable chill. She was in a country lane somewhere in Gloucestershire, in the Cotswold hills. And although Doll hadn't transported her as far from the robot-induced Armageddon as she would have liked, in contrast to her dreadful morning, there was almost the faint promise of peace here – other than the steaming green car and the fumes that were still quietly emanating from her head. She took a few breaths to calm herself. At least she'd been able to chug into a parking spot and hadn't fizzled out in a winding country lane leaving a tailback of beeping tractors or angry sheep. There were *some* small mercies. It was almost as though old Doll was willing her to stop here and take in the view.

Now she came to look, the scenery below was almost magical, if she'd been in a better mood for it. A blanket of mist hung low through the deep green and autumnal gold valleys, a few smatterings of Cotswold stone houses hugging together in what she guessed were small villages. Hills rose up around her, clusters of trees on their tops. The fields seemed to cascade down the hillsides, a patchwork blanket of shapes and shades, divided by ancient stone walls and gates.

There she was, a town girl in a peacoat, perched somewhere in the middle. She hadn't come far – but in that moment, it would have to do. Rosie moved around the car, narrowing her eyes at its frontage. Not that she'd ever admitted it out loud, but she'd always had the feeling that Doll's front view was like a face. The two bulging headlights were the eyes, and the grille at the front looked just like a mouth. Right then, she could have sworn Doll was winking at her. A car, winking? It *had* been a pretty weird morning.

Rosie put her hands on her hips. 'I don't find you funny. And we're going to have words about this later on.'

As tempting as it was to crawl into the boot and hibernate until at least next century, it was time to find help. Her phone battery had died on the journey, which she should have been annoyed about. Yet part of her gave an internal cheer that *hardware* wasn't as all-powerful as it thought it was, without a human to plug it in.

Had Rosie landed in the outskirts of Stroud? Doll was far too antiquated for satnav – not that Rosie would have been in the mood to consult it, as she'd zoomed away from the scarring sexbot fiasco. She'd had no real plan, other than to bolt.

Rosie grabbed her holdall containing clothes, her laptop

and essentials from the boot, half-registering the bags of stuff for charity that hadn't quite made it to a shop, even though she was definitely charitable. Then she locked up Doll and made her way along the country lane on foot. Her toes felt bruised inside her boot after dropping Cassius's stupid vase on it. It had taken all of her composure not to clonk him on the nose with the thing – although adding a police officer with handcuffs to that surreal bedroom scene would not have improved her day.

Rosie limped along the quiet country road, trying not to snag her beige coat on the hedgerows, realising she should have checked her face. Her sobs had no doubt left her with mascara cheeks, and she'd given up trying to readjust her sad ponytail. Much to her mum and sister's disappointment, she'd only ever half cared about looking well groomed.

Why were there never enough toilets in the countryside? Rosie felt like she'd been walking for days with her heaving bag, even though it had probably only been about ten minutes. She was bursting for the loo, her foot was throbbing, and she could really do with a cup of something warm for her nerves. There hadn't been a single car or person. Where was everyone?

She stuffed her hands into her coat pockets, wondering if some of her coldness was caused by shock. Her fingers brushed against the collection of now crumpled envelopes that she'd grabbed on her exit from the flat, and she pulled them out. Probably bills. Urgh. Not that she had a job to help pay them, or even a roof to live under unless a car counted as a fixed abode. Surely, they weren't all bills? She deserved *some* positive news today. What was this orange one? She stopped and pulled it open, noticing it smelt of a perfume that was oddly familiar, even if she had no idea why.

The letter inside was handwritten, on orange paper too.

Anyone would think it was a love letter. But as her eyes devoured it, it became clear it was anything but. Her mouth dropped open.

Oh *God*. A whirlwind of emotions spun through her, twisting her insides and making her want to yell with the stupid, frustrating pain of it. Was this some kind of crass joke? Hadn't she been through enough today? She shoved the note back into her pocket. Because somewhere, deep inside her, the words registered as something she'd long suspected but didn't have the courage to admit. And after everything the world had fired at her that morning, one more truth bomb might sink her.

She felt herself wobbling and thrust out a hand. All she got was a prickly hedge ... and a voice?

'Rachel?' A woman bustled out of an overgrown entranceway and made Rosie jump. The woman glanced at her watch and tutted. 'You're a bit bloody late.'

Rosie blinked back the tears that she really hadn't invited, and glanced behind her for a Rachel, even though it was obvious there was no one else around. 'No, I . . . I'm Rosie,' she stuttered, forcing up her reluctant shoulders as much as her holdall would allow. If nothing else, her mother had taught her not to blubber in public.

The woman screwed up her face, as if she was trying to remember something. She reminded Rosie of the squat, scary-looking woman from that film *Misery*. The one who'd kidnapped the writer and bashed his legs with a sledgehammer to make sure he wrote a novel without escaping. That would be just about her luck today. Rosie shook her head. The writer in her always did have an overactive imagination.

'I was sure he'd said Rachel,' the woman continued, scratching her head. 'But he's a forgetful old beggar, and I ain't much better. Well, you'd better come in and I'll show you around. I'm rushed for time now. Let's go.'

The woman beckoned her with an urgent hand and turned to walk away.

'I'm not sure . . .' There was clearly a mistake, and Rosie *wanted* to explain herself. But she was also desperate for a wee, and perhaps she could ask to use a phone. And anything that distracted her from the contents of that letter could only be a blessing. As she plastered on her brave face and hobbled around the hedge and into the opening of the entrance, she spied a huge, ramshackle house that would surely have room for at least five toilets.

'Teapot's warm,' the woman shouted back at her. 'I'm not one for idle chit-chat over bone china, but you look like you need something hot before you keel over. Nerves got to you, or something? Anyway, I'm not having the death of an employee on my hands.'

An employee? But there was no time for questions. The woman marched off along the dirt track towards the big house. And there would be a *cup of tea* at the end of it. It wasn't quite a pumpkin-spiced latte, but what she wouldn't give for that ritual of calm, right then. The small, cup-shaped thought filled Rosie with a flutter of hope after the worst morning ever. There would be plenty of time for explanations when they got to the house. Although maybe she should get her jittering hands around that cuppa first.

As Rosie limped past the partially overgrown wooden sign at the entrance, she noticed the name carved into it. *Autumn Meadows Farm*. She probably shouldn't follow strangers onto unknown land, when not a soul knew where she was. It had Scary Hostage Situation written all over it. Though quite honestly, Rosie didn't think her morning could get any more atrocious than it had already. What was there to lose?

4

'I'll put your tea in a flask. Chop chop! No time to hang about like bats.'

Rosie did her best to keep up with the older lady, as she swept down the dirt-track driveway like a whirlwind in a wax jacket and welly boots. If she'd been hoping for a bit of sympathy with her sweet tea, it didn't look like she was going to get it.

They were almost halfway to the tumble-down house when Rosie saw him. She had to blink a few times to check she wasn't imagining him.

His long, dark hair was tied back from his face, which looked kissed by the sun and nature's elements, but rugged in a way that made Rosie's breath catch. It was like watching a wild, untamed beast as he heaved his way along the path with a stern determination, and actually grunting. Though, in fairness, she might have done the same if she'd been carting *that* on her back. It was a pumpkin. A ginormous orange one, which looked like it belonged in a prizewinning competition and would have squashed most people like a pancake. Who even grew them that big? And why? Well, at least someone was playing the alpha role in their own story, and she was already doing her best not to cast him in one of hers.

Seeming to sense someone was staring at him, the man, who was probably a similar thirty-something age to Rosie, stopped to look up. His eyes were like the darkest shade of wood, and Rosie instantly wished she knew more about trees so she could put a word to them. As they met with hers, she had the overwhelming sense she wanted to write a thousand words. About eyeballs? She shook herself off and cleared her throat. Her wayward writer brain was playing tricks again. *Walnut* would do. It was rude to ogle strangers. The walnut-coloured eyes narrowed at her and then darted a look towards the woman in charge, who was now at the door of the house.

'Come on, Rachel. You're already late!'

'No, it's . . .' Rosie didn't have the energy to shout.

Walnutty pumpkin man grunted again and strode off, still carrying the world's largest squash as though it was a perfectly normal pastime. Maybe it was, at Autumn Meadows Farm.

Rosie was soon inside the house, and after she'd reiterated that her name was Rosie, her host introduced herself as Agnes. On closer inspection, Agnes still looked worryingly like the woman from the film *Misery* – although in truth, she seemed brusque rather than mean, and Rosie hadn't yet spotted any sledgehammers. After a bit of huffing, she'd even let her use the ancient downstairs toilet.

Now she'd done that, of course, Rosie knew she should ask to use a phone to call the car breakdown people and be on her way. Though in all honesty, she had no idea where *her way* was. She couldn't face being towed back to the family home, with her half-sister, Flick, gawping and saying, *'I told you Cassius was a nerd-geek.'* The curious inside of the farmhouse was more intriguing – and there *had* been mention of tea.

'Come on, come on. Let's not dawdle.' Agnes ushered Rosie towards a tattered curtain that hung in a doorway, and they ducked past it, into a kitchen.

The kitchen was a jumble of mismatched furniture and yet more pumpkins – of all sorts of strange sizes, colours and knobbly shapes. Rosie was a big fan of autumn and those cosy baskets of tiny pumpkins you saw in cute deli shops and cafés, but these were something else. She had never seen such an array of them. Some were pretty shades of amber, peach and fiery ginger. Others were unashamedly warty and bordering on gruesome – yet there was something fascinating about every one. Her fingers itched to reach out and touch them, but fondling other people's vegetables might come across as peculiar. Or were pumpkins classed as fruit?

As she pulled her gaze away, she spotted something else that was curious, through the dimly lit room. Various sets of eyes were appraising her. They belonged to cats, and lots of them. Not unlike the pumpkins, they came in all shapes and shades, yawning on rocking chairs and stretching on worktops. Strutting across the broken floor tiles as though they were great kings and queens of who knew where.

'My strays,' said Agnes, who must have been busy filling a Thermos flask with the promised tea while Rosie was taking in her surroundings. She handed it to her. 'They keep me company.'

'Wise choice,' said Rosie, nodding her thanks for the flask. The place might have seemed a little unusual compared to what Rosie was used to, but she'd take the company of cats and misshapen fruit or veg over the tech-nerd hell she'd just stormed out of.

There was a loud mewing as one of the cats began swinging from the doorway curtain.

'Door fell off,' said Agnes matter-of-factly. 'Could probably get Zain in to fix it.' She tipped her head in the direction of the dirt track where they'd seen the guy hulking the freak pumpkin. 'But I couldn't put up with all the swear words and testosterone.'

Zain. So that was his name. Rosie imagined Cassius trying to replace the missing door with a swipe-card entry system, which didn't quite have the same appeal. Not that she'd found walnutty eyes appealing, of course. 'Sometimes you're better off without men altogether,' Rosie agreed.

Ruuuuffff. Rosie jumped, glad there was a lid on her flask. For the first time, she spotted a small, scruffy brown and white terrier curled up in his basket in the corner, his eyebrows raised at her.

'Apart from you, Onions. But you ain't no good with a hammer.'

With Agnes's Gloucestershire accent, the dog's name sounded more like Un-yunz. Even though Rosie's family spoke with an excessively well-to-do air, the local accent always made Rosie feel more at home. Rosie's own lilt was somewhere in between.

'He won't hurt you. He's as deaf as a post and he's only got three teeth,' said Agnes. 'And there are the others, of course.' She swept her arms around. 'Fourteen stray cats, six unfortunate mongrels and . . .' Before she could say the word, a chicken flapped through the kitchen. 'A whole lot of hens. The place has become an informal sanctuary for waifs, wild things, and anything that needs a home.'

Agnes gave Rosie a quizzical look, like she was wondering which of those categories Rosie might fit into. She wasn't far wrong.

'Anyway, you haven't got time for my sob story. We must get on. You carry your tea; I'll take your bag.'

And with that, Agnes grabbed Rosie's bag and bustled her towards the rear of the kitchen and out through a back door.

'I'll show you around the lake,' said Agnes, pacing off again like she wasn't the kind of woman who took no for an answer.

The lake? 'I really should explain,' shouted Rosie, hobbling to keep up. She still wasn't sure what this was all about, and she should really ask to use a phone and be on her way.

'Yes, yes. More time for your yapping when we get there.'

Rosie sighed and limped onwards. Well, the woman had her bag, which was stuffed with clothes and her laptop, and at least all of this was providing a welcome distraction from her Monday from hell. In this curious place she could almost forget all of that other stuff had even happened. In fact, she might get another glimpse of the gruff guy if she followed on. The more she thought of it, the more she could see him as the hero in a future romantic novel. And didn't a writer need to embrace a bit of bookish research?

5

They pushed their way through wild undergrowth and prickly bushes, Agnes taking it in her stride as though her frog-eyed wellies were on autopilot. Something told Rosie that this woman would push on through anything, and before Rosie knew it, she was lifting her own chin a little. Perhaps Agnes's no-nonsense determination was just the tonic.

The fresh country air was certainly working wonders in quietening Rosie's busy thoughts, and she couldn't help noticing the contrast from the false lights and busyness of town life. Though in the distance, she did see a glow of something. Adjusting her eyes, she could make out fields in all shades of autumn. They were filled with row upon row of pumpkins, in shades of burnt orange and warm maple, like something from a seasonal photo. To her wild imagination, they spoke of autumn hopes and Cinderella dreams, and she wanted to pause and soak it all in. But her host didn't look like she was in the mood to whip out her wand and play fairy godmother, and she certainly wasn't stopping.

With her bruised toes and heeled boots that didn't work in

the countryside, Rosie couldn't quite keep up. She'd never walked well in heels, but when she'd tried to sneak around the office in ballet pumps, Kelvin had told her off for wearing 'slippers'. After several fields of trudging, with Rosie never quite managing to get level with Agnes or get her to stop and listen, they arrived at a rickety wooden gate.

Agnes frisked her own pockets and seemed to realise they were empty. She shook the lock on the gate and tutted. 'Head like a sieve. Never mind, there's no going back.'

'Actually, I probably should,' said Rosie, taking a moment to gather her senses between worn-out breaths. She didn't know what was going on here, but she should put a stop to this burgeoning mistake and get going. There was no burning need to go snooping after Pumpkin Man or do impromptu novel research.

'Frogs don't jump backwards.' The woman looked down at her wellies. 'And nor should you.'

Rosie scratched her head. Didn't they?

Then, like a champion hammer thrower, Agnes threw Rosie's holdall over the gate. Rosie winced, hoping she'd bundled enough clothes around her laptop to cushion the fall. In hindsight, most of that stuff could have stayed in the car. Though if she was honest, Agnes was right about one thing: Rosie was in no rush to go back anywhere. Even this odd march through the cold and brambly countryside with a slightly scary stranger was more appealing. Maybe *ever onwards* was as good a plan as any.

Agnes climbed onto the gate, which creaked a little in protest. Before Rosie could work out exactly what was going on, Agnes had somehow swung her not unsubstantial frame over the top of the thing in some kind of wobbling gate vault and had landed swiftly on the other side. She waved at Rosie to do the same.

Rosie stepped back. 'No, I shouldn't. I mean...' She pointed in the vague direction of her broken-down car, which was probably a good few miles out of sight.

Agnes beckoned again. 'Come on, girl. Who's eaten your self-belief? If you're one of those employees who slacks off at the first hurdle...'

'I'm a very good employee,' Rosie heard herself bite back, even though she was not here to fight for a job she knew precisely nothing about. It was simply a matter of principle. She straightened herself.

'Glad to hear it. Now, prove it and get your short arse over this fence. I've got cats to groom, and this interview wasn't meant to take all day.'

'I'm not actually here for...'

'Shh! You're surely not going to be beaten by a pensioner.'

Agnes leaned over the fence to relieve Rosie of her flask, grabbed Rosie's bag from the ground, and began to walk off, once again leaving Rosie with little choice but to go after her – because now Agnes had her stuff *and* her cuppa. If she could just get her *short arse* over that gate.

'Honestly,' Rosie muttered as she climbed onto the first rung, trying to remember how Agnes had hauled herself over. Something to do with swinging one arm, and then a leg, and then... 'Ohhhhhh! Bugger it.'

Rosie crash-landed into a heap on the mud, which was not particularly soft on a cold day. Her bum cheeks felt it, and who on earth thought it was a good idea to wear beige? At least she'd got over the fence, which was probably the only thing she'd succeeded at all day. Maybe that was a good sign.

'Bloody nice try,' came Agnes's surprised voice, having turned back to face her. 'Didn't think you had it in you. Maybe you and your backside have passed the first hurdle after all.'

As Agnes began to chuckle to herself, Rosie felt one of those *laugh or cry* moments bubbling up inside her. She'd woken up that morning thinking she was going to have a quiet day at her desk with a laptop and a calorific cupcake. She'd ended up getting fired, eating all four of them and walking in on her boyfriend getting naked with a sexy android. Now she was on her sore behind in a field, with no idea what the heck was going on.

For reasons she couldn't explain, Rosie felt a ripple of laughter forcing its way through her. The sensation shook upwards from her belly and burst into her throat, taking her whole body by storm. Great tears of absurdity began rolling down her face and she was absolutely letting them. It was quite possibly the most cathartic, desperately needed laugh Rosie had ever experienced.

Agnes strode over, yanked her up by the arms and swiped the stray grass from her coat. 'I knew you were a frog,' she said, looking Rosie up and down as if she'd only just noticed how out of place she looked in her office clothes. 'Welcome to the country. You're not what I expected, and I'll have to have words with Farmer Wilbur about his unlikely recommendations. But nature doesn't judge.' She shrugged. 'And Agnes loves a trier.'

'Thank you,' said Rosie, even though she wasn't quite sure what for.

Then as she took a deep breath and straightened up, her eyes were drawn to something. It was impossible to miss it. *The lake*.

Parts of it were hidden by the autumnal wisps of bulrushes, but as she stepped forward to take a look, she could have sworn the sun came out in celebration, even though she hadn't seen a blush of it since first thing that morning. Much like the balm of the pumpkins in the far-off fields, the sight of the lake took her breath away. Its water rippled and shimmered, deep olive with hints of gold where the light kissed its tiny peaks. It seemed to hold a majestic stillness, even though under its quiet surface she guessed there must be life.

And suddenly, Rosie was imagining herself walking wildly along the wooden jetty under the warmth of a setting sun. Inviting depths, cool water fresh against her skin. Somehow there was laughter too, and the whistle of birdsong, and glowing pumpkin lanterns...

Rosie shook her head, because that was verging on ridiculous. Her cantankerous writer's head was having a field day. She could barely swim, and she'd never liked her fleshy thighs in a swimsuit. And who on earth were these people she could laugh and swim with? Perpetually shaking off acquaintances who asked too many questions and preferring the sanctity of books, she didn't have many close friends these days – or certainly none around here. Maybe she should break free from Autumn Meadows before any more strange ideas intoxicated her. Next thing, she'd be imagining Zain the walnut-eyed pumpkin carrier diving in, looking broad-shouldered and burly in a pair of swim shorts. *No.* Neither men, nor her choice in them, could be trusted one tiny bit. Her life had no room for any of that.

'Well now, the sun hasn't come out in days. Something around here likes you.'

As Agnes said it, Rosie heard movement on one side of the lake. Beyond the bulrushes, she caught the outline of the dark-haired, huffy man who she definitely hadn't just been imagining in Speedos. This time he was standing outside a log cabin, stripping off a lumberjack-style coat and kicking off his work boots in a way that made Rosie stare for just a little too long. What was wrong with her? There was nothing exciting about a man in a jumper. She shook her head. To her great relief, he disappeared inside the cabin without noticing that her eyeballs were inexplicably out on stalks. When she managed to peel her gaze away from the door he'd just closed behind himself, she noticed there was an almost identical hut on the opposite side of the lake.

'There's Zain again,' said Agnes. 'Zain Kay. He used to be a farmhand, back when my late husband farmed crops here. Zain's the only one who stuck around when the money ran out. That's life, I suppose.' She shrugged. 'He built the cabins himself, and I let him live in one of them. He grows the pumpkins. Speciality ones too, though he's very precious about them. He got some fancy seeds from America. Think he had family there, but he's very hush-hush about his past. And good luck getting your hands on his knobbly ones.'

Rosie's eyes widened. 'I certainly wasn't planning to . . .'

'Anyway, he doesn't like people and he's as moody as an ox without a turnip – but he's good with nature, so he probably won't kill ya.'

'Right,' said Rosie, unsure how to answer any of this, or why she wasn't running for the hills as fast as her dodgy boots would carry her.

Yet despite Agnes's odd revelations, she found herself following the woman around the lake, like this whole place had a pull she couldn't quite resist. Serenity. That was what she sensed here, and she couldn't say when she'd felt that last. An extraordinary awareness of peace that hugged Rosie like a coat and began to ease into her skin. She knew it was probably some kind of post-shock reaction after her traumatic morning. Her brain had surely released funny chemicals to help relieve the stress of having the bottom fall out of her world. And of course, she would explain to Agnes that she wasn't here for any interview, or whatever.

She definitely, absolutely would.

But what was the harm in soaking up some much-needed

tranquillity before she was forced to get back to her actual life? The one where she had no job, no home, and a long list of outrageous ex-boyfriends. And that was before she considered the contents of that dreadful orange letter, which for all she knew could have been scripted by a cunning chatbot too. Yes, her writer self was enjoying this distraction. Perhaps she needed it.

'The job comes with accommodation, of course. It's basic, but it does the trick. And it's the sort of thing some folk would pay a fortune to holiday in, even if it's just a glorified pile of old logs.' Agnes pointed towards the wooden hut they were approaching. It was the one at the opposite side of the lake to that *moody ox*, Zain, with his woody walnut eyes.

'Accommodation?' Rosie repeated.

Agnes turned and looked at her strangely. 'Well, you brought your stuff, didn't you?' Agnes waved the holdall that she was still holding hostage, even if she probably didn't mean to. 'If you take the job, you can move right in. No point in wasting more time.' She checked her watch again. 'Didn't Wilbur tell you nothin'?'

They were just a few footsteps away from the log cabin now, and Rosie had always wanted to see inside one of those things. She had no idea who Wilbur was, or even what this job was all about. But somehow, the frog eyes on Agnes's wellies were staring up at her. If frogs didn't jump backwards, surely it wouldn't hurt to bounce in and take a look?

6

The log cabin, which was apparently accommodation for whoever took the mystery job at Autumn Meadows Farm, fitted in so perfectly next to the lake it looked as though it was part of nature.

The hut's simple wooden construction had been stained a deep shade of russet, which blended with the oaky browns and burgundy reds of the bushes it nestled into. There were slatted steps up to its front door, and solar lights strung outside. Rosie could almost imagine them twinkling in the twilight, their reflections bouncing off the lake like fireflies. Not that she'd be there to see that, of course. As she looked up, she noticed the hut had one of those grassy roofs like she'd seen on pretty postcards. Maybe flowers would grow there, with a little encouragement. If it just had an awning, and maybe a little outdoor table and chairs for sunny breakfasts, and ...

Agnes poked her head out from inside the hut. 'You coming in, or what?'

Rosie blinked, glad of the disturbance from her incorrigible thoughts.

'Erm, I suppose.' What if Agnes had been in there unpacking her bag? She would need to intervene and end the charade, in case she accidentally ended up with this job, whatever it was. But she'd come this far on what was already an extremely odd goose chase. It would be rude not to have a quick look.

Inside the hut, there was barely room to swing a butternut squash compared to what she was used to – especially with Agnes taking up a good chunk of the floor. Though the space was surprisingly warm and inviting. It was just... *lovely*. She felt a wave of emotion rushing upwards and filling her throat, though she quickly swallowed it back. What was wrong with her today? She was not going to cry over a fancy log shed.

Yet the more Rosie moved, the more loveliness she saw. The interior had been painted a rich creamy colour and smelt gloriously like fresh wood. There were sheepskin rugs on the wooden floor, cosy blankets on the high cabin bed – which had been built into the wall like a grotto – and even a wicker basket of logs next to a wood burner. She imagined herself lighting a fire there and burning the stupid orange letter that was still in her pocket. Not that she'd be staying.

And was it a mirage, or was there an old-fashioned typewriter in that small workspace beneath the bed? A collection of partly melted pillar candles huddled close to it and Rosie tried to blink away the vision of herself writing there, in the peaceful semi-darkness. She could almost hear her fingers tapping at the small round keys, her romantic novel unfolding itself like magic. Something inspired by nature, with a lake and a wooden hideaway, and a strong, dark hero. He'd be called something like Zain or Cain, and would have dark eyes and carry huge pumpkins on his muscular bare back, looking brooding and moody...

'You all right?'

Agnes's voice broke through her daydream, which was just as

well. Her delinquent thoughts were about to steam up the windows.

'Mmm hmm,' she managed.

This whole place was like a hug on an autumn day, and goodness knew, Rosie could do with one – even if today she was particularly needy. She blew out a tense breath. Because with every passing minute, it was becoming worryingly more difficult to shake off the misunderstanding she'd been oddly acquiescing to.

'The last employee, Krista, decorated the place,' Agnes explained, thrusting the Thermos back at Rosie and motioning that she should drink up, as though she didn't have all day. 'Liked her home comforts but didn't have room to take it all in her backpack. Buggered off travelling with no notice and left me in the lurch. That's why I'm in a rush for someone to take over the wild swimming and get the place ready for the retreats this autumn. You know.' She made a shushing noise and lowered her voice. 'The pumpkin retreats.' She mouthed the P word like it was something taboo.

Pumpkin retreats? Rosie scratched her head.

'It's been a heck of a job to find anyone to sort these retreats. Did Wilbur tell you about my roof?' Agnes didn't wait for an answer. 'The house needs a new one before winter or never mind raining cats and dogs. It will be raining *on* my cats and dogs. My poor animal sanctuary will become a swimming pool. And cats don't like to swim.' She was wringing her hands now. 'You're our only hope of bringing in some money.'

Rosie could feel her story senses twitching. Something to fight for. The chance to be the heroine of her own life, rather than a forgettable minor character, always dumped or replaced. But no – that was beyond silly. And what on earth were pumpkin retreats anyway?

Rosie gulped. 'I'm sure there are other ways.' She tried to ignore the thought of drowning animals that was tugging at her heartstrings.

'This is the best we've come up with,' said Agnes. 'We've got to use what we have to make that money. No question. Wilbur said you were an expert at planning wild retreats with a very limited budget. *Extremely creative*, he called you. Then he came up with the idea of using the pumpkins as our ... what was it now ... UFO? BRB?' She huffed. 'USP! That was it. Our Unique Selling Point. He says people are going wild for these *autumn vibes* and pumpkin-spiced whatchamacallits. Photos in pumpkin fields and cooking marshmallows around campfires wearing pumpkin face packs and singing about the harvest moon.' She waved a hand. 'Or whatever. Your job to come up with something, you being the expert.'

'I don't really know about ...'

But her unlikely host wasn't letting her get too many words in. 'It's a miracle we found you. No time to waste.'

Agnes opened a cupboard and threw in Rosie's holdall like it was a done deal. Rosie's eyes widened. She tried not to think about the wooden lodge from that film *Misery*. This woman made a lovely cup of sweet tea and was surely not a hammer-wielding kidnapper.

'If we don't get moving with the plans, I'm going to have to sell off the land.' Agnes slumped backwards against the small copper sink. There was a hint of desperation in her eyes, and Rosie couldn't help but feel for her. 'The only buyer who's shown the slightest interest is some tech giant who wants to tear the place up to build factories. They want to make robot cats. Robots replacing real pets? Whatever next?'

Rosie felt every hair on her body stand on end. 'Whatever bloody next,' she agreed, even though she'd just had a good eyeful of what could well be *next*. Robot girlfriends and chatbots that nicked your job.

'There is one slight sticking point.' Agnes cleared her throat. 'Zain doesn't yet know about the pumpkin UFO. I mean USP.' She shook her head. 'And let's just say, he might not be over the harvest moon about it.' She waved her arm towards the hut on the other side of the lake. Rosie found her errant eyes following. 'He's not fond of crowds or fuss, and he's like a grizzly bear protecting its offspring if you try to get your hands near his big ones.'

Rosie blinked.

'Or indeed his little lumpy ones,' Agnes continued. 'He's very particular. Though I'm sure you youngsters could work it out. He's got a good heart under those funny tattoos and that hair that needs a good chop.'

'Tattoos,' Rosie heard herself saying, as images etched themselves onto the rugged skin of the bookish hero she'd just been imagining. They suited him.

Agnes shot her a strange look and then lowered her voice, even though the Zain guy definitely couldn't hear. 'Though he'd be even moodier if I had to sell the land to a bunch of tech folk. He doesn't even use a smartphone, and I can't see Cyber Purrz caring about his kooky crops or his bats. Not that I've dared to mention the threat of selling yet.' She shuddered. 'So it's in his interests for the pair of you to work together and not fight – even if the stubborn oaf doesn't yet know it.'

Agnes straightened herself. 'So, can I leave it with you? I trust Wilbur's judgement, and you seem respectable. A wild retreat expert, no less. And your lake swimming experience will come in handy. In fact, you'd be wise to pretend to Zain that your retreats are all about wild dunks in the great outdoors, until you dare to mention his pumpkins.' She gave Rosie another visual sweep. 'Though you may want to dress down a bit. Think Krista left some spare wellies and other crap in one of the cupboards, if you get stuck.'

'No, I . . .' Rosie gulped. It was high time she stopped trying on this fantasy life and made her confessions. The longer she left it, the more ludicrous it would be. She knew nothing about swimming or pumpkins or planning retreats, especially with *a very limited budget*. She was an expert in precisely nothing, and she certainly wasn't keen on bats, whatever *that* was all about.

None of this was her problem.

Yet she could feel a fizzing frustration at the thought of tech weirdness winning yet another battle. Then there were Agnes's poor cats and dogs, and she did love all things autumn. And her traitorous eyes must have been staring longingly at the typewriter whilst thoughts danced, and fresh ideas about running writing retreats started to bloom, uninvited, even if she was sure she'd once imagined them in one of her daydreams. Stupid, of course. But Agnes pounced on her apparent interest in the typewriter.

'Think Krista left some paper.' Agnes began opening cupboards. 'She used that thing to start typing up retreat plans. None of that Wi-Fi around here, you see. No outside world to trouble you. Pure peace. Though Wilbur said you were more into painting, not writing. I'm sure you could bring some of your artiness to the retreats too. Painting seasonal scenes and carving pumpkins around the lake.' Agnes gave her a buoyant clap on the arm, like it was a brilliant plan.

Rosie spluttered up the tea she'd been sipping. 'No! I mean, honestly, I don't think I'm the person you were looking for.' Enough was enough. She could not hang around here pretending to be a retreat-organising, wild-swim-conducting artist extraordinaire. She had none of those skills. What was she still doing here?

'Oh. You've changed your mind? Don't like the accommodation? The pay's not great, but it's enough to keep you alive and kicking. I'm not even fussy about proper references. Wilbur said you were good.' There was a tinge of despair in Agnes's voice.

'Well, I'm not good. I'm . . . *mediocre*.' Her ex-boss had said as much, and he hadn't even witnessed her attempts at swimming or holding a paintbrush.

Agnes shrugged. 'Aren't we all. Look, you're here now and I don't have time to find anyone else. It was a struggle enough to find you – you're our last chance. Just give it a go for a day or two. The swim ladies will be here on Wednesday, and I can't get in the water with my impetigo.' She scratched her leg, like it was an after-thought. 'And you won't catch Zain parading around the ladies in a pair of swim shorts.'

'Right.' Well, that was probably for the best, as Rosie had no desire to see any more male nakedness or have any more unbidden thoughts about strangers in Speedos this week. Or, in fact, ever.

Of course, she *should* explain that this had all been a terrible mix-up. Rosie knew that. Though it was getting trickier by the second. Now it would involve admitting to Agnes that she'd been drinking her tea and stringing her along for a whole hour, like some complete oddball. No. It would be easier to say the job wasn't for her.

Which she definitely would. Very, very soon.

But would it hurt to pretend to try it out for a day or two? Just to appease Agnes and prove she'd given it a shot. Then she could bow out politely before she got rumbled, and everything would be *fine*.

Rosie was needed here. *Wanted*, in fact. Even if it wasn't

exactly Rosie that Agnes had been expecting, and the real interviewee might still appear at any moment. Feeling needed, however fleetingly, was intoxicatingly good. Especially when she'd spent the morning facing the truth that in her own life, she was nothing more than a loser.

'There's running water,' said Agnes, turning on a tap that screeched and spluttered in protest. 'Just needs a bit of encouragement. And the electrics work some of the time. There's a bed. It's warm. I provide the food, as it's not so handy for shopping out here.' She pointed to a basket of supplies on the small worktop. 'And did I mention the peace and quiet?' Agnes was smiling with every single one of her teeth, even if it looked a tad frantic. 'Nothing better for your soul than the great outdoors.'

Well, Rosie's soul *was* in a mess. And she didn't have a bed to call her own. She couldn't face slinking back to the family townhouse, with her sister gabbling about her misfortunes to her fifty squillion Instagram followers, and her mum saying, *'I knew you always picked buffoons.'* Her car wasn't working. She had no trusted friends to call on, because she often distanced herself when people pointed out her boyfriends' flaws, and her ex-colleagues probably only liked her when she bought cakes. In truth, she'd never really felt like she'd fitted in with anyone, other than Vix, who'd rudely gone to live in Portugal when they were both in their teens.

Staying here and pretending to be the real interviewee for any length of time would be outrageous. *Obviously*. And she wasn't an outrageous person.

'Just one night. See how the place grows on you.' Agnes's voice was getting a little more desperate.

Just one night. Right then, the fantasy of hiding in a remote, Wi-Fi-free hut for just a little longer was luxurious compared to facing reality. On the other side of the farm's boundaries, she had nothing but a list of troubles. But here? Here there was a typewriter that was calling her fingers, and a log burner that needed logs. And that intriguing man in the hut across the lake...

So perhaps just a short while longer, then she'd leave tomorrow. Unquestionably. She could sleep on things and then get up, ask to use a phone, arrange something with the breakdown people and be on her not-so-merry way.

'Just one night,' she heard herself whispering.

'Great! Or maybe two. I knew you wouldn't let me down.' Agnes checked her watch again. 'Right-ho. Must be off.'

Rosie exhaled a long breath. Because she knew she would have to let Agnes down at some point. Perhaps she was *extremely creative*, like the person Agnes had been hoping for – but it had never amounted to much. She wasn't right for this job like she'd never been quite right for anything. And yet somehow, Rosie felt compelled to stay here. Just for one night. Or maybe two...

7

Rosie watched Agnes dash off around the lake, back in the direction of the wooden gate and the big house beyond. *Just a bit longer, and then, seriously, I have got to get out of here and face things.*

She clapped a hand over her forehead. What was she even doing? She was all but trespassing here. Masquerading as someone she wasn't, because it was marginally easier than confronting who she really was – a jobless, homeless *Raggy Dolls* reject. If Agnes found out she wasn't the potential new employee she'd been waiting for that morning, she might set her deaf dog on her or come for her feet with a *Misery*-style sledgehammer. And Rosie only had one set of un-bashed toes left.

Yet somehow, agreeing to stay here felt like the least surreal thing that had happened that day. If someone had told her yesterday that she'd be fired in favour of a chatbot, find her boyfriend naked with a robot called Zoe and spend twenty-four hours hiding out in a wooden hut, the part about the hut would sound the most likely. At least, that was one way of convincing herself that being here wasn't *completely* absurd.

Agnes had left her with a tatty guidebook to who knew what, before marching off in her frog-eyed wellies, insisting she had things to do. 'Zain's around if you've got any questions,' she'd said, in a slightly too breezy voice that suggested she didn't believe Zain would help her if her bum was on fire. In fact, Agnes's exit had been surprisingly sharp, as though she'd known loitering a moment longer would give Rosie the chance to change her mind and bolt. 'We'll talk more about the job tomorrow,' Agnes had shouted over her shoulder as she'd practically legged it.

Tomorrow. Rosie sighed and kicked off her boots. That would of course be the day when Rosie would say 'no thank you,' and be on her way.

She took off her coat and flopped down on the sheepskin rug by the wood burner, its soft fleece seeming to welcome her in. Her fingers wove themselves through it, as if trying to anchor her. Her whole universe had shifted, and here she was, clinging to a borrowed rug like it was a life raft, while her world still tremored. If earthquakes had aftershocks, that was where she was.

Although a thought kept tugging at her consciousness. Shouldn't she feel . . . *sadder*? She'd just lost everything that she'd thought made her who she was. And yes, she was wobbly and hurt, from her blackened appendages to her streaked mascara. She felt like she'd just done ninety minutes in a tumble dryer on an extra hot spin. Though she wasn't quite mournful. Was there something wrong with her? Why wasn't she *heartbroken*? Maybe losing James, and the collection of disastrous relationships that had followed, had numbed her. She let out a gasp. *Oh God*. What if she'd grown immune to love? Was that why her scribbled love scenes had been *oddly lacking*? No. That didn't bear thinking about.

Her eyes flitted towards her coat, the ludicrous orange letter still stashed in its pocket. Even the letter's contents hadn't completely floored her, as though some part of her had known the truth would always come for her. The truth about her deceased *sort-of* fiancé, James. Couldn't she just have one past relationship that remained sacred, without having it tarnished with suspicion?

But was the letter's author telling the truth, or was she simply a gold digger, hoping to nab the contents of *the box*, which Rosie hadn't even brought with her? She pulled the envelope from her coat pocket, registering again its faintly familiar whiff.

Her fingers toyed with it. She *could* read it again and try to piece things together. She could have her own Jessica Fletcher moment and attempt to solve the mystery of who was lying and who could be trusted.

Or she could just rip the damned thing up.

Before she had chance to change her mind, her hands quickly set to work. *Rip, rip, rip.* Such a satisfying tune. With a small chuckle that probably wasn't *that* maniacal, she threw the tiny pieces into the air and watched them land around her, now as flimsy as feathers.

There. That was how you sorted out junk mail. She'd faced quite enough problems for one day. Her heart feeling lighter, she crawled around collecting the torn shreds and throwing them into the unlit wood burner. Now that Rosie had no particular address, surely no more of these strange-smelling accusations could find her.

Now all she had to do was get her head straight and get ready to leave this place first thing in the morning. And above all else, not get any floaty, carried-away ideas about hiding out here, like her other real-life issues didn't matter.

Because she could already sense her writerly imagination settling itself in. She was a hopeless swimmer, and yet she was sure the shimmer of the lake had tried to charm her. Zain and his pumpkins wouldn't want her here, yet this cosy hut was doing its best to cuddle her in. And as for the call of that typewriter...

No. There would be absolutely no getting settled. She tried not to dwell on the fact that a hunk of 1980s Citroën metal was the only thing that would be missing her. Cassius wouldn't have told anyone she'd caught him with a sexbot and fled. He'd probably assumed she'd scurried back to the Featherstones, so he'd be happily entertaining Zoe. She was rather bendy, and Rosie definitely couldn't do the upside-down bicycle for *that* long.

Rosie huffed and stood. Nature called. Must be all that tea. She shuffled around the hut, opening doors – but all she found behind them were cupboards. Where on earth was the bathroom?

She consulted the tatty guidebook, which wasn't much help. 'Come to the house and grab food and supplies when you need them,' Rosie read. 'Cottage pie available on Wednesdays, and I sometimes do sausage and pumpkin hotpot on a Friday, though don't count on it. Likely the dogs will beat you to it. Or feel free to forage. No shooting.' Rosie let out a giggle, imagining Agnes's no-nonsense voice as she read. 'Spare toilet roll is kept at the house. And sawdust. Helps with the stink.'

The stink? Rosie sniffed the air. Everything smelt OK to her. Where exactly was she going to put this sawdust anyway? She'd only ever seen it used for guinea pig beds or to cover piles of vomit at primary school. This place got curiouser.

As she peered out of the window wondering if she'd missed something bathroom-like on the way in, she saw Zain darting out of his cabin. Surely he'd be able to explain the facilities?

Agnes had suggested he was completely unsociable, but there was something about him that made her story sensors twitch like a mouse's whiskers. Nobody was hostile for no reason. Maybe he'd be perfectly nice when you got to know him. Not that she'd be sticking around. She craned her neck to get a better look, but he was gone. And for some reason, she couldn't help getting up to follow.

'He might be scary, but my eyes can't possibly witness anything more terrifying than what I've already seen today,' she reasoned. And if he was already starting to inspire a character for her novel, she'd better get out there and poke around. Plus, she *really* did need a wee.

She eased her feet back into her boots and rescued her coat from the floor. It was time to meet her fellow lakeside dweller properly – even if they wouldn't be sharing a lake for long. He grew and cared for cute mini pumpkins, for goodness' sake. There was nothing at all to be frightened of.

8

'Aaaaaaaah!'

Rosie's hands flew to her mouth, trying to cover her own scream. It wasn't the first time she'd shrieked at a naked body that day, and perhaps she should have been covering her eyes instead. But somehow, she couldn't pull her gaze away...

'Who the hell are you?' the gruff voice belonging to the well-sculpted, muscular body responded, as he turned towards her.

And perhaps *he* should have been covering his private parts. But as rivulets of lingering shower water cascaded down his tanned skin, weaving through his twisting black tattoos and prickling his flesh into goosebumps, he made no attempt to hide his nakedness. He simply wrung out the water from his long dark hair, pulled an elastic from his wrist and wound his locks into a knotted bun. Rosie was vaguely aware she was scrutinising the streams of water that were snaking from his shoulders and making their way down his rippled chest towards his fairly substantial...

She gasped and turned away. Why had it taken her so long?

'It's cold,' the voice huffed again, as though trying to make excuses for the size of things.

From what Rosie had inadvertently seen, no excuses were needed. So this was what Zain Kay looked like close up. She hadn't meant for her *novel research* to have been quite so thorough.

'And you've had a good stare at everything now. Bit late to look away.'

'I was not staring.' Although she probably had been. It didn't seem like the time to explain she might put him in a book.

Anyway, it was surely impossible not to fully appraise your surroundings. It was basic human nature. You never knew when alpha-male nudity might pop up and pose a threat.

Though the only thing in crisis right then was her wildly beating heart and her red-hot cheeks. Not to mention the sudden influx of cave-woman hormones that seemed to be screeching *take him to your hut*. Which was, of course, ridiculous. She'd only ventured out to find a loo.

In her peripheral view she saw Zain reaching for a towel, and she heard the swoosh of it wrapping around his toned body. It seemed she'd stumbled upon him using an open-air shower behind some bushes, which was quite a lot more than she'd bargained for. She certainly hadn't set out to judge the best sculpted bottom competition. Although if she had . . .

'Find what you were looking for?' His voice interrupted her thoughts, which was probably just as well. 'You can at least turn and show your face, now you've witnessed every inch of me.'

She'd been trying her best not to count the inches. She straightened herself, took a deep breath, and dared to turn around, her boots skidding about in the mud. 'I was just looking for something. I got lost.'

'Thought you'd find it inside a running shower?'

'Well, what kind of person takes a shower in the middle of the day?' she replied, even though she knew that was none of her business. She had to say *something* to make herself seem like less of a nosy-eyed voyeur.

'Someone who has a job that gets them dirty.'

There was a spark of rebellion in his eyes, which were even more *deep, dark wood* on closer inspection. They sank into his square, determined face, and she found herself wanting to wander into them, even though nobody got that intrigued about eyes outside the pages of a love story. He could have been a model in some sort of burly farmers' magazine, all gruff-looking and at one with the land. Despite him now being tightly towelled from the waist down, Rosie decided his face was the safest place to look.

'We don't all keep office hours,' he added wryly.

His visual sweep of her work clothes sent a pang of annoyance through her. Her heels, that were sinking into the earthy ground beneath her feet, weren't doing her any favours. Why hadn't she grabbed those spare wellies?

'I don't work in an office.'

He grunted, like he didn't believe her. 'Then where do you work?' There was a tinge of suspicion in his voice. 'Are you trespassing? Because if you are . . .'

'No, I am not!' She jutted out her chin. 'I work . . . here.' Even he noticed the small gasp she let out after the last word. Why on earth had she said that? She did *not* work here. Was this her stupid compulsion to try and fit in rearing its annoying head? She'd be bringing him fancy cupcakes next. Though he looked more like he'd eat squash stew around a campfire. 'You saw me with Agnes earlier.' She waved her arm in the vague direction of where she'd seen him hulking a pumpkin.

'Work here doing what?' His eyes narrowed a touch,

although he was still playing it cool. In fact, Rosie wondered why he wasn't freezing his nipples off, seeing as he was dripping wet and only half covered. Perhaps he was like a Bear Grylls superhuman. Or more likely too stubborn to back down and find a jumper.

'Swimming things. And retreat stuff.' Oh *gossshhh*, what was she even saying? Rosie rubbed her forehead, wondering if it was too late to take that back. She was digging herself an idiot-sized hole. *Retreat stuff*? What did that even mean? At least she hadn't accidentally mentioned getting her hands on his pumpkins.

'Right. So you're Krista's replacement.' He exhaled sharply. 'She was a thorn in my arse too.'

Rosie blinked a few times, trying her best not to recall the sight of his particularly nice rear end, or to get even more flustered at the thought. This semi-bare man was doing all sorts of strange things to her, and even though it was all in the name of *novel research*, it really needed to stop.

Falling for mysterious men was Off. The. Table. She got herself in enough mess with the ones she thought were an open book, let alone a slammed-shut one.

Though somehow, she couldn't bring herself to walk away. And it wasn't the muddy floor that was gluing her.

Zain shook his head, clearly deciding to be the *bigger person*. He gave the shower tap a final crank to halt the last drops, stepped into some nearby work boots and moved towards her, like he was readying himself to pass. If she thought her heart was beating quickly before, his approaching semi-nudeness was setting off at least twelve drummers drumming in her ribcage – and it wasn't even Christmas.

'If you came for a shower, it's all yours. If you *work here*, we share it. Next time, you'd better yell if you don't want to see me naked.' He quirked an eyebrow, like the final bit might have been a question. 'Or listen out for the water, like any normal person.'

'I am normal!'

Zain stopped when he got level with her, turning his body towards her, his face tantalisingly close in the confined space. He smelt of cedar and spice and raging male nakedness, and she hadn't realised the last one had a smell, until that moment. It beat the hell out of Cassius, who in hindsight had always had a faint air of talcum powder and polos. Maybe this was what fresh pheromones smelt like.

Intoxication by way of human chemicals. That could be the only explanation for her legs feeling a touch wobbly and her skin tingling like a kaleidoscope of butterflies was on the loose. She felt her mouth opening as if it wanted to do who knew what, even though she had not given her brain permission. His breath felt warm against her face, and his eyes were almost reading her. Or perhaps that was her strange imagination again.

She shook her head to break free from her trance. It really was rude to stare.

'You're normal,' he repeated, as though mulling it over.

She knew that her cheeks must still be streaked with mascara, and her hair was only half tied in its ponytail, the rest having given up entirely. She probably looked like she was auditioning for a part in a ghost train, not here to do *retreat stuff*.

But he simply shrugged. 'Glad somebody is.' He turned and began to walk away.

'Toilet!' she yelled after him, instantly wishing she hadn't. 'I was actually out here looking for the . . . I need to . . . you know.' Smooth, Rosie. Very smooth.

'Over there.' He pointed, without turning back towards her. 'The sawdust is in a bucket outside.'

'Sawdust?' It had been mentioned in the tatty guidebook, but what was it for?

He sighed. 'Use the sawdust if you're . . . doing anything more than a pee. It's bad enough that I have to share the damned shower with you.'

'I see,' she said quietly, although he was off towards his hut, his discarded clothes now over his arm. Well, at least he hadn't been too descriptive over the toilet situation. Perhaps she was right that there was more to him than a grumpy guy in the wilderness.

And suddenly, her fingers were twitching. Not to touch him, of course. He was too far away now, and poking strangers was wholly inappropriate. She was a woman who should be nursing a wounded heart, with no time for wayward digits. No – her hands were trembling to type. A story was emerging in her mind, and she needed to get her thoughts on paper. Sometimes, it was the only way to stop them getting completely carried away.

9

Rosie had no idea it was possible to be a hot mess in such fresh autumn weather – but that's exactly what she was by the time she rushed back through the door of her cabin. She'd found the compost toilet, which lived in a cobwebby wooden hut that looked like it might fall down if you sneezed on it. The floor of the loo hut had nettles sprouting from its earthy ground, and she'd have to remember to take a toilet roll. At least she hadn't yet needed the sawdust.

Though it wasn't her foray with outdoor urination that was sending her whole body into a fluster. It was her first *up close and too personal* encounter with Zain. It was like she had entirely forgotten she was a red-blooded human until she'd set eyes on *him*. The way he'd stood in that open-air shower, barely fazed by the screaming, ogling woman, in no particular rush to cover up his nakedness. He'd seemed more bothered at her seeing the full length of his wet, dark hair than . . . well, anything else.

And though his body had looked almost sculpted from rock, with its twists of firm muscle and the pattern of black tattoos that laced down his arms and across his broad chest and back, she had a sense that even if he'd been standing there in a dressing gown and bobble hat, he would have emanated something impossible to ignore.

What was it about him, exactly? Yes, he was head-to-toe heavenly – and she'd even seen his toes. But she'd met plenty of attractive guys, especially with her mum and sister being such about-the-town social floozies. They knew everyone magazine-worthy within a sixty-mile radius, and her own previous boyfriends had all been reasonable-looking. Yet in all the time she'd spent with any of them, she couldn't remember feeling as hot, dizzied and alive as she'd felt in just a few minutes of Zain's moody presence. And there she'd been, panicking that life had numbed her. At least some parts of her were still sentient.

Or was she just fantasising? Was this her creative head taking hold of an awkward, embarrassing situation and turning it into some kind of sexy naked shower fest? She seriously hoped so, because with the day she was having, her poor, reeling mind had precisely no space for anything beyond a fantasy.

Rosie threw off her coat and moved instinctively to the old-fashioned typewriter, which lived on a small oak desk under the mezzanine bed. The tiny study area was nestled there like the cosiest writer's nook. As she ducked to sit on the pink padded chair, she felt something magical embosoming her. In her mind's eye there was stardust wisping around, whipping up ideas and sending energy to her fingertips. If a fairy godmother of writing had arrived in that moment, waving her wand and wiggling her hips to a charming Disney soundtrack, Rosie probably wouldn't have even blinked.

From her wild imagination to her excited hands, something special was happening. Like a conductor in front of an orchestra, Rosie's fingers knew the way.

'I'll show them my writing isn't *robotic*,' she whispered to herself, thinking back to all of those publishers who'd rejected her previous attempts at writing a novel. 'And that my words are better than something churned out by a chatbot.' With no internet out there, Kimberkoo Chat could go and *chatter off*.

She pulled some paper from the desk drawer and fed it into the typewriter. Usually, her writing sessions would begin with a whole lot of faffing. She'd make tea and prepare snacks. Light candles. Gather notebooks. Line up lucky gonks. All these things she would cling to, as though she couldn't write a word without the moral support of a pink-haired troll and three varieties of biscuits.

Yet today, there was no preparation. She noticed there were fairy lights strung around the writing cubby, but she didn't stop to flick them on. When the paper was ready, she began to type.

Rosie wasn't even sure what was spilling out onto the page. She vaguely registered there was someone not unlike Zain, who was now ingeniously called Cain. There was showering outside in the elements, surrounded by the glory of nature. Trees and water and birdsong. Nakedness and goose-bumped flesh and feelings she'd never quite experienced but was starting to imagine. Her fingertips felt like they were buzzing with inspiration, as did every single part of her. When she paused to remember intimate moments from her past, she couldn't recall ever having felt truly alive. Had things always been . . . *robotic*? Had she been no more animated than android Zoe, and her false, cat-like emissions?

She shook her head and rewound her thoughts back to the full, eye-watering form of Zain, and her creativity sprang back to life. In reality, the man was infamously grouchy, and he'd made it abundantly clear that she was another thorn in his bottom – but her imagination didn't care about that. Or maybe it liked him all the more for his lack of compulsion to people-please. No doubt he never felt obliged to buy toilet roll if it wasn't his job or laugh at his colleagues' mundane jokes, even if most of Zain's colleagues were probably pumpkins. What tonic was he drinking? Because she wished she could get a mouthful of that.

If she didn't keep her distance, Zain would no doubt quickly suss her out for being an impostor. He didn't seem like the type to care about throwing her under the Agnes bus for being the big porkie-pie liar that she was. Though again, her imagination had no care for harsh realities. Or perhaps it enjoyed the tingle of danger.

As she typed, her emotions pouring onto the page, the strangest thought began to emerge. She shook it away at first, because who would believe in such a thing? Yet it was almost undeniable. Here she was, writing in the now semi-darkness, words flowing from who knew where, like she was some sort of thing possessed. If she was willing to see magic wands and cloak-clad fairy godmothers in her mind's eye, perhaps she was going to have to accept this curious truth.

Zain was her muse.

Nooooo. Could that really be right? She stopped for a moment and scratched her head. Hadn't Virginia Woolf had a muse? And Shakespeare had apparently treated himself to a few. Not to compare herself to great bards, or anything. She had yet to write a manuscript that hadn't been scoffed at and stamped with '*get this crap off my desk*'. Even her attempts at writing about periodontitis were *mediocre*.

Maybe a muse was exactly what she'd been missing. Would she still be able to write if she wasn't around him? The panicked thought gripped her chest. No, that was silly. She'd be leaving here tomorrow, and she had no capacity for such concepts.

Rosie felt a growl in her tummy. It was probably the only sound she'd heard in hours, other than the rhythmic tapping of her fingers against the typewriter's keys. The peace out here was incredible. No car alarms or horns beeping. No jolly banter from pubgoers outside her window. It was no wonder Zain was so prickly at having to share his tranquil lake, because there was something to be said for solitude. It was like her very own writing retreat.

She checked her watch. It had been hours, and writers deserved food. There was a spell at work here, though even spells allowed time for tea breaks, and she was sure she'd spied cake in Agnes's basket of food.

Rosie switched on the fairy lights and desk lamp, realising typewriters didn't light themselves up like laptops. Perhaps she'd find matches for those candles too, although she'd have to be careful of the small wadge of typed manuscript that had now amassed. Even the sight of it filled her heart with glee. Some days it was hard to believe she was a *real writer*, when she'd been faced with publisher rejections and a boss who made her write about rotting teeth.

But here in this moment, she had the tiniest sense that anything could be possible, away from the noise of real life and the shadows of doubt that other people cast on her. *'It's not a proper job though, right?'* That one had been Cassius's sister, queen of doing not a lot. *'You're not bloody Jane Austen.'* Kelvin, her delightful ex-boss. She was probably only fifteen miles from it all, and it had only been a few hours. Yet somehow, in this remote, Wi-Fi-free serenity, it felt like a lifetime away.

She leaned across and gave her perfect pile of papers a stroke. Of course, it wouldn't be the easiest thing to edit. Not like a computer, where you could move text around, or quickly delete the dreadful bits. But she'd always loved to edit on paper. Somehow, it made the process feel more real.

Rosie unfolded herself from her writing cubby, taking care

not to bump her head. She filled the kettle and found the softest, sweetest-smelling ginger cake in Agnes's basket. It was wrapped in a brown bag decorated with little gingerbread people and looked like it was from a homely café somewhere. Grabbing what she needed, she reinstalled herself at her desk.

It was gone midnight when Rosie finally climbed into bed, cosy in her flannel pyjamas, belly full and thoughts emptied onto paper. It had been the most surreal day, and she ought to be sobbing into her pillow about the state of everything. Her lowly writing role hadn't given her enough spare cash for savings, and she had no intention of sponging from her parents when she'd had more than three decades to sort her life out. The thought of having to slope back there and live like she was on the set of a Cotswold reality TV show gave her palpitations.

Though somehow, none of that was troubling her right then. It felt so far away that she could barely even reach it. If she closed her eyes tightly enough, she could pretend that messy life belonged to someone else entirely, and that hers was just rosy.

As she curled up under the fresh-smelling duvet and pulled the soft, clean blankets around her, she almost felt . . . *happy*. It was probably still part of the strange aftershock. Maybe she would wake in the night screaming and worrying about robots taking over the world, and about never finding a job that couldn't be done better by some software package with a stupid name.

But for now, she would take *happy*. Because who knew what tomorrow would bring?

10

'Brrrrrr! That was cold.'

Rosie bounced back into her hut, the excitement of her mini morning adventure fizzing through her. It had only been an exploratory trip to the compost toilet, wearing a big jumper over her PJs, and some borrowed wellies. But for someone who'd always lived in a busy town and had never even been camping, sneaking out in the six a.m. torchlit darkness had felt like a thrill. She'd made it there and back in one piece and had managed not to bump into any naked men en route, even if a tiny part of her was secretly disappointed about that last bit. Purely for research purposes, obviously.

'Right. I should pack up soon, ready to get a move on.' Rosie wondered if people got used to talking to themselves, living out here. Not that she'd be sticking around to find out. She swallowed down the sadness that pulled at her throat.

Before she could dwell on it, she heard a series of thuds on the wooden steps leading up to her cabin. Her eyes widened. The footsteps seemed to retreat again as quickly as they arrived, and as Rosie rushed to the window, she saw the dark shape of

Zain retreating. Even though it wasn't yet light, he was unmistakable, with his long black hair tied up in a scruffy knot, his figure carved like solid wood against the promise of morning. What had he been doing there, outside her front door? Why hadn't he knocked?

Rosie ducked back from the window in case he turned around and caught her spying on him again, even though he was clearly the intruder this time. There was a strange tug in her chest to know more about him – but the more sensible part of her knew she ought to stay away. He didn't like her being there and would probably soon work out that she was all but trespassing. Anyway, he was better off kept as a fantasy, because when you got too close to people, you saw all of their flaws. You found out they collected underwear-stuffed dingoes, or got kinky with cyborgs, or . . . Her eyes flitted to the wood burner where the torn-up fragments of an orange letter lay. *Other stuff*.

No. Zain was better off kept at arm's distance. This whole bubble would have to burst soon anyway. That morning, she would check in with Agnes, politely decline the job, and get out of there.

Guessing he'd now be safely back in his own hut on the other side of the lake, she opened her front door a crack to see if there were any clues as to what he'd been doing out there.

'Oh.' Rosie didn't know what she'd been expecting, or indeed why she was now talking to a basket of pastries. But that's what he'd left behind.

She picked it up, then straightened herself, her eyes seeking out Zain's home across the water. A dim light was on, as though he didn't like to waste things. It was a comfort to know he was there, even if she may never see him again. She imagined Cassius at this time of day, with his flat full of voice-activated lights and two million gadgets to make his morning run as efficiently as that scene from Wallace and Gromit's *The Wrong Trousers*.

'Live simply,' she heard herself say. She looked down at the basket again, noticing it was filled with croissants, fresh bread and those little pots of jam that you got with a hotel breakfast. 'And stop talking to baked goods.'

Zain must have brought the food over from the main house, unless he was a secret artisan baker as well as a speciality pumpkin farmer. She was touched he'd brought it to her door, even though he'd probably wanted to hurl the crusty rolls at her head and shout, *'Get off my patch.'*

'You have a beating heart under that firm torso, huh?' she whispered. And this time she wasn't speaking to the pastries.

When she'd thrown together a quick breakfast, she cosied back into her writing cubby. She hadn't been meaning to write that morning. But even a fleeting glance of Zain was enough to make her creative mind twitch, and before she knew it, she was deep in the flow.

'You in there?' The loud voice and sharp knock pulled Rosie from her writing alchemy. It was Agnes.

How long had she been typing? Rosie jumped up and pulled her hair into a wonky bun, smoothing down her pyjamas like that would make Snoopy and Woodstock so much tidier. Why hadn't she even dressed yet? She rushed to open the door.

'Oh gosh, I'm all behind,' Rosie explained as Agnes bustled her way in. Rosie scooped bits of leftover breakfast back into the basket, realising she'd left the kitchen in a crummy state.

Now was meant to be the part when Rosie gathered her things and insisted she wasn't a good fit after all. That *had* been the plan. Yet with every moment she spent here, it became harder to peel herself away.

'Sorry about the muddle,' Rosie heard herself saying, while

her logical brain screeched: *screw the mess – tell her you can't take the job!*

'Tsssk, woman,' Agnes chided. 'I'm not one to judge.' She held her hands out and Rosie noticed she had her jumper on backwards under her patched-up wax jacket, and she was sure that was strawberry jam on her cheek. 'And if you think I'm scruffy, wait until you clap eyes on Steve.' She held her sides as she laughed.

Who was Steve?

'And when you meet Mags and the swim ladies, that quirky bunch will make you feel right at home.'

At home. It was outlandish to entertain the idea, though part of her was terrified about leaving, just as her precious new story was coming to life.

'I take it you're staying,' said Agnes, in a way that did not sound like a question. 'The swim lot are coming tomorrow, and I'll never find anyone else to coordinate before then.'

Rosie gulped. She could swim a few metres and like most things in her life, she could just about tread water. But she'd never dared to swim in a fresh lake, where the depth wasn't clear and there were no handrails. Her mind was reeling. And that could be the only reason that her errant mouth decided to take over.

'I'll stick around.' Wait, what? When exactly had that been decided? 'I mean, just for a week, to see how it goes.' Yes, that was more sensible. She'd get the essence of her story down before the whole thing slipped away, then she'd be out of there. Because stories were delicate like that. You couldn't disturb them when they were settling in. 'As long as I don't need to be a lifeguard, or anything. I'm limping at the moment, so I shouldn't be in charge of anyone's safety.'

'Don't be daft. You're not David Hasselhoff.' Agnes did a

slow-motion running impression. 'They're seasoned swimmers, and they'll show you the ropes. There's tow floats and spare kit. And make sure you put on a good show in case Zain's watching. If he thinks you're all about the swimming, it'll give you chance to charm him before he realises you've got designs on his big, bulging squash.'

'I'm pretty sure Zain is not for charming, and I may not be here long enough to get a grip on anyone's . . .'

Agnes waved a hand. 'Give it a week and you'll never want to leave. This place gets under your skin.'

That was *not* going to happen. It was a pumpkin farm, not a parasitic infection.

And yet, there *was* something about this place. The freedom of it. The enchantment of waking up to the sound of nothing but birdsong. Pure darkness, other than the solar lights reflecting on the lake. The distant glow of the pumpkin fields, warm and almost mesmerising – even if she hadn't dared venture there yet, for fear of being impaled on a certain farmer's pitchfork. Autumn Meadows was a riot of everything she loved about her favourite season. It *would* make the perfect backdrop for all sorts of retreats – theoretically. Not that she'd be the one stupid enough to brave it.

Agnes straightened herself and checked her watch. Rosie had no idea what she was always in a rush for, unless disappearing in haste was her canny method of getting her own way before Rosie could organise her thoughts.

'Just a week,' Rosie repeated firmly, hoping her message was loud and clear.

Rosie had spent her whole life winging it. She could surely style this charade out for another week without making any preposterous mistakes or blowing her own cover.

11

So that was who Steve was.

Rosie was sitting on the edge of the wooden platform that jutted out into the lake, when the hairless, three-legged cat approached her. She'd never quite seen anything like him. He was like a grey, bony bag of skin with the greenest *what are you looking at?* eyes. Someone had fashioned him a denim jacket out of what looked like a coat for a trendy baby, but with the arms yanked off. He hopped towards her and sat down, the silver name tag on his collar catching the cool September sun.

'So you're the one Agnes mentioned yesterday. Well, I'm pleased to meet you.' Rosie would have shaken his paw, although with his back leg already missing, that might have toppled him over.

She looked down at her own bare feet, which were dangling from the edge of the platform, one set of toes still blue-green from having dropped Cassius's vase on it just two days before. What a difference two days made. 'At least I only came away with an injured soul and a few bruises. Our wounds are what make us real though, aren't they?' she said, stroking a cheek that was warm enough to prove he wasn't a Cyber Purrz robot pet. Perhaps he was another of Agnes's waifs and strays, which Rosie had seen skulking around, as if conspiring to make her feel guilty enough to stay and fight for their new roof.

Rosie had no idea why she was confiding in a cat with no hair, as she sat by the lake in a slightly too small swimming costume she'd found in the spare kit box, with a towel wrapped around her shoulders. It was beautiful out here, with the brightness bouncing off the water and taking the chill from the air. Her plan was to brave a practice dip before the morning's swimmers descended, but so far, it wasn't happening.

She hadn't seen anyone since Agnes had left yesterday, although Zain must have stealthily dropped her breakfast basket again that morning. It had had a note in it from Agnes, reminding her that the wild swim gang were arriving at ten a.m. and that she'd cook up a vat of leek and potato soup for collection. The '*seasoned swimmers*' would be here in one hour. Rosie put a hand on her stomach, which was clenching at the thought of convincing them *and* the potentially snooping Zain that she knew what the heck she was doing. Was it too much to hope that Zain was off stroking his precious pumpkins or disappearing into those mysterious polytunnels she'd recently spied?

'At least this lovely lake will be warmer than the open-air shower,' Rosie whispered. 'Did you know that thing spits out freezing cold water? If I was sticking around, that would be the first thing to get sorted. In fact, I'd need to make *quite* the list.'

Her first foray with the outdoor not-so-private shower the day before had ended in a lot of yelping and absolutely no showering. Legging it half-undressed from the compost toilet that morning, with a huge spider on her trouser leg and evidence of a stinging nettle attack on her bare bottom, hadn't been her finest hour either. A muffled guffaw from beyond the nearby trees had made her wonder whether the elusive Zain had witnessed some of that one.

'Do you think I was romanticising when I thought a short stay in the country would be the perfect thing?' She looked at Steve, not sure what she was hoping for. Maybe the solitude was getting to her. 'I'm used to town life. I can't even swim that well. It wasn't something we did growing up, other than if one of Mum's friends had a pool party. And then I did my best to hide behind a plant pot or help the staff chop cucumber for the Pimm's. My thighs are a bit too chubby to look good next to Mum and Flick. Flick and I have different dads, you see. Though she's got most of Mum's golden genes. Not sure whose genes I've got.' She cocked her head at the feline, whom she guessed didn't fit into many circles either. His *stare if you dare* attitude was so freeing. Not that she was the sort of person who took life lessons from a cat.

'Want to join my gang?' She held up the corner of her towel in case he fancied hopping under. Even for a denim-clad trendsetter, autumn was still on the chilly side.

The cat narrowed his eyes at her and took a jump backwards, landing a little too close to the edge of the jetty.

'Steady,' Rosie warned. 'We don't want you falling in.' Maybe she should take him back to the house in case he shouldn't be roaming too close to the water. She had no idea if cats with three legs could swim. 'Who's your human? Do you belong to Agnes, or are you a wanderer? Not sure where I live now.' She checked over her shoulder. 'In all honesty, it's got a little complicated. Though I'll be on my way before I cause any mayhem here.' It sounded quite exciting when she said it out loud.

A breeze nipped around them as she spoke, rustling through the vegetation and leaving her with a twinge of panic that someone may have overheard. But who was there, other than Zain, who seemed to do his best to keep his distance?

'Anyway, I need to rip off the bandage.' Rosie nodded towards the water. The sun was shining between the odd cloud, so the temperature surely wouldn't be *too* terrible. There was no way she could experience her first plunge in front of all those hardcore swimmers who'd soon be arriving. They'd sniff out her ineptitude like wolves on a pumpkin pie. 'It's this or get my *short arse* out of here. And I don't really have a home.'

She stood up and stretched her limbs, the too tight swimming suit pinching at her bottom.

'I've got this toe float thingy. I guess you attach it to your toe?' Rosie wriggled the strap around her non-bruised big one. 'Though it's not a great fit. Maybe I have weird appendages.' She bent down to scoop up the bright orange inflatable float part and hugged it to her churning belly. 'No, this is stupid.' She dropped the float and held her arms out to Steve. She should *not* be jumping into the water without a clue.

Weoooooooow.

'Oh my God!'

Suddenly, it was too late for decisions. Rosie's abrupt movements sent Steve scarpering further backwards. His surprised body plopped into the water, and it didn't look like he was ready or able to swim.

He was sinking.

Before Rosie could think better of it, she grabbed her orange float and jumped after him. Adrenaline pumped through her as she flew through the air, but then her body hit the lake. It was as cold as ice against her skin, making her cry out in shock. Her arms managed to grab Steve, her legs thrashing under the water, panic filling her mind. She gasped uncontrollably. The float shot away from her, freeing itself from her foot and darting out of reach. She kicked and flapped frantically, trying to keep her head and Steve's above water.

In her struggle, she felt herself gulp in a mouthful of liquid, and then another. Somehow her body was sinking, down beneath the water's dark surface, its chill filling and surrounding her. She used her feet to try and propel herself upwards, desperate not to pull the cat down with her nor to let go and risk him descending out of sight.

Then suddenly she heard a crash against the water and there was a shape overhead. Instinctively, her free arm reached out. She felt the hardness of something and clamped onto it. Then her head was above the water, her body coughing and gagging as though it wasn't quite hers.

She was being pulled from the lake and onto the platform and wrapped in something. Bundled into someone's arms and rubbed and squeezed and held. Steve the cat was there too, cradled against her stomach. He was shuddering, but she could sense he was safe.

There were gruff words, which sounded like '*idiot*' and '*what the hell?*' though everything was muffled and watery, like part of her still belonged to the underworld.

'We're alive,' she heard herself saying, through gasps and splutters, her body shaking with cold, her heart racing. She was rubbing the cat's thin body. And she was smiling – which really was the oddest thing. 'I feel so . . . *alive*.'

This made the warm, wet person who was enveloping her tense with crossness. 'Reckless, stupid . . . Why the hell did you jump in there?'

It was Zain's voice.

'Steve fell in, and I think it was my fault, and . . .' Her teeth were chattering, much like her busy brain.

'And even though you can't swim, you thought you'd be the bloody heroine?'

How did he know she couldn't swim? But it was the word *heroine* that her mind latched onto. Yes, that was exactly it. She looked down at Steve, who seemed to be gazing back at her like he knew she'd just salvaged one of his nine lives. For once, she had played the lead. Not a side character or a pointless, walk-on part. She'd jumped in, feet first, and saved something. And she might be freezing cold and jabbering complete nonsense, but like never before she felt *vital*. The sense of it was growing inside her and filling her up. As another of Agnes's cats sauntered past, its eyes wide with wonder, she knew what she had to do.

'I c-can swim,' she lied, because this was no time to go blowing her own cover. 'And I *am* going to do this. For the w-waifs and strays. Of which I am proudly one.'

'The cold water has shocked you,' she heard Zain saying. 'Maybe you're hallucinating.' His strong arms continued to rub her, her body curling into his warmth and wrapping around the cat.

If anything, the cool water had stunned some sense into her. She'd never had a real cause to fight for, other than a job writing about bad teeth. But at Autumn Meadows Farm, there was land to be saved from mean developers. There were cats, dogs and an eccentric older lady who needed a new roof, or they would *all* be drowning. And this would make perfect material for the novel she'd been beginning to write. Real life could be her inspiration, couldn't it? Here was her chance to prove she *could* write better than any stupid chatbot. And if she could do whatever else Agnes needed, she could get one over on the tech company and their scary-sounding robot cats too. Of course, there was the thorny issue of convincing Zain to offer up his prized crops – but that was a worry for another day.

Rosie's vision came slowly back into focus, like actual life was a tad inconvenient. She already knew her mind was trying to wind back and remember everything that had just happened, ready to weave it into her story. The smell of woodiness and water on her rescuer's skin. The way his comparative heat seeped through and slowly became hers. Some kind of strange, soul awakening...

'I'm a fish out of water,' Rosie heard herself utter. Even Steve got bored of her nonsense at that point. He jumped out from between them, shook himself off, and walked away.

Had she always been a fish out of water? Yet for a moment, she had been a fish *in* water. And even though her swimming was atrocious, and she didn't know much about retreat planning or pumpkins, there was something intoxicating about feeling so alive. With that one simple choice to jump in and do a worthwhile thing, something had changed in her. And she didn't want this feeling to end.

'You're talking gibberish.'

'G-g-gibberish,' she repeated. It really was a good word.

'We need to get you warm.' Zain stood, lifting her with him. 'Do you trust me?'

It was the strangest question, when she had no real idea who he was, other than a gruff pumpkin farmer called Zain. But her response was instinctive.

'Yes.'

He'd been trying to keep her alive, after all. And people who spent their time getting finicky about their flora were inherently good, weren't they?

'Then let's go.'

12

'Should be me checking whether I can trust you,' Rosie heard Zain huff as they reached the door of his hut and he kicked it open, cradling her chilly body against him, still wrapped in a soaking towel. 'You're the one who creeps up on naked people in showers.'

She tried her best to hide her smile at the thought. At least she didn't have to conceal the mental images his words had just created. That beautiful, tattooed skin, the ripple of muscles...

'Still not sure you should be coming in here,' he said.

With her head against his torso, every word he spoke rumbled through her.

'You make it sound excitingly d-dangerous.' Her jaw was still shivering. Why did she suddenly like that idea? Hadn't she had enough risky encounters for one morning?

He raised his eyebrows at her like she was the strangest creature, stepped over the threshold, and kicked the door shut behind them.

After the surprising cold of the lake, the warmth of Zain's hut was like a huge great hug. She couldn't see much, with her head nestled into his firm chest, but with the heat and the smell of burnt wood and smokiness, she guessed he'd been using his log burner. There was something magical about that scent. Homeliness mixed with the wild outdoors, with a hint of perilous possibility. She smiled into his torso.

'You OK?' He was looking at her as though she'd gone a bit delirious.

She wasn't sure if that much was true. But something *had* changed when she'd jumped into that water. She'd found a cause to fight for. Of course, Zain had done his fair share of the rescuing. But it was OK for heroes and heroines to take turns in saving each other.

And since she'd emerged, every inch of her tingled. Her skin throbbed, her heart was racing and each one of her senses felt magnified. Though maybe some of that change had begun the moment she'd first seen Zain.

She looked up at him. She was fantasising and she knew it. He was a burly grump who didn't want her anywhere near his patch, and she was a recently dumped homeless impostor who needed to sort out her life and stop ogling strangers. Yes, he made the perfect muse. But when you got to know the bare reality of people, the magic soon disappeared. If Zain was going to inspire her to write, she needed him to stay magical. And if she was going to keep juggling her precarious secrets without dropping any balls, she couldn't get too friendly.

She could absolutely keep her distance.

'We should take our clothes off.'

He said it so matter-of-factly that Rosie heard herself splutter.

Zain exhaled as though he knew he hadn't phrased that well. 'You're half freezing. This towel's making you colder. I'm leaving a wet puddle on the floor. I'm not suggesting anything creepy. Just survival.'

'Oh.' She tried to hide the disappointment in her voice, because *of course* it was better that he wasn't suggesting naked antics. If he was, she'd poke him in the eye and scream the hut down. Probably.

He moved to the bed and dumped her down unceremoniously, whipping the wet towel from around her and throwing a nearby blanket over her body.

'The bed's clean,' he said, with an edge that suggested he didn't like to be judged.

And his still-warm sheets did smell good. Somewhere between that cedar scent she'd smelt on him during the nude shower incident and a fresh linen fragrance that made her wonder if he was a little less feral than she'd assumed. Was a wild-looking man with a penchant for cleanliness even more appealing?

He scratched the back of his neck and looked away. 'You should probably get out of that costume. Do it under the blanket. I've got better things to do than look at you. I need to take this off.' He pointed to his dripping clothes, which clung to his body, making him look all parts statuesque farm god. And that was definitely her writer head getting carried away with things. 'Then I'll find you something dry.' He looked around the hut, seeming to realise that with everything open plan, taking his clothes off was a *no privacy* situation. His glance flitted to the window. 'That swimming lot will be here any minute. I can't strip off out there without them rubbernecking like a bunch of synthetic chickens.'

'Promise not to cluck at you,' she said sagely. She wasn't quite sure why she was crossing her fingers under the blanket, because she could surely manage to keep her eyes to herself for two minutes. And if she accidentally caught a glimpse . . . well, she'd seen it before.

He moved to the other end of the hut, peeling off his jumper as he walked, barely giving Rosie time to look away. *That back.* Every part of it rippled with the motion of him easing his clothes over his head, like he was water itself. Did he use the lake to swim much between all that pumpkin prodding, she wondered? And why was she still staring? The black ink markings that decorated him were mesmerising. Twisting patterns interwoven with dark vines, and creatures she couldn't quite make out.

'Just research,' she muttered to herself, as she tore her eyes away and began pulling off her swimming costume under the warmth of the knitted blanket. It felt soft against her as it touched her bare, goose-bumped skin. Almost sensual. She shook her head. She was not going to get all kinky about a blanket. What was happening to her today?

Rosie tried to stifle a laugh. She sensed Zain's head shoot around, then turn away again.

'I wasn't looking,' he said quickly.

She was safely hidden under the blanket anyway. But now his movement had caught her eye again, she could see there was nothing hidden about him. The bottom half of his clothes were on the floor, leaving his rear view deliciously naked. When did she become the sort of person who described nude men as delicious? She really should stop.

Rosie looked away. They'd promised each other privacy, and she was going to respect that, like the decent human being she was. She'd be outraged if he'd been trying to spy on her.

She heard him move across the floor and open a cupboard. From her peripheral 'definitely not gawping' view she could tell he was grabbing out clothes and pulling them on.

'You decent?' he asked.

Apart from the places her mind was wandering to. 'Yes.' She gulped.

He turned to face her, and she turned her head too. Their eyes locked. Just for a moment. His beautifully dark – even darker than her own. Something seemed to fizz across the cabin between them. An energy. A connection amid the chaos.

He took a few steps forward and threw a pile of clothes towards her feet.

OK, maybe she'd imagined the connection bit. And her eyes were not a pair of Barratt's Refreshers – there was absolutely no fizz.

'You should get some clothes on.' Did his gaze just sweep over the shape of her? He cleared his throat. 'People are going to be arriving. I forbid you to get back into that water today. Or maybe ever. But if you're here to oversee the wild swimming, however temporarily, you'd better show up.'

She exhaled a long breath, wondering if he'd been the noise in the bushes, while she'd been confiding in Steve the cat. How much had he heard and was he the type to tell tales?

'I'm going to look for Steve. He's probably still cold and confused after his dip in the lake.' His eyes scanned the room. 'Don't touch anything. I don't usually let people in here.'

'Is the cat yours, or one of Agnes's strays? He's . . . cute.'

He narrowed his eyes at her, like her question was overstepping. As if being completely unclothed in his man-hut wasn't already quite familiar.

'Cats don't belong to anyone.' His gaze flitted to the cat bed which Rosie now noticed by the fire, not far from two bowls, which presumably weren't for humans to eat their beans on toast from. 'One minute,' he said, by way of warning. He pulled on a dry pair of boots and left the hut, banging the door behind him.

So he didn't let people in here. She guessed that meant he didn't have a girlfriend, unless he was a strictly outdoors type of guy. Her eyes widened. Maybe that was a thought for her romantic novel – with or without the outdoor shower.

And what was it he was so keen for her not to snoop at? He'd said don't touch anything, but looking from a polite distance was surely fair game? She let her gaze drift around the hut. It was similar to hers, but with fewer fairy lights and a lot of weird-shaped pumpkins. Unlike the ones in Agnes's kitchen, they weren't randomly strewn. His were arranged on shelves, some in size order, and others grouped in shades. There were jars and jars of carefully labelled seeds too, and a big stack of books that she couldn't quite see the spines of. She cocked her head, wondering where his fascination came from.

Then her eyes landed on something even curiouser. A collection of tiny wooden houses that lined the hut along one wall. Some were tent-shaped with holes in the front instead of doors, and others looked like little houses with grooved panels underneath for something to use to climb in. Was he living with gnomes?

Before she could fathom it, Zain was back, with Steve under his arm.

'Cat's fine,' he said. 'Just needs a dry-off and a clean coat. But your people are here. You going to get some clothes on and try to convince them you belong? Or are you getting out of here before you *cause any mayhem*?'

The pointed look he gave her told her he *had* overheard at least the tail end of her heart-to-heart with Steve. Her stomach dropped. Was she at even more risk of getting turfed out now, when she'd only just decided that she wanted to stay?

As though sensing her thoughts, he blew out a breath. 'Look, I'm in no rush to grass you up. You're a pain in the arse, and you make some remarkably stupid decisions for someone who's not a complete numbskull.' He nodded down at Steve. 'But you saved this little guy's life. And if you're planning to leave soon, I don't need to completely ruin yours.' His eyes held a warning, even if she had no idea how to interpret it. 'As long as you stick to your lake and steer clear of my pumpkin patches and polytunnels, we can agree not to murder each other. *For now.*'

She nodded. Though knowing she couldn't really promise that, perhaps murder would end up on the menu. 'Thank you. And thanks for jumping in after both of us too.'

He shrugged. 'Anyway, looks like you'll have enough on your plate with this lot.' He tipped his head towards the window. 'They're waiting for you.'

Rosie gave a few rapid blinks. Part of her wanted to hide in a cupboard or call in sick, or head for the hills in search of the person called Rachel, who'd been meant to apply for this job. But a bigger part of her felt her shoulders straightening. Because she was becoming a woman who took action – even if she wasn't sure whether it was outlandishly absurd. 'Well then. I'd better get on.'

Rosie made a grab for the spare clothes Zain had chucked onto the bed. She had no idea what she was doing, but she had an intriguing new role to play. She just hoped she could fake it until she could make it.

13

'So you're the new wild swim retreat superhero?'

The woman standing in front of Rosie with her hands on her hips reminded her of Miriam Margolyes in a floral swim cap. Rosie had worked out that her name was Mags. She was short and apple-shaped, with wayward grey curls bouncing out from under her headwear, and eyes that looked like they didn't miss a trick.

Rosie gulped. 'Well, I wouldn't quite say superhero.' She just had to get through overseeing her first session without giving away that she could barely swim, knew nothing much about retreats and was absolutely not entertaining thoughts about Zain's pumpkins. Or indeed Zain.

Easy. *Right?*

'You're coming in though?' another woman asked. She was a similar age to Rosie's mum and had grey-blonde hair that had been chopped short, with the sides shaved like a mohawk. From their quick introductions, Rosie knew her name was Bonnie, and she was here with her daughter Luna, who had the same hair but dyed pastel pink.

'Not today, she's not. Injury.' Zain arrived near the group and pointed at Rosie's bare bruised foot, even though she hadn't told him about her run-in with the vase.

They were standing outside Zain's cabin, Rosie dressed in clothes he'd lent her after the lake rescuing incident, from the combats and knitted jumper to the dark green boxer briefs that were actually quite comfortable, apart from the flappy pouch at the front where she could probably keep half a dozen crumpets. Not that men's private regions should be measured in terms of a griddle cake.

Zain gave Rosie a tight-lipped look that said *don't you dare do anything else stupid, or murder is back on the cards* and stomped off towards his precious fields.

'A man of so many words.' Luna put a hand to her heart and made a swoony look behind Zain's retreating back. Her accent was fiercely Bristolian, like Bonnie's. 'Hot though, isn't he? Like the perfect chisel of Orlando Bloom, whipped up with the rugged hairiness of Jason Momoa.'

'You don't stand a chance,' said Mags. 'Unless you turn yourself into a butternut squash. He doesn't like people. Just wildlife and pumpkins.'

'Oh, I can be wild,' said Luna, pulling her swimsuit out of her bottom and beating her chest, with a giggle. Her arms were tattooed with what looked like phases of the moon, which Rosie thought suited her. 'But I'm with Ellen now.' She shrugged. 'I don't think she'd want to share me.'

Bonnie gave her daughter a side-squeeze. 'She's the best thing since sliced bread, that one. I forbid you to make eyes at Zain the Grouch. Even if I do think there's more to him than you'd guess.' She cocked her head like she was trying to work it out.

'I think he lives with gnomes,' Rosie blurted out, before she could think better of it. She put a hand over her mouth. She'd promised him no snooping, and that should probably extend to no telling tales, if she stood a hedgehog in hell's chance of him not annihilating her chances of sticking around. 'Sorry, forget I said that. It's not like I've been inside his hut, or anything.'

'Yeah yeah,' said Bonnie. 'Don't think we didn't see you coming out of there dressed in his clothes.' She tapped Rosie on the upper arm and winked.

'No, it definitely wasn't that!' Rosie could feel her cheeks burning.

'Right down to his camouflage pants.' Mags pointed to the waistband of Zain's underwear, which was protruding above the combats. 'Taming Mr *Grump*kin. We like you already.'

'I don't reckon he's grumpy,' said Luna. 'Just misunderstood.'

Rosie was coming to see he had hidden depths too, and she couldn't stop wondering what his story was, or the hush-hush past Agnes had mentioned. She just wished she wasn't so inquisitive to find out.

The swim ladies were soon joined by a few others. Once the swimmers had taken their cool dips and dried off inside their towelling ponchos, they noticed that Agnes's supply of leek and potato soup had arrived. Rosie hadn't even had to hobble over and collect it. She assumed Zain had had a chivalrous moment, though that suggestion was met with guffaws and *not on your nellies*. But they hadn't seen him pull her out from the water earlier that day, bundle her up and take her to his warm cabin, before rushing off to check on Steve the denim-clad cat, even if their relationship was still on seriously shaky ground.

The other swimmers peeled off to get on with their days, leaving Rosie chatting to Mags, Bonnie and Luna outside her cabin. She wasn't sure what the etiquette was, but Luna was shivering, so Rosie beckoned them inside. They took a moment to appraise it, before Mags set about stoking up a fire in the log burner, and Luna dropped cross-legged onto the mat, emptying out the impressive contents of her backpack, from baguette rolls and spreads, to various pots with beany salads.

'She likes me to stay healthy,' said Bonnie, who grabbed a cushion and sat down gracefully next to Luna, in a similar lotus-like position, rearranging her floaty dress. 'But I can't live my life like the Saint of the South West.' Her ribs tinkled with an infectious laughter, and she pulled a bag of custard doughnuts and a large clip-top bottle from her wicker basket. 'Elderflower wine. Made it myself, last year. It's been nicely fermenting.'

'A little bit of what you fancy does you good,' said Mags, pulling a stool over to the fire and setting herself up as the unofficial fire poker. 'Or a lot of what you fancy.' She chuckled.

Rosie was secretly thrilled to see the torn fragments of the orange letter about her late fiancé going up in flames. If only all of life's problems could be dealt with so efficiently. She'd barely had time to think about James, or any of her hopeless exes, since she'd been here – other than the odd cutting detail that had wriggled into her story.

Rosie brought an assortment of mismatched glasses and plates, and even found herself remembering how to fold napkins into quirky leaf shapes, which she'd once learned from one of her mother's housekeepers. They were soon tucking into their impromptu cabin picnic, with Agnes's soup on the side. After Rosie's eventful morning even a few sips of the home-brewed elderflower wine was whizzing to her head. Rosie realised she was inadvertently hosting something – and enjoying it. Add a bell tent and a few pumpkins, and it could almost be an autumn retreat.

The ladies told her they lived in the nearby Cotswold village of Mistleton, which sounded like a lovely place. Maybe she'd have to borrow a bike someday.

'What do you love so much about wild swimming?' Rosie asked, keen to pad out her research in case Zain dared quiz her about swim retreat plans. She'd seen the elation in their faces since the moment they arrived around the lake. Their joy was compelling.

'I love the camaraderie,' said Mags, giving the other ladies a smile that lit up her whole, rosy-cheeked face. 'The in-it-togetherness.' She stretched out her legs in front of her and flexed her toes inside her rainbow-striped tights. 'And it does wonders for my aches and pains.'

'Brr. Cold though.' Rosie shivered. The three women stopped to look at her with slightly confused faces, so she quickly backpedalled. 'I mean, I'm used to the wild swimming bit, obviously. But I do prefer a nice hot shower!' She hated to fib, but she could not go outing herself as a woman who'd stolen someone else's job.

'It gets easier,' Mags replied. Was she giving Rosie an almost knowing look?

'Helped me with my anxiety too.' Luna was picking at her baguette as she said the words. 'Some life stuff triggered it again a couple of years back.' She glanced at her mum, her various piercings glinting in the firelight. 'The cold of the water and being out in nature helps to bring me back to the present moment. It's incredible.'

'Yeah, nothing like freezing your tits off in an ice-cold lake to bring your thoughts slap bang back to reality.' Bonnie threw her head back and laughed.

'Some things you shouldn't joke about, Mother.' Luna tutted.

Bonnie squeezed Luna's arm. 'It's been a right couple of years, love. Sometimes you've gotta laugh or you'll cry.'

'The water's a great leveller,' Mags added. 'It doesn't care about your arse size or your cellulite. And goddammit, I look gorgeous in a floral swimsuit. I shouldn't keep me covered up!' She threw her arms wide, spraying crumbs everywhere. 'Ooh, sorry, Rose. I'll clear that up.'

Rosie loved how Mags was shortening her name already, like Vix often did.

When it was Bonnie's turn to share her reasons for loving the water, a look passed between her and her daughter. Rosie thought she detected a sadness in Luna's eyes. Instead of speaking, Bonnie nodded at Rosie. 'What about you, love? What brought you to the water and why do you like it so much?'

Rosie felt her chest tighten. 'Erm.' How could she find an answer that wasn't a big stinking lie? She cleared her throat. 'Troubles, I guess.' She pondered it for a moment. 'And you're right. I did forget them the moment I hit the water earlier today. It makes you feel so effervescent, doesn't it? Like before that second, you'd only been existing.'

Bonnie squeezed her arm. 'Exactly that, gorgeous girl. Life can be short. Make sure you taste every delicious moment.' She had doughnut sugar around her mouth and a blob of custard on her chin, and her eyes shone with a twinkle.

'How about the swim retreats?' Luna asked. 'Any thoughts?'

'Oh yes, Agnes said you were a whizz at planning these things, and that soon enough this place will be a retreat paradise,' said Bonnie.

'She did?' Rosie scratched the back of her neck. She really must find Krista's old notes and pray they held something useful. 'I mean, of course!'

'With not much of a budget,' said Luna. 'It's a clever thing to pull off.'

'Especially with Zain on patrol,' said Mags. 'Not to spook

you, but he wouldn't agree to Krista chopping so much as a blade of grass to accommodate her plans.'

'Right,' said Rosie, trying not to sound deflated. She was beginning to worry that her brush with watery danger earlier that morning had given her false confidence. Some of it was beginning to wear off.

Not to mention all of the pretence she was struggling to keep up. She'd need a cheat sheet to remind her of her various awkward untruths.

'But you're an expert, Rosie love,' said Bonnie. 'And didn't Agnes say you were a painter too? You'll make the whole place come alive with creative magic.'

Rosie gulped.

'We believe in you,' said Luna, topping up Rosie's glass. 'And Zain's a sausage dog in wolf's clothing.'

Rosie gave a smile because what else was there to do? When she took a minute to think about logistics, the whole idea was terrifying.

Maybe that was why her wayward mouth decided to overspill.

'What do you think about the idea of pumpkin-themed retreats? Do you reckon people would be into them? And strictly between us and these walls, or a certain farmer might bury me in a distant meadow, where would you start?' The words had escaped before Rosie had chance to censor them. But she came to be glad they did.

The afternoon stretched out lazily, with more treats appearing from bags and cupboards, and a whole lot of excited chatter about pumpkins. Rosie hadn't felt brave enough to confide in her new friends about *all* of the secrets she was hiding – but at least the truth was out about Agnes's unusual retreat USP, and the swim ladies had promised not to spill the beans.

They'd even challenged her to start drawing up a few ideas. It was petrifying, but if she wanted a splinter of hope at saving things, she could at least grab a notebook and get nosy.

Once they'd said their goodbyes, Rosie knew she had words to type. She felt so enlivened that she knew she'd be writing well into the night, better than any insentient Kimberkoo Chat. Her novel was coming together, and somehow, she'd have to stick around at Autumn Meadows to find the inspiration to finish it – whatever the *mayhem*.

She would need to let Agnes know she was ready to give this a real shot – beyond the one week she'd promised. Then it would be time to start phase one of her pumpkin retreat missions.

14

It was difficult to have a serious conversation with someone when they had a one-eyed chicken under their arm and a plethora of toast crumbs down their misbuttoned cardi. Luckily, Rosie was fast becoming the sort of person who didn't run at the first sign of ridiculousness. She guessed that was a must if she was going to stick it out at Autumn Meadows Farm.

'So I thought the new shower and toilet block could go right here,' Rosie said, gesturing with her arms to the place where their open-air, poor excuse for a shower was.

Rosie had sketched up her new idea in her notebook and had tried showing it to Agnes, but her boss was too busy making clucking noises at her latest unfortunate stray. In fact, Rosie hadn't got much sense out of Agnes all morning. She'd gone to the farmhouse to tell her boss she'd be staying, to which the woman had said, 'Well, obviously,' as though this unconventional role was the best thing since sliced pumpkins. Then she'd brought Agnes out here to talk through her winning concepts, but it was proving difficult to hold her attention.

Rosie cleared her throat. In fairness, she did feel a bit bossy, waving her pad around and suggesting a bunch of changes, but if she was going to start getting the place ready for retreat visitors this autumn, she ought to get a move on. And part of her was anxious to prove herself as a proactive, sparklingly brilliant employee, after being cruelly replaced by a piece of dumb software just a few days before.

'The new shower and toilet blocks?' Rosie said, in a louder voice, trying her best to sound assertive rather than nagging. 'Retreat guests are going to need a little more than *this*.'

Agnes looked up from her conversation with the chicken. 'No budget for it. But this shower works perfectly, and they're welcome to share your compost toilet. I can get hold of more sawdust.'

Rosie blew out a long breath. 'This water is freezing cold, and there's barely any privacy for people to get changed.'

'There's nothing wrong with this shower, although I refuse to start sharing it with half of the Cotswolds.'

The brusque voice behind Rosie made the hairs on her neck stand on end. Zain bloody Kay. Of course it was. It seemed she couldn't have a confidential chat about anything without him rocking up.

'And your swimming people can get changed under their weird poncho towels. It is swimming retreats you're here for? Like that annoying woman Krista.'

'Definitely just *swim* retreats,' said Agnes, giving him her best, *absolutely not lying* smile, and trying to distract him by flaunting her one-eyed charge.

He briefly fussed the chicken's head, before turning to eyeball Rosie and the notebook she was now sweatily clutching. He stepped forward and snatched it from her. Her heart sank. At least it only contained a few drawings and a list of general items, and probably didn't mention the word *pumpkins*.

'So what, you're planning to knock down trees and fill the place with breeze blocks?'

'Not exactly.' She bristled, putting out her hand for her notebook. It didn't sound great when you put it like that, but that hadn't been her plan, exactly. 'It's just that guests might prefer nicer facilities. Lovely warm power showers, somewhere to plug in their hair straighteners, full-length mirrors...'

'They'll get clean enough in the lake,' Zain huffed. 'And aren't they coming out to nature to escape all that superficial, plugged-in bullshit?'

It was true that Rosie had happily shunned the expectation to do anything with her hopeless hair since she'd been here, but she wasn't ready to concede that point.

'I haven't used a full-length mirror since 1983,' said Agnes. 'Seeing the whole picture ain't what it's cracked up to be.'

Rosie resisted the urge to punch the air when she saw Zain's eyebrow quirk at Agnes's wrongly buttoned cardigan, even if it was clear neither of them would ever mention it.

'What else is on your list?' Zain asked, thrusting Rosie's pad back at her.

At least he wasn't going to snoop through her notes.

'Those big, stinky piles of rotting junk need to be sorted.' Rosie waved an arm in the direction of the next field. 'They're an eyesore, not to mention a health hazard. I'm sure I saw a snake writhing out of one of them.' Rosie shuddered.

Zain's face twitched into the briefest smile before going back to its stern look. 'Snakes. Good. The heaps must be in active decomposition. Grass snakes are ectothermic, so they need its warmth.'

Rosie gave him a puzzled look.

'Don't get him started on his compost,' said Agnes. 'Or his natural habitats for wildlife.'

'Wouldn't want to bore you,' Zain said, with more than a hint of sarcasm. 'Or prompt you to destroy their home, so you can make a fancy dressing room.'

Rosie did not like the thought of snakes, but she had to agree they'd been here long before she had. And compost *was* a good thing, now she realised that was what the junk was. She would have to concede that point and learn to keep her distance.

'They're harmless and rarely bite, if you don't go poking. And wear wellies.' He pointed to the borrowed autumn-leaf-print ones she was wearing, and she could tell he was trying not to smirk.

'Well, I'm glad something rarely bites,' she muttered.

'Anything else?' He prodded a finger towards her list.

'Better lighting around the lake,' Rosie replied, holding her chin up, in readiness to be shot down.

Agnes gasped and put a hand over her chicken's one eye.

'Nature. Needs. Better. *Lighting*.' He overpronounced each word with a level of incredulousness that Rosie thought was particularly uncalled for.

'It gets so dark at night-times, and certain creatures have a tendency to fall in.' She gave him her best triumphant stare.

'Steve did not start toppling into the lake until *somebody* turned up, talking too much and spooking him. And it's a flat *no* to digging up the land to lay more cables. Plus, more lighting would confuse the bats.'

'Don't get him started on the bats,' Agnes whispered to her chicken.

Zain spun to face the older woman. 'You've employed her to look after your wild swimmers and set up some kind of great outdoors swim retreats, and she knows nothing about nature. And as for her swimming . . .' He shot Rosie a glance. 'Have you even checked her references?'

Agnes cleared her throat and looked at her watch. 'Anyway, I ought to dash. I'll leave you to it.'

'No!'

Rosie and Zain shouted the word at the same time. At least they were agreed on something. Rosie did not feel good about pushing her luck with her new boss, so soon after losing her last job. Everything still felt so fragile here. But she was not putting up with Agnes scurrying off again and leaving her to fight this out with Zain.

'I do not need to spend any more time with this woman.'

Zain looked at Rosie, holding her gaze just long enough for her to feel another fizz of something pass between them. It had happened in his cabin, although this time it could only be his wrath. She felt herself flush.

'Likewise,' she confirmed, even though a small part of her relished feeling vexed, after worrying that life events had numbed her. At least not *all* of her emotions were dormant.

'And we don't need these retreats,' Zain added, still watching Rosie, like his words were a dare.

Agnes shifted awkwardly in her frog-eyed footwear. 'We could do with the extra money,' she said, more quietly than her usual no-nonsense tone.

Zain stiffened. 'Money. That's all anyone ever cares about, isn't it?' Then he exhaled sharply, his shoulders dropping. 'I've got work to do.' He turned and began walking in the direction of his pumpkin fields, his stride becoming more purposeful.

Rosie couldn't help watching him for a moment, his body silhouetted by the rising sun. His dark, messy hair dragged into a bun, his lumberjack-style coat pulling tight across his broad shoulders, which suddenly looked as though they were carrying the weight of something.

Agnes cleared her throat, which was totally unnecessary, as Rosie had not been *completely* transfixed.

'Money's a touchy subject with him,' Agnes explained. 'Something happened in his past, I think. But you can see why I find it impossible to tell him anything. He's like an undetonated bomb.'

'That's the undetonated version?' Rosie whistled. 'But if you just told him the house needs a new roof, and you can't go on like this...'

'He'd be up there himself trying to fix it, with precisely no health and safety. Then I'd have no decent roof *and* an obstinate oaf falling through it and breaking half of his limbs. Or worse still, he'd order me to get out of there and go and stay somewhere safer.' She shuddered. 'I don't want to do that. And who would have me, with all my waifs and strays?' She hugged her latest fowl in closer, two cats now circling figures of eight around her feet. Onions barked from somewhere in the distance.

'And the threat of Cyber Purrz wanting to buy this place?' Rosie asked, though she already sensed it was hopeless.

Agnes sucked in her breath. 'Zain belongs to this land. Whatever has gone on for him before, this farm is his stability now. I can't stand to mention the risk of selling it, unless we absolutely have to.' She grabbed one of Rosie's hands and squeezed it with a strength that was almost scary. 'He's like a son to me, even if I'd never dare say that to him. I know you can find a way of making this work without us having to threaten *concrete.* You'll respect an old lady's wishes, won't you?'

Rosie sighed. Agnes knew how to lay it on thick, with her puppy dog eyes, housed in the determined body of a Rottweiler. But Agnes was her boss, and Rosie did not want to go losing her job, home and chance at writing her best romantic novel by disobeying her wishes, however far-fetched they seemed.

'The key will be compromise,' said Agnes, like such a thing would be a breeze with the guy she'd just likened to a weapon of war. 'And baby steps. If you can get him to accept the idea of the swim retreats and all that extra footfall, it will come as less of a stretch when you mention bringing the odd pumpkin patch into your retreat plans.'

'Let's hope so.' Rosie could hear the deflation in her own voice.

'I have faith in you, girl.' Agnes gave her a hearty clap on the arm. 'How do you eat a pumpkin farmer? One bite at a time.' She laughed at her own joke.

Rosie rolled her eyes. She was sure the saying was about eating an elephant, not a pumpkin farmer. Although right then, she was fed up at having quite so many elephants in the room.

Rosie looked at the notebook in her hand, which now hung limply at her side. It had been filled with ideas about shiny new shower blocks and enhanced lighting. It had been full of her first wave of hope. But even though it stung to admit it, Zain had a point. Perhaps they should be trying to attract the sort of retreat goers who would respect the land, rather than demand somewhere to plug in their gadgets. People who wanted to get away from it all, much like Rosie had.

She would just have to magic up new ways to make the farmland retreat-worthy, without the mod cons and upheaval. That was the only chance she had of winning Zain around.

15

'So, let me get this right. You're going to fix your problems of denial . . . with a bit more denial?' asked Vix, her voice sounding sceptical through the phone's tiny speaker.

Rosie had just fully charged her mobile and walked for miles to find a half-decent signal. For *this*. The fact that she was back at the spot where she'd parked her broken-down car, which she still hadn't arranged to be towed, was *not* another sign of denial. Life admin was just boring. And if she sat on a bench with her back to the car, she barely had to think about it.

She'd been putting off making contact with the outside world, though after yesterday's doomed planning meeting with Agnes, she'd been *so* looking forward to chatting through her struggles with her best friend. Vix was usually the voice of reason, but now Rosie had filled her in on everything, she almost wished she hadn't.

'Rosie, I'm worried about you,' her friend said gently. 'Could the reason that your life keeps going off track be because you put your blinkers on and ignore the inconvenient stuff?'

'No.' Rosie tried not to bristle, because she knew her friend always meant well.

'You're telling me you caught Cassius googling bot sex, but you smiled and carried on eating your cornflakes?'

'I didn't smile, exactly.'

'And let's not start on the guy who filled your bed with knicker-stuffed dingoes, because I could have flown over and throttled him with a thong for that. And the bloke you swore wasn't impersonating a lollipop lady, even though he literally kept the sign in your wardrobe.'

'Hmm.' Rosie shifted on the wooden bench, which wasn't the most comfortable.

She begrudgingly wondered whether her dearly departed fiancé James ought to be added to the growing list of cockups. Well, he hadn't *exactly* been her fiancé at the time he'd died, because he'd split up with her about a month before, and he'd never *exactly* given her an engagement ring. But he'd often dumped her and then changed his mind. He'd been fickle like that.

'Look, lovely,' said Vix. 'I don't mean to panic you, I just hope you're not hiding from real life. It's natural that you want to take time out. But not letting people know where you are, when they may be worrying? And masquerading as a wild-swimming, pumpkin-retreat-organising super-guru? You don't need to pretend to be anyone else, Rose. You're bloody magnificent as you are.'

Rosie made a non-committal sound. 'I'm not hiding, I'm just . . . finding myself. Taking a moment to work out who I really am away from the noise of town life, and the AI and robots who were threatening to take over my existence.' She knew that was melodramatic, but she'd been loving not spending her days logged in to anything or arguing with a voice-activated pest called Serena.

'So what are you going to do about Zain and his pumpkins?' Vix asked. 'Because you can't keep avoiding them. Or him.'

Rosie let the thought settle. 'Damn it, you're right.' Perhaps she did sometimes side-step the tricky issues. And if she was going to make some new, improved pumpkin retreat plans, she at least needed to get an eyeful of Zain's big ones. No more denial or beating around the stupid bush. 'I'm going to get my hands on them.'

Rosie felt her spirits lift. Yes, there would still be subterfuge, because Zain could *not* catch her getting her hands on his speciality crops. But you couldn't make a retreat-worthy pumpkin face pack without breaking a few pumpkins, and in fairness, Zain had *plenty*.

Vix giggled. 'Do I detect a certain something in your voice when you mention him?'

Rosie's forehead creased. 'Rage?' She joined her friend in laughing. 'Don't worry. After my various dating disasters, I've concluded that I'm probably immune to love.' The only tears she'd shed for Cassius had been humiliated ones, and this thing with James and the orange letters should have hurt a whole lot more. 'Though being out here in this beautiful place has made me better at writing about it.'

'Glad those birds and bees are inspiring you.' Rosie could almost hear her friend winking. 'And take care on those clandestine missions.'

Rosie was still nervous about *all* the secrets she was juggling, not to mention that the real interviewee for the retreat role might show up at any time, or Farmer Wilbur could arrive in his tractor and out her as a fraud. But she had a strong feeling that this new creative challenge was worth the jeopardy.

As they said their goodbyes, Rosie found herself agreeing to check in with the Featherstones. Her mum and half-sister were sometimes frustrating, but they were good people, below their layers of showing off.

Rosie stood up from the bench, took a deep breath and opened their group chat. She hadn't missed the constant pinging or her phone's insistence on letting her know what a phenomenal job everyone else was making of their lives. She hadn't realised how demoralising that had become until she'd had chance to unplug.

She ignored the tens of unread messages from Cassius. At some point she'd have to arrange getting the rest of her things – but it was only stuff. Half of her clothes had probably never suited her, and she was doing just fine without a multitude of unnecessary face creams.

Instead, she braved the unread chat with her sister and mum.

> Mum:
>
> Where are you?
>
> Flick:
>
> Why is Cassius forwarding your mail here? Did you dump him? What's this letter in the orange envelope? It reeks of cheap perfume.
>
> Mum:
>
> Sweetheart, are you all right? Please get in touch. Your father is in a tizzy.
>
> Flick:

> 😂 Like you even know who her dad is!

Mum:

> Don't be so crude, Felicity.

Flick:

> Anyway, glad you dumped Cassius. He was so weird. Let us know you're OK though. Ooh, the Devonshires are holding an epic party next week. We could snag you a new boyf. Come along and we'll flood your Insta with pics of you and ALL the hot guys. That will piss off nerd boy. You did dump him, right?

Rosie sighed. This was precisely why she'd been putting off getting in touch with her family and why she hadn't wanted to go back and stay with them. A million questions, a handful of jokes at her expense and the expectation of putting on a fake smile to be seen at a bunch of parties. Her sister and mother loved all of that – but Rosie hated it. She always felt like the less shiny one, and after two glasses of fizz, she was usually desperate to go home and read a book.

And another orange letter? She let out a tense breath. She *would* face it at some point. Though it would be filled with more uncomfortable words and requests for the contents of *the box*.

Rosie bounced a few thoughts around in her head before typing a response to her mum and sister.

Rosie:

> Yes, I've split up with Cassius. All fine. Just staying in the countryside for a bit. Thank you for the party invite, but things are quite busy here. Sending love.

She could see the message had been opened almost instantly and that her sister was typing a response. Flick did live on her phone and thrived on the constant stream of notifications as though that was her air.

> Flick:
>
> Did he cheat on you? I'll brain him. Not that there's another human on earth who would agree to do the funky monkey with that geek. No offence.

> Mum:
>
> I did say you could do far better. Don't worry, sweetie boo. We'll find you someone. Who are you staying with? You're always very welcome here. Your father would love someone to play backgammon with.

Rosie laughed. Neither she nor her stepdad had a clue how to play backgammon. They'd once realised that if they got the board out, Farrah and Flick would grumble, call them boring, and leave them alone.

> **Flick:**
>
> OMG, tell us where you are! Somewhere swanky? Can we visit? Send pics!!!

Rosie could just imagine those two turning up with an army of Louis Vuitton suitcases, lodging a formal complaint about the compost toilets and demanding Martinis by the lake. Her chest tightened. That could *not* happen. She should turn off her phone quickly, in case they were trying to track her down to the nearest phone tower.

> **Rosie:**
>
> I'm signing off now, but I'm absolutely fine, I promise. I'll check in with you again soon. Happy partying. Xx

Now she'd bitten the bullet and spoken to her family, Rosie made a call to the breakdown people to tow Doll back to her parents' house, before the poor thing got clamped or confiscated. There. This was a day for progress, after all.

That being sorted, it was time to tackle the next phase of her important pumpkin missions.

16

The weather was fair with a few clouds and the odd tease of autumn sun as Rosie made her way back across the farm towards one of the pumpkin patches, hoping not to be seen. When she'd left her hut earlier that morning before her chat with Vix, Zain had been busy on his porch with a hammer, some nails and his strange little gnome houses. She could only pray that he was still occupied and not in the mood for nosing after her.

Rosie felt almost countryish, in her leaf-patterned wellies and green, swirly-patterned dungarees that Cassius had once looked at strangely. She'd even grabbed another bag of barely worn clothes from the boot of her car, which had been destined for the charity shop in one of those donation bags. An assortment of quirky garments she'd enjoyed collecting, like there had been another person inside her, trying to get out.

Against all the odds, was she actually starting to feel at home here? She let the long wild grasses tickle the tips of her fingers as she walked. She'd always loved this season best of all, for its gorgeous colour palettes and its sense of slowing down to cosy up. But being out here in nature gave it an extra sprinkle of magic. She bent to sweep up a handful of wildflowers that had fallen, admiring their clashing colours.

Her writing needed more of this too. She took a moment to tune in. Birdsong – though she couldn't tell a bullfinch from a barn owl. A soft, floral smell, perhaps from the chamomile she recognised from her mother's tea, or the fiery flowers that could be marigolds. And not for the first time since she'd been here, her mind wandered to the fantasy of running writing retreats, in this wonderfully stirring wilderness. She shook away the thought because she clearly had enough on her plate.

'Pumpkins,' she reminded herself, like a mantra, ploughing on towards them, trying to ignore the nervous flutter at her plan to steal a few. She had some experiments up her sleeve, and she hoped the swim ladies would be her willing testers.

Rosie arrived at a wooden gate and stile between fields, stopping to take it all in. Just *wow*. The sight of so many golden winter squash, like happy sunshine faces peeking out from their leafy beds, was a balm to her eyes. She wondered how anyone could be grumpy out here. Did it bring a smile to even Zain's sulky lips? As she turned and began to climb the stile, the opportunity to check out his lips for herself was thrown at her.

'Whoa!' The sight of Zain so surprisingly close made Rosie jump. Her body began stumbling backwards from the wooden stile and her bag of clothes dropped to the floor. He reached forward and grabbed her.

Rosie blew out a breath and willed her heart to slow down. It must have been the near fall that had set it racing.

Zain had been climbing up the other side of the stile in her direction, perhaps on his way to the mysterious polytunnels she'd just passed. Or maybe just to spy on her.

It was acutely, cheek-burningly apparent that they no longer needed to be clinging to each other like a pair of vines. So why on earth were they? Why were his deep brown eyes drinking her in, like she was *actually* a mug of pumpkin-spiced latte? Why were his strong hands still gripping her, and his intoxicating manly scent still filling her nostrils, when she'd been quite happily sniffing his marigolds just moments before?

If she didn't know it was completely impossible, she'd wonder whether the universe kept flinging them so embarrassingly close for a reason. At least they were both fully clothed this time.

'What are you doing out here?' he asked, his eyes narrowing. 'I thought your domain was strictly around swimming and the lake?'

'Oh, it definitely is,' she said breezily, waving a hand, which she then realised was brandishing some of his wildflowers. *Damn it*. 'I'm just . . . *lost*. So many fields, so many primroses.' At least stolen flowers might put him off the scent of her intention to nick a few of his precious pumpkin babies.

'They're nasturtium,' he said, through gritted teeth. She'd never seen them quite so close up. They were pearly. 'One of the useful flowers that attract pollinators for my Cucurbitaceae. *Pumpkins*. But that doesn't work if town people come here and tear them up.'

'They'd fallen!'

At least that much was true.

They looked at each other, their reddening faces still close, his hands clamped to her upper arms, her fingers still clenched around the chest of his jumper, now almost angrily. She could feel cross heat emanating from him too.

'And it's part of your new role to come out into my fields and tidy up?'

'If you must know, I thought they'd brighten up our compost

toilet, if I can trouble Agnes for a vase.' The idea had only come to her when she'd spotted them, and it seemed a shame to waste them. 'Seeing as you vetoed my suggestion to build a new shower and toilet block, I'm coming up with ideas to make use of what we have, *without* trampling on nature. Yes, you can thank me. You'll get to carry on enjoying your open-air ablutions.'

He raised his eyebrows, and she was sure the memory of her barging in on him stark naked in the shower passed between them.

Then he huffed again for good measure, and they let each other go, both climbing in his direction because it was far too awkward to cross over on the wobbly wooden stile.

'What's in the bag?' he asked, his attention brought back to it now it was by their feet, his eyes registering the writing on its side. 'You stealing from charity too?' There was the tiniest tinge of humour in his voice this time, as though he knew not even she would stoop that low.

She tutted. 'More clothes. Like these.' She flapped a hand towards herself, then felt a bit silly. 'Hopefully more suitable for being out here. Or whatever.'

He seemed to weigh her up, before giving her a curt nod. 'Nice dungarees.' It would usually have made her feel self-conscious, but for once, she didn't sense sarcasm. 'They suit you.' He seemed as surprised by his words as she was. 'I mean, probably more practical than the beige coat and the boots you couldn't walk in.' He quickly bent to pick up the bag and thrust it towards her.

'Thanks. I think.' Sometimes it was OK to accept a compliment, wasn't it? She'd seen her sister do it a million times, without her own peculiar impulse to bat it away. Her shoulders relaxed, though not for long.

'Anyway, I don't want you roaming around near my crops.

Some are rare breeds and all of them are precious to me. I don't want anyone traipsing where they shouldn't.'

'It's not as though I'm likely to squash one,' she scoffed. 'Anyway, I'm really not interested in a bunch of gnarly old, boring vegetables.' She didn't want to rile him, exactly, but perhaps she should throw him off the scent of her guilty intentions.

His jaw clenched, like he took that as a challenge. 'Scientifically, they're fruit, not vegetables. They have seeds. Although nutritionally, they are closer to vegetables. And they're *not* boring.'

Rosie nodded slowly. 'Right.'

She noticed his slight wince, as if he knew the conversation was getting weird already. Something inside her wanted to keep him talking. Perhaps he wasn't *always* strange.

'I didn't know there were so many shapes, colours and varieties,' she continued, deciding that if she could get him talking, it would be handy for her pumpkin retreat research – even if it would go against maintaining a safe distance to avoid accidentally spilling any secrets. 'What can you tell me about them?'

Rosie could almost see the conflict playing out across his face, his desire to share something about his beloved pet subject having an almighty row with his craving to be left alone.

Then with a resigned nod, he beckoned her to follow him, in the direction of the pumpkin fields. Her heart skipped with glee.

'But only because if I show you, you're less likely to snoop or steal,' he said over his shoulder.

'I never would,' she replied sagely, crossing her fingers behind her charity donation bag, which in theory, could probably hide a few.

'Cinderella,' he announced, when they arrived, waving an arm a little awkwardly at row upon row of the bright orange sort, growing fatly on their twisting vines. 'Medium to large, deeply ribbed, predominantly ornamental. But moist and creamy inside.' He cleared his throat, apparently realising that sounded a bit rude. 'That is, when you cook them.' He eyeballed her. 'Which I do not permit you to do.'

'Noted.' She tried not to giggle. 'No pumpkin muffins for me.'

He gawped at her like she'd just suggested manslaughter.

As they kept walking, him reminding her to stick to the designated paths and begrudgingly helping her where the walkway had become overgrown, he continued to explain the varieties, almost softening a touch with each fleshy friend he introduced.

And perhaps it should have been boring, hearing Latin terms or learning half a dictionary of different types, from Autumn Gold to the little white Baby Boo, to the pretty spotted Carnival or the frighteningly blistered Warty Goblin. Ordinarily she would have switched off ages ago, nodding, smiling, and disappearing into her own creative thoughts. That's what she'd done when Dave had raved about dingoes or James had droned on about conferences in Telford.

But listening to the surprising fondness in Zain's voice and witnessing the way he knelt gently to touch the fruits' skin or check how it was growing was strangely addictive. Rosie found herself following him, keen not to interrupt his flow. She'd never seen nor imagined this side to him. Had many people? Never mind complicated retreat activities, like hayrides or carving jack-o'-lanterns – although she wasn't writing those off. But guests might pay good money to have their souls soothed by Zain's enamoured words.

Despite still clinging to her charity donation bag, which would have been *so* handy for swag, as time passed, she realised she was struggling with the idea of stealthily nabbing his pumpkins to boil into retreat menu stew.

'The ones that seem rough on the outside are misunderstood,' he said quietly, as she crouched next to him to stroke the gnarly skin of a variety called Goosebumps. 'They keep people at bay, but they're often sweeter.'

They looked at each other, then quickly turned their heads away.

'Then there's the symbolism,' he went on, more cautiously this time. 'The cycle of life and fertility, the connection to the earth, hollowing them out to make room for new beginnings...' He paused, seeming to inwardly groan. 'Well, some of it's probably bollocks.' He stood up sharply, brushing down his clothes.

Rosie blinked a few times and then stood up too.

'No, honestly. It sounds fascinating. What else can you tell me?'

He sighed heavily and turned to her. 'I can tell you that I've been working on these fields, breeding, cross-breeding, trying to improve varieties and bring back species that my North American ancestors once grew. I don't know what your plans are for these *swim retreats*.' He said the term as though he didn't believe that's all they were going to be. Rosie felt a pang of guilt, because he wasn't wrong. 'You luring a bunch of middle-class, retreat-hungry hipsters in swimsuits onto this land is going to stomp over everything I'm trying to achieve. If you were planning to encroach on my fields to erect a bunch of fancy yurts and start singing around campfires, I suggest you find somewhere else.'

Yurts. Now that was a nice idea.

Although something else had been bugging her.

'What are all these pumpkins for?' Rosie asked softly. She didn't mean to offend him, but even her inner dreamer knew when to get real. 'Have you got anyone to sell them, or any way to make good use of them? Or are they all going to live, die... and rot?'

A twitch in the vein in his temple told her she'd hit a raw nerve.

'I have no wish to trample over *anything*, but like Agnes mentioned, she could do with the funds that my swim retreats would bring.' She was allowed to say that much, even if it was more than her job was worth to mention crumbling roofs, the threat of a cat factory, or indeed the pumpkin-themed USP. 'Maybe we could compromise over where I could set up camp for the guests and where people can safely wander?'

She willed herself not to mention carved pumpkin lanterns or turning his rare-breed squash into soup.

The question hung in the air, the faint idea of mutuality dancing between them through the autumn haze.

'Nature has been compromised by humans enough.'

His pumpkin-headedness ought to have vexed her more, but there was something magnetic about the spark in his eyes. He was the hero in his own story, and *this* was his fight, even if she was only just coming to learn of it.

'And why do people put money before . . . *everything*?'

There went another of his touchy subjects. Rosie's story senses began twitching, but she feared if she prodded for reasons, Zain the '*undetonated bomb*' would explode in her face.

'Money doesn't have to be a bad thing,' she replied calmly, because she was coming to see that *sometimes* his bark was scarier than his bite. 'People do good things with it too.' Granted, her mum spent it on sequinned dresses – but he didn't need to know that.

Zain didn't look convinced.

'We were getting along for a moment. I don't want to ruin things.'

He looked away. 'I was boring you with Latin words and freaky gourd facts. I'll go back to keeping my mouth shut.'

'Honestly, I enjoyed it. You're passionate about this. Don't feel embarrassed.'

'I'm not. Passionate or embarrassed. It's just a bunch of fruit. No point in getting attached to anything.'

She could tell he didn't mean that.

Then he turned and stomped away, and it was clear he wasn't going to turn back.

Rosie decided she'd go back to her cabin too, though she'd find a different route. And frustratingly, she no longer had the heart to steal Zain's pumpkins. For now, she would have to find another way.

17

'It's sink or swim night,' Rosie whispered, crouching down to talk to the tiny creatures in her new bug hotel, which she'd named Buggingham Palace.

In truth, that evening's sunset swim was more of a decoy, whilst she worked out how to break it to Zain that the retreats would involve parading around his pumpkin patches more than freezing your nipples off in a lake. He was *not* going to like it.

'After the dip, I'll coax the ladies inside and wow them with a few pumpkin-themed retreat ideas. Good, hey?' She'd been to the library to do some research at the same time she'd sneaked out to buy pumpkins. On the plus side, she didn't have to feel guilty about pinching anything from Zain.

The insect house was one of the projects she'd found herself toying with since she'd been at Autumn Meadows. She'd seen people make them on TV once and had remembered this was a good time of year to help wildlife find a home. She'd made *Wingsor Castle* for Zain, though she'd have to leave it outside his cabin silently, because he probably wouldn't accept it with much grace. He'd hit the roof when he'd caught her appropriating items for it from his log shed. As if anyone got so territorial over chunks of old wood.

Rosie had been adding more of her own little touches around the place, like she was setting the scene for her brand-new Rosie-led adventure. A solitary chipped vase had appeared in the once scary toilet hut, which Rosie had taken as Zain's sign that he wouldn't kill her over her idea to add bunches of fallen autumn wildflowers in there. Seeing as she'd dropped her plans for a swanky new toilet and shower block, it was the least he could do.

She'd made paper bunting from old ribbon and discarded manuscript pages to brighten up the toilet hut too, which he hadn't even torn down yet. And remembering something else she'd learned from her mother's housekeeper, she'd made cinnamon-spiced soap for their shared shower, which had definitely gone down a bit even before she'd started using it.

The incident where she'd got stuck on the grassy roof of her hut whilst trying to plant wild daffodil bulbs had earned her a stern telling-off from Zain, but she couldn't win at everything. It wasn't her fault if Steve the cat had knocked her ladder over, and the flowers *would* look lovely when it came to spring, if they were still there to see it. Zain's surprised face when she'd shimmied down the drainpipe instead of waiting for him to replace the ladder had been worth the bruises.

Rosie had the growing sense that making this place special for the promise of future guests might actually suit her. Her imaginative mind was happy, and if she could magic up holiday lodgings for a bunch of beetles and the odd ladybird, maybe there was a chance she could work out where to start with these retreats too.

Whatever others might say about the slightly borrowed, completely unconventional life she was forging, nobody could call it dull. She glanced across to the horizon, which she found herself doing more these days, rather than checking her watch. The sun was beginning to settle towards the distant hills, and any moment, her swim friends would arrive. There would be plenty of excitement for her first group dip, though Zain wouldn't be around to drag her out like a freshwater prawn this time. He was still keeping a sulky distance after their debate in his pumpkin fields.

'Will he ever come around?' she asked her bugs.

How would she even broach the subject of the *real* retreat plans, when he was already cross enough about any sort of intrusion on the land? His pumpkin patches could be so valuable – especially when he was currently doing nothing with his crops other than stroking them and whispering sweet nothings. Didn't such magnificent *gourds*, as he'd called them, deserve to be shown off and celebrated? Maybe she'd have to get fearless with Agnes and insist he was told a few home truths, even if her boss had been obstinate that some things were better left unsaid.

Rosie looked absently at Zain's cabin before going inside her own to get changed.

She was still pretending to the swim gang that she knew the ropes of wild swimming, because that was part of what she'd been employed for. But being ratted out for her rubbish swimming wasn't quite as terrifying as overcoming her hurdles with Zain.

Rosie's eyes flicked to her predecessor Krista's retreat planning notes, which she'd found slung inside one of the cupboards. They said things like *Zain is an obstructive twat* and *this is never going to work*, before launching into pages of plans for her ultimate trip around the world, which Rosie guessed she had promptly disappeared on. At least they agreed on one thing:

Zain was the source of considerable conflict – although every story needed a good dollop of that.

With the windows open in her hut, she heard the swim ladies' voices in the distance. She knew that Mags, Bonnie and Luna would be there, and a few others too.

Rosie popped a towel poncho over her swimsuit and opened her front door.

'Oh!' She put a hand to her mouth at the slight shock of finding a bright orange float on her doorstep, with hairless Steve curled up next to it in his usual denim attire. He looked up and yawned at her. As she bent to stroke him, she noticed a note tied to the cord of the float.

The strap goes around your waist, not your toe, it read. Followed by: *It's a TOW float. AND PLEASE DON'T DROWN* in large, insistent capitals. The corners of her mouth twitched into a smile, and she dared another quick glance towards Zain's cabin. The lights were off, although she'd worked out he often slunk about in there by candlelight. She swallowed the rising guilt that the swimming was partly pretence.

'Who knew he cared, huh?' she asked Steve, giving his bald head an extra rub. 'I bet he's a big old softie really.' Steve purred, like he was trying to agree. But cats often did that.

The swim ladies were soon outside Rosie's hut, hugging Rosie and shedding off their outer layers with wild abandon. The sky was turning shades of butterscotch and burnt orange as the sun began to set over the Cotswold hills, a soft blanket of clouds overhead to keep in a touch of warmth on the crisp autumn evening. As chatter and giggles laced the air, some of Rosie's nerves began to dissipate. If she could get through this swim and then share her latest retreat ideas with the ladies without them thinking she was hopeless, she'd have ticked two courageous, action-taking things off her list. Her confidence would need it for the long haul.

The often-intuitive Bonnie, grey mohawk tied in bunches that evening, seemed to sense Rosie's nerves when it was her time to get into the water. She came over and squeezed her arm.

'Not feeling it?' Bonnie whispered.

'I'm not really . . . I don't usually . . .' Rosie sighed. 'It's a long story.' Should she just tell them she'd ended up here by mistake? Would they feel compelled to tell Agnes?

Rosie looked into Bonnie's big, aqua blue eyes. They were just like her daughter's.

'Stories, hey. We all have 'em,' said Bonnie, quietly. 'Our lives are made up of them. Sometimes they change in an instant and we find ourselves in a brand-new one, wondering who the heck we are, don't we?' Her laugh was delicate, like her words. 'It's all right – no need to share. If you're having a fresh start, we respect that. Now, I'm getting into this water before that sun goes down. You coming? Nothing better than this to wash off life's crap and restore you to factory settings. And I promise you, whatever's bothering you will soon feel a whole lot smaller.'

Everything the others had said about wild swimming had been right. With her body immersed in the lake, surrounded by these women she'd been thrown together with, Rosie felt held, supported, and so inexplicably brave. It was so gloriously removed from her previous existence of town life and world-dominating chatbots that her soul was positively singing. Bonnie was right. With every immersion she felt more alive. And somehow, this was sweeping her mind clear of the debris that had been piling up like an old junk yard since she wasn't sure when.

'Takes your breath away, doesn't it?' Mags said, as they pulled themselves out of the water, the last of the apricot sun having slid down behind the hills, silhouetting the trees like distant lollipops.

'And your troubles,' Luna added.

Rosie hoped so.

'It changes from minute to minute,' said Rosie, marvelling at the sky as they wrapped themselves in towels. As the sun descended, it cast different shadows, the shades of the sky altering in each moment. 'Blink and you'll miss it.'

'You know it, dear girl. Just like life.' Bonnie's voice sounded sad but happy all at once. 'Grab it with both hands. Live it like you mean it. And don't let the pumpkin farmers get you down.'

Luna let out an inexplicable sob and threw her thin arms around her mum.

'You daft sod,' Bonnie giggled.

Their teeth chattering, Rosie invited her new friends inside, with the promise of a warm fire.

'And I might have an ulterior motive,' Rosie confessed, as Mags, Bonnie and Luna moved towards her cabin.

'If it's got anything to do with that food I can smell, I'm in,' said Mags.

'It certainly does,' Rosie replied, bundling them through the door and closing it behind them, keen for Zain not to see from wherever he might be moodily lurking, because he could *not* clap his eyes on this.

'Welcome to the world's smallest pumpkin farm retreat! You're my chief testers.'

18

'You massacred his pumpkins!' Luna gasped, her eyes landing on a Magic Lantern variety that Rosie had quite badly carved with a smiley face and filled with a tealight.

Rosie had packed her cabin with lots of them, like a mini pumpkin-themed grotto. The glow from them was wonderful, although she was acutely aware that decorating one small hut was a million miles off organising successful retreats. She didn't even know where retreaters would sleep, or how she'd cater for them, what activities she could arrange, or if she could do any of that without Zain committing first-degree murder.

'Oh, you *are* brave,' Bonnie breathed, as though in the midst of someone heroic.

'Nooooo. All of these are from the nearest village shop,' Rosie rushed to clarify. 'He'd carve *my* head if I butchered his precious Cinderellas without his say-so.' Her forehead creased as she wondered how on earth she'd ever secure such permission.

'He'll come around, love,' said Bonnie. 'And it does look incredible in here. So inviting. You're a natural.'

'It's not like he does anything else with them,' Luna reasoned as she sat herself on the rug, drying her pink hair with her towel. 'I mean, he just grows them all – massive ones, weird ones, multi-coloured ones – and they end up as compost. Surely, he has bigger dreams for them than worm food?'

'A pumpkin deserves its moment of transformation into a carriage, if only for one night,' Rosie added wistfully, her mind wandering off into a world of fairy tales.

'Or to shine brightly in a pie,' said Mags, rubbing her belly.

And it was time to dish some food.

After stripping down to her swimsuit and plunging into a cold, dark lake, sharing her tentative pumpkin farm retreat ideas with the others didn't feel as daunting as she'd expected. There were *mmms* of delight at the pumpkin and spiced apple soup she'd made earlier in Agnes's extremely disorganised, cat-filled kitchen. Bonnie was soon suggesting she could make pumpkin wine instead of elderflower, and Mags chipped in with thoughts on pumpkin bread and sweet treats. Luna became animated about Rosie's pumpkin pampering ideas, from face masks to hair treatments and maybe a spot of peaceful pumpkin painting.

With the warm glow from Bonnie's wine, they were soon chatting like they'd always known each other. Rosie couldn't remember when she'd last felt like this. She would usually duck away from socialising, because past friends had been too vocal about her iffy choice of boyfriends, even if she now knew they'd had a point. Being at home with a book had always felt easier, but maybe there was something to be said for opening up to more real-life friends.

As the evening went on, Bonnie confided that her illness had brought her and Luna to the water, both determined to enjoy every moment, because you never knew what lay ahead. 'C word,' she said simply, touching one of her breasts. 'Though I'm all right again, for now. They thought it was stubborn. But it hadn't met me.' She winked. 'I come here to feel skin-tinglingly alive. And because Luna vetoed mountaineering. Though she'll have to learn to let go at some point.'

There were a few tears, and some words from Mags about how bloody brilliant they'd both been.

Rosie could already feel the guilt of her own omissions bubbling up inside her, mixing with the sadness of all that beautiful Bonnie and her close ones had been through. Bonnie had shared something so personal, and Rosie was still pretending to be someone completely different. Even if it might put her job and home in jeopardy, could she really go on being dishonest with these women?

Just as she was grappling with her conscience and panicking at the thought of Agnes drop-kicking her over the farm gates for being Fake Rachel, Mags picked up a slip of paper that Rosie had hastily thrown on the fire pile before their swim.

'Hey?'

Rosie saw Mags's eyebrows raising and realised in a belly-dropping instant what she was holding.

'You thought the float went on your toe?' Mags asked, looking at Rosie. Then her eyes widened, and she clapped a hand over her mouth. 'Ignore me,' she mumbled. 'Nothing to see here!' And she swiftly threw Zain's note from earlier, about tow floats and not drowning, into the log burner.

Bonnie and Luna looked over, only half-registering. Rosie's mind raced through her options, mentally packing her bags, facing rollockings, and going to live in a cardboard box, before realising that she might be catastrophising. If her secrets got out to Zain, that might well be her fate. But tonight, with these women, she felt drawn to release some of her baggage. Because a problem shared was one less problem that could eat you alive.

'Look, I need to tell you something. Feel free to judge me or hate me for not coming clean before. But I'm not who you think I am.'

Telling Mags, Bonnie and Luna the truth about who she was and why she'd ended up here hadn't been nearly as dreadful as Rosie had imagined. She opened her mouth and let it all spill out, and to her immense, slightly sweaty relief they were nothing but kind.

'No offence, but I guessed you weren't a wild swim expert,' said Luna, with a cheeky half-smile. 'Anyway, I like you just as you are.'

'And not to be nosy, but where did your ex get his sexy robot from? And do they do one who looks like George Clooney? Because I could be in the market for one of those.'

'Mags!' Bonnie shook her finger. 'Don't be such a dirty old dog.'

'Less of the dirty,' Mags replied, as she tittered into her mug of soup. 'No harm in a single lady checking out her options.'

Bonnie shuddered. 'It's all a bit creepy.'

'And that's not the worst bit,' said Rosie, giving a quick look around. 'Don't tell Steve, but the future of this place could be given over to robot cats, if I don't pull in the crowds and create some pretty impressive pumpkin farm retreats, in record time. And guess what? I'm not a retreat expert either. Apart from a few ideas from the library and a bit of pumpkin soup, my plans are looking sparse. I have no clue how to bring this all together. Will you help me brainstorm some more?'

Rosie filled them in on the dangers of Cyber Purrz and their ugly factory plans, and the three suited men she'd seen poking around the farm and taking measurements.

'Well, we're not having that,' said Mags.

'Jeez, does Zain the sworn technophobe know about this?' asked Luna.

Rosie sighed. 'No. And I'm not allowed to tell him. It's more than my job's worth. Agnes thinks he'll hit the roof or do something dangerous.'

'You need to get real with him, if you want a cyber cat in hell's chance of getting him onside.' Luna gave Rosie an apologetic look, because clearly nobody wanted *that* scary job. 'But whatever you decide, we need to make plans.'

'I have to get things up and running this autumn. And there's hardly any budget. This land and Agnes's crumbling house depend on it,' said Rosie.

'And what is it that *you* want, love?' asked Bonnie.

It was true that every main character wanted something. 'I want to help. To do something that makes me feel worthwhile. And to keep my cosy little home, and the headspace to write the novel I've been working on.' She pointed towards the typewriter in the corner. 'I've never written the way I write when I'm here.'

It felt too fanciful to float the idea of the writing retreats that kept bobbing into her mind, but maybe one day – because surely they couldn't run pumpkin retreats all year round?

'So you write novels?' said Luna. 'Wow.'

'Ahh, not a painter then?' said Mags.

'Nope,' Rosie replied, feeling a little sheepish.

'Then grab that typewriter, Rosie,' said Luna. 'We have some lists to make.'

And once again, Rosie's fingers were typing like the wind. But this time, she was creating list upon list of ideas, resources, areas of expertise, friends in the know, random talents, dates and deadlines, and all sorts of things she had never even thought of. Her writer self *loved* a list. They would need plenty of pruning and perfecting, and lots of it would evolve as they went. She'd have to run things past Agnes and perhaps put a firm foot down, and to reach a *whole* bunch of nail-biting compromises with Zain.

But somehow, a plan was coming together. Rosie's mind was bouncing with brainwaves, and she was relishing every moment. It was just like crafting a story – but this one wasn't make-believe. Who knew real life could be as much fun as fiction?

She also knew that when she got back to her writing cubby, her own storytelling powers would be elevated by the friendship and feelings she'd experienced tonight. Any chatbot would have its work cut out to replicate these emotions and turn them into meaningful words that would change people's hearts.

Rosie smiled as she sipped her elderflower wine, watching the others become enlivened too. Perhaps they were onto something with these retreat logistics. Maybe, just maybe, Rosie could pull this off. There was just the not-so-small matter of Zain. But she'd let some of her secrets out tonight, and it had gone surprisingly well. They'd made progress *and* she was feeling like much less of a guilty fraudster. If she could somehow convince Agnes to let her be similarly honest with Zain, surely there was a tiny, glimmering hope of winning him around?

19

'My bathroom looks like a duckpond. And I haven't even got any ducks!'

When Rosie reached Agnes's farmhouse, fully intending to put her foot down about them getting honest with Zain, it seemed the woman had enough on her plate. She was scurrying around her kitchen trying to find buckets and bowls. Hens were flapping, Onions and his pack of quirky mongrels were barking, and Agnes seemed to have forgotten about the soup she'd been cooking as it bubbled and spat green liquid, giving off the smell of burnt broccoli.

Rosie rushed to the hob to turn it off, then did her best to shoo the hens out of the back door. Goodness knew what they were even doing in the house, but Agnes had her unconventional ways.

'Why are all my buckets as holey as a block of Swiss cheese? Can you collect rainwater in an ancient cracked *Le Creuset*?'

The dogs continued yapping, and between that, the stress emanating from Agnes, and the one-eyed chicken that was running around in circles rather than finding the exit, Rosie could barely hear herself think. Maybe today was *not* a good day to negotiate with her boss about letting her tell Zain some home truths, in the hope he'd be less ferocious about her retreat plans. Agnes clearly had enough to deal with. If Rosie dared to harangue her, she might get thrown out of Autumn Meadows on her ear.

'Agnes, what's going on?' Rosie yelled above the noise. 'And how can I help you?'

Agnes flung open a saucepan cupboard and pointed inside. 'Grab what you can and follow me upstairs.'

When they reached Agnes's bathroom, Rosie could see that her duckpond analogy had been a slight exaggeration, but there were several damp, dripping patches on the ceiling.

'Is your roof leaking?' Rosie asked.

Agnes turned to look at her. 'Well, I knew I didn't just employ you for your brilliance in a swimsuit or your excellence in retreat planning.'

Rosie gulped, acutely aware that she was secretly still fairly shoddy at both. She moved around the bathroom, placing saucepans under drips and trying to say reassuring things to Agnes, even though she knew nothing about dodgy roofs.

'Can you ring a specialist to come and patch it up for you?' asked Rosie. 'I know you can't afford a proper job until the retreats bring in some money, but if it's just a few roof tiles that need replacing?'

'Not unless I can pay them in eggs.'

'Do you know anyone with the right equipment who would do you a favour?'

Agnes put down her collection of bowls and scratched her head. 'Farmer Wilbur! Of course. He's got a cherry picker and he's always fixing things at his lavender farm, isn't he? Come downstairs and you can call him. He'd be round in a jiffy.'

Rosie's stomach flipped.

'No!' Her yelp was so loud that she set off the dogs again, somewhere below. She could not have the person who'd apparently recommended her for the job showing up here and shouting *'Who the blazes are you?'* There were surely rules against misappropriating other people's jobs. 'He's probably far too busy with harvesting, or whatever. We won't bother him.' Rosie had no idea when folk harvested aromatic bushes, but it was definitely the time of year for tractors.

'He does that in late summer,' Agnes huffed. 'You ought to know.'

'Obviously!' Rosie squeaked, clapping a hand to her forehead. There was no getting away from it. For once, a certain pumpkin farmer was the lesser of two evils.

'Time is of the essence – we need to get Zain. I know you don't want him bullheadedly trying to bodge your whole roof or insisting that it's not safe for you to stay here, but he's got a long ladder, and he did build our cabins. He can surely help with a quick repair job.'

Agnes made a grunting noise, which Rosie was taking as affirmative. And now that she'd got one vague *yes* out of her, she may as well seize the moment.

'If we're going to tell him about your roof troubles, it makes sense to confess that this is why pushing on with the retreats is vital. Can I have your permission to divulge everything I need to, to try and get him onside? The threat of Cyber Purrz buying you out and the fact that the pumpkin USP is the only thing that might save us?'

Agnes stood in her dripping bathroom, her messy hair wet, her usually formidable face crumpled. As much as Rosie didn't like to pester a woman when she was down, this was for Agnes's own good if she wanted to keep her home.

Agnes clasped and unclasped her hands a few times and then gave a small nod. 'Do what you have to, though my advice still stands. One bite at a time. If you throw everything at him at once, he'll be the one chomping *your* head off. And I don't want to be around to see that.'

It didn't take long for Rosie to rush to the nearest pumpkin patch, where luckily, Zain was busy working. He must have sensed the urgency enough not to put up a fight, and at the words '*Agnes needs you*', his face fell, and he rushed after Rosie, up to the house. When they reached Agnes's cramped bathroom, its floor littered with saucepans, the sound of dripping water punctuating the air, he broke his own tense silence.

'What's going on?'

Agnes garbled out the bare minimum about a few roof tiles probably having fallen, and that a quick repair should do it, and that maybe Farmer Wilbur could help after all. Rosie grabbed the edge of Agnes's old, cracked sink, trying to disguise her fresh wave of panic.

'Wilbur will be away,' Zain barked. 'Always takes a long break in autumn, after his harvest.'

Rosie mouthed a silent thank you in the direction of the dribbling ceiling. She hoped it would be a world cruise that he wouldn't be back from any time soon.

Zain paced to the window. 'I can probably get onto the roof from here.'

'What are you going to do, tie a few tiles to your head and hook the hammer through your belt loop?' Agnes shot Rosie a look. 'You see what I mean?'

Zain turned to them, his eyes narrowing. 'You two been talking about me?'

Agnes blurted out 'no' at the same time Rosie put her hands on her hips and said 'yes', which really didn't help matters.

'How long's this been going on?' Zain pointed upwards, his movements abrupt. 'This isn't the first you've known about your roof having problems, is it?'

'The whole thing needs replacing by the winter,' Rosie said hastily, before Agnes was able to waffle her way out of it. 'A swift repair might do for now, but a plaster won't fix a broken leg.'

Zain's dark eyes began filling with something that looked like fury. Rosie could almost have sworn she saw flashes of red. 'Why does she know about this, and not me?' he asked Agnes, through gritted teeth. 'Is she an expert with a slate ripper now, as well as a whizz in the water?'

Rosie forced her shoulders upwards. 'I'm not here for home renovations. But I *am* here to help Agnes use her land in a profitable way so that she can repair this roof and save her home. That's why getting my retreats up and running quickly is so important. Because without them . . .' Rosie raised her hands to make her point, a plop of water landing on her head in full support.

'And you thought you couldn't trust me knowing your business plans?' His glare swept to Agnes. 'You confide in her, over me, without even checking who the hell she is?'

Rosie swallowed hard.

'Like I'm just some stupid farmhand?'

His eyebrows pinched together, and Rosie felt a pang of something for him.

She stepped forward. 'Nobody thinks you're stupid. Just . . .' she chewed her words '. . . exceedingly cross.'

'You haven't seen cross,' he said, his face almost giving off steam. A drip of water landed on his shoulder, and he batted it off, moving quickly and thrusting a spare saucepan under it. 'I do not like being lied to. What else have you been hiding?'

'Oh nothing,' said Agnes shrilly, checking her watch. 'I'll just pop and make some tea!'

Rosie opened her mouth to protest, but her boss was off like a shot, singing loudly about raindrops falling on her head, as though to block out the sound of objections.

Just great. It was clear Agnes was leaving the rest of the revelations to Rosie, though perhaps her boss was right about one thing. Eating an elephant – or indeed a pumpkin farmer – one bite at a time, was probably the wisest way. Their immediate issue was to get the roof patched up. And if Rosie dared to mention robot cat factories or getting her hands on his precious gourds right then, he might just blow the roof off.

20

Thank *goodness* for a quiet evening in the log cabin, writing by the soft glimmer from her carved Magic Lanterns. She needed it, after her stressful morning holding ladders for Zain and listening to him turn the air blue over being kept in the dark about Agnes's roof fiasco. After that, she'd spent the afternoon dodging him, conscious that she still had more truths to spill, but desperate to give them both time to cool off.

Curiously, the robot cat tech company were soon on the phone to Agnes, upping their offer by an amount that had made Agnes's dispirited eyes bulge. The suspicious part of Rosie wondered if they'd sabotaged those tiles themselves. Unluckily for them, Rosie was done with being beaten by the likes of technology and idiots.

But first, there were words to write. Wood crackled lightly in the burner, its smoky scent teasing the air. Rosie was cosied up in her Snoopy pyjamas, a cup of tea at her side. She stretched her fingers over the old typewriter keys, closed her eyes, and breathed in all that peace – at last.

If nothing else, it had been a good day for inspiration. As

real-life dramas unfolded, she felt moved to weave them into her fiction. Hot farmers brandishing tools. A heroine with sizzling secrets. Coming together to defeat the bad guys. With a few embellishments and some wishful thinking, life was ready to become art on the typewriter paper in front of her.

'Ahhhh, yes.' Rosie breathed out gently. Everything was perfect and quiet and still, if only for this moment. 'Whoa!' She jumped up, nearly spilling tea over her manuscript. What on earth was that noise?

There was a loud, fast-paced clacking sound coming from outside in the darkness, as if a small army of castanet players was having a fiesta. It was interspersed with high-pitched quacky-squawking. Had the castanet players brought a dolphin? Rosie clambered to one of the windows overlooking the lake and twitched her curtains.

'What the actual . . . ?'

From the gentle glow of the solar string lights outside her cabin, she could just make out the dark figure of Zain, crouching by the water, with a screen. She knew from his previous grunts that he didn't bother with smartphones or devices out here. Presumably there wasn't much point without reception, and he didn't seem like the kind of guy who had friends.

So what was he up to? The curious noises sounded like they were coming from the semi-lit screen. She pursed her lips. If he was a secret tech geek, his days as a muse were over. An image of a bare-bottomed lady robot popped into her head. Urgh. Zain's past was a mystery, but he surely wasn't *that* weird.

Her sensible head wanted to keep her distance. Yet Zain's unexplained magnetism had Rosie pulling on her wellies and a hoodie and creeping out into the night.

'It's just novel research,' she muttered to herself, for the eleventy-billionth time. And perhaps she *could* build on her brave morning and broach some more touchy subjects. Anyway, it was surely her duty to check he wasn't out there disturbing the water voles with images of robot porn. Maybe he'd found a secret Wi-Fi hotspot by the lake and was watching something dodgy.

Click clack click click clickkkkk...

It certainly sounded dodgy. Rosie drew back her shoulders as she paced towards him.

His head shot up as she approached, one finger moving crossly to his pursed mouth. From the dim light of the screen that was illuminating his face she could see he didn't like being disturbed, which meant he *must* be up to trouble. She put her hands on her hips.

'Bats,' he whispered, his full lips pressing against his finger as he spoke.

They really were nice...

'*What*?' The word finally computed at the same time as another round of quaketty-clacking. Rosie ducked, her arms shooting over her head. Her feet lost grip in the slipperiness of the mud, her wellies sliding. She felt the thwack as her bum hit the earth, a traitorous whimper escaping her.

'They're more scared of you than you are of them,' Zain whisper-hissed. He looked like he wanted to stay cross with her but was struggling to stifle his laugh. 'Bat detector.' He nodded at the screen. And perhaps he was also too enamoured with his flying Halloween creatures to keep up his best Zain fury. 'Their calls are usually too high-pitched for us to hear, but with this...' His eyes lit up, as if he'd discovered the very best kind of secret. 'With this we can get a little closer to nature, without disturbing it.'

She pondered his words, knowing that was exactly what they needed for the retreats. Maybe out here, where he was more at peace and less likely to start yelling, was the best place to raise it. Because if she could just get Zain on board . . .

She flinched again as the bat clacking restarted.

To her surprise, Zain moved his crouched body towards her. She almost felt herself moulding to his warmth, like ice cream around particularly hunky jelly. Hmm. She'd have to work on *that* description before it got anywhere near her novel. Zain showed her the screen, which was displaying the noises, almost like a heart monitor. 'They're here to eat the insects over the lake, not you. They'll hibernate soon. Nice to get a last look at them.'

Rosie shuddered. She didn't know much about bats, other than their association with eerie darkness and vampires, neither of which were on her *nice* list.

'Fear of the unknown,' said Zain, as though he was somehow in tune with her tremors. Which he *obviously* wasn't. 'Like the spiders, you'll get used to them. You might even grow to . . .' He looked up at her, his walnut-brown eyes seeming to consider something.

'Like them?' she asked.

He frowned and looked back at the screen.

The contours of his face really were something, and it wasn't her fault if she often found herself studying them because he didn't say a lot, outside of his specialist subjects. What else did she have to go on, besides those angular lines that tried to radiate annoyance but gave occasional glimpses of the passions beneath? Even if it was a touch unusual to get passionate about bats.

'There they are,' he whispered with an excited urgency that would have knocked Rosie onto her bum if she wasn't on it already.

He wrapped one strong arm around her and pulled her back

up into a crouching position, and with the other he pointed towards the sky whilst his bat detector went wild with noises.

They huddled by the water, watching the swoop and soar of the tiny, dark-winged creatures as they hunted for flying insects. Zain's stifled excitement was strangely infectious, and bats *were* sort of cute when they kept their distance.

'Some species are at serious risk of extinction, Rosie.' Had he even used her name before? It sounded so soothing as it danced across his tongue. 'Sorry if I was harsh earlier, but I'm not just a dumb guy who obsesses over pumpkins – I'm here for *all* of it. Even Agnes, in all her saucepan-wielding ridiculousness. And I care about this land. These little guys play an important part in the bigger system, and humans are screwing up their habitat. I'm just trying to do something good. My bat houses are working, even if it's only a small thing in a messed-up world.' He exhaled an almost despairing breath.

'Oh, they're bat houses! So you don't live with a bunch of gnomes.' That explained those funny wooden boxes she'd seen in his cabin.

His eyebrows twisted. 'Gnomes?'

'Please tell me you put the bat houses in trees, and that there aren't breeding bats lined up near your sock drawer.'

'What?'

'Nothing.' She giggled, and they both looked up to the sky as the bats began another round of clacking and diving through the air.

'They have their own traffic rules up there.' His voice was full of wonder, like he was lost in his own thoughts. 'To avoid crashing. They use echolocation to find their prey, but also so they can follow each other's flight paths.'

How was he making the least sexy subject ever seem so fascinating?

'We need them for insect control. More bats, less pesticides,' he continued, his voice still a barely there whisper. She might have thought he'd forgotten her presence if his arm wasn't still around her. Maybe he didn't want her to move and frighten his bats. 'And more bats, more chocolate.'

'Really?' Now she was interested.

'They play a big role in pollination. Not that we're growing cacao around here, obviously. But they take over flower pollination when the butterflies and bees are sleeping. Kind of like night duty. I grow flowers and herbs around my patches, to help with pollination and pest control. Told you I was a fun guy.'

His serious face relaxed into a smile, and he turned his head towards her, their noses almost touching when she mirrored his turn in. She sensed herself smiling too and drinking in this moment. His warm breath against her lips, his eyes slowly moving down towards them. Watching her so intently. She was overwhelmed with an urgency to kiss him – and it wasn't just so that she could write about it.

What? She blinked a few times. Where did *that* thought come from?

'Sorry.' He shook his head and moved it back a few inches. 'Shouldn't have invaded your space.'

'Erm. I think I invaded yours. Maybe it was my echolocation.'

'And now I've got you telling bat jokes.' He clapped a palm against his head. 'Which is exactly why I should keep myself to myself.'

He stood then, nearly toppling her, but catching her quickly and pulling her up with him.

'Getting overenthusiastic about nature, like a big kid.' He pushed his free hand through his long hair. It was as black as the night and not tied back like it usually was. The thick curls lifted and fell like a sigh. 'Not that I really got to be a kid.' He said the last part even more quietly.

Was he about to share something about his past? Rosie held her breath, wanting to know more about him. And for once, it wasn't for the love of a good story.

But he shook his head. 'Honestly. I should go,' he said, pointing to his cabin.

'You were here first.' She shrugged and looked back at hers.

An extremely errant part of her wanted to grab him and pull him there with her, if the notion wasn't completely absurd. They barely knew each other, outside of their constant clashing, and she was still trying to navigate her topsy-turvy new life and bewildered heart. And she could not go losing her job and home for one shameless night of *research*.

'Do you want to come inside?' Damn. Had she said that out loud?

The moment stretched out, more unsaid words dancing between them, until finally he responded. 'Yes.'

Something inside her bounced.

'I mean no.' He exhaled again.

Then he leaned towards her, his arm outstretched. And at that last delicious moment when she thought he was going to cup her face and kiss her, and she was getting ready to sink right in and taste him, to grasp at his long waves and feel the silkiness between her fingers, he moved his hand swiftly towards her hair and made a grabbing motion.

'Leaf in your hair. Sorry.'

She watched his hand pull away. She couldn't see him drop a leaf, but the night was dark. Had he been going to kiss her, or had she completely imagined that? It was like something from one of her romcom novels. Realising her mouth was still open in readiness, she clamped it shut.

The brief touch of his fingertips against her ear had left every nerve ending tingling. Except, more than anything, she'd wanted his lips on her mouth.

'Goodnight,' he said, sounding more flustered than usual, before turning to walk away.

Why was her heart sinking? Kissing him had never been part of her plan. He was meant to be inspiration for her wild and free story. This man belonged safely locked in the confines of her imagination. Yet somehow, her thoughts and feelings were beginning to spill out.

'Wait,' she hissed, not wanting to disturb the bats and their bug-shaped dinner. Despite everything reeling around her jumbled head, she didn't want him to leave yet. 'Will you . . . show me your bat houses?' She tried not to inwardly groan, because that had to be the worst line ever.

21

Wow, had she really just come out with a terrible line about bat houses? Not that she was trying to pick Zain up – especially not after the awkward *leaf in your hair* incident. She was just curious about flying mammals. And she did have pumpkin-shaped truths to discuss with Zain, whether he wanted to hear them or not.

'You want to see my bat houses? Out in the fields?' He seemed surprised.

Well, she'd half hoped they could inspect the ones in his hut, which were presumably empty. Somewhere warm, that smelt like cedar and manly musk, and where she might cadge a cup of tea, if teabags weren't too cutting edge for him.

She held up her chin, pretending she wasn't wearing Snoopy pyjama bottoms with a mud patch on her rear. 'Of course in the fields. I'm not scared. The other day, I didn't even scream at the snake in your pumpkin compost.' He hopefully couldn't see she had her fingers crossed behind her back or hear her heart racing. 'And I make bug houses. I care about this place too, you know.'

'I did receive Wingsor Castle,' he said, clearly fighting the edges of a smile. 'As strange as it was.' He shrugged and paced back towards her, eyeing her patterned wellies doubtfully and grabbing her hand. 'Walking boots would have been safer, but you'll be all right.'

Now she had her hand tucked inside his, she had a strong sense she would be – even if the thought seemed peculiar.

Click clack click click clickkkkk . . .

She jumped and moved closer into him. If she could only get used to these funny bat noises.

As they crept around the edges of the fields, their path lit only by the screen of Zain's bat detector and the iridescent moon, they slid into all kinds of unlikely chat. Zain pointed out the bat boxes he'd apparently made from old wood and fixed into the trees. When he launched into a lively whisper about bat roosting and mating seasons, he was quick to apologise, mumbling something about his lack of conversation skills and being an oddball.

Rosie squeezed his hand, which she was only still holding for health and safety reasons. 'Nothing is odder than the couple of weeks I've had. I feel like I've literally seen and heard it all.' And while there was no way she was going to admit that she'd misjudged every single man in her whole history of relationships, including, perhaps, her late sort-of fiancé, she did find herself spilling the tale of walking in on her ex trying to conjugate with a life-like sexy robot.

Zain turned to look at her, his eyes dancing with confusion. 'What?'

'Exactly. And that was just moments after I lost my writing job to a computer chatbot thingy called Kimberkoo Chat. Artificial Intelligence that's more creative than me.' She huffed into the night, her breath producing a cross little cloud, which made her want to laugh at the sheer stupidity. It felt like a lifetime away now she was here. Zain's decades-old bat screen was surely the most state-of-the-art thing she was *ever* going to contend with at Autumn Meadows, and she didn't mind if technology had better ears than her.

'K . . . K . . . Kimberkoo?' Zain seemed to have trouble getting the word out.

'I know, extraordinary name. I didn't even dignify it with a Google search, because I don't want to see the thing in action.'

'Right,' he said, scratching the back of his neck.

'My old boss reckoned it could probably script whole love stories. Can you imagine? It's just nonsense, isn't it? Talk about technology overstepping the mark.'

'*Overstepping the mark*,' he grunted back. 'Wait. Your job was writing? Thought you were something to do with organising retreats?'

'Yes!' she said quickly, trying not to grimace. 'That too. I do all sorts, really. Creative things. Did I mention I'm writing a novel?'

His eyes widened. There, that usually distracted people. She didn't need to admit that her previous attempts had been rejected for being strangely bereft of romance, or that her current fictional hero was based almost entirely on him.

'I'd better not be in it.'

'Nooooo. Writers never use people they know.' *Much.*

They walked on for a while in silence, Rosie behind Zain, his usually strong shoulders appearing slack. She'd expected more of a grilling on her slip-up over job roles, but presumably her full-blown robot-sex revelation had trumped the fact she liked to write stuff. That was bound to turn even the toughest person a touch queasy. She wasn't usually such an over-sharer, but Zain had been sharing some of his heart too, even if he hadn't meant to.

Rosie tried to turn the conversation back to bat chat, but it didn't engage him. Zain's arms hung at his sides, the bat detector almost forgotten. Even the bats had gone eerily silent.

Since the mood was already broken, maybe it was a good moment to tackle the other subject that had been filling her with dread. They weren't going to get anywhere talking about kinky androids or winged mammals.

It was time to get real, and she finally had Agnes's permission to do so. She took a deep breath and balled her fists.

'I need to start laying down plans for these retreats, here on the farm. As you saw today, it's getting quite urgent.' She winced, fully expecting a backlash.

Instead, she got another huff.

'Agnes didn't want to worry you, but if we don't use the retreats to scrape together the funds to fix her roof by winter, she'll have to find another option. Right now, the only obvious one is to start selling off the land.'

Zain stopped abruptly, his back stiffening. 'Sell it to who? What about my pumpkin fields?'

'The only people interested are a tech company. I think they're more into mass-producing robo-creatures than preserving anything that's living.'

He spun around to face her, his eyes feral in the moonlight. 'What?'

'They make robot cats, and they want this land to build a factory.'

Zain's face was a knot of angst, and if it was possible to see a heart breaking through all those layers of jumper, she was seeing it now.

'A factory?' His voice was still low, but every part of him was shaking like he might just explode. 'A dirty big concrete mess over the top of everything I've been trying to grow? And not for the first time, why has nobody breathed a damned word of this to me before now?'

Rosie remembered Agnes calling him an undetonated bomb, but it probably wasn't prudent to mention that.

'Agnes hoped it wouldn't come to that, and she didn't want to upset you.'

'Upset me?' The flashing red eyeballs were back. 'What am I, a child? What *upsets* me is everybody lying. So if there is *anything* else you've been hiding from me, I suggest you tell me now. It works out well for you that I don't want to disturb the bats, because you do not want to hear the full force of my fury.'

Rosie swallowed hard, thinking of the other bombshell that would cause even more wreckage.

He took a step back and exhaled, as though realising that even his quiet aggression was a lot. He rubbed a hand against his temple.

'There is one more thing,' Rosie said slowly. Well, one more thing he *had* to know. She'd still be harbouring her own closet skeletons, if she didn't want to get the sack.

'The thing is . . . Agnes had some advice. The best way to create real interest for the retreats is to offer what this farm does best. We need to give people the sort of retreat experience they can't find anywhere else around here.'

His forehead creased. 'What the hell? Not *naked* wild swimming? I was pissed off enough about hipsters in swimming pants, but if they're going to be parading round with their balls on display, hugging trees and getting pubes in the lake . . .'

'No, Zain. The farm's Unique Selling Point isn't nudist swimming.' She braced herself for the storm. 'It's *pumpkins*.'

Zain's jaw dropped, his eyes widening like a pair of Baby Boos.

'No. *No way*. I am not having people trampling around the place, poking their noses into my precious Warty Goblins, carving up my Crown Princes and wanting to turn my Casperitas into pumpkin-spiced latte.'

'It would be nothing like that!' Now wasn't the time to mention that she really missed a pumpkin-spiced coffee. 'I honestly think we can work together on this. Reach a compromise that suits everyone. Because it's got to be better than the alternative.'

His face tightened.

'The sort of people who'd want to visit would respect and love nature. They'd come to switch off from the outside world and to bask in these glorious surroundings. Doesn't everyone deserve that chance?'

'What others need is *not* my problem.'

'But this land is. It's a farm, Zain. And Agnes tells me it used to be a profitable one, in the days when her husband was alive. You worked with him too, didn't you?'

His look was incredulous.

'Everything you've been doing here is so impressive,' she continued. 'I've never seen so many pumpkin varieties. They're *beautiful*. I've been learning more about them too, and their potential uses. But isn't it all wasted if the crops aren't being enjoyed or used for anything?'

She sensed the fields had become his own, slightly self-indulgent project, though she didn't dare say it.

'Just like us, a pumpkin doesn't simply want to exist and then die. It wants its chance to *be a pumpkin* and do all of the things a pumpkin was born to do.'

A vein twitched near his temple, and was he actually baring his teeth?

'A pumpkin wants its chance to *be a pumpkin*? Well, now I've heard it all. Sounds like Kimberkoo Chat doesn't have a patch on you.'

She was surprised he'd remembered its name.

'All I'm saying is that farms should be productive,' she replied, trying to sound calm. 'Pumpkin patches can be hugely popular during autumn. And if we can offer wild retreat experiences with the glow of the pumpkin fields as a backdrop, we could really be onto something.'

He glared at her. 'I came here for peace.'

'Surely we could reach an arrangement that respects your privacy and your work, but still brings the retreats to life? You and me against the robot cats.' She let out a nervous laugh.

'There is no *you and me*,' he replied firmly. 'I'm a lone weirdo who gets excited about bats and gourds. And that's exactly the way I like it. Gourds don't lie or let you down.' He stepped around her, passing the bat screen to her, presumably as a source of light. 'I'm heading back, and so should you.'

There was probably nothing out there but a few flying creatures and the odd fox, though at least it seemed he didn't wish death upon her. Surely that was *something*?

As they walked, Zain's shape solid against the dark, starry sky, Rosie couldn't help but feel for him. Despite the fact she would never have had herself down as a nocturnal beast expeditioner, seeing Zain so animated about the bats had been a rare and magical treat. She'd enjoyed spending time with him. They'd almost been getting along, until she'd had to ruin it.

But needs must.

And much like him, she didn't have space for any *you and me* in her life – even if, now and again, in her wild, fictional imaginings, she did enjoy wondering.

22

'I'm *siiiiiiiiinging* in the shower.'

Rosie had to sing, to stave off the nerves. She flicked the tap off and grabbed her towel, throwing it around her and stepping towards her wellies. Her new friends would soon be arriving to make a start on the retreat plans, and she was a buzz of tension and excitement. She could only hope that Zain wouldn't be obstructive, because although she'd spilled the truth about the pumpkin USP, he hadn't yet given his blessing. In fact, she couldn't be sure he wasn't plotting to destroy her with a giant orange cucurbit. But it wasn't his land, and she had a job to do.

'Lovely weather for a cold blast,' she half-yelled to the very man, who'd appeared at the entrance to the open-air shower wrapped in his own towel, paired with a teasingly tight T-shirt and woolly hat.

He gave his usual grunt.

It was still pretty dark and crisp at six a.m., but Rosie had been learning to embrace the autumnal outdoor cold showers with loud singing to counteract the sting. It was the only option, with no bathroom in her wooden hut – and it wasn't hygienic to wash her private bits in the same sink where she cleaned her teacups.

Zain's eyes were wide, on his usually nonchalant face. He'd probably never seen her taking the cold shower by storm, as she often sneaked in later, when the day was a few degrees warmer. But today Rosie had plans, and she was keen to get started, come what may. She reached for her heart-patterned dressing gown, which was on a makeshift hook, and swung it around her shoulders.

'Oops. Mustn't forget this.' She bent to pick up the upside-down glass and slip of thin cardboard that she'd left on a nearby tree stump. 'My humane spider catcher. You get some real biggies in the toilet hut. Don't worry. I've got them all out for you.' She gave him a wink. 'I'm popping to the house as soon as I'm dressed. It's bacon and egg Saturday, so I'll bring your rolls back for you, if you like?' Kill him with kindness was as good a plan as any. 'Save your legs.'

She pointed to his, which were bare below his towel. She tried to ignore how inviting the soft dark hair along his firm calves looked, because calves were surely not meant to be sexy. And those rugged work boots, undone and ready to be pulled off, much like that fluffy grey towel...

Rosie shook herself back to her less steamy reality. This shower did uncommon things to her. 'Probably my turn to get the breakfast, anyway. Black coffee?' She didn't dare mention pumpkin spice.

It was the understatement of the season to say it was her turn, considering there was a tray of food and coffee outside her front door each morning, and she was fairly sure Agnes wasn't ambling over in the dark, followed by fourteen stray cats and a one-eyed chicken. Though every time she'd tried to thank Zain, he shrugged it off.

Rosie blew Zain's still-surprised face a kiss, before hurrying back towards her hut to get warm and dry.

Wait. She'd blown him a kiss? She tried not to wince as she stomped across the grass. *Get back in control, Rosie.* It must have been the shock of the cold shower making her brazen, or the fact she'd secretly enjoyed his bat-watching company a few nights ago, until the point she'd started talking about robots and the threat of his prized pumpkin fields being sold.

She arrived back at her hut and pushed through the door, sitting herself by the toasty log burner, thinking about that night again. They hadn't spoken since, other than his reluctant huffs of acknowledgement. She guessed he needed time to brood about her revelations, and even she was glad of the breathing space after that curious *is he about to kiss me?* moment. Had there really been a leaf in her hair? Had he wanted more than a bit of foliage removal too?

Whatever was going on, when she had some more solid retreat plans, she would have to approach him. At least he hadn't downed tools or fled, even if she'd seen him slope off in the direction of the farm's exit a few times. Had he been going somewhere?

Rosie checked the clock and began pulling on her clothes, opting for her swirly dungarees. It was still early, but she had breakfast to collect, the next chapter of her novel to write, and a whole lot of highlighted lists to bring together.

In moments of wildness, she was still wondering if she could combine her passion for writing with her growing love for the great outdoors to offer writing retreats. She knew people would come for the nature, pumpkins and the promise of peace, but they surely couldn't harvest juicy pumpkins all year long. Out of season, they would need other ideas. This place helped her to switch off her mind from the busyness of real life, and write.

Could she make space for other budding authors to do the same? It would be one in the eye for chatbots taking over.

The trouble was, Agnes still thought that if anything, Rosie would be whipping out blank canvases and teaching people to paint. That was what the real interviewee for Rosie's job loved to do. Rosie still prayed that *Rachel* didn't show up, or she'd be homeless without a cause – and this place was coming to mean everything to her.

Not long later, Rosie's new friends were tearing towards her cabin in a flurry of '*coo-ees*' and waves. Her heart swelled at the sight of them. Like a true protagonist, she'd gathered her team – and she couldn't have dreamed up a better one.

Mags had brought flasks of tea because she didn't trust Rosie's intermittent electrics. Bonnie had her big smile, and no doubt a collection of sweet treats. And Luna had brought her girlfriend, Ellen. Luna and Ellen had spent a summer working in North America making teepees, which apparently made them a dream camp-making team. Ellen was pushing a wheelbarrow of goodies they'd managed to gather.

'Everyone was so generous in the village, especially when we mentioned how vital it is that we make these retreats work,' said Luna, giving Rosie a hello hug.

Ellen bounced over for an introductory squeeze too. She was tall, slight and naturally beautiful like Luna, but with long blonde hair that had been dyed blue and green at the tips. 'And I'm sure there will be plenty more donations when word gets around. Nobody wants to see the big house crumble, especially with those cute cats and dogs needing shelter.' She bent down to give Steve a stroke. He seemed to have appointed himself as overseer already, somehow wearing a lumberjack-style cat coat today. Did Zain have a range of outfits for him?

'Luna might have painted a worst-case, *imagine if the land got sold for a dirty great factory* situation,' Bonnie whispered. 'That soon got people keen to help. I'm surprised they didn't follow us down like a rescue crew. They're loving your mission, Rosie. Everybody's rooting for you.'

Rosie blinked a few times, feeling a rush of something. She realised she was trying to hold back tears. Maybe this was how it felt not to be a spare part. To be out here making a difference, rather than writing about periodontitis for a numpty named Kelvin. *Make yourself irreplaceable*, he'd told her. She wouldn't quite say she was that, but she was fighting for something – even if it was still extremely precarious.

'Thank you,' she mumbled into her sleeve as she tried to swallow a sob. It was a lot of weight on her shoulders, even if she did have the world's loveliest helpers.

'At least the Gingerbread Café in the village sent emergency ginger and rum cake,' said Mags, settling herself down on Rosie's cabin steps. 'Here, at your service.' She kicked off her wellies and stretched out her toes, not looking like she intended to do a great deal any time soon.

Bonnie tutted and dragged a huge pile of canvas from the wheelbarrow. 'You'll be helping me measure and cut this for the teepees, while Luna and Ellen sort the poles.'

'I've been thinking about how you could spread word of the retreats,' said Luna. 'There's a local woman called Lexie who runs a popular blog and knows loads of other bloggers. She's happy to share what she can.'

'We could all shout stuff out on social media,' said Ellen.

Rosie thanked her. If she was honest with herself, her sister Flick could probably drop a few posts and make the retreats a hit. Though that would involve letting her family know where she was, and she couldn't cope with her mum and sister turning up and blowing her cover – or the fact that if they arrived, they'd surely bring more orange letters full of hurtful words and possibilities she couldn't face.

'Bea from a gorgeous shop in the village sent bunches of dried lavender for the teepees,' said Luna. 'Great for tranquillity and sleep. She sent honey too.'

Rosie inhaled a deep breath of the lavender. It certainly was calming.

'Pumpkin waffles and cinnamon honey butter,' said Mags, as though she was already creating her perfect retreat breakfast menu. 'Bea is Farmer Wilbur's daughter. Do you know him? He's good friends with Agnes.'

Rosie gulped. 'Well, people have been kind.' She put her hand on her heart, which did feel touched, even if it was now beginning to race at the mention of Wilbur. She hoped he was still on the long autumn holiday Zain had mentioned. 'But maybe we won't call in the rescue crew just yet.'

In fact, all of these details were giving Rosie more ideas of her own and reminding her that she was good at things too. She could add her own tweaks and creations to make guests feel at home. She'd learned all sorts from her mum's staff through the years, from towel sculptures to making chocolates for pillows, and she could hand-craft more soaps like the ones in the shower that she was sure Zain was still sneakily using. And of course, there would be all manner of cute pumpkins, when she finally got her hands on them.

They set to work outside Rosie's cabin, the late September sun warming their backs and reflecting off the lake like it was a large, glittery mirror. Birds sang from the trees and coppery-coloured bushes, seeming happy with their company. Rosie couldn't help wondering where Zain was, though she was trying not to panic about how he might react *or* to have wayward memories about his full lips in the moonlight.

Luna and Ellen pulled out lengths of rope and various supplies from the trolley. Agnes had agreed to them using logs and planks from the woodshed, with or without Zain's blessing. Mags ambled around barefoot, pointing a lot and pretending to look busy.

Bonnie helped Rosie to lay her plans out across the grass, weighing the sheets of paper down at the corners with pebbles. Rosie knelt, took her coloured pens and scribbled more notes. How would she divide these jobs up? Where would these yurts even go, if they needed to work around Zain's fields? Would they provide enough sleeping space? Her head filled with more questions than answers. Just as she looked up to quiz Bonnie, she realised that the person kneeling next to her was Zain.

23

Zain laid out a sheet of paper of his own on the grass, next to Rosie's. 'Brainstorming. Not my usual thing, but ... you know.'

Rosie's mouth dropped open. Did she dare to believe he'd come out here to help with their retreat preparations – even if they had to involve his pumpkins as the USP? Maybe her home truths about Cyber Purrz had finally filtered through. Her heart lifted.

'I saw them,' he blurted out. 'Some guys in suits, sniffing around. Pointing at my fields and talking about destroying everything. One said they could pour concrete in the lake, and the other said my pumpkins were a pointless waste of space.' Anger sparked in his eyes.

'Concrete?' Rosie uttered the word like it was tinged with wickedness. This place was fast becoming part of her soul, and she was damned if she'd let anyone fill her lake with rock so they could build a fake cat factory.

'The worst thing is,' he said quietly, 'they have a point. Just like you warned me. Farms should be productive; I know that. And Agnes's husband was good to me. I should be doing better by them both.' He blew out a long breath. 'My crops *have* almost become a waste of space. What's the point in my experiments if I churn out speciality pumpkins and do nothing with them? I've been selfish. My ancestors wouldn't have squandered good produce like this.'

'You're not selfish.' She squeezed his hand, noticing his fingers curl back around hers for a second. They both pulled away. 'Look, you're helping us now, aren't you?'

He gave an almost imperceptible nod.

'What are your experiments? If you don't mind me asking.'

'I do,' he replied. 'Mind you asking. I just came to give you my thoughts on these retreats.'

Well, you couldn't blame a girl for trying.

'Fair enough. Let's look at these plans.' Rosie busied herself with Zain's notes, which to her surprise, were pretty impressive. It was as if he'd swallowed the encyclopedia on how to create the perfect wild retreat – which *obviously* he hadn't. That sort of thing didn't even exist. For someone who shunned a smartphone and presumably didn't bother with Google, he'd compiled quite a list – even down to some quirky ways they could incorporate his pumpkins.

'Are you saying you're OK with these officially being pumpkin farm retreats?' She held her breath.

'Mmm.'

It was more of a growl than a *'woo hoo, let's do this'* – but it was beyond what Rosie could have hoped for.

'Thank you.' She kept it simple, conscious a gushing response might send him stomping off. 'How did you come up with all this? It's brilliant. Did you . . . go to the library?' She could barely imagine his gruff exterior and muddy boots among the bunting and books.

He huffed. 'I do have a brain, you know.'

'Of course.' Perhaps Zain was naturally good at this sort of thing. Some people used search engines and chatbots, but Zain didn't need to. What other hidden talents did he have?

She put a hand on his bare forearm and immediately wished she hadn't. It was warm and firm, and she had the sudden feeling that touching him might become addictive. She allowed herself a moment before pulling away. 'This . . .' She placed his list down next to her list collection, weighing its corners with pebbles too. 'This might just save us.'

He shook his head. 'You're doing all the saving. It's just a few extra thoughts from . . . well, me. Logistics. You're the one with the details. Flowers in the loo. Stinky soaps. Making people feel special.' He scratched the back of his neck. 'Or whatever.'

Did she really make people feel special? Had her small gestures started to make him feel that way? Rosie had always been told it was rude to stare. Yet here she was, getting lost in Zain's gaze for what seemed like the longest time, even though it could only have been a few heartbeats.

She cleared her throat, and they went back to looking at their lists. Though as their elbows touched as they rearranged paperwork on the grass, she heard his surprised intake of breath. Had he felt that spark too? As she accidentally caught his gaze, there was something in his deep, woody eyes that she hadn't seen before. And his look made her *feel* something. Like a swooshing. Once again, she kind of liked it, and would definitely put that in her book.

Rosie heard Luna making a low wolf-whistle sound from across the grass and could see from the corner of her eye that she was nudging Ellen and pointing at her and Zain. Rosie quickly pulled her gaze away from his and fiddled with her ponytail.

'My experiments,' he said hurriedly, as though he might

change his mind. 'We might as well be honest with each other, if we need to work together. At least if I tell you, you won't need to go poking around.'

'Honesty!' she said breezily. 'Always the best policy.' Other than she wasn't going to divulge that she was an impostor, that a woman called Bianca was trying to hunt her down with mean orange letters, or that at least one of her ex-boyfriends had been on *Crimewatch*.

'I'm trying to bring back some all-but-lost varieties. I got hold of rare seeds from distant relatives.' He shrugged, like he didn't want to go into it. 'My family history is complicated. I've also been cross-breeding, to make varieties of my own. Crops that are hardier, so they can grow better and stronger, even out of season. And some I'm just toying with, to see how quirky I can make them.' His lips twitched into an *almost* smile. 'It all goes on, in those polytunnels.'

'Could some of these experiments help us?' said Rosie, the cogs in her brain turning. 'It's been bothering me that the pumpkin retreats might not work outside of autumn. Are you saying we could extend them to other seasons to?'

'Possibly, in time. If I can get my head around people being here, in theory, we could involve visitors at different stages of the year – spring planting, summer growing, autumn harvest. I guess a pumpkin patch is for life, not just for autumn. And it's better than the alternative.' He gave a small shudder. 'Hell, I could probably do with some help out there, if we're going to get *profitable*.' He said the word as though he still didn't like it. 'We can move with the seasons too. Wildflower meadows, sunflowers . . . Those might attract people in *and* help with pollination. We can work it out as we go.'

Rosie grabbed his arm again. 'You're right. But first, the pumpkin retreats. Are you in on helping too?'

He sighed. 'Happy to do what I need to, I guess.'

'He's happy,' Rosie heard Bonnie whisper not quite quietly enough to Mags as the pair of them wandered over. 'She's put a spell on him.'

'That's one word for it,' Mags not-so-whispered back.

Zain shot them a look and then stood, shaking himself down.

'Why don't you show me this field you've suggested for the retreat base camp?' Rosie said quickly, jumping up with him. 'We'll size it up for the teepees. And I love your idea about treehouses.'

'Treehouses? I'll never get myself up into a horse chestnut,' said Mags, offering Zain a parcel of cake.

His eyes widened, like he wasn't accustomed to kind gestures. After a slight hesitation, he exhaled and took it. 'They'd be more like wooden huts built onto the trees' structure and strengthened from below by stilts, rather than something you need to swing into, like Tarzan.'

'Knew he reminded me of someone,' Mags muttered.

'On stilts?' said Bonnie.

'It gives a true immersive experience,' said Zain slowly, as if trying to remember something. Then his words picked up pace. 'Being up there in nature, the rustle of the trees as you sleep. The views of the pumpkin fields to greet you as you wake.' He swept his arm in their general direction. 'A small balcony for al fresco dining on a hearty pumpkin stew, while you gaze at the stars. A set of binoculars to take in the birds as they peck happily from the pumpkin bird feeders. Not to mention the health benefits of forest bathing, or *shinrin-yoku*, as the Japanese call it. It reduces stress hormone production, boosts your immune system, awakens your senses, brings your creative soul to life . . .'

Rosie scratched her head. Who was this, and what on earth

had they done with Zain? Now he was definitely starting to sound like he'd inhaled a brochure on the perfect pumpkin retreat lifestyle, complete with a few tomes on health and well-being. But like he said, he had a brain. It would be rude for anyone to assume he hadn't.

Yes, Zain Kay had hidden depths. And the more Rosie saw of them, the more she liked.

Perhaps she should get him to write the retreats' promotional material. He was certainly selling it to the others, who had all gathered around. Luna was looking gooey-eyed, and her girlfriend Ellen was tutting at her, good-naturedly.

'And fewer creepy-crawlies and slithering creatures up there too,' said Mags. 'I don't want any adders up my ladder.'

Zain shrugged. 'Maybe Rosie will lend you her humane spider catcher. The best thing about the treehouses is that they'll be a compromise.' He turned to Rosie and held her with one of his looks, that were fast making her feel like she was the only other person in the universe. 'They won't take up precious meadow space or encroach onto the habitats of the farm's wildlife. It will be more about co-existing in harmony. Growing to understand each other but still respecting the other's space. I used to think people just brought problems – but I'm starting to learn that some have good hearts.' He stopped for a moment, as though trying to remember what came next.

'He gives a lovely speech,' Luna breathed. 'He should be an actor, or something.'

'They're all my own words.' Zain's response was a little on the gruff side, but he shook himself and blinked a few times, his face looking like he was trying to compute something. 'Respecting each other's space, good hearts,' he muttered, checking things off on his fingers. 'Yes, that was it.' He lifted his head. 'Some people want to make things better, even if they seem out of their depth and they wear the most unsuitable wellies. I respect that.'

Rosie tried not to grin.

He really did have a lot of words today, and not all of them sounded like the version of Zain that Rosie had come to know – but she could get used to the compliments. Rosie could only guess that seeing the men in suits sizing the place up and threatening to bring concrete had lit a fire under his particularly firm backside. That couldn't be a bad thing.

'We need to talk more about this compromising,' said Rosie, grabbing Zain's arm and pointing towards the fields. 'Shall we?'

She experienced an unmistakable pull to hear more of his intriguing words. Suddenly it felt like, together, there was a growing possibility they could get somewhere.

Though there was a tug of fear that she ought to curb her mounting desire to be dangerously close to Zain. When she'd arrived, she had carefully constructed reasons to keep her distance. She had too many secrets. He was her mysterious muse. Her romantic life always ended in spectacular disaster. But the more she spent time with this intriguing hermit with the hidden heart, the more parts of that fell away. If she wasn't careful, she'd have no walls left.

If they worked together, could she still keep a colleague-safe distance? And if she didn't, would their newly found level of compromise come crashing down?

To everyone's surprise, he took her hand and squeezed it. How long would this fascinating new version of Zain be sticking around?

24

Rosie heard a shuffling outside the door of her cabin, followed by a muffled cough.

'Your smile lights up the sky. And ... erm ... it's kind of dark out here.'

She thought she heard a rustling of papers, although she might have imagined that bit. In fact, she was half-convinced she was imagining the whole thing. Was that Zain's voice out there in the darkness? It sounded like him. But like on a few occasions during that day, it didn't seem like the sort of thing he would usually say. Maybe everything that was going on was changing him too.

Rosie stood in the candlelight, hugging her mug of milky tea. She'd been about to sit down and write, after a busy day of helping to build teepees and plan treehouses. Through her written words, she'd wanted to explore the tingle of *something* that had been growing between her and Zain that day.

'Don't make me do the *baby it's cold outside* line.' He coughed. 'Not that I have any actual lines, obviously. Erm. Anyway, the weather's pretty mild. Are you in there?'

Rosie couldn't help a grin as she opened the door to the person who was definitely Zain, albeit an unusually nervous version.

He looked a little dazed at the sight of her, like she'd thrown him off script. Maybe he wasn't accustomed to fully-grown women in embarrassing Eeyore pyjamas.

'I . . . erm.' He looked over his shoulder towards the lake and then back at Rosie. 'I don't usually forget what I was meant to say.'

'Must be my sky-lighting smile, putting you off.' She gave him a wink to let him know she was jesting.

'I think it was the donkey,' he said, pointing to her top. 'Cool character, that Eeyore. Grumpy, but misunderstood. Shall we . . . start again?'

Rosie nodded, not quite sure what they were starting again, but keen to find out. Was he planning more bat watching?

Zain held out his hand. 'The stars are incredible tonight. I'd like to share them with you.'

She laughed and took in the view beyond him, suddenly feeling like she was on a film set. The dark sky above was beautiful, studded with more glittering stars than she'd ever seen. They reflected and shimmered across the lake, which she now noticed was edged with carved pumpkin lanterns.

What – *he'd taken a knife to his pumpkins*? Rosie blinked a few times. Didn't he have strict rules about his precious vine fruit?

And was that a wooden rowing boat bobbing next to the jetty? She knew there'd been one stuck in the overgrown bullrushes, but she'd never properly seen it.

And then there was Zain. Standing on her doorstep, wearing a navy suit, the white shirt underneath pulling tight across his firm chest like the buttons wanted to break loose. She'd never seen him in anything that wasn't fit for labouring outdoors, as much as she secretly loved to ogle him in his tight T-shirts and work boots. Tonight, his hair was scraped back neatly into a low bun, even though a few wavy strands had already pulled away.

Yet more than anything she could see, was the feeling swelling up inside her. The *floating-to-the-top-of-the-world-ness* that filled every part of her as he held her gaze, his solid hand still outstretched like a question. If somebody didn't tie her down, she might just glide away.

Was she being *wooed*? It was a thing she'd read about in scores of love stories. Heroines being swept off their feet by swishy, romantic gestures – but it had never happened to her in real life. She'd come to believe that sort of thing was reserved for fiction or the glamorous few. The ones who took the starring roles, not the forgettable extras. Perhaps her luck was changing.

Well then, she'd better put down her cup of tea and go with it. If Autumn Meadows had taught her anything, it was that if she never stopped to smell the rambling roses, she couldn't truly write about them. Was that why her own love stories had always fallen flat? Rosie Featherstone needed some first-hand experience of being wooed.

She let her hand slip into Zain's and felt the warm deliciousness of it closing around hers, encircling her fingers. With her other arm she pulled down a coat from the hook near the door. Looking down at her feet, she realised that fluffy slipper socks weren't ideal for whatever nocturnal pursuits Zain was planning. Before she had time to locate her wellies, she heard Zain mumbling something about being her chariot, and suddenly he was sweeping her up into his arms like on the day he'd rescued her from the lake. Only this time she was giggling and calling him silly, and he was smiling, his eyes shining as her legs kicked with glee.

'Where are you taking me?' Rosie managed to ask, through

her laughter. She tucked herself into his warmth, his usual cedar scent embracing her.

'Dinner on the lake.' He tipped his chin towards the boat she'd noticed. 'I think the bats have just about finished feeding so we shouldn't bug them too much.' Then he winced, as though realising the bat part wasn't quite so romantic. 'I wasn't meant to say that.'

'According to whom?!'

But he didn't answer. Instead, he strode purposefully towards the water. She looped one arm around his strong neck to steady herself. Her other hand landed on his chest, and she couldn't help noticing that the buttons on his white shirt were undone just enough to allow a glimpse of the black tattoos stretching across his tanned honey flesh. Her fingers twitched to touch them.

Much to her disappointment, they arrived at the jetty too quickly, and he was soon placing her down. Her legs had never felt so unsteady – and it was nothing to do with where she'd landed. She took a few deep breaths and looked around her. The sight would have made even one of Jane Austen's romantic heroines weak at the knees.

The jetty had been lined with more tiny jack-o'-lanterns and there were solar string lights woven through the bullrushes. Solar-lit autumn flowers bobbed across the water and the calming sound of crickets was being played from who knew where. The boat itself had received a repaint and was now called *Rosie and Him*, which was so cheesy that it made her chuckle again. A low table had been placed on the middle with a carved Sweet Dumpling pumpkin acting as a lamp. And to top it all off, she spotted a picnic basket, a blanket and a bottle of what looked like Bonnie's elderflower wine near the end of the jetty.

'Are we eating?' asked Rosie, really hoping so.

'Yes, of course. When surveyed, seventy-four per cent of people agreed that a date should include food. Although only twelve per cent suggested the food should be seasonal. Clearly, they don't understand the nutritional benefits of a pumpkin.'

'You did a survey?' Rosie laughed.

'No! Obviously not. I just read something, and . . .'

'You've been reading up on dates?'

'Also no.' He straightened his collar. 'Ignore me. I was just thinking out loud.'

Rosie nodded sagely. 'Seventy-four per cent of people probably do it.'

She tried to hide the glimmer from her eyes at the thought that this must be a date, because it was almost too perfect to be true. Even the fullness of the moon and the blanket of stars was on their side tonight.

And unless she was imagining things, he'd just suggested he'd been cooking up his prized gourds, in her honour. This *was* a surprise.

Zain seemed to remember himself, and the boat. 'Allow me to help you in.'

25

Rosie wondered if Zain had speed-read the dictionary of dating etiquette as he offered her a stable hand into the boat. It wobbled beneath her slipper-socked feet, nonetheless. She swiftly sat to avoid a woman-overboard situation. Zain stepped in steadily with the supplies, almost like he'd been practising his newly found finesse.

'I prepared us a meal,' he declared, still not sounding quite like himself.

Rosie guessed it was nerves, which made her heart melt for him even more. He'd gone to such huge lengths to do something special for her. Something way out of his usual, people-repelling comfort zone. Just like her feelings for him had been growing, maybe his had too. Though if she pondered the thought too much, it would terrify her.

She reached over and squeezed his arm. 'Thank you. And it's OK to just be you.'

He gave her a strange look. 'I . . . I am. I just don't want to get this wrong.' His hand inched towards his pocket and then snapped back. 'I'm sorry. This is not my usual thing.' His dark eyes looked lost for a moment. 'My usual thing is pretty rubbish.' He blinked, perhaps not meaning to have said the last bit.

Rosie reached over for a double squeeze, rocking the boat again. 'I love your usual thing.' The bat boxes, the quirky pumpkin facts, his passion for things she'd never even thought about. She was coming to see that she really meant it. His way of seeing the world was stretching her imagination, and his kindness beneath the grumpy exterior was warming her more each day. But it was far too soon to start spurting all of that. So she settled on: 'It's cute.'

Did he seem the tiniest bit disappointed with *cute*? If he did, he quickly reset himself.

Zain used the oars to row them further into the middle of the lake, his arms moving rhythmically, the water swishing gently in tune. Rosie let her fingers trail along its dark, glassy surface, the autumn coolness calming the unexpected date nerves that were starting to build. No one had ever done anything quite so special for her and she could barely get her head around what it meant.

'Hope you like pumpkins.' Zain's random statement broke through her thoughts.

'Pardon?'

'Sorry, I'm getting this all backwards.' He put the oars down inside the boat and blinked at her. 'I was meant to say that tonight's meal will whip you up into a whirlwind of pumpkin deliciousness. Get ready to sample the delights of pumpkin hummus with a light and fluffy pumpkin bread, followed by a baked pumpkin fondue, and finished off with a pumpkin and ginger cheesecake that will set your taste buds racing. And luckily, your friend Bonnie thrust her wine at me, because I didn't have time to think about that.'

He began pulling supplies from the picnic basket and arranging everything on the makeshift table between them. 'I thought your retreat people might enjoy getting into nature for some seasonal foraging too, with a little guidance.' He smiled at her. 'As long as they don't kill themselves on a poisonous mushroom.'

'Always better not to.' Rosie chuckled. 'This is incredible.' She cast her eyes over the spread being laid out in front of her. 'And you've actually cooked your own pumpkins? I thought there would be strict rules about that sort of behaviour.'

He shrugged. 'There are rules about who gets their hands on my special ones. But I have a whole lot of pumpkins.'

Wow. He was changing.

'Where did you get these tasty recipe ideas?' she asked, willing her thoughts not to wander to where her hands dreamed of drifting to.

'They're all my own,' he said quickly, not for the first time that day.

Rosie added *inspired menu choices* to his list of unexpected talents.

'And the food's nothing much. Just simple stuff.' He motioned for her to try something.

As she sank her teeth into the soft, sweet pumpkin bread with its delicate nutty flavours, she thought her taste buds would dance straight to heaven. 'Where did you learn to cook like this?'

'It's just basic. I grew up looking out for myself.' His quietening voice was almost swallowed by the night. 'But my complex life is another story.'

'I'd like to hear it,' Rosie said softly.

'But it's not part of . . . tonight.'

'We're not sticking to a script. Are we?'

'No, of course not.' He cleared his throat. 'I grew up in care. I was bounced around from foster home to foster home and although the people were nice enough, I rarely felt . . . *wanted*.

You know? More like I was an inconvenient spare part. My mother was an addict of anything and everything. She was born and lived in the south-west of England – but never anywhere stable. I never properly knew my dad. He was from Montana in the US, from a long line of pumpkin farmers. His family and my ancestors were good, honest people. But I came to learn that he's nothing like them.' He shook his head. 'Not that I know much about him.'

'And you? Did you manage to settle anywhere?'

He looked at her as if he was weighing things up. Like he'd already said more than planned. 'There was one family I nearly stuck with. They were kind. Dennis taught me to care for the land, to sow seeds and watch them grow. To listen for the call of the birds.' His voice faltered. 'But I messed it up. Like I always do. I break things before . . .'

'They have chance to break you?' Rosie completed Zain's sentence when it seemed he'd lost the courage to finish it.

'Yes, that. Stupid hey?'

'Not at all.' Rosie wished she could clamber over the boat and hug him. Maybe a date on the water wasn't that convenient when you didn't like falling in. 'Some of my relationships have been interesting. You're not alone.' She wasn't going to confess they'd all ended in full-scale disaster, or that her favourite one so far was her fictional version, with a hot hero called Cain who was very much inspired by him.

'Look, I'm sorry if I was quick to judge you as just another townie, and if I spent too long fighting against your retreat plans. Maybe life has conditioned me to be wary and expect the worst. But you. You've shown me that people can be genuinely good. And not just because they want to use you.'

Did she see that flicker of pain across his face again? It disappeared quickly but left her wondering what else had happened in his past, and perhaps feeling a touch guilty about the Cain-Zain thing, even if she didn't class it as *using* him, exactly.

'Anyway, forget my history. I just wanted you to know that now I've looked into it, I guess having people here on retreats could have its positives. A chance to encourage folk to care for the land. I could even consider showing them the ropes of pumpkin farming and make it more hands on. It's worked in other places.'

'I love that idea.' Rosie could feel the excitement of it bubbling up inside her, the boat swaying a little more every time she nodded in agreement. 'You looked into it?'

'No,' he said quickly. 'Not exactly. It's not like we even have Wi-Fi. I just . . . had a think about things.'

He rubbed his temple.

Rosie grinned. 'It looks like all that thinking hurt.'

His eyes sought hers, across the flicker of the lantern. 'I'll admit being wrong was painful. You turned up here, all well groomed and bossy, and you tested my views. Thank you for waking me up from my slumber. For being . . . *you*.'

Rosie let the words hang in the air. Was he really thanking her for being her? Not that she was sure about the bossy bit. 'Well, nobody's ever called me well groomed.' She gave an embarrassed laugh and rearranged her scruffy ponytail. 'I could never work my straighteners, and I usually had lip gloss on my teeth. It's refreshing not to worry about those things anymore.'

'Whatever you're doing now, it suits you,' Zain said simply.

Rosie would usually have put herself down and pointed out her ill-suited pyjamas or the fact her nails needed a date with a nailbrush. Though tonight, she allowed herself to accept the easy compliment.

It felt like they had been out on the lake for hours, eating and talking by the light of the moon, and sampling Bonnie's elderflower wine in tiny cups. Maybe they had been. Time rarely seemed to matter here, other than the metaphorical clock that ticked above them, against which they'd need to race to get the retreats up and running by sometime next month. Though nothing about this night was being rushed. It was like they were floating, somewhere between 'before' and 'after'.

When it was time, Zain rowed them back to the jetty and helped Rosie out of the boat. She wasn't going to argue with his chivalry, even though she knew he'd have passed over the oars if she'd wanted them.

'Need me to carry you again?' Zain pointed down to her slipper socks. 'Or I could lend you my boots?'

'How about a piggyback to my cabin? If it won't ruin your suit.'

Zain smiled and shrugged off his jacket, taking a moment to open his slightly too tight white shirt a little more. Rosie felt a flush of heat to her cheeks. If he undid any more buttons, it would be the undoing of her.

'I've never worn anything less comfortable. Climb on.'

Rosie beamed as she clambered onto Zain's back, trying not to get too excited about the firmness of his muscles through the cotton as her hands grabbed his waist and shoulders, trying to find somewhere good to hold. Except that every part of him was far too good. He was solid and warm, and so ridiculously stable for someone who would swear they were the opposite. She trusted him. And was it wrong that she wanted to climb onto him and never get off?

'Who knew you'd end the evening being my valiant horse? I'm sorry.'

'Who says this is how we'll end it?' His voice rumbled deep against her body as she wrapped herself around his back.

She heard herself sigh involuntarily at the thought. If he

knew what he was doing to her, who knew how this night would end, or whether they'd even make it as far as the cabin. Suddenly Rosie felt like she was wearing far too many clothes.

Each step Zain took towards her door vibrated through her, making her cling more tightly. His body felt warm as his muscles worked hard to support her. Her own body was almost melting. The anticipation of what those steps meant was building with every second. Did getting closer to her hut mean she was about to be dropped off chastely? Or was this the beginning of a journey that would end who knew where?

Before she could work it out, they were at the bottom of Rosie's steps. Zain climbed them swiftly, as though she were weightless. When he got to the top, he twisted his arms and swivelled her from his back to his chest and held her against his front. Their faces were almost touching, his hands gripping the tops of her thighs to hold her steadily against him. She gave him a gentle, breathless nod to let him know that everything he was doing was more than OK.

He took one final step to rest her back against the door, and she used its firmness to push herself into him.

'Is there a leaf in my hair?' she asked with a gentle tease, as he looked at her in that intense way of his.

'There was never any leaf in your hair.'

And then his mouth found hers in the half-light, their lips sinking together and moving like the ripples of the lake, gently and rhythmically, making her feel out of control and yet safe. Her whole body was trembling, and she wanted more.

She pulled at his shirt buttons, eager to put her hands on his naked flesh, to feel his firm, tight muscles against her. His chest half bare, she wrenched up her top, groaning as her skin touched his. He glanced down, his eyebrows rising at the sight of her bra and the swell of her nipples beneath it. His mouth opened as if he wanted to taste one but couldn't quite reach. Then his eyes were drawn back to her lips, and he kissed her again, deeply, like everything was about this moment. He rocked his body against her in a slow, tempting rhythm as their mouths moved. Her legs still wrapped around him, she was now pulsing, tingling, aching to be touched.

Ohhhhhhh.

When the kiss came to an end, Zain's arms shaking and Rosie's wrapped around his neck, it was like returning from another world.

'Not yet,' he whispered into her hair, as though he knew she was equally desperate for more. As out of character as deeply indulgent sex on her doorstep was, she would have welcomed it then, in this shadowy, secluded space, the chill of fresh air against her skin, the calls of the wild echoing in the distance. 'I want to know you first.'

'OK,' she replied, reluctantly, taking a moment to get her breath back. She knew he was right. 'I know what Juliet meant now when she told Romeo that he kissed by the book. Where did you learn to sweep a girl off her feet like that?' Not to mention the other parts of her that had been willingly drawn to life. 'Seventy-four per cent of people surveyed would have just had their worlds rocked.'

Zain placed her down gently and they smiled at each other for a moment, as though their kiss had unlocked a secret that was just for them.

Then he straightened himself and gave his crumpled clothes a pat-down.

'I feel like you've got this all figured out,' said Rosie.

'How do you mean?'

'A perfect plan for the retreats, a flawless date on the lake. A pretty exciting finale. You're full of surprises.'

'I'm not sure I'll ever have it all figured out.' He sighed. 'Like I said before, I just came up with a few logistics. I can throw the shell together, but it's you who knows how to make the people inside it feel treasured. Does that make any sense?'

This time their kiss was softer. And like time had stretched out when they'd been out on the lake, she wasn't quite sure how long it lasted. She just knew that with every moment, he was filling *her* with something treasured. And when it ended, he watched her go inside and went back to his own hut, alone. He'd whispered in her ear that he didn't trust himself to stay and that the best presents were unwrapped slowly. As agonising as not rushing things was, she knew exactly what he meant.

26

Dancing. On. Air.

That was how Rosie had felt since that first kiss with Zain, just a few short weeks ago. And that was how she still felt right then, as she took her morning stroll around the pumpkin fields, the burnt-orange radiance of Zain's beautiful fruit like warmth for her soul.

He was happy with her strolling freely here now, as long as she respected the vines. She was even allowed to poke around in his polytunnels, which were like a farmer's version of a science lab but stuffed with all manner of gorgeous gourds. This calm morning walk was exactly what she needed before the first unofficial retreat practice weekend that was about to kick off.

The last few weeks had floated by like a dream. Zain had surprised Rosie with more romantic dates that had felt so perfect they could have been extracted from the textbook of dating. They had stargazed under cosy blankets with flasks of pumpkin-spiced hot chocolate. They'd ambled around Autumn Meadows, listening to the chatter of birds and spotting water voles. Yesterday they'd made marshmallows that looked like little Cinderella pumpkins, which they'd be toasting around a campfire later on, as part of their retreat test run.

Zain had tried to pass off their perfect dates as research for retreat activities whenever Rosie had gently teased him about the effort he'd put in. Sometimes she'd wondered if he'd lined up the wood pigeons for an immaculate dawn chorus. Even the things he said seemed poetically word-perfect, even though she hadn't had Zain down as a talker. Most of their dates ended with ever-intensifying clinches that she hoped weren't part of any wild retreat research.

Rosie stopped to pull out a notebook, remembering one such hot embrace that definitely deserved a place in her book. She barely needed to magic up a scene from her own imagination these days, as everything Zain said and did would make any romantic fiction fan's heart do somersaults. She smiled as she recalled just how alive Zain made her feel, when she'd once worried that she was immune to properly falling for anyone after her run of romantic catastrophes.

With a flourish of her pen and a few scribbled hearts in the margin, she popped her notebook away and took a moment to breathe in her surroundings. She'd always loved autumn, for its stunning shades and the promise of cosiness. Being here had made her appreciate it in brand-new outdoorsy ways. The crisp, dewy mornings, when the smell of rich earth seemed to rise and fill her lungs. The way the trees gently dropped blankets of gold and russet leaves that she would sweep and gather for compost. The sheer joy of watching the crops fatten and grow ripe. After a wobbly start, she now couldn't imagine not being here, and she was excited to share some of this with their future retreat guests, if they could just pull it off.

Her mind wandered to the retreat preparations, which had been coming along nicely. She and Zain had busied themselves collecting wood, building treehouses, and trying to beg, borrow or barter for what they needed. Rosie had rounded up kind locals to chip in with spare materials, and she'd been writing marketing bumph for local businesses in exchange for old tin baths or material for teepees. Zain had swallowed his pride and helped on local farms as a trade-off for borrowing expertise or spare hands.

With the meerkat-like interest from locals, and the infinite pompom energy of the swim ladies, word was spreading like butterflies. Rosie had even reluctantly set up social media profiles for the pumpkin farm retreats, so they could build excitement as preparations unfolded, because she couldn't switch off from technology forever. Luna and Ellen were doing most of the social media posting, as Wi-Fi was still No-Fi around Agnes's land, but Rosie had been using Agnes's old bike to ride to the library with her laptop and do whatever promo she could.

With a pang of nerves, Rosie wondered again about whether all the exposure could end in her mum and sister soon tracking her down. Not even an envelope could open in the Cotswolds without those two hearing about it and turning up in their glad rags, and Rosie desperately didn't need them to blow her cover when things were starting to go well.

She exhaled a long breath. Taking control of your own story wasn't always easy.

'Everything OK?'

Rosie turned to see Zain behind her, his hair still wet from his shower, but to her slight disappointment, fully clothed. He locked Rosie with his *I could do wild things with you* stare, before moving in to put his arms around her. His steady warmth was exactly what she needed.

'Ready for your big weekend?' he asked.

'Mmm hmm.' In his bear-like hug, her nerves were already

melting. 'And it will be good to finally test one of the treehouses tonight.'

'Well, if you need anyone with you, to help check yours is stable...' he whispered into her ear.

Rosie's giggle escaped into his neck, and she loved that it tickled him.

'What, with Mags and the gang?' Rosie teased.

'If you prefer,' he joked back. 'But I'd rather save my energy for you.'

With the closeness of his body against her, she was getting a feel for the energy he was talking about. If he wasn't careful, she'd be demanding a demonstration here, in his pumpkin fields. What she wouldn't give to get down and muddy with him right then, if they didn't have a busy day planned.

Their collection of film-set-worthy dates had left her imagining all sorts of intimate, explosive endings. Back in her old life she may well have slept with him on date one, out of some hollow desire to please. But she wasn't in that superficial world anymore, and none of what she'd *always* done had worked out for her. So with Zain being gentlemanly and never rushing things, she'd been enjoying the skin-tingling anticipation of waiting.

Though Rosie was only human. There was only so long she could keep her suddenly quite hot hands to herself.

'Tonight?' she whispered back, her breath against his ear making him groan. 'Tonight, I might just be available.'

'Only if you want to be.'

Oh, she wanted to be.

27

'These retreats will be the best thing since pumpkin toffee pie,' said Bonnie, putting down her wicker basket and looking up at the treehouse she was going to share with Mags for the weekend.

Luna arrived at her side, having already thrown her backpack at the bottom of the one she was sharing with Ellen. 'I thought you were trying to be healthy, Mother.' She put her arm around her mum's slight shoulders and gave them a squeeze.

'I am being healthy. I'm on a pumpkin farm retreat, aren't I?'

'Then why did you bring your custard doughnuts?' asked Mags, coming up behind them, already wearing her flowery swim cap, even though swimming wasn't strictly on the day's schedule.

Rosie smiled and watched on as her friends chatted among themselves, seeming relaxed and at home already. The treehouses were finished and looking lovely in their simplicity, like little huts of happiness. Not that it had been simple to get them built, with all the tree specialists, health and safety and borrowed muscle power. Though somehow, with a lot of favours and a bit of credit, they'd pulled it off. She'd been working hard to try and make this first practice run as smooth and joyful as possible. Real-life guests were already grabbing spaces and paying for the proper retreats, which would begin later that month.

Of course, Rosie would usually have felt the pressure of something that huge weighing down on her like the arse-end of a robot cat. Yet being surrounded by fresh air and space, and having Zain on her side, *at last*, had given her the strength of ten ginormous gourds. Yes, she was still nervous, but they'd have time after this weekend to iron out the creases. And if the baddies of the piece were those suits from Cyber Purrz, then they would just have to make sure these retreats were a winning success.

Rosie rearranged her ponytail and straightened herself, trying to ignore the belly butterflies that were going on under her new pumpkin-patterned dungarees. 'We won't let you starve, Bon,' she said, taking a deep breath and going to join the group.

'Still not sure how I'm going to get my aching limbs into one of those treehouses,' said Mags, placing one hand on her back.

'Then you need to try my candlelight yoga,' said Bonnie, beaming from ear to ear. 'I've just finished my teaching certificate, so I could show you all later. And I'd be happy to do sessions at future retreats, by the light of pumpkin lanterns.' She gave Rosie a hopeful look.

'And I brought my hurdy-gurdy for a campfire singalong.' Mags opened the case of a stringed wooden instrument that looked almost medieval.

Rosie smiled, her heart feeling warm. They were an eclectic bunch, but she wasn't sure how she would have managed without them. 'Thank you, everyone. I might just take you up on those thoughts.'

'You could bring your writing into the mix,' said Luna, giving Rosie a nod. 'I mean, who doesn't feel creative out here? I've only been among the weeping willows for ten minutes, and I already reckon I could write a poem.'

'She couldn't write a poem,' Ellen mouthed.

'Part of me would love to.' Rosie sighed. 'But I've got enough on my list for now, juggling all these pumpkins. I don't want to rock the boat.' There were only so many brave steps a person could take at once, without tripping over. She checked over her shoulder. 'What if I mention writing and Agnes says, "*Ooh yes, and what about your painting?*" and wheels some canvases down here?'

She kept her voice low, conscious that Zain didn't know that the real interviewee for her job was a woman called Rachel, because there hadn't been a good moment to bring it up. She didn't feel great about that, but it had taken them so long to reach a truce, and now they were working brilliantly together, how could she possibly jeopardise things? Not to mention that their budding relationship was delicate, and he did *not* like having the wool pulled over his eyes. She would have to tell him when things were altogether more stable. In the meantime, she was being the best retreat-organising employee she could possibly be, so surely that was something.

'When life gives you canvases, paint pumpkins,' said Mags.

It sounded like as good a plan as any.

Then Zain appeared, making Rosie jump, and she quickly changed the subject. To her relief, Mags accosted him about carrying her luggage to save her creaky bones.

'Welcome to our Pumpkin Farm Retreat,' Zain said, when he'd finished with the bag chat. He extended his arms around himself, like he was introducing an autumn-themed show. The camping area was next to Zain's largest pumpkin patch, giving the guests the most fantastic view. 'A place where pumpkins reign and all things wild are celebrated.' He gave Mags a wink and she giggled like a teenager. 'I'm sure your host will make your stay seamless.' His gaze landed on Rosie. 'She has a special way of making everyone feel...'

Until that point, Zain could almost have been reading his word-perfect speech from an autocue. He was charming and confident, and had their guests' hearts and minds stuck to him like jam on a sandwich. Not for the first time, Rosie almost didn't recognise him. But when his eyes met hers, he faltered.

'Umm...'

'In love?' Luna whispered, finishing his sentence and giving Ellen an animated nudge.

Rosie felt the heat rise to her cheeks. 'Shall we get everyone settled into their treehouses?'

Zain nodded.

The treehouse where Mags and Bonnie would be sleeping was called Woody and had a spiral staircase that wound its way around the tree's trunk. Like Squirrel, the treehouse next door where Luna and Ellen would be staying, it was held aloft by the strong branches of an oak tree and strengthened by stilts secured into the ground. There were more treehouses dotted in the trees in each corner of the camping meadow. She and Zain had compromised on a setting that was close to both the pumpkin patches and the lake, with clusters of trees, and a natural glade where they'd set up the teepees, campfire area and more pumpkin lanterns. Rosie had even made autumn-leaf bunting, which she'd twisted with fairy lights and strung from tree to tree. It would be even more magical when night fell.

They made their steady ascent up the spiral staircase to Woody, with Zain carrying Mags' and Bonnie's bags, and Luna and Ellen insisting they'd stay at the bottom and keep a watch out for wolves, of which there were definitely none.

'Each treehouse has just one room,' Rosie explained, when they were safely inside Woody. 'This is where you'll sleep.'

'Wooooow,' said Bonnie, letting the word whisper around the wooden space.

Mags gasped and nodded furiously in agreement, her lungs still out of puff from the stairs.

Rosie watched as their eyes bounced around the room, taking everything in. The low beds with their cosy bedding and blankets, the pumpkin-spiced chocolates she'd made for them and left on each pillow, in hand-decorated boxes. Their orange towels, which she'd twisted into pumpkin shapes, complete with cinnamon sticks for stalks. The wicker baskets filled with local toiletries in seasonal fragrances, which Rosie had sourced. The strings of paper bunting she'd made from discarded manuscript pages. They couldn't afford to put heating or lights up in the trees yet, so they were making do with swapped or borrowed camping equipment, which Rosie hoped would add to the sense of adventure.

As her guests noticed each detail, Rosie felt a sense of elation when their eyes lit up. Even Zain was taking it all in, his mouth slightly open. He hadn't had chance to see the finishing details. Those home comforts that Rosie hoped would make up for everything being pretty rustic.

'We'll use the teepees as our communal areas, and you can grab water and reusable bottles on ground level.'

They knew about the compost toilet, and Rosie would tell them about the open-air bathing area later. Now it was set up, she knew it was so much better suited to the land than the jarringly modern shower block she'd once naively imagined. She almost couldn't wait to sell the idea of a warm soak in a wonky tin bath under the starlight, with the solar string lights exuding their gentle glow.

'And then there's your treetop balcony,' said Zain, seeming to remember his lines, even though *of course* he didn't have any. 'Let's show you.'

They filtered out onto the small balcony and stopped to take in the view. It was another *wooooow* moment, only it took a while for anyone to formulate the words.

'Something inside us was born to live in the trees,' said Zain quietly, looking out over the view as he spoke. Rosie stood next to him, Mags and Bonnie at her side. Luna and Ellen were at the foot of the tree, looking up. 'Our ancestors found safety and shelter here, and many still do. The pumpkin farm is already a special place, but coming up here will give you an instant disconnect from busy life.'

He turned to them. 'That's one of the reasons we decided on no flashy amenities or tech up here. Whenever I leave this place, I see half of the planet with their faces glued to screens. Being elevated invites you to look up. To see the bigger picture.'

His words made Rosie want to float. As his eyes met hers, she slipped her hand into his, feeling his warmth and wanting to keep it there always. He squeezed it lightly and pulled away. Well, that was probably more professional.

Their retreat preparation jobs had caused Zain to leave the land more and more, to work elsewhere or to collect things. Rosie had never seen Zain outside of the farm. In her imagination, he existed only here – the place that was perfect for him. She was intrigued to hear what he thought of the world outside and wondered if being out there was changing him. He was certainly coming back with more ideas and a lot more to say for himself.

But she knew it was silly to want him to only be here, in the bubble they had created. Could their blossoming relationship work outside of these hedgerows, and would the influx of new people change their peaceful dynamic? Or would her skeletons start catching up with her?

Rosie shook herself and smiled. There was no need to over-analyse. They had their first day of pumpkin farm exploring, foraging and campfire cooking to look forward to, and Zain had suggested that tonight could hold something even more incredible for the two of them. She'd chosen to sleep in a treehouse called Wild, which was in a secluded spot away from the others. Every inch of her hoped Zain would be joining her.

28

Other than the odd hiccup over missing toilet roll, or retreaters getting lost in the autumn meadows, the first practice retreat day played out perfectly. Even the weather was smiling on them. They'd helped Zain with a spot of early pumpkin harvesting. They'd refuelled on a picnic of roast pumpkin lasagne and an autumn salad that Rosie had thrown together. Zain had even let them carve a few pumpkins and paint faces on them, although Rosie was sure she'd seen him wincing.

Now they were building a campfire, where they'd cook the pumpkin flatbreads they'd made, to eat with their butternut squash risotto.

'Watch your feet,' Zain said to Mags, as he dropped an armful of firewood near where she was sitting, barefoot and waiting to toast her toes against a fire that wasn't yet ready.

'Will do,' Mags mumbled, through a mouthful of Rosie's home-made chocolates.

What Rosie liked best about her new group of friends was that their rebellious differences gave Rosie permission to be herself too. *And* they didn't nag on about her choice of boyfriends.

She took in the scene, knowing she had mud on her knees and twigs in her hair. Her nails bore no sign that she'd ever had a manicure and the only thing on her face was a smattering of seasonal freckles. And she felt *happy*. No, it was more than that. She breathed it in, trying to find words to describe it so she could write about it later. She felt *full*. Not in a *too many chocolates* way, though she had sneaked more than a few. But full to the brim with something she couldn't quite pinpoint. Like sparkly joy dancing with a peaceful knowing, and a spirit so grateful it might burst.

Then there was Zain. Her gaze was drawn back to him looking all parts romantic hero, hulking firewood and swiping moisture from his brow. Who knew scenes this flawless could exist in real life? And that falling for someone had little to do with being head over heels, and everything to do with her tumbling heart. She couldn't wait to be closer to him tonight. Would it be their night? Because right then, everything felt just *perfect*.

'You all right, love?' asked Bonnie, arriving at her side and giving her back a rub with the one hand that was free from sticks.

It was only then that Rosie noticed her eyes were welling up. She was so full that she needed to overflow. If she'd been living her life on the sidelines before, then at last she was truly part of something.

She smiled at her own silliness and wiped her face with her sleeve. 'I'm fine, honestly. Just having a moment. A joyful one.'

In her old life, Rosie would have passed off the tears as a mascara malfunction. She was coming to see that real friends weren't people you needed to put on a brave, powdered face in front of or buy cakes for every Monday, even when it was surely their turn. They were people who you could *have a moment* in front of, without judgement.

'I'm not surprised you're emotional,' said Zain, arriving at their side. 'Look at everything you've brought to life.'

Rosie nodded. As a writer, she created whole, imaginary worlds. She'd just taken the next step and helped to build something real. She was beginning to prove that she wasn't just a dreamer who floated through life with her blinkers on.

'You're a natural,' said Mags. 'I've been spoiled, right down to my very toes.' She gave them a wriggle.

She took a deep breath and allowed herself to say, 'Thank you.'

Before she knew it, everyone had pulled together to build the campfire. And then pumpkins were sizzling, more of Bonnie's elderflower wine was flowing, and Rosie was learning how to pan-fry her first flatbread.

When it was time to toast the marshmallows she'd made with Zain the day before, Rosie made her excuses and moved to be next to him. She'd spent all evening catching his eye over the flicker of flames, feeling giddy with possibilities every time they'd held each other's gaze. Even without the campfire, every inch of her would have been white hot. Their relationship wasn't secret, but they were on work time. She couldn't have spent the day fondling him, as much as she'd wanted to. The almost forbidden nature of being near him was making her desire burn. If he was still intending to sneak into her treehouse, she'd be the one melting like a marshmallow.

Rosie settled herself in next to Zain, no longer able to play *hands off*. The look in his eyes as he moved his head to acknowledge her told her he felt it too. She reached out to touch him, allowing her fingers to wrap around his as she took a marshmallow from him. He was warm from the flames and sparks of something flew through her, like electricity lighting a torch. From the twitch of his hand, she knew he was right there with her. He'd been quiet tonight, but sometimes their chemistry spoke more than any words.

They speared her marshmallow onto a long toasting fork, watching as its softness resisted momentarily before giving in with a barely audible pop. Rosie could feel her mouth watering. Their hands intertwined, they guided the fork towards a patch of orange embers, spinning it gently while its edges bubbled and crisped.

Of course, she could have worked out the perfect toasting method for herself. Or she could have joined in with Mags and Bonnie's marshmallow-eating contest, or Ellen's game of setting hers on fire and using it to write her name in the sky. Goodness knew, Rosie wanted to sear the darkness with a million looping hearts. Though there was nothing stronger than her ache to be close to Zain.

Chatter carried on around them, Rosie being only fuzzily aware. The fire crackled and smoked, and there were definitely stars overhead, if only she could tear her eyes away to look at them. Mags pulled out her hurdy-gurdy contraption and played something that made Rosie want to sway. Arms swished in the night air, and Luna and Ellen were telling Mags to start a band.

Rosie and Zain moved away from the fire, letting their limbs wrap around each other as they began to dance. The music had a pull that made Rosie feel powerless. And it was lucky for her that she trusted every part of Zain, because so did he. He felt warm and solid against the midnight chill, their hips pressing into each other. As their bodies swayed, his hands wove into her hair, drawing her face towards his, their mouths softening into a kiss she'd longed for all day. His lips against hers. The marshmallow-sweetness of his tongue. It was almost too much to bear.

She pulled him behind a tree and crushed herself against him, guiding his mouth towards the nakedness of her neck. The sweep of his lips against her flesh made her groan.

'I could stay here forever,' she whispered into his hair as his tongue traced a trembling line along her collarbone. So much for keeping things professional. Right then she didn't care.

'For . . . *ever*,' he repeated back, the word almost getting stuck as his mouth found its way back to hers. It was thirsty work all this kissing. Maybe he needed more water too.

He stopped to look at her, his eyes seeming to be processing something.

'Well, you know. Not necessarily against this knobbly tree. Maybe somewhere more comfortable. Later.' She allowed her eyes to flick towards the treehouse where she was staying, knowing he'd already alluded to it. And so had the hotness of that kiss.

He ran a hand through his hair, but it got lodged against his bun and he pulled it away, a few black strands falling loose. His gaze travelled back to the campfire, where they could still hear singing and laughter, above the buzz of the hurdy-gurdy. Did the instrument sound almost melancholy now?

'We should tidy up,' said Zain, straightening himself. 'We're meant to be working. It's getting late.'

'Oh.' Rosie straightened herself too, feeling the cold bite as Zain moved away. She pulled her clothes back into order, the warmth in her chest evaporating. 'Yes, you're probably right.'

Zain strode back to the others, moving silently around them as he cleared things away. Rosie followed suit.

At some point, perhaps when Rosie was busy talking, Zain disappeared into the night without saying goodbye. Rosie had sensed it was coming, though she wasn't sure why. Had she said the wrong thing? Had he overheard something? Perhaps if she was harbouring fewer half-truths about who she was, she wouldn't feel so edgy. She *would* tell him at some point, when they'd saved the land, and they could laugh about it all. But right then, it was too risky.

She wondered whether he'd be back later to climb up to her treehouse and into her bed, or whether he'd been spooked back into his cave.

Once they'd retired to their beds, Rosie couldn't help keeping watch for him. Hoping he would come yet preparing herself in case he didn't. Her eyes became heavy with tiredness, and she heaved a sigh and began tearing off her clothes, throwing them into the corner. She pulled the blankets around her to keep the night chill from seeping through her underwear and into her bones.

Just as she could barely keep her eyelids open, there was a flash of something. She moved quickly to the treehouse window to look out. And there it was. Her light through the darkness. Steady, determined, coming boldly in her direction. Her spirits soared.

Then the light stopped near the dying embers of the campfire. They illuminated Zain, in all his rugged glory. He looked dishevelled, like he'd been trying to sleep but failing. His hair was ruffled. His body seemed as restless as hers. Had he only come back to check the flames were out or to pour water on them and watch them smoke?

He looked up towards her window, like an animal that sensed he was being watched. Hot ash reflected in the darkness of his eyes. A burning red that scorched through the night and landed firmly on her, pinning her, in a way that set her imagination on fire. She let the duvet slip from her shoulders, showing him that underneath it, she was down to her bra. If he wanted to see what was on the bottom half, he'd have to come up there. She hoped the look on her face made the invite clear.

29

If Rosie had been worried Zain wouldn't accept her brazen challenge to hurry himself to her treehouse, she didn't have to worry for long.

With a quick look around him to check nobody was in sight, he made a swift pace towards it, taking the steps two at a time like he'd been born to climb to her. As he arrived at the hatch to get in, he slowed a little, allowing her time to change her mind. She wasn't going to.

'Come in,' she said hurriedly, keen for him not to back away again.

Half through, he didn't move fully into the treehouse yet.

She was aware her body was shivering now. Perhaps in anticipation for what was surely about to happen, in this small, secluded space, between two people who'd been desperately falling for each other. Or maybe it was the fact she was wearing nothing but thin frills of underwear on such a cool autumn night. His gaze finding her erect nipples through the lace confirmed he'd noticed how cold it was too. He returned his look to her eyes, apologising.

'It's OK, I invited you here. I want this. More than anything.' She hoped her voice conveyed the depth of feelings that were bubbling inside her. 'Did something spook you earlier?'

Rosie was conscious that he'd acted strangely after her mention of *forever*, even if she'd only used the word jokingly. At least she hoped it was only that. If he'd rumbled her about anything else, it was better she knew before this night moved on.

He shook his head.

Or not. Not talking could also be good.

It was odd how Zain fluctuated between having no words at all and then finding plenty of line-perfect ones. Though right then, it was hot that he was lost for them. And she was completely available for *hot*.

His eyes explored her, his mouth slightly open as though he couldn't quite believe he was here, that she was almost naked, and that there was one clear direction this was going.

'You seem . . . *ready*?' he asked, nodding towards her underwear, which was delicate and perfectly matching and obviously not the sort of thing you pranced around in every day. She was relieved she hadn't worn it in vain.

She nodded, strands of hair falling from her scruffy topknot and settling on her bare shoulders, like something from a romantic tale. 'Mmm hmm.'

Rosie didn't want to talk anymore, or to delay the moment she'd been secretly longing for since that day she'd seen him unclothed and dripping in the shower. *Ready* was exactly how she felt. They'd waited so long for this moment, through weeks of heated squabbles and even more heated dates, the growing feelings, sharing their hearts and worlds. She was ready to share *all* of her, and to savour all of him.

Her body was still tingling for him since their kiss against the tree earlier that night. Since his tongue had teased her collarbone and made parts of her pulse.

At last, he pulled the rest of his body through the hatch, his muscles tensing with the movement, his gaze never leaving her. The light from the carved lanterns threw him into an orange glow, making him look almost magical. He cast shadows as he moved slowly towards her. The look on his face made her melt – like yearning mixed with lust, with a hint of something animal. And a knowing that the further he stepped to her, the less likely he would be able to turn away.

Rosie lowered herself back onto the bed, her skin prickling with goosebumps and buzzing with pure, unadulterated longing for him. A craving to be touched and held by those firm yet gentle hands that she'd seen lovingly tend the land, and that she'd daydreamed of being caressed by. To smell his musky, cedar scent on her, to taste the sweetness of him. To explore new parts of him and bring some of her wildest fantasies alive, right there in the treetops. The wind was rustling, and owls cried out in the distance. She yearned to howl into the darkness too.

The blankets felt soft beneath her skin, but she wanted his warmth on top of her. She let her knees drop open, her body inviting him in. He climbed slowly onto the bed, peeling off his top layers, bringing his heat. Rosie pulled him onto her, wrapping her arms around him, her cold body shivering against his. His closeness felt like *everything*. Her heart was filling.

She could feel at once how part of him was stiffening eagerly against her, straining against his jeans. The brush of his hardness against the soft place between her legs made her groan. He rocked against her, the tease of material still between them. She gasped, her heart racing.

And then he was kissing her on the mouth, breathing in her rhythmic moans, and she was fantasising about his lips in other places. His tongue was so firm and intent, if it travelled to the throb between her legs, she surely wouldn't last another moment.

But right then, she wanted his face against hers, her eyes locked with his. The look in them showed her just how much he wanted her, how much he almost couldn't wait for her. She'd never felt so longed for. His desire was completely intoxicating.

She took his hand and guided it inside her lace underwear, encouraging his fingers to touch her. She groaned in pleasure as he found the exact spot between her legs. The place that had been aching for him, since she didn't know when. His fingertips teased lightly as if they had all the time in the world, but she did not want to wait. Her back arched up off the bed, keen to feel his firmness, desperate for him to push his way inside her. His eyes drifted closed for a moment like the pleasure was all his, as the length of his fingers penetrated, up inside her, taking her somewhere she couldn't wait to be.

She moved against him, more and more urgently, until she felt the burn of his skin against hers, his fingers so deliciously deep. Sheer, tormenting heat, her whole body vibrating, her mouth open against his, tongues exploring. It was happening so quickly and there was no pulling herself back. She *wanted* this. His touch was sublime. As she yelped his name into his mouth, asking him not to stop, his free hand found her breast inside her bra and pulled softly against her nipple. Every nerve ending came alive. The world went white. She was his.

When her body finally finished shuddering, she lay there for a moment, feeling his reassuring weight on top of her, observing him watching her with half-dazed eyes. He was beautiful. And wherever he'd just taken her, she wanted to take him there too.

She moved out from under him and rolled him onto his back, watching his eyebrows quirk in question. His top half was naked, his own dark nipples erect on his tanned, patterned skin. She was desperate to undress the rest of him, yet keen to take her time and watch him writhe with the want of her. His eyes were wide as she unbuckled his belt, and she took a moment to drink in his craving. His hunger to be touched by her, his body twitching with every slight brush of skin, his manhood growing again beneath taut denim. She pulled open his jean poppers with a playful slowness, enjoying his nods of encouragement. Words had clearly escaped him.

He'd given her so much pleasure that she was still reeling from it. Her skin tingled, her pulse sped. It was time to make him feel this too. All of it. To watch his face. To sense his raging heart. She pulled his erect penis free. It was the first time she'd seen it fully ready for action, and it was bigger than their cold shower run-in could have prepared her for. She caressed the warm length of it with her hands, enjoying the way it trembled and jolted as though it couldn't get enough of her. As though *he* couldn't get enough of her.

'Rosie.' At last, he'd found a word. It seemed like the only one he could manage, as his body contorted on the bed from her touch, moans of sheer lust escaping him.

She'd been planning to find a condom and climb onto him. For their bodies to rock backwards and forwards in this rustic hut beneath the stars. To feel him inside her, his hands on her breasts, his hips thrusting upwards and hitting her intimate spot. Them coming together...

But like her, his excitement was hastening. They'd been tempting each other for so long. And like a gift, she didn't want to keep it from him. She was desperate to watch his pleasure reach its climax in her grasp. So she kept her hands moving, so rhythmic it was like the most intimate trance. The pleasurable angst in his face, the rise and fall of his body, the increase of intensity before his final, thrusting release. From his wild, feral cry of her name, she knew he was as ecstatic as her, to be right there, powerless in her hands.

Soon she was climbing up next to him, bringing tissues and pulling the duvet and blankets over them, curling her body into his warmth. She felt perfect and satiated and oh so tired.

'I'll be ready again in a moment,' he whispered.

Though she sank into a deep, delicious sleep so quickly she barely heard him. Sometimes talking was completely over-rated.

30

'Anyone for pumpkin waffles?'

It was Bonnie's voice that woke Rosie and Zain from their treehouse slumber. There hadn't been many hours of the night left after their urgent but incredible exploring of each other's bodies, but they must have slept through them like logs. Zain's suggestion, before they drifted to sleep, that he'd soon be ready for more action would have to wait.

Though he was out from under the duvet and hurriedly tugging his clothes on before Rosie could rub the sleep from her eyes.

'Everything OK?' she asked him.

'Not really. It sounds like the guests are making their own breakfasts. That's our job.'

Rosie could tell he was trying to dial down the frustration in his voice, but he wasn't doing the best job of it.

'It's OK, they're our friends. This is just a practice run.' Rosie sat up and ruffled her messy hair, smiling at him. He really was gorgeous, even when he was passive-aggressively cross. Almost as sexy as last night's face of complete surrender. She knew that would make it into her book, if she wasn't careful.

'They're *your* friends,' he corrected her. 'I barely know them. And that's no excuse for us not to do our damnedest to get this right. We'll have nowhere to live if these retreats don't work out, and my pumpkin fields will be flattened like pancakes.'

'Yes, boss,' Rosie teased, rooting around on the floor for her jumper in an effort to show support for his haste.

'No, Agnes is our boss. We're not meant to be . . .' his voice paused as he looked around the inside of the treehouse at the strewn clothes and crumpled bedding '. . . letting her down.'

He pulled on a coat, buckled his belt with a more exaggerated clunk than it needed, and shot down through the hatch of the treehouse without another word.

'Well, good morning to you too,' Rosie said after him, still half-smiling at his strop. Not everyone was a morning person, and it probably wasn't professional to be having so much fun on the job. Though in fairness they'd clocked off before anyone started getting naked, and at least their treehouse called Wild wasn't in earshot of where their guests had been sleeping. And they could avoid doing that when paying customers arrived. They weren't offering *that* sort of holiday.

Rosie popped on her own clothes, downed half a bottle of water, and climbed from the treehouse to join the others. Checking her watch, she could see it was late, and she and Zain appeared to be the last ones up. The fire was already going, and Mags was doing a good job of burning bacon whilst Ellen tried not to scald herself boiling a pan of water for coffee.

It wasn't ideal that their visitors had been left to fend for themselves. It wasn't the sort of service that would go down well on Tripadvisor, if wooden huts in trees had that sort of thing.

She apologised to her friends, but they waved off her worries and hugged her good morning. Rosie noticed Zain's jaw tightening at the not discreet enough whistle from Luna about Zain and Rosie having just emerged from the same treehouse.

So when Mags made a throwaway comment about them being like one big, unlikely family, Rosie was only partly surprised to see Zain's shoulders stiffen, before he let out a huff and moved off to rearrange his trusty pile of logs.

'You're quiet this morning, Zain,' Bonnie sing-songed. 'I was hoping for one of your dreamy speeches about treetops and nature. You have such a way with words.'

Rosie could see from the sparkle in Bonnie's eyes that she was trying to be friendly.

Just like Luna was, when she put her hand on her heart and said, 'Too many word-perfect speeches like yours, our Zain, and you'll have us all falling for you. And we'd always thought you were the quiet and broody type.'

But Zain was clearly not in the mood for their banter. He dropped the chunk of wood he was holding back onto its pile and walked away, in the direction of his hut by the lake.

Rosie's mouth dropped open. Where was he going? Was he honestly OK with visiting her in the middle of the night to get pretty damned intimate, actually, then stalking off without even saying, *'Oh, that was nice'*? And it looked as though she was going to have to get through the rest of this retreat day without him too.

She wasn't sure what had gotten into him, but *some of them* had work to do. Perhaps she'd try talking to him later. She was used to turning a semi-ignorant eye on other people's odd behaviour in the hope it would pass, because that's how she'd navigated most of her relationships. Though that had always ended badly.

If the first real retreat was going to kick off in just a few weeks, she and Zain needed to work together. And more than that, she had feelings for Zain. Not just *let's roll around in a treehouse* feelings, but something undeniably deeper. A connection that was worth fighting for, even if some people might be too obstinate to admit it.

'Trouble in the camp?' Mags whispered, looking at Zain's retreating back.

'I'm sure it will be fine,' Rosie answered. She hoped she was right.

After juggling a day of retreat activities and pretending she was on top of things, Rosie was soon seeing everyone off. Bonnie was jabbering wildly about making pumpkin fizz for future guests and Mags may have said something about hurdy-gurdy entertainment. It seemed like the retreat had enlivened them in more ways than they'd bargained for. It was just a shame that something had sent Zain heading for the hills.

At least Agnes's dog Onions had bothered to come outside for the send-off, together with a few helpless-looking cats and a stray chicken who looked a bit confused. They wouldn't have been out of place waving a *save our roof, save our home* banner, if animals could write.

They pulled in for a group hug, trying not to trip over Onions or squash the ginger moggy that Mags was hugging, who Rosie thought was called Orangeade, but it could have been Pumpkin.

'We'll make sure these retreats take off. Those cyber cats won't take over on our watch,' Mags half-whispered to her ginger charge, like they were living in a sci-fi cartoon.

Though Rosie had other things on her mind.

When the others had left and Rosie had shepherded the various animals back to their homes, she made her way back to camp to tidy up the treehouses. Even though she was thinking about him, she jumped when she saw Zain climbing out of Squirrel with Steve under his arm.

'Sorry,' Zain muttered as he stepped to the ground, avoiding eye contact. 'Lost my cat. Didn't even remember to feed him last night.' He grimaced.

'I thought cats didn't belong to anyone,' Rosie replied, her hands on her hips. She wasn't usually this confrontational, but as much as this was stretching her comfort zone, they needed to talk. He'd left her in the lurch today, and she couldn't bear going back to everything being awkward.

Zain shrugged. 'True.'

He tried to step past her, but she blocked him.

'Did I do something wrong?'

'No, of course not.'

'Then why did you spend the night butt-naked in my bed and then strop off without even saying toodle-oo? I mean, at least it wasn't a total shag and run, but still. I think I deserve a bit more respect than that.'

'Of course you do. No question. Which is why you're better off if I just . . .' He let his head drop.

Rosie placed her fingers under his chin and gently tilted his face up. She'd expected some resistance and one of his huffs, but he seemed strangely powerless. When their eyes met, an energy danced between them.

Then she remembered something. 'It started when I talked about *forever*, didn't it? And then Mags's joke about us being like a family. They were just throwaway comments. No one was suggesting . . .'

He shook his head. 'It's not as simple as that. *I'm* not as simple as that.' He rubbed the back of his neck. 'Though if you're looking for *forever* or someone to play happy families with, you need to know that's not something I'm sure I can do.

It's not in my nature *or* my nurture.' He sighed heavily. 'I'm not programmed that way.'

'You're not a chatbot.' Rosie allowed a small smile. He didn't return it.

'I'm sorry I came to your treehouse last night. I shouldn't have let this thing between us snowball. I know what I'm like when things start to look serious.'

'Snowball? You make us sound like an inevitable disaster.'

He shrugged. 'Look, we're meant to be protecting this place. How can we do that properly if we're too busy jumping in and out of each other's beds?'

'Is that all it was to you?' she asked, shaking her head as if it would help things make sense. 'A bit of bed hopping? I thought last night was special.' Even though they'd fallen asleep before the main event, the starters had been to die for.

'It was too special,' he said quietly. 'And I don't know how to deal with that.'

She felt her shoulders sinking. Where was this all going wrong?

'Anyway, I've mucked in as much as I can with the treehouses and setting up the retreat camp, and I'll do my bit with showing off the pumpkins – but you can take most of it from here. You don't need me to help fluff people's pillows or toast stuff around the campfire. I'd only mess things up. Put people off with my grumpy face or sabotage your chances of doing a great job. And you *are* doing brilliantly.'

'You looked happy enough last night. It felt like we all belonged. Didn't it?'

Zain shrugged. 'Must have been that weird fizzy wine. Belonging is not my thing. Life was simpler before. Please.' He stepped backwards. 'Trust me, I'm doing this for you too.'

The look that passed between them was heavy, like a big old

sack of sadness. Rosie didn't know how to deal with this either, other than to let Zain step away. It would be even harder if they let themselves fall deeper. If she'd slept with him last night, her soul would be breaking in two.

Though something inside her wanted to have one last word.

'That thing about forever,' Rosie shouted after him as he walked away. 'Nobody knows how to do that.' He stopped. 'It's just one day at a time, isn't it? And you keep going like that. Trying to do your best. Promising not to hurt or mislead anyone. In case you're wondering.'

He turned back to face her, still keeping his distance. 'I would never mean to mislead anyone. Just so you know.'

Then he turned away and kept on walking. Rosie thought she heard him say something about being sorry, although she couldn't swear it. She felt like she couldn't swear to anything anymore. Who was she to even mention misleading, when she hadn't confessed how she'd deceived Agnes to get this job, or that she couldn't hold down a single, sorry relationship, or that she had no expertise in running retreats, or even writing a half-decent love scene without using him as inspiration?

And just like that, Rosie was back to being a loser in love. Though that didn't mean she was destined to fail at everything. Did it?

31

Rosie was just finishing a morning swim in the lake when she heard them. The water had its usual refreshing chill and there was a blanket of grey clouds looming. It was probably going to rain. She was later than usual, having treated herself to a lie-in after their busy trial-run retreat. *People need rest*, she'd told herself. Mainly because there'd been no one else to listen, with Zain back to being a grump. As she pondered the thought of a quiet day in her writing nook typing something steamy about treehouses and large, quivering manhoods, the uninvited voices broke through the bullrushes.

'It's just one woman and a few tatty treehouses, isn't it? What difference will it make?'

It was a man's voice, but Rosie didn't recognise it. She kept still in the water, hugging onto her inflatable float.

'It's the guy too,' said another male voice. 'And his fields of ugly pumpkins.'

'What, the hermit in the hut?' said a third guy.

They all laughed at that.

Rosie resisted the urge to climb out of the water and shout at them, even if Zain was sometimes a bit *hermitty*. She wanted to know what was going on.

'Whatever it is, it's no better than a cottage industry, with no cottage. They're just trying to run a few retreats for wannabe, pumpkin-stroking nomads. All this wildlife crap is just a fad, anyway. They can't compete with a factory.'

Wildlife – a *fad*? Rosie gawped.

'The old bird isn't as keen on selling though, now she sees funny dungarees lady and the hermit as a viable option.'

Rosie clapped her hand over her mouth to hold back her gasp. *Old bird? Funny dungarees lady?* Who were these ageist outfit-shamers? And yes, she *could* compete.

'Then maybe we need to up our offer again. Buy the old woman out of that ramshackle house too. I know she wanted a new roof, so her mangy cats didn't drown. But wouldn't she prefer enough cash to get out of here and buy a new place? Then we can dig everything up and have free rein. The trees, the crops, the lake, the house. So much easier if we flatten it all and pour in the concrete.'

'You're all heart, Reginald,' said one of the voices, with a quite annoying chuckle. 'You'll be offering to replace her foul felines with a batch of cyber cats, next.'

'That's not a bad shout,' Reginald replied. 'They don't need feeding, and you can switch them off when you get sick of them.'

'Yeah, and they're not full of bloody fleas.'

'That is enough,' Rosie heard herself shout, her voice loud enough to carry over the lakeside foliage.

Even Steve, who'd been waiting patiently for her on the jetty, was hissing now – and she wasn't even sure if hairless cats could have fleas.

Rosie was done with trying not to make a noise. In fact, everything she'd just heard made her want to make more noise than ever. If she wasn't submerged in cold water, her blood would have been boiling. She swam quickly to the jetty, her arms and legs thrashing like the sails of a very cross windmill. She hauled herself out and marched around the bullrushes, not caring that she was now standing in a too small, borrowed swimsuit in front of three men in smart suits. They could take her as they found her.

'I don't know who you are, other than you're clearly from Cyber Purrz. But I do know that you're behaving like very rude people. This is not your land, and anyone who doesn't care for *faddy wildlife*, our precious pumpkins or cats with real hearts does not belong here. You need to leave, before I call security. And you do not want to be set upon by six dogs and an angry hermit. It won't end well for you.'

Rosie had no idea where she had just found her bolshiness from, or even whether these men were trespassing. And she wasn't sure Agnes's collection of friendly mongrels would scrub up well as guard dogs, with their limited number of limbs and teeth. The cats were probably scarier. But she wasn't putting up with this nonsense on her quiet day off, because there was no excuse for bad manners.

The three suited men stood staring at her, their mouths open. One scratched his comb-over.

Rosie had felt like that little cartoon dog Scrappy-Doo marching over there, her fists almost circling, veins pumping with defiance. Though now she was in front of them, they merely looked at her like she was a little bit odd. It was a look she was used to, growing up next to her glamorous mother and sister. A look she'd spent her life aiming to avoid, by trying to *fit in*. And it was a look she'd barely thought about since she'd embraced life at Autumn Meadows. Until today.

Rosie felt her shoulders droop. Standing there with a tow

float hanging limply from her waist, her body shivering, she began to sense the ridiculousness of it all. This place had a way of sweeping you into a fantasy. Of making you believe that anything was possible. Though maybe she *was* just one weird woman who couldn't make a difference with her tatty treehouses.

As the men looked at each other, Rosie felt a swoosh of material around her shoulder. A towel had been thrown around her and firm hands rubbed warmth into her upper arms. A throat was clearing itself to speak.

'The lady's right. You shouldn't be here. Unless you want to join us as paying guests.'

Rosie could hear the sarcasm in the voice, which was coming from behind her. It was Zain's.

'Though we're not officially open yet.' Zain stepped in closer behind Rosie, looking over her shoulder at the men's feet. 'If you're coming, you might want to reconsider your footwear. The farm's not a shiny shoe kind of place.'

One of the men harrumphed and the other two shuffled awkwardly. The sky above them darkened. Now Rosie came to look at them, they were quite comical, huddled together in their *don't get any mud on me* single-breasted suits. They were markedly different in height, as though they were going for the bronze, silver and gold award in being uncivil, without the podium. And it was *them* who didn't fit in here.

'We're just doing our jobs,' the smallest one muttered, half-apologetically.

The middle-sized one elbowed him in the side.

'So am I,' Rosie replied, straightening herself and lifting her chin. If nothing else, her mum had always reminded her that nobody took you seriously if you spoke to your feet – though her sister would add that she needed a pedicure. 'And I'm getting quite good at it.'

'She is,' Zain warned. 'And even I'm embracing it.'

Rosie's heart swelled; was he back on board? There was a great thundering clap overhead, as if the whole planet was agreeing with them – and moments later, the sky lit up like a silvery smile matching hers. Rosie would usually have groaned at the arrival of thunder and lightning. Like the three men were doing now, her head would have darted around, looking for shelter, because it was a pain to get your nice clothes wet. But since she'd been here at Autumn Meadows – with Zain, and sometimes without him – she'd felt more connected to the ground beneath her feet and everything that grew here. Even to the vast sky above, which brought a kaleidoscope of weathers that all now had their places in her heart. And right then, with the elements cheering her on, she had never felt more of that oneness.

As the clouds began to drop rain onto the men's dry-clean-only office attire, Rosie couldn't help the triumph that was filling her. It only looked like a passing shower, and maybe like her, it couldn't change much in the long run. But just then, it was making them use their briefcases as umbrellas and make haste off Agnes's land.

'Next time you trespass, we'll call Steve,' Rosie shouted after them, trying to keep the giggle out of her voice. 'Then you'll be sorry.'

When they were far enough away, she allowed herself to burst into laughter at the thought of the denim-waistcoated feline seeing off Small, Medium and Large, like a much better version of Scrappy-Doo than she had managed. Though she knew her laughter was covering a whole lot of nerves. Everything they'd been trying to throw together here *did* pale into insignificance against the might and money of a company that could afford land and factories and all manner of tech.

'You need to get out of this rain and get warm,' said Zain.

It wasn't like her to forget his presence, or not to notice the rain that was now pelting down around them, soaking Zain too. Perhaps she needed it to wash her thoughts clear. They looked back towards his hut and then hers. There was smoke coming out of her chimney. Rosie sensed a battle going on behind his eyes, like he wanted something, but needed to resist.

'You have your fire on. You should go.' He pulled off his jumper and wrapped it around her towelled shoulders, then turned her in the direction of her hut. 'And don't worry about The Three Tuxedos. We'll think of something.'

She laughed again, probably in mild hysteria. 'I think they were wearing normal suits, although I'm pretty sure the small one had a cummerbund to hold his belly in. Though the name fits them. And will we? Think of something, I mean. Are you really going to embrace things again?'

'After that?' He took a deep breath. 'Yes. I'm not letting them come in here and try to trample over everything you've worked so hard for.'

Wow. Was he putting her higher up his list than fighting for his pumpkins?

He began rubbing her shoulders again, tentatively at first. Even if someone had put a typewriter in front of her, she couldn't describe how much she wanted him to come back to her hut. To hold her again, to undress her by the fire, to make her feel warm and whole, like the night she'd slept next to him, drinking in his testosterone and heat.

She didn't need anyone to fight her corner anymore – but it was bloody nice to have someone, and to make a stand for them too. To have *him*, even if she sensed it might only be as workmates from now on.

And if he really was in, they had a bigger mission now.

After seeing *The Three Tuxedos* and hearing their threats to make Agnes a more enticing offer, Rosie had the strong feeling they had to up their game with retreat plans. They needed to make a bigger stand.

She wriggled away and turned back to face him. 'It's time to take off the tow float.' Her hands found the tie around her waist and loosened it. She let the loop drop to the floor and stepped out, feeling like a learner driver taking off her 'L' plates.

Though as much as she was ready to throw caution to the wind with retreat strategies, she'd have to rein in her emotions for Zain. Maybe he was right. If they were going to bring in enough money to save the house and land, they'd need all their energy and focus. Trying to juggle their confusing feelings – not to mention her unfortunate fibs – would throw them off track, as they'd recently proved on their retreat trial weekend.

'Nothing dampens your determination, does it?' He laughed, a little sadly.

'Well, thank you for backing me up. You always know the right thing to say these days.'

He winced and took a step back and scratched the back of his neck. 'No. That's just it. I really don't. I . . .' He seemed to search the horizon for something, before looking back at her. 'I'm just a stupid-arsed gourd farmer, OK? Sometimes I mess things up. And I'm *really* sorry for running out on you the morning after we . . .' His look was intense. His hand reached out as though he was about to have another *leaf in your hair* moment. But he quickly snatched it away. 'Please know it's nothing to do with you. The way I feel about you . . . oh God. There's a lot you don't know.'

'So tell me.'

Maybe if he had something hidden to share, she could offload some awkward mistruths too.

He shook his head. 'Look, you're shivering. You should go. I'll do what I can to help with things. I owe you that much. As a colleague. And . . . friend. But right now, that needs to be all – because I can't be the person you think I am.' He gave her upper arms an amicable squeeze and turned her gently towards her hut, which was almost harder than him saying *bugger off*.

And what did his cryptic words mean?

She began her wet walk back to her cabin for one, willing her head not to look back. She knew he'd be standing there in the rain, watching her, instead of stomping back to his hut to get dry. She also knew he wouldn't follow. But that would have to be OK too. There was work to do, wasn't there?

32

It was surprising how quickly the thunderstorm cleared after The Three Tuxedos had fled, using their briefcases as umbrellas. It had been a ridiculous sight, although Rosie wasn't naive enough to think that would be the last of them.

'We need something more,' she said to Steve, who'd been the first to escape the rain to come and curl up on the rug in front of her fire. It seemed cats were more sensible than humans. 'The retreats will be great.' She walked to her window and looked out at the parting clouds, remembering the clap of thunder. 'But if they don't go off with a fundraising bang, those guys will buy out Autumn Meadows and the farmhouse too, filling everything with factory fumes. Then we'll have cyber cats *and* chatbots taking over the world.'

It sounded dramatic, but the threat of losing everything they'd worked for was real.

She looked back at her cat friend, like he might have groundbreaking answers. He simply lifted his head, treated her to a silent meow, then resettled himself.

'Well, I see you're not feeling talkative.'

Rosie's eyes moved to the drawer where she kept her mobile phone buried, because she had a strong feeling she needed to talk. To thrash around ideas and get sense from someone other than a denim-clad feline. And it wasn't just her fears about the farm that were playing on her mind.

'Time to call Vix.'

Rosie would brave any risk of rain – and she would walk.

She wasn't quite sure when she'd become the kind of person who spoke to a borrowed cat wise enough to only answer at mealtimes. Somehow, he'd convinced her into keeping spare bowls in her hut for him and buying him moggy treats. At least he might keep her warm on lonely nights when she was dreaming of his owner.

'And no more pointless fantasies about Zain.' She grabbed her phone and threw on a raincoat. 'We've got bigger fish to fry.'

This time, Steve's meow was audible. Oh, to have the simple life of a cat.

Rosie rushed along the lane and out of the farm's gates, keen to catch up with her oldest friend. The time was the same in Portugal, and if she got it right, Vix might be on her lunch break.

Rosie allowed her mobile to ping to life as she made her way to the parking spot where she'd broken down in Doll the Citroën, all those weeks ago. It was still the closest place for a hope of decent reception.

The Cotswold hills were aglow with the glorious shades of autumn, from earthy reds to honeyed golds, with fading green fields and round hay bales dotted between. She could spot the lavender farm in the distance, even though its season had passed, and she could recognise the little village of Mistleton where her swim friends lived, with its large central spruce tree and its shops and gingerbread-themed café. Being up here usually gave her a sense of peace. Though right then, it was a sharp reminder that there was real life beyond Autumn Meadows – and some of it was crying out to be dealt with.

Hastily, she opened her thread of messages from her ex-boyfriend, Cassius. She'd just seen off three idiots who ran a robot empire. She could absolutely deal with one sexbot pervert, rather than continually burying her head. She clicked onto the latest message, which, as expected, was about when she would collect her stuff. Her fingers hovered, before swiftly typing *Soon* – because she was all about learning to conquer things, even if she had more immediate fires to fight first.

Rosie briefly considered contacting her family, and even dealing with the contents of the orange letters, which had probably still been arriving with them, even if she'd burned the one she'd brought. Would the words hold less power over her if she faced the truth of them? Did mistakes from the past really matter, when you were striving for a better future? She held a hand to her head, the thought making her dizzy.

'I've got enough going on,' she concluded. The letters would have to be a worry for another day.

She jabbed her phone screen and waited for the call to connect.

'Finally!' said Vix in a voice so loud it nearly pierced Rosie's eardrum. 'Rosie Featherstone, anyone would think you're living in a desert cave. I can never get hold of you.'

'Sorry,' Rosie replied, trying to keep the wobble out of her words. She hadn't realised how much she'd missed her friend. 'My phone's usually off now, but I reply when I can.'

'It's not the same as having a proper chat. Are you OK? Let me see you.'

Rosie pressed to accept video. 'It's so nice to speak.'

'So nice that you never do it?' Vix's face appeared on the screen, her eyes big and dark, her hair pillar box red today. It fluctuated. She was smiling, her words never cross ones. 'Ooh, you're looking good though. Did you use fake tan?'

'No, I saw some sunshine.' Rosie laughed. She'd always been rubbish with fake tan, ending up with streaky bacon legs and palms the colour of an orangutan.

'And look at your hair all naturally wavy. Are those real freckles? Country living suits you.' Vix's tone was warm and encouraging. 'My heart feels good seeing you with a smile on your face.'

Rosie felt her grin falter.

'Is there a *but*?' Vix never missed a trick.

'I don't mean to only ring you when I need something...'

'Nuh-uh.' Vix waved a *who cares* hand. 'I like *big buts*, and I cannot lie. What can I help you with?'

Rosie filled her friend in on the latest with the pumpkin farm and the bucketload of extra jeopardy, with the leaky roof and The Three Tuxedos adamant they'd up their offer again. And she hadn't meant to share her conundrums over Zain, but somehow, they spilled out too.

'It's a big mess, isn't it?' Rosie concluded.

'Well, I love that you're noticing the issues,' Vix replied. 'I mean, the old Rosie would have been hiding in a cupboard, distracting herself with a paperback novel and possibly eating cake.'

It didn't sound like a *bad* plan.

'Now you need to start asking questions,' Vix continued. 'Because words don't *just* belong on paper. Did you ask Agnes if she'd want these Tuxedos to buy her a new house? Surely her Plan A isn't seeing her treasured home turned into a factory for battery-powered cats?'

Rosie let out a small laugh. 'You're right. I should find out exactly what she wants and how much we'd have to raise.' She scratched her head. 'Though we'd need a cash injection to fund Agnes's new roof. I thought that would happen when the retreats kicked off, but we've had so many expenses. Health and safety, insurances. Then there will be food, laundry, extras . . . We can only keep going on credit and kindness for so long.'

'A cash injection. What resources do you have?' Vix's brown eyes were still large on the screen.

'Umm.' Rosie tried to think of it like a problem in one of her novels. 'Some land, a lake and a lot of pumpkins?'

'So how could you get this venture off to a flying start? Hint – you're a Featherstone. This is probably in your DNA, if you can just trust yourself.'

Rosie felt herself inwardly groan. Because she *knew* the answer. They didn't have time for this project to grow slowly, or for money to trickle in. It had to take off like a rocket and bring in cash – and that could only mean one thing.

The idea bubbled in her mind, part inspired by her dates with Zain, mixed with things she'd pored over in novels, and life skills she'd gleaned along the way. Zain wasn't going to like it, and it would be an extreme stretch of her own comfort zone. But the butterflies in her stomach told her she was onto something. And butterflies didn't lie.

'I'm onto it,' said Rosie, sounding far more confident than she felt. She wouldn't trouble her friend with the details yet, because it would need some fleshing out.

'Always here if you need me.' Vix's eyeballs were smiling. And if eyeballs could wave pompoms . . . 'Whatever you decide, you'll smash it.'

Rosie wasn't sure about the *smashing it* part, though she was about to give Zain the fright of his life, when she told him. She let out a sigh.

'Want to talk about Zain?' Vix asked.

Was it that obvious?

'You know my advice is going to be much the same, right? Just face the music and talk.'

'If only. I mean, sometimes he has heaps to say, and other times, barely a word. I sense there's more to him than he's letting on.' She just hoped it didn't involve horny hardware or toy dingoes stuffed with his ex-girlfriends' knickers.

'I think you like this guy,' said Vix. 'I mean *really* like him. Before, you've always measured men in terms of a boring tick list. Has his own flat. Not wanted by the police. Parents don't hate him.' Vix counted things off on her fingers. 'But when you spoke about Zain earlier, your eyes went all melty, and you used words you usually reserve for your romantic heroes. If you think there's more to him and you're as keen as I think you are, keep talking. The answers will come. Between you, you'll work things out.'

'Do you reckon?'

'Hell yes, my capable, kickass friend. And before you thank me, please know that the answers were already within you. You simply needed a nudge to help you find them.'

Now, Rosie just needed to nudge her nervous self back to the farm and hit Zain with her controversial new plan.

33

'So we'll need more boats,' said Rosie, pointing her pencil at Zain, before adding it to her party to-do list. In truth, her insides were still reeling at the thought of her scary new launch party idea, but they needed something *big*. And she did love a list.

'Still no,' said Zain, his face stony.

And she hadn't even mentioned the jack-o'-lanterns.

He'd not long come back from his daily patrol of the fields and was taking off his boots outside his cabin. In fairness, she probably should have waited until he'd had lunch before accosting him with ideas about a launch event and auctioning tickets for candlelit meals on little boats on the lake. It wasn't unreasonable to be a touch *hangry*.

Though maybe it was unreasonable to growl. Rosie huffed back at him.

'Look, it's only one night. After that, everything will be tranquil again. I promise.' She'd known he wasn't going to jump up and shout *yippee* about the extra footfall across his once peaceful home, but it wasn't as though she was planning party poppers or everybody dancing to 'Agadoo' on his precious patches. It would be a serene celebration, with eating and gentle music and people appreciating nature, and they wouldn't even encroach onto his fields other than for a hayride or two. She had explained all of that.

Zain sighed. 'Where would we get more boats?'

'There's that guy at the boating lake. He doesn't use his boats in the evenings, and we're getting good at calling in favours.' Zain hated asking for help, but they'd come to learn that needs must.

Zain didn't reply, which was a whole lot better than a flat 'no'. Rosie took heart and continued.

'Once people have looked around the campsite and taken in the view of the pumpkins, I'm seeing picnic blankets around the lake, with guests eating. Maybe campfires to create atmosphere and warmth.'

'Who's going to cook all this stuff?' Zain sat down on the step of his porch and looked out across the lake.

'That's a great question. Have you heard of Lukas Knight?'

Zain shrugged.

'He runs a supper club above the café in the local village. His place has got a Michelin star now, and people pay a fortune to eat his food, even though his style is down to earth and rustic.'

'So we need to ask for another favour?'

'His girlfriend Gretel from the café is already a big fan of what we're doing, and I bet he wouldn't want an ugly cat factory springing up in his backyard. If we can get him on board it would give us a huge boost for ticket prices.'

She was met with silence again, albeit a contemplative one.

'You did say you'd still help me, even if . . .' She let her words trail off. Even if he couldn't bring himself to fall for her.

'Have you spoken to Agnes?'

'Actually, yes.'

Rosie had marched to the house to speak to her earlier, after her video chat with Vix. Agnes had admitted that some days she felt tempted to give up the pressures of farm life, and the big house with the nippy breezes and knackered rooftop. But she'd shown Rosie her quote for a new roof, plus her costs to keep the place running. The figures had made Rosie's eyes water – yet nothing was impossible. If she could just convince Zain to get on board with her launch ideas, surely, they could fight for this?

She pushed her notebook of figures under his nose.

'This is why we need a flying start.' She pointed to the amount for the roof alone. 'We need to make this sum before rainy winter, unless Agnes and the animals turn into amphibious frogs. Either you're with me, or you can say hello to your new job with The Three Tuxedos, filling in the lake with rock.'

Well, there was no point in beating around the bush.

'I can't think when I'm hungry.' Zain stood up sharply. 'Have you eaten?'

Rosie shook her head. She'd been on the go since they'd seen the men from Cyber Purrz that morning, and her stomach had been a knot of nerves.

He eyed her for a moment, then exhaled. 'Then you'd better come in.'

Rosie nodded. She remembered Vix's advice to keep the lines of communication open with Zain if she wanted to get to the bottom of things. Although right then, it was enough of a mission to get him onside to save their home.

Rosie followed him into his cabin, trying to ignore the heady scent of cedar and general manly Zain-ness that hung in the air. Steve was curled up on the foot of his bed, and she resisted the urge to tickle him and whisper *traitor* into his large, bat-like ear.

He lifted his head and seemed to raise his eyebrows at her, if a hairless cat even had them.

And was that a row of Steve-sized denim waistcoats drying on a makeshift line near the sunny window? Zain would never cease to surprise her.

'You've got it good,' Rosie giggle-whispered, giving Steve's bald head a gentle rub.

Zain was busy pulling out bread and hunks of meat and cheese from cupboards and his small fridge. He looked at his ingredients as though he was considering making something and instead threw it onto a tray with some knives. He pushed a collection of gnarled pumpkins aside and dropped the tray onto a table.

'I'll get beers,' he said, pacing back to the fridge.

Rosie half-expected him to crack them open with his teeth, but he came back with a Swiss army knife and used the gadget. He put it down and took a swig. The word *Dennis* was inscribed on it and Rosie remembered Zain mentioning a foster parent with that name.

Inscriptions. Her mind bounced to *the box* and the thing James had left behind with the inscription that had surprised her. She was thinking of her late not-quite fiancé more lately – generally not in a positive way – and for some reason he'd crept into her manuscript and had been sized up against *Cain*. Though she had the feeling she'd delete James when she got to the root of what was bugging her. And she was in no rush to ever mention him, or her embarrassing naivety, to Zain.

'I didn't steal it,' said Zain, making her jump from her thoughts by plonking down his beer and sinking into a chair. 'He died. His wife Pru gave it to me.'

'Do you miss him?' Rosie asked gently, as she sat opposite Zain at the table.

He busied himself cutting bread, more roughly than he needed to. 'Didn't see him much in his later years. Staying in touch isn't really a thing when you bounce from home to home. Anyway. I think I disappointed him.'

'Don't say that.' Rosie reached her hand across to touch his arm, then pulled it back. Maybe it was safer if they maintained their boundaries. 'I'm sure you didn't.'

'No need to be sad.' He dropped a chunk of bread in front of her. 'I disappoint people at times – which is why you're better off out of it. You're too good for that.' The look he gave her seemed loaded with apology. 'It's just one of life's facts. Like the grass is green, or like Steve has the same number of legs as a tripod.'

Zain was clearly trying to make light of it, so she allowed him a smile. 'I wish you wouldn't think like that.'

'What? He's the fastest cat in the land. I wouldn't have him any other way.'

'Not about the cat.' She rolled her eyes. 'About yourself. And you should let people make their own judgements.'

His abrupt headshake told her the case was closed.

They prepared their meat and cheese in silence. Rosie still had her notebook for the launch party planning, but it didn't feel like the moment for that either.

'Do you want to talk about your parents?' Rosie asked, before she'd had chance to overthink it. If she ever wanted to understand him, it was a good place to start. She'd wondered about his background since he'd briefly mentioned it.

He looked up at her from his sandwich, seemingly impressed with her boldness. A few strands of dark hair hung around his face, framing his strong jaw and dancing in front of his eyes. She felt an urge to reach across and tidy them back into his bun so she could see him properly, but she clamped a hand around her beer.

'My mum died when I was eleven, though I was in care before that. She had addiction problems. Drugs, gambling, alcohol. Anything she got her hands on she couldn't get enough of. Except me.'

The final two words came out so softly, Rosie wasn't even sure that he knew he'd said them.

'I wasn't enough. I guess I'm nobody's addiction.' The small smile on his lips didn't fool her. He was trying to make light of things again. That he had to tore a piece of her heart.

She reached across and squeezed his hand, resisting the impulse to jump up and throw her arms around him and tell him how easily she'd become addicted to every fibre of him. He was so much more than he gave himself credit for. How could she even express that? She longed for him, as much as she tried constantly to suppress it.

'Never say that. You have no idea.' Her eyes welled up, the pressure of tears and sadness almost excruciating. 'I . . . I'm sorry you had to go through that. I can't imagine how tough that must have been.'

'Tough.' He said it like he was mulling something over. 'My mum's sister used that word at the funeral. *She was a tough woman to love. You're better off without her.*'

'That sounds . . . harsh?'

'Yeah. Or stupid. I don't think anyone ever got it.' He rubbed the back of his neck and exhaled. 'I didn't love my mum one bit less for anything that she ever did. We're not programmed like that. It didn't cross my mind to blame her. I blamed me. I loved *me* less. I was the one who wasn't *enough*. Not even for my slightly mean aunt, who had a big enough house and no intention of sharing it.'

'No, no, no.' Rosie squeezed both of his hands with hers, having none left to stop the flow of tears from her eyes.

'Hey, it's OK.' He pulled a hand away and used the corner of his sleeve to wipe her cheeks. 'It's just life, isn't it? We weren't all built to last the race. My mum's probably better off sitting on a cloud. At least she can't spend all her time swearing at slot machines up there. And the view must be fantastic.'

They both knew that wasn't why Rosie's heart was slowly breaking. Her thoughts went out to the mother who'd lost her way. But sometimes it was the ones who were left behind who struggled to find their path again.

Zain was trying to avoid the heaviness, and something in his eyes told her she should respect that. Dark humour was sometimes his way.

'I suppose you want to know about my dad now?' His smile was wry. Almost playful.

'No! I honestly didn't come here to be nosy.'

He raised his eyebrows. 'Well, before you ask, Montana is a long way.'

'Oh. You didn't ever think about . . . ?'

Zain placed a finger on her nose, which was almost certainly a little snotty. She would normally have been self-conscious, but somehow, in that moment, they were beyond that.

He took a swig of his beer. 'Some things can't be fixed.' He pointed the bottle towards her notebook. 'Anyway, we were meant to be coming up with plans for your thing. Maybe that's something we *can* have some control over. But the past? The past is done.' His look said he didn't want to hear any more about it. She could hardly blame him for that.

'OK. But if you ever want to talk . . .'

'Understood. Now, work. Sometimes you and your notebooks are a welcome distraction.'

'Right, yes.' Rosie shook herself down and grabbed her pen. She needed to get back onto safer territory. Territory where she didn't want to throw her arms around Zain and make everything all right. Much like Steve the cat, maybe the things he'd been lacking had made him stronger. And it wasn't her place to try and fix any parts of him that needed healing, as much as her instincts begged to. Zain had made it clear he didn't want that, and it was tricky enough to get him onside when it came to work matters. If they were going to come together to save their homes, she couldn't risk rocking their already precarious boat. And she didn't want her heart to be thrown overboard by him again.

'Maybe your partygoers would be drawn in by magical sunsets and stargazing. And your chef could do a pumpkin harvest feast theme.'

Her heart gave a little skip. And there she'd been, hoping that talk of work would make her want to hug him less. Why did he come up with ideas that made her swoony?

'Great.' She busied her hands with adding items to her list.

'And your hayrides. I can organise that. I have ideas from stuff I've seen at my paternal family's place, in the US. I mean, it was a long time ago. I was only there briefly, and it didn't work out.'

His voice had trailed off a bit. Rosie stayed quiet, wondering if he wanted to talk.

'You know, they could trace their history right back to the early settlers, who learned how to cultivate the fruit from Native Americans. Can you imagine? Hundreds of years of belonging to something and farming one of the oldest known crops. Deep roots. Hard toil. The joy of watching something grow. Something you planted and cared for, with your own bare hands.'

Now and again, Zain disappeared into something that sounded like the perfectly written musings of his soul. That had been one of those moments. Where did it come from? It was a far cry from the reclusive, huffy Zain she'd first met, who'd made her believe he'd barely seen a classroom. Though she knew he couldn't be harbouring a secret library of poetic pumpkin verse.

'Maybe that's why you're so connected to the land, Zain. It's in you.'

She thought she saw the smallest inkling of pride wash over his face, before he quickly straightened his features.

'Maybe I have too much time on my hands, and I get on better with plants than people.' The corners of his mouth lifted.

'You're improving with the people thing.'

'Hope not. Must put a stop to that.' He took a swig of his beer and stood. 'Did you know Agnes has a back kitchen? She never uses it, though the equipment in there isn't so bad. With a good clean-up it might work for your chef guy. If we're going to do this thing properly, we'll need more than a few burnt campfire offerings. I don't know whether we can beat The Three Tuxedos, but I do know that giving up is not in my blood. And nor is pouring concrete into lakes.'

At that, Rosie jumped up and allowed herself to throw her overjoyed arms around him. She was only human, after all.

34

'You grate the spices; I'll stir the chocolate.'

Zain took the grater and did as Rosie had suggested, starting with the cinnamon sticks. The two of them were in Agnes's back kitchen, making pumpkin-spiced chocolates for their retreat launch party, which was just a couple of days away – although, thankfully, the weekend retreats didn't start until a week after that.

Rosie was dizzy enough with nerves at the thought of hosting this huge do. She had to keep reminding herself that she didn't *hate* parties, she'd just been to a lot that weren't her cup of tea. Surely hosting would be better – and this one was for an extremely important cause. She focused on Zain's hands as he worked swiftly with the spices, taking care not to break them or grate his knuckles.

He looked up at her. 'Shouldn't you be stirring? Or am I distracting you with my impressively large stick?' He waved the cinnamon at her.

His lips were teasing into the smallest smile, even though she could see he was trying for a poker face. It wasn't her fault he had such mesmerising kitchen skills – among other things. She tried not to remember that night in the treehouse, now that getting naked with him was apparently off limits.

'I was looking at your apron, actually,' she replied, hoping to draw attention away from her cheeks, which she could sense were darkening like a pair of Baby Red Hubbards. 'I hadn't realised you'd been officially crowned *The Queen of Cat Snacks*.'

Zain was wearing one of Agnes's novelty aprons, which looked more like a postage stamp against his broad shoulders and chest. It had a picture of a cat's head poking out of the front pocket, and a swishy tail that even Steve would have been proud of.

'The chocolate?' he repeated calmly, one eyebrow rising to match his half-smile.

In truth, his cool sense of direction had kept her going, over the last week or so, as they'd worked together to bring their opening event plans to life. Zain had been great at seeing the bigger picture and turning her inspired ideas into some sort of strategy, and she'd enjoyed coming up with the *thoughtful stuff*, as Zain called it. The little details that she hoped would make their guests feel cared for and special. By popular demand from Mags, the chocolates were making an appearance in the launch party gift bags.

Zain was so unrufflable that she lived in a constant temptation to reach out and ruffle him. And the more time they spent together...

'Right yes, the chocolate.' She'd better get on with it before he needed to remind her for a third time. 'My scatty head.' She busied herself with breaking off chunks of dark chocolate and dropping them into a glass bowl, ready for melting. She was using a simple recipe she'd learned from one of her mum's staff. Rosie might never have been much of a partygoer, but she had enjoyed being behind the scenes making sure everything was just right.

She and Zain had worked together to scrub up the back kitchen the previous week, ready for the catering. She *loved* being near him, even if it was only doing something dull, like attacking grubby cupboards with a sponge. As strange as it was, she was sure he felt that too, though he'd been fighting it. She looked at him, smiling to himself as he worked. Was he nearly out of fight?

In the spirit of teamwork, they'd even arranged for Agnes to have internet installed at the house, because it wasn't practical to run online bookings and enquiries by constantly nipping offsite. Rosie's laptop sat on a table in the corner of the room so they could keep an eye on the auction for exclusive tickets to dine at their opening night.

With a bit of persuasion, Rosie had managed to get local chef Lukas Knight and his team to donate their time to cook for the guests who would be dining on and around the lake. His proposed menu had mouths watering and people bidding for tickets already, and Bonnie had even agreed to become their official supplier of pumpkin fizz. When Rosie had visited the nearby village of Mistleton to talk to Lukas, she'd ended up with even more generosity than she'd bargained for. Some of the shop owners had offered gifts and services to be auctioned on the night, to help to boost funds for Agnes's roof.

As Rosie began melting the chocolate, she felt Zain's presence behind her, his head peering over her shoulder. His body was close and warm, and she couldn't tell whether it was the steam from her bowl that was sending her into a flush, or him.

'Mmmmmmmm.'

There was a depth to Zain's groan that made her want to liquify too.

He was breathing in the smell of the rich, dark chocolate, and as Rosie turned her head a touch to look at him, she could see his eyes were closed, his thick eyelashes fluttering gently against his cheeks. It reminded her of watching him sleep, that night they'd spent together. Peaceful and unguarded, even if the next morning had been a confusing far cry from that. But still, the urge to lean in and feel her lips against his skin again was almost uncontrollable. Like nothing she'd ever felt.

His hair was tucked perfectly inside a bandana, which only accentuated his solid features. His skin was so velvety, and . . .

Her nose twitched. Hang on. What was that odd smell?

Her head swung back quickly to her stirring. 'Oh crap. It's nearly burning.' She pulled the pan off the heat and tried to grab the glass bowl without thinking, scalding the pads of her fingers. 'Ouch!'

Where was an oven glove when she needed one? As she flapped around looking for it, Zain cranked the cold tap onto full blast and pulled her hands underneath it. The relief was almost as instant as the universe's stark warning. She exhaled sharply. If she didn't want their plans to go up in smoke, she had to stay in control of things. And that included errant thoughts about Zain. Didn't it?

'Thank you.' Rosie tugged her hands back and turned off the tap. 'It's fine. Just a blip. Do you want to get back to the spices?'

'Yep. Sorry. My fault for putting you off your stride. I couldn't help myself. Smelling the chocolate, I mean.' He moved back to his workspace.

She inspected her fingers. A little red, but probably not as bad as her embarrassed face.

Keep your body parts to yourself if you don't want them burnt. That was surely a good motto to live by. And who on earth had velvety skin, other than teddy bears? That had simply been her romantic writer's head getting carried away with itself.

'You're doing a great job, you know,' Zain said quietly, his back to her as he worked. 'I would never have thought of these extra details. This stuff seems to come naturally to you. That and your boundless optimism, even when our chances seem slimmer than one of Agnes's rescued moggies.'

'You're good at a lot of stuff too. The original date on the lake was your idea. That night was . . .'

She brought her attention back to her chocolate, letting her words taper off.

'Right, yes,' he replied. She could sense him shuffling awkwardly. 'Not sure where the date ideas came from. Must have appeared to me in a dream.'

Rosie's laptop chimed from the corner. She guessed it was a notification for another launch party ticket bid. As inspired by her lake date with Zain, she'd borrowed more boats and they were auctioning tickets to dine on them, as well as a lakeside picnic option, Zain's pumpkin patch hayrides and fizz and nibbles under the stars.

Now they just had to hope for no rain, no disasters, and some decent bids to save the day. And that was before she contemplated what on earth she'd do if Farmer Wilbur or anyone from her past showed up and dropped her in it.

The laptop chimed again.

Zain looked up. 'Someone's popular.'

'Actually, I'm not.' Rosie shook her head.

'Nor me. It's over-rated. I don't even have devices for people to reach me on if I can help it. The Hermit in the Hut.' He winked at her.

'It's people bidding on our tickets. We'll have a look when I've poured the chocolate into moulds.' Now it was cooling, she motioned for him to bring the spices so she could start stirring them in.

'Is that where you've been writing your novel?' He nodded towards her screen. His bandana came loose, and he threw it aside.

She felt the heat rising to her cheeks again. 'Usually, but not this time. I used to rely on Wi-Fi for my work to save to a cloud, and we don't get that in our cabins.' It had been enough to get Agnes to agree to it in the house. 'So I've been using an old typewriter. At least I can't keep rewriting every word or deleting things in a huff.' She shrugged. 'It's almost freeing.'

Zain tipped his spices into Rosie's chocolate, and they watched the motion of her wooden spoon as she stirred them in.

'I'll have to edit my manuscript when I've finished the first draft, which I would have done on paper anyway. Once I've done that, I'll type up the edited version on my laptop. And then heaps more edits. Though a chatbot could probably have written the whole thing in about fifteen seconds, of course. Not that Artificial Intelligence could possibly create anything heartfelt.' She rolled her eyes. Being at Autumn Meadows Farm with Zain had convinced her that the best words came when you felt truly alive, which AI never would be.

Zain cleared his throat. 'A chatbot. No. Of course not. I mean, who knows.' He waved a hand. 'Maybe some people would need that, but not you. I'm sure you're better than that. Erm . . . Rosie?' His body tensed and he seemed to be considering something.

Rosie looked up. Whatever it was, it was making deep furrows on his beautiful forehead.

'Something up?'

He blinked a few times before bringing his attention back to the chocolate moulds he was meant to be lining up. 'No, of course not.' He cleared his throat. 'Is the first draft of your novel nearly finished?'

Rosie sensed that wasn't the real topic that had been playing on his mind, but she continued anyway. If it was important, he'd come back to it when he was ready. 'Actually, I think it might be. I'm just not sure of the ending yet.'

She'd been letting art imitate life, inspired by what was happening at the farm, with a fictional twist and a bit of artistic licence. Though it looked like she'd have to compose her own fictional ending, as there would be no romantic finale between her and Zain.

'Am I in it yet?'

'No!' Rosie yelped, almost too quickly. He wasn't, exactly. Her main male character was called Cain, rather than Zain, although he did look suspiciously similar, and had treated her main female character Josie to exactly the same romantic dates. She'd obviously have to change some of that but writing it had been like reliving it – and what she wouldn't give to experience those moments again.

'Good,' he replied. 'I would hate that. Anyway, I'm not sure anyone would get me.'

'You'd probably stir up too much trouble,' she teased.

'Though maybe you could combine your passions and run writing retreats here? I bet they'd go down a storm.'

'See what I mean about trouble?' She laughed. 'Maybe one day, in a dream life. But one thing at a time, hey?'

Rosie grabbed her wooden spoon and dolloped a splodge of chocolate onto his nose. Then she plonked his bandana back onto his head and ducked away quickly, before he could mount a revenge attack. 'Now please keep your clothes on in my kitchen.'

He raised his eyebrows at her. 'I'll do my best.'

It was hard enough being in a confined space with him. There was no way she could cope if he started removing outer garments and swishing his hair like that guy from *Poldark*.

Ping, ping, ping. Ping, ping, ping.

Luckily, they were saved by the bell.

'What on earth?' Rosie rushed to her laptop and clicked the mousepad. 'Oh . . . *wow*. I think there's a bidding war.'

The Cotswolds was an affluent place. It seemed some people would remortgage their summer house to be seen at this sort of exclusive event. She tried to ignore the niggling worry that her mother and sister could be two of them. If they showed up, her cover might be seriously blown.

Zain's arrival at her side swiftly distracted her. They leaned over the screen.

'How much?' Zain asked, blinking a few times and looking more closely. 'People are bidding wild amounts for these tickets. Are you putting on a secret Take That concert? Or is the Duchess of Gloucester handing out canapés?'

'Nope. Just you in your borrowed Queen of Cat Snacks apron. I guess you must be hot right now.'

'You do know I'm not wearing this on the night?' He gave her a nudge.

Their eyes stayed glued to the screen as the figures rose, the notifications chiming like an overenthusiastic fruit machine.

'That must be all your extra promotional stuff this week. Well done,' said Zain.

Since Agnes had agreed to get internet at the house, Rosie had been popping over to update social media and build excitement about the launch event and auction. Their following was rising, and local bloggers and media were taking an interest.

If it wasn't for not wanting the Featherstones to track her down, Rosie would have considered contacting her sister, who with her huge Instagram tribe, could make anything go viral. But Rosie's nerves had enough to deal with. And for once, she wanted to succeed at something her way, instead of feeling like the slightly rubbish relation.

'Thank you,' said Rosie. 'Technology certainly has some uses. Although we're definitely not getting Kimberkoo Chat to write our promo material. That wouldn't fit in with our ethic of bringing people back to nature. And I'm sick of that thing nicking my job.' She giggled and nudged him back, feeling almost dizzy at watching the numbers take off. Could they actually do this?

'Hmm, yes. No chatbots,' Zain replied, absently.

Though she guessed he didn't know much about those, being a self-confessed hermit.

'I think our luck is finally changing,' said Rosie, straightening herself and taking a moment to breathe it in.

Zain stood too, and as he turned to face her, she noticed that in the excitement, he'd forgotten about the blob of chocolate on the end of his nose. She reached up and wiped it with her finger, trying her best to keep a straight face.

'I was saving that.' His hand encircled itself gently around her wrist and he drew her finger towards him, his mouth slowly opening.

She could have pulled away and made light of it. She could have smeared the chocolate onto his cheek or wiped it on his cat apron or even eaten it herself. Though as he moved her finger towards his lips, it was as though time stood still. Or perhaps that time couldn't move quickly enough. So when he made to put her finger into his mouth, she let him.

He didn't break eye contact as his tongue teased the chocolate from her fingertip. It shouldn't have felt quite so sensual. It was just Zain, licking a bit of stray chocolate from her skin, for goodness' sake. Yet the warmth and softness of his mouth mixed with that strange sense of longing deep in his eyes must have fired up a million nerve endings. She was probably glowing so brightly that she could be seen from outer space.

When his lips finally released her, it took all her willpower not to leap into his arms and kiss him. There were so many reasons not to, but the more time they spent together, the more those details seemed to melt away, like the chocolate in her bain-marie.

'We make a great team, don't we?' she heard herself breathe.

He was nodding slowly, almost as if his head was moving against his will. And then his lips were travelling towards hers, and she was leaning into him, their mouths meeting in a way that caused fireworks. Rosie's whole body felt like a launch party celebration, filled with sparks and joy and the hope of all things magical. She had no idea where this moment would lead to, whether her heart was about to be broken or fixed or taken on the ride of its life. But right then, she just wanted to sink into him. To be devoured by her own lust for him, and the emotions that were growing inside her. From the way he was cupping her face in his hands and whispering sweet, sensual words between his kisses, she sensed he was feeling them too.

35

Rosie spotted Zain sitting in one of his pumpkin patches, silhouetted against the indigo night sky, a solar lamp at his side. He looked peaceful under the stars, resting on the rugged earth between his vines. It was the field where he grew his Prizewinner pumpkins. The huge ones, like he'd been hulking on that first day she'd seen him. He'd since admitted that he'd always held back from fighting for life's prizes. She hoped she was helping him to change that.

She took in the sight of him, leaning back on one hand, a bottle of beer in the other, facing away from her. She'd been taking an evening stroll as she often did, when the weather was gentle, and she had things on her mind. Though she'd guessed he might be somewhere out here.

Zain's dark hair was tied scruffily, and Rosie had a craving to go over and set it free, run her hands through it, use it to pull his face towards hers...

Their kiss in Agnes's back kitchen earlier had signalled a new shift in their relationship, although neither of them had suggested taking things further on their boss's laminate worktops. And as mind-altering as the kiss had been, there had been something unspoken between them that they needed to retreat and think about their next actions, rather than getting swept up in the moment and going on to regret it.

It all seemed more complicated, with them having to work together and live across the lake from each other. And the fact that their last physical encounter had ended with Zain fleeing and Rosie feeling rubbish, even if he'd apologised and had sworn it wasn't about her. If she was going to let things go further, she wanted to know she could trust him. That he was all in, if he wanted more too. And they would only find that out by talking, so she resolved to disturb his peace.

He didn't seem surprised when she crouched near him on the hard mud, and he pulled off a few large leaves and made ground cover for her to sit. He was wearing dark jeans that pulled tight around his firm thighs, as if they wanted to burst free.

She resisted the urge to touch him.

'I've been waiting for you.' He signalled to an open beer bottle next to him. 'I know you often walk this way.'

'Confident,' she said, taking it and sipping. 'What else have you already prepared for?'

'Nothing.' He shrugged. 'But after earlier . . .'

'You guessed I'd be back for more?'

'I'm not that self-assured.'

For a man who was so virile and hotly mysterious, he probably should have been.

'I guessed you'd want to talk,' he said.

She did. And *so* much more.

An owl hooted in the distance, taking her right back to their night in the treetops, when they'd trembled under each other's touch. If she was ever going to feel that way again with him, he was right about the talking.

'I'm falling for you,' she blurted out, before taking another swig of her beer. 'And I can't make it stop.' She hadn't meant to lay her cards on the table so easily, but she was bored of this metaphorical poker. Life was precious and they'd been wasting too much of it.

For the first time since she'd sat down, he turned to look at her. His deep brown eyes seemed to weigh her up.

'So don't stop,' he said quietly.

'And risk getting hurt again?'

His beautiful, usually strong face crumpled. 'I'm sorry I backed off like that, after that night. It meant something to me too. I was cowardly. Stupid. I was scared of so many things, and . . .' He put down his beer and ran a hand through his hair, his black band pulling free. His hair fell in dark waves. Even though Rosie had never usually been into the untamed mane look, its mirror-like shine was mesmerising in the moonlight. *He* was mesmerising. It was getting harder not to touch him.

'What's changed?' she asked. 'Aren't you frightened anymore?'

He studied her face for a long moment. 'I'm terrified. I've made mistakes and I've not always been myself, and some days I wonder who I am at all. I'm sorry for that.'

'You have nothing to be sorry for.' She put down her own bottle and grabbed his hand. 'Well, a few things.' She gave a small grin. 'But you don't have to apologise for being human. We all mess things up once in a while.' She thought back to earlier in Agnes's back kitchen, when he'd seemed as though he wanted to say something, then didn't. 'Whatever you want to share, I'm listening.'

His sigh left warm breath on her cheeks. 'In answer to your question, nothing's changed. I'm pretty sure I'm still the same person who's made the same messy mistakes. As much as I've grappled with the guilt of things, I can't go back and change them. So maybe we could ... start again? From right now, in this moment. Because I'm falling for you too. And I don't want to make it stop.'

She smiled at him softly and he took it as a cue to continue.

'God, Rosie, I love everything about you. It makes no sense.'

'Why, thank you,' she joked.

'No, I don't mean that. You see how bad I am at this? I mean, I love being with you, even when we're just dragging logs around, or making lists about toilet roll, or grating sodding cinnamon sticks.' He ran a hand through his hair. 'And I love your *funny dungarees*, and the way you encourage me, and support my extremely weird pumpkin obsession.'

'I love your pumpkins.' She treated him to a wry smile. 'I can't get enough of being with you either, and understanding how you see the world, and even catching scary spiders so that you don't have to. And I love how you make me feel safe to just be *me*.'

He nodded slowly. 'Me too.'

She squeezed his hand, brought it gently to her lips for a kiss and then let it go.

'Do you know what I also love?' she asked quietly. 'When we stop talking and let our bodies speak.'

'Mmm hmm,' he agreed, as if words had once again escaped him.

There *would* be a time when she'd confess her niggling secrets. But it wouldn't be before they got through their launch event and saved this farm. And it wouldn't be tonight.

Then slowly but steadily, she began peeling off her clothes, one layer at a time, right there in the dirt like she'd fantasised about more than once. Her eyes didn't leave his as she relished every minute of the look on his face, like he was hungry for her.

'And I love it when you touch me,' she said, when she was down to her underwear, which this time didn't match.

He began pulling off his clothes too, to make a bed for her in his Prizewinner pumpkin patch. The look on his face said he was ready to claim his prize.

'And I love touching you. Just show me where.' His voice was almost a growl.

In a different world she would have worried about her body, or being almost naked in a field, or the fact she fully hoped to have shuddering, muddy sex right here, under the stars. But her time with Zain, in this wild and incredible place, had dissolved some of those fears away.

He knelt near her, swallowing hard, his eyes taking her in. They roamed over her curves as she lay back on his nest of clothes, his pupils dilating. She used to have hangups about her thighs, but now she just wanted to wrap them around him. He was still waiting eagerly for her direction, and after a deep kiss that left her whole body trembling, she pushed his head gently downwards. She wanted his full lips between her legs, like she'd imagined in many a wayward daydream. She was throbbing for him already.

His tongue worked its way down her body, caressing and kissing her nipples like he was tasting her. Then he descended, his tongue trailing a slow, sensual line down her centre, flicking her bellybutton, teasing her stomach, passing the spot where she wanted him, then nuzzling her inner thighs.

'If you don't get there soon,' she gushed, pulling his hair and guiding his face between her legs.

'There?' He pulled her panties aside, his breath warm

against her soft, intimate skin. The tip of his tongue found the perfect spot, as though he already knew her.

Her deep groan of pleasure told him that was exactly the place. She raised her hips to him, pushing into him, slowly at first, then more insistently, finding her rhythm. He murmured his encouragement, his lips vibrating against her tingling flesh, sending tiny ripples of pleasure through her. His fingers pulled at her underwear again, to make more space for himself.

'Oh *gosssssshhhhh*.'

She didn't know what he was doing with his tongue, other than it was exploring wildly, his mouth sucking, her skin pulsating, her mind getting ready to explode. She had never felt anything like this. She wanted a *lifetime* of it.

But tonight, she wanted to reach her ultimate pleasure when he was inside her. She wanted to move as one with him, feeling every twitch of his lust for her. And she'd come prepared for exactly that.

He looked surprised when she wriggled out of her underwear, motioning for him to do the same and pulling out a condom from the pocket of her thrown-aside jacket.

'Another thing I love about you is that you make me feel like anything is possible,' she said as she raised her eyebrows about whether she should open the packet. He nodded. 'Even my pretty weird pumpkin farmer fantasies. Do you mind a bit of trampling of your fields?'

This time he was shaking his head.

She slipped the condom onto the end of his penis, which was now harder and huger than she'd ever seen it – and she'd yet to properly touch him. She savoured the way his eyelids fluttered shut as she unrolled the rubber down the length of him. It felt good for her too.

'What do your fantasies look like?' he asked, his voice a low rumble.

She beckoned him down to her, whispering a few of her wildest ones into his ear. She could feel him nodding against her.

'But first, I just want you to take me here.'

He lowered himself over her, her legs parting, more than ready.

His naked chest was solid, his black, twisting tattoos sweeping up his biceps and across his sun-kissed torso, winding around etchings of vines and all things nature, like his bare body was a map of him. Her hands reached out to them. She heard his sharp intake of breath as her fingers traced his chest, touching a hard nipple, trailing downwards through the firm grooves of his abs, teasing the line of black hair that led to his erection.

He closed his eyes. His deep groan was unmistakable.

She pulled him down further towards her, their arms wrapping around each other, their hands gripping flesh. Hers was raging. Their lips came together greedily, urgently. He tasted of sweet beer and deep longing, their tongues moving in a way that felt so right she could almost cry. His mouth was rhythmic and sure, an excruciating tease of everything that would surely come. Her heart screamed. If kisses could leave an imprint on a person's soul, Rosie knew this one would mark hers forever.

Her hands rode up Zain's firm back, memorising every curve of him. His muscles were tense, and so was his penis, which was pushing against her leg. She used her hands to guide it inside her, pushing her hips upwards, making him groan. His hands slid under her buttocks, clenching her rear and tugging her up to him, as though she was the most incredible, addictive thing. With one more exquisite push, he was fully inside her. *Ohhhhh.* It was everything she'd fantasised about and so much more.

They moved together, gasping into the night, the ground blissfully hard against her back, dustings of dirt kicking upwards as Zain thrust deeper inside her. It was as rousing and animal as *all* of her imaginings.

His hot mouth moved to her neck, tasting her, groaning into her, tormenting her skin with his tongue. Having him inside her was electric. She was burning and shivering all at once, and the depth of emotion that was flowing through her was almost too much to bear. His head moved to her nipples and his mouth was on them, sucking them carnally until she could have sworn that would be the end of her.

Oh wow.

The moon shone over them and animals called in the distance, but none of it mattered, compared to the feeling of being under Zain's body, his desire pulsing through her.

She wrapped her legs around his back, thrusting herself up to him, desperate to feel him deeper and deeper. Frantic for her throb to be satisfied but longing to feel this way forever – with him – balancing on the edge of pure, exquisite bliss.

And then she was coming and coming in the most sensuous waves, and so was he, hot and fast, desperate and feral, pushing himself into her and gasping into her hair. She felt alive. So very, intensely alive. And she never wanted to stop feeling like this.

36

'Of all the ways to get warm, that was probably my favourite,' said Rosie, her gentle laugh filling the space around them as she huddled under a blanket against Zain's chest.

They'd drifted off to sleep in the pumpkin field after Zain had brought some of her pumpkin farmer fantasies to life, and when they'd woken not long afterwards, Rosie shivering into the October night, he'd carried her back to his hut to warm up.

They were now in his bed, the morning hour still early. Her mind couldn't stop replaying images from what had undoubtedly been the most intimate night of her life, which had continued more slowly and deliberately when they'd reached his bed. Of course, with previous boyfriends, she'd had reasonable amounts of sex before. As a woman of thirty-six, she knew where everything went. But suddenly, it felt like none of her earlier encounters had been *genuine*.

After all those years of assuming that she knew what love and lovemaking was, in a few precious hours, everything she thought she understood had been turned on its head.

Because last night had been something else entirely. It had

felt *real*. Her body had moved with Zain's as though they were one complete person, with one beating heart. When their bodies were connected in the very deepest way, it had felt like he was part of her. Like every shudder, every pulse, was connected directly to her soul. It had been beautiful and magical and almost terrifying. To lay herself so completely bare, to gasp his name as if it was the only word she could remember. The sound of it coming from somewhere deep within and guttural. Her body was flushing again at the thought.

At last, she was sure that previous relationship disasters hadn't left her immune to feeling or falling deeply – she'd just always chosen the wrong men for her. And Zain was oh so right.

Rosie glanced at the clock. They would need to be up soon, to push on with preparations for the official launch party and auction, which was happening the next evening. Until that time, she would cherish every inch of him. Her fingers tracked the artwork on his body. The collage of etchings she'd been so desperate to pore over since that morning when she'd accidentally barged in on him in the shower.

'Do they mean anything?' Rosie asked, the pad of her finger tracing the outline of a mountain. Vines twisted out from it and a bird flew above.

'Not really. A tapestry of things that I've added over the years. Me finding parts of myself, and hoping that by searing them onto me, I'll keep them close.' He shook his head, taking her hand off the small bird and placing it over his heart. 'Though it doesn't work like that. Belonging, I mean. You can't carve it onto you. You have to feel it inside you.' He shrugged. 'I guess. Still trying to work it out.'

'They're stunning. And I hope you can belong with me,' she whispered.

'I hope so too.'

He turned onto his side to face her, and as her hand trailed downwards his eyebrows rose. She remembered him making a throwaway excuse that first morning in the shower, about the cold water having an adverse effect on the size of his manhood. She could now vouch that everything he had to offer was particularly generous.

'You're chuckling again,' he whispered into her hair, which was now completely wild from the best-ever night. The way she was feeling, the wilder the better. Had she ever even lived before she'd arrived on this farm?

She tilted her gaze towards him, hungry to see his face, his smile. Desperate for her eyes to sink into his.

'And blushing a little.'

There was his smile again. She felt like she'd seen it a surprising amount since they'd been working together on their projects, but it had never come so easily nor shone so naturally as it did this morning. He was lighting up the world.

'Are you hot for me?' His gently teasing tone was setting her on fire.

All she could do was nod. For a writer, she had relatively few words to answer with. Though she knew that when she stole some time with the typewriter later, her heart would spill. In fact, everything she'd written about love until recently suddenly felt like drivel. Maybe those terrible rejection letters from publishers had been right. Perhaps her romantic scenes had been oddly lacking – because much like a piece of chatbot software, she *hadn't* known what love was. But something had changed.

His gaze was still on her, his eyes delicately sweeping her face as though they were enamoured with everything they saw, even though her eyes were probably puffy, and her cheeks creased from the sheets. He was looking at her as if she was his world, and his mouth twitched like there was something he couldn't *not* say.

Suddenly, she felt it too. The overwhelming surge of it. Filling her up and threatening to burst from her. Her lips opened and the words tumbled out.

'I love you.' They were followed by her own small gasp. She hadn't meant to say it so early, although somehow, she hadn't been able to stop it.

'I love you too.' His words were quieter than hers. Slower. More considered. 'And that thing you said before about no one knowing how to do *forever*. You're right. Forevers are created one day at a time.'

She could feel his heart beating under her hand, steady and strong. Getting faster as her other hand teased up his body towards his face. And once again she was climbing on top of him, even though, in a past life, she wasn't usually confident enough to take the lead. She loved the look in his eyes as he drank her in, the swell of her breasts, the delicate dip of her navel. His tongue traced his lips, and she remembered the deep pleasures of it from last night. He'd made every part of her glow.

As they both grew ready, Zain searched around for protection and put it on. And soon Rosie was easing herself onto him, both of them gasping with sheer, uncontrollable *want*.

The look in his dark, hypnotic eyes as they moved steadily together told her he'd found everything he needed to belong.

She felt it too.

37

Rosie was sitting at the typewriter, deep in thought about the magical night and morning she'd just spent with Zain. She hadn't *planned* to turn their lovemaking into a steamy new scene for her novel, but somehow the words had emerged onto her page. In fact, it had taken up quite a few pages. She smiled. Perhaps she should change a few details and delete the part about the pumpkin field, so it wasn't so obvious that naked Cain was naked Zain. Or more likely, she should keep this scene to herself. She would never want to embarrass him.

They'd spent the rest of that day getting ready for the official launch party and auction, which was happening the next evening. There was still a lot to do, but they had tomorrow. Rosie just hoped the event would grab enough attention to get retreat spaces filling up, and that the party and auction would raise enough to fund Agnes's roof.

'This is the life,' Rosie breathed to herself.

Her hair was tied up in messy buns, damp from her quick swim earlier. She still had her swimming costume on under her flowery dungarees, and there was a wet patch on her bottom from where she'd sat down without drying properly. Her socks were odd because she hadn't had much time to worry about things matching. And she didn't care a dot.

Everything felt *wonderful*. Like anything was possible.

Maybe one day she could start thinking seriously about her writing retreat ideas after all. Her novel was coming together, and she was even starting to think of herself as a *real writer*. She was working on her manuscript every day now – her own words, not something about periodontitis or horrible teeth. And definitely not anything that could be churned out by a chatbot.

Zain seemed to be growing and changing too. From the antisocial grump in the hut, to a man full of romantic words and plans. And more recently, to something almost in the middle. Like he was settling into himself. Or to her.

Yes, she was a woman in love. Her heart sped at the thought. She and Zain had said the words out loud to each other, and for the first time in her life, she *knew* she meant them. Even her relationship with James, which she was coming to believe hadn't been what she thought it was, had never been a patch on this.

Finally, she was winning at life.

The loud knock at the door surprised her. She'd been tucked into her writing nook for longer than she'd realised, pages of her manuscript spread out on the table next to her, whilst she tried to work out where her story was going. Was it weird to keep basing her plot on real life, now that Zain was so much more than a muse?

'Rosie, it's me,' came Zain's rushed voice from the other side of her front door. 'Can I come in?'

'Of course,' she shouted back. It was sweet that he still asked, although she guessed it made sense to keep some boundaries.

The door opened and Zain strode in, running an agitated hand through his hair.

'Have you seen Steve?' he asked. Rosie shook her head. 'He hasn't touched his food, then I realised I haven't actually seen him for a couple of days. With everything that's been going on, I didn't notice. I've looked everywhere. Agnes hasn't spotted him. He likes to pretend he's his own boss, but he doesn't skip a mealtime.'

Rosie put her papers down and stood up, making her way to the coat hooks. 'Right, we'll split up and look again. I'm sure he'll be fine; he always is. Three legs and nine lives. He's my kind of superhero.'

Zain tried a smile, but it didn't reach his eyes.

'Hey.' She stepped towards him and squeezed his hands. 'We're in this together, OK? And we'll find him.' She grabbed the pet snacks and gave a handful to Zain. 'Cat bribes at the ready. Let's go.'

They set off around the land, taking separate routes. Zain disappeared towards the camping meadow to check the treehouses again. Rosie paced around the lake, calling into the bullrushes and shaking the box of treats. She knew without him saying it that Zain worried about Steve falling in. He could swim in a wobbly sort of way, but not for long and not without starting to gulp water.

'*Steeeeeve?* Where are you, little man?'

It was cloudy overhead, and the sky felt grim and grey. Rosie pulled her raincoat tighter. A knot of guilt began forming in her stomach. They should have noticed he was gone, but they'd been too wrapped up in their own bubble. Would they be forced to suffer the price? If anything happened to Steve when they should have been looking out for him, maybe it would shake Zain's confidence about letting people into his once solitary world.

She took a few deep breaths to calm herself, and when she

was sure she couldn't see him by the lake, she headed to the woodsheds. She knew Zain had checked all around the farmhouse and across the pumpkin fields – but the only thing to do was keep looking. Then she'd check the road. Neither of them had mentioned it, because it would be like admitting the worst.

It must have been an hour later when Rosie got back to the lake. Zain's cabin was closest, so she decided to go in and look for him. If he wasn't there, she'd put the kettle on and wait. Then they could plan what to do if Zain hadn't found Steve.

'Zain?' Rosie knocked on the door and put her ear to it. There was no light coming from inside, even though it was starting to get dark. Zain didn't reply.

Then Rosie heard a crash from inside, like something falling and hitting the floor.

'Steve?'

She pushed the door open and flicked on the erratically buzzing light. Something scurried across the floor.

'Steve, was that you? Are you OK?' She rushed towards the table where the shape had darted and dropped to her knees. 'It's you! Come here, you silly thing. What are you hiding from?'

Rosie felt her eyes fill with tears at the sheer relief of finding him. He must have let himself in through the cat flap. The awful images she'd been imagining of the poor thing struggling for his life in the water or being injured on the road began to evaporate as he hopped into her arms. She kissed his bald head and breathed him in – even if his cat waistcoat did now smell a bit like a pond.

'We should get you changed. Have you eaten?' She had no idea what she was expecting him to answer. Stickleback sandwiches by the lake? But she'd become so accustomed to talking to him, and he seemed to like it. 'What were you running from, anyway?' Rosie stood, Steve still cradled in her arms. 'What was the crashing noise?'

Steve wriggled to get down and Rosie realised he must be hungry. She moved to the full bowls and crouched with him, letting him climb down. And that was when she noticed it. A laptop, in an awkward upside-down position on the floor near Zain's bed, as if it had fallen there. That must have been the loud noise she'd heard. *A laptop?*

Rosie's forehead creased. Zain had never mentioned having a laptop. In fact, he'd grunted and pulled a *no way* face when she'd asked him if he used a smartphone or any devices. Which had seemed unusual – but that was Zain. And it had made some sense because the phone signal was patchy, and Wi-Fi didn't stretch this far even now Agnes had it in the house. Even Rosie still used a typewriter – though she now preferred it.

So what was Zain using it for? And what were all those papers? Some were strewn across the bed and others had apparently fallen to the floor when the laptop had landed. She guessed Steve had jumped onto the bed and knocked things off.

'I should tidy up. Don't want you to get into trouble.'

Rosie paced to the bed and picked up the laptop, hoping the fall hadn't done it too much damage. The screen was black, and she didn't want to start pressing buttons. It wasn't her business, even though she felt curious for an explanation, when its presence niggled against the version of Zain she'd come to know. She knew Agnes had a dusty old desktop, but not a laptop that Zain could have borrowed, and he'd never mentioned using one for their projects. Not that it would matter if he did. So why hadn't it come up in conversation?

Rosie sighed and put the laptop onto the bed, before bending to pick up the fallen papers. She wasn't *meaning* to read them because she definitely wasn't a snooper. She'd never spied through her partners' phones or rifled among their stuff for damning clues about anything. Although in hindsight, maybe that had been her downfall. If she'd stopped turning a blind eye to Cassius's sexy robot Google searching, or if she'd asked more questions about where her on-off fiancé James had always been disappearing to, and why he sometimes smelled of strange perfume, or the unusual inscription on his new-looking watch that he'd sworn was an heirloom...

The knot began to reform in Rosie's stomach, only this time it was tighter. Had she always ignored the signs, even when signs were surely there for a reason? Friends had warned as much. Had her naive way of trusting people, or perhaps ignoring the obvious because she didn't think she deserved better, been her undoing? Her eyes were filling up. She tried to blink back the tears, but a few escaped onto one of the papers she was holding.

'Oh goodness.' She tried to rub it off, but the paper had been scribbled on and highlighted. The ink smudged.

And there were only so many times you could keep sidestepping the signs – especially when they were glaring in front of your eyeballs, highlighted in a *warning* shade of orangey-red that might as well be screaming *read me.*

There came a point when it would simply be reckless not to.

38

'Zain *Kimberkoo*?' Rosie stared at the papers she was clutching as though they were bare-faced lying. And sheets of A4 printer paper definitely didn't have faces. 'As in Kimberkoo *Chat*?'

She could feel the tightness in her chest as the words swam in front of her. They were copies of emails sent to a Zain Kimberkoo. He'd said his name was Zain Kay. Hadn't he? Well, that was a load of buggering ruddy bullshit. If a person couldn't even be honest about their name, what else were they lying about?

Thoughts flew around her head, and she felt powerless to stop them. *Kimberkoo*. Clearly, he must be connected to that AI software thing that had stolen her job at KJ Marketing. Even though she'd come to see she was better off without that damned job that had never suited her nor filled her with any confidence, why the hell hadn't Zain said that he was somehow linked to it, when she'd spilled her heart out about losing her role? Why had he pretended that he was some kind of *hide in a log hut technophobe*, when he quite possibly had his hand in the latest in artificially intelligent chatbots?

Because surely, there couldn't be that many Kimberkoos kicking around. What was a Kimberkoo anyway? Was that one of the creatures he had tattooed on his chest, that she'd traced with her loving fingers? She winced. How many times in her life was she going to miss the blatant signs?

And if Zain was nothing to do with the chatbot company, he could at least have said, *'Now there's a funny coincidence – same surname as me!'*

Yes, *that* would have been the normal, innocent human being thing to do. So what else was he covering up?

Rosie swiped away the fresh lot of tears that were forming and prepared to read. A tiny part of her was still clinging to the hope that the emails would say: *'Only joking. My name's really Zain Kay and I love you to the moon. Tut tut for snooping.'* But she knew that was ludicrously wishful thinking. She sank onto the bed, which was a sea of messy papers. Whatever she was about to read, she had a feeling it would be better tackled sitting down.

Her eyes scanned the first page, still heavy with the guilt that she was reading Zain's emails without having been invited. But she'd come this far, and she couldn't unsee the glaring truth of his real name. There was no going back.

Rosie scratched her head. From what she could work out, these were printouts of questions to the chatbot Kimberkoo Chat, together with the chatbot's answers. Zain must have emailed them to himself so that he could keep them. Where had he been doing all of this? Because Agnes didn't have a printer. He'd clearly been sneaking off somewhere computer-friendly. Yet another thing he hadn't mentioned.

Question: Give me the best ideas for romantic outdoor dates. Include a few pumpkins. And tell me what to say to her!

Tell me what to say to her? Rosie balked. It was bad enough that he couldn't even plan a genuinely heartfelt date. Assuming these date ideas were for her, that was. Maybe he was hiding secret sodding girlfriends too.

Answer: So great to see you back, Zain! We've missed you.

So he used this thing often? Of course he bloody did. For all she knew, he could have invented it – and if he had, he was probably also a secret millionaire. Her eyes darted to Steve, who was still gobbling his dinner. If it turned out her darling cat friend was a robot too, she would never trust a living being again. And she certainly wouldn't trust a non-living one. Steve looked up at her and mewed gently. No. He was genuine. She'd felt his warmth, his breath, the steady beat of his heart. Not that any of that had meant much for the trustworthiness of Zain.

Here are some ideas for romantic outdoor dates. We hope you manage to woo her.

Woo her? Urgh. She'd been suckered by the dating prowess of a computer programme. She had definitely felt wooed.

Idea 1: Romantic evening dinner date on a lake – including a few pumpkins.

Well, at least it was their date – this one was engraved onto her soul. She'd felt like she'd stepped onto a movie set that had been created just for her. She should have known it was too good to be true.

For this date you will need a lake and a boat.

In advance, prepare the lake by lining the jetty with carved pumpkin lanterns. You may also wish to source string lights and/or floating lights for heightened romance.

How ridiculously contrived. Her heart plummeted. She'd thought those perfect details came from Zain, with her in mind. She was surprised the chatbot hadn't added an Amazon link to buy floating solar-lit autumn flowers and taken a commission.

The boat should be ready with a picnic basket on board. The basket should be filled with pumpkin-themed food that your date will enjoy. We suggest pumpkin hummus with a light and fluffy pumpkin bread, followed by a baked pumpkin fondue, and finished off with a pumpkin and ginger cheesecake that will set her taste buds racing.

Make sure you tell her that you prepared this food yourself (even if you did not). This will impress your date and make her feel like you care (even if you do not). This will put her in the mood for wild romance. (You're welcome.)

Now her blood was beginning to boil. If she'd been kidding herself that it was almost sweet for Zain to seek online advice to create the perfect date, *that* had put an end to any such mercy. He was using the chatbot to line her up for *wild romance*? This had been the night of their first proper kiss. Had that been scripted somewhere too?

Maybe the chatbot had churned out a list of sexual positions – no doubt that seventy-four per cent of people surveyed thought were chuffing brilliant.

When the scene is set . . .

Arrive at your date's door and take her by surprise.

Check.

When she answers, sweep her up into your arms and tell her you are her chariot. She will like this.

By the bloody book, Zain Kimberkoo. This was outrageous.

Make sure you are wearing a suit and that you're looking handsome and well-groomed. Keep the top two buttons of your shirt undone, to show a little chest. This will appear enticing. (Prepare to be touched. We do not know how this feels, but we are told it can be magical.)

Seriously? He needed that much detail to get through one single date with her? And he'd followed it too. She remembered with a pang exactly how she'd felt at the sight of his *enticing* chest, and how that whole, feet-sweeping date had felt. That was the first point she'd realised she was falling hopelessly in love with him. But she hadn't been. As she read the next section of the chatbot's reply, entitled *'What to say'*, the dreadful truth hit her. She'd been falling in love with a chatbot. Because the things he'd said to her weren't his thoughts or feelings at all. They were a computer-generated script.

She swallowed hard, remembering that it had all felt just a little too perfect. Recalling his hand occasionally moving towards his pocket, as though there was something inside it that he'd been desperate to consult. She'd even joked that he seemed worried to go *off script*. At that point, he could have taken the opportunity to confess he'd had some help to plan things, but that he was ready to chuck the stupid instructions and be his honest, genuine self. Whoever the hell that was.

As she rifled through the other papers, it was like reading a well-constructed game plan of their whole relationship. Stargazing dates under cosy blankets with flasks of pumpkin-spiced hot chocolate. Early morning walks where they'd listened to the birds chatter and spotted water voles in their burrows by the lake. Making marshmallows together and toasting them around a campfire. She had *known* all that had felt like something from the perfect dating textbook. And she had loved every disingenuously planned minute of it, without thinking to question it.

And it was one thing to get dating ideas from a chatbot. In itself, that wasn't much different to a bit of internet searching for inspiration. But to follow it word for word like an actual script, and pretend you've never even heard of Kimberkoo Chat when it comes up in conversation, even though Kimberkoo is in fact your pissing surname. And then to use exact lines that had been spoon-fed to you by a piece of software. *'Your smile lights up the sky.' 'Baby it's cold outside.' 'The stars are incredible tonight. I'd like to share them with you.'*

He'd even been having Q&As with Kimberkoo Chat for retreat ideas. Oh look, and there was that whole spiel he'd given to her swim friends when they'd stayed in the treehouses for the practice retreat. *'Being elevated invites you to look up. To see the bigger picture.'* Those words had sounded so poetic she'd probably gone weak at the knees. And she should have known he hadn't come up with *shinrin-yoku forest bathing* or dining *al fresco*.

Never mind being a pumpkin farmer. This guy was a first-rate actor. He'd learned his lines without missing a beat. He'd pretended to be someone or some*thing* that he wasn't. And yet again she'd fallen for a man who had an extremely strange relationship with the truth.

No wonder that night in his Prizewinner pumpkin field, when they'd talked before making love, he'd asked if they could start again. He'd wanted to pretend that everything before that moment hadn't happened. Because he *knew* he'd made her fall in love with a lie. He'd taken her for a prizewinning idiot.

She'd come here to get away from all of this. The chatbots, the robots, the pointless tech that was getting too big for its artificial boots. Talk about stepping from the frying pan into the raging electrical fire.

So when Zain barged through the door of his cabin, looking red-faced and ranty, clutching a wad of papers himself, Rosie was fit to explode.

39

'What is this?'

They spat out the same question at the same time, whilst waving their respective wads of A4 paper towards each other. It was absolutely not a sign that she was in sync with this man. If Rosie had ever thought for a second that she was, that had been a *gargantuan* mistake.

She wasn't even sure if she could articulate what she'd just discovered or how furious she was, so she glared at him, almost daring him to speak. She had no idea what was on the paperwork he was gripping, but she was sure it wasn't going to trump the Kimberkoo Chat exposé. For once, she was going to win – even if winning would feel exactly like losing everything. She was having quite the season for that.

'You've been documenting our exact relationship, and turning our private life into a novel for the whole freaking world to see?' His look was incredulous.

With what she'd just discovered, he had some serious cheek.

'No, I have not,' she bit back, realising he was holding pages from her latest manuscript. Because she hadn't, exactly. 'It's the story of Josie. And Cain.'

'Oh, so expertly disguised. No wonder you're a writer. What a bloody wordsmith.'

Well, that was below the belt. 'How dare you. It's just a working draft. I can change anything I want when I do the editing. Shows how much you know.'

'I do know that this appears to be the same story as a certain Rosie and Zain, other than some bonus sex scenes, which I'm pretty sure didn't happen – although the one in the pumpkin field did. I expressly told you I would *hate* being used as fodder for your novel. And why am I being compared to some dead bloke called James?'

'James is nobody.' She had no idea how he'd crept into her work, but she'd soon realised he'd never belonged. It was OK to explore things, before deciding to delete. 'And as for the sex scenes.' She felt her cheeks flame red. 'They call it artistic licence – because I *do* have an imagination. Unlike some people.'

He exhaled sharply and ran a hand down his face. 'Rosie, I understand that you're a writer. And I'm sorry about the wordsmith comment. You *are* good – I've just seen that. But I'm an extremely private person. I do not want my intimate life – and parts – described in full technicolour detail for everyone and their uncle to read. You'll have to use that imagination and create your own storyline. Isn't that what authors do?'

'Oh, so now you think I'm not a real author?' She stood up from the bed and put her hands on her hips, one hand still gripping tightly to the printed-out emails she'd been reading. Some of the papers from the bed slipped to the floor as she moved.

A look of realisation began to dawn on Zain's face, but Rosie wasn't finished with his accusations yet.

'And you don't think I can make up my own storylines? What's wrong with taking inspiration from real life?'

She cocked her head angrily, trying to get his attention from the floor by her feet. Though now he was pointing at the papers, his forehead creasing. She didn't know why he looked so confused. They were his sodding emails. Reams and reams of fully scripted dates, planned with precision like a military operation to conquer her heart. He'd used her own chatbot nemesis to make her fall in love with him. Or perhaps, more accurately, to make her fall in love with a chatbot.

Which is when another thing occurred to her. All that time she'd been thinking she was writing a love story straight from the depths of her heart, she'd been disillusioned. Because if the chatbot had contrived their dates, the things they did together, the words Zain had used to make her fall for him – then Kimberkoo Chat had more or less written her novel.

She'd based pretty much everything on what had happened between her and Zain, yet all of that had been scripted to sickening perfection by a piece of stinking software. Not only was she helping to prove this tech could take over from real humans, but she wasn't even sure if she could write a decent story without it. Her blood went cold. That manuscript Zain was clenching had been her best-ever attempt. The one she'd been *sure* wouldn't be rejected. Her first ever hope of reaching her published author dreams and becoming the heroine of her own story – in more ways than one.

She leapt towards him, trying to snatch it back. He pulled away, his stare landing on the papers she was still holding, before locking with hers.

'You've been going through my stuff?' Something behind his eyes seemed to be processing thoughts at lightning speed, like his head was an actual computer. Right then, nothing would surprise her.

'Yes, Zain *Kimberkoo*. I happened to stumble upon your emails – even though I had no idea that you were an email kind of guy, or a laptop kind of guy, or that your name wasn't actually Zain Kay, because you're related to a chatbot.' She glared at him, past caring that most of that made zero sense.

'Related to an artificially intelligent computer program? Yes, that seems likely.'

He could keep his stupid sarcasm. 'It sounds like you know a lot more about the whole thing than you were letting on. "*So great to see you back, Zain.*"' She gave the line from the chatbot the mocking air quotes it deserved. 'And why did you lie about your surname?'

'I never told you my surname.' He pinched the bridge of his nose and screwed his eyes shut, as if this was giving him a headache.

Rosie searched her memory. 'Then you must have lied to Agnes about your surname. She was the one who told me.'

'No I didn't!'

'So your surname isn't Kimberkoo?'

He sighed and opened his eyes. His lack of response told her it was.

'And you're not the kind of person who enlists a robot computer thing to make women fall for you, so you can shag them in your pumpkin field?' Blood was rushing to her outraged face so quickly it felt like her eyeballs might pop.

'What? No! It was nothing like that. And I *did* try to tell you, and to distance myself...'

'It was exactly like that. And here's the full-blown proof. Every date you ever wowed me with. Every romantic sentiment you ever used on me. *Take her on a date to a lake, carry her to the boat like you're her chariot, arrange a pumpkin-themed picnic basket.* It probably gave you blow-by-blow instructions on how to grope my boobs and snog my face off, before disappearing into the night like some chivalrous, non-sex-hungry prince of the bloody gourds. Well, I am *not* charmed. Because it was all mapped out. Every single sordid step of it – and none of it came from you. None of it was from the heart. That's if you even have one.'

'Is that what you honestly think of me?' His eyes were searching her, and with every second that she didn't answer, they became a little colder.

'I have no idea what I think of you.' Her hands dropped to her sides, the papers falling like dead autumn leaves. 'Or even who you are.'

Something inside her clung desperately to the hope that he was about to explain it all. That there would be some dramatic plot twist, where he was secretly saving the world in his underpants, and Agnes was the real Zain Kimberkoo in cunning, Mrs Doubtfire-like, latex disguise.

But he simply looked at her, his face sinking like his once strong shoulders. 'So you thought you'd go through my stuff to find out.'

'No, actually. I just happened to . . .'

'*Stumble* across my paperwork, whilst you were busy going through my laptop. Nice.' He raked a hand through his hair, dark waves tumbling. 'You know, I spent my whole childhood longing for a bit of privacy. Praying for a home where people weren't always checking up on me, going through my things, treating me as though I couldn't or shouldn't be trusted. My so-called father couldn't be arsed to stick around. My mum couldn't even be bothered to stay alive for me. I thought you . . . I thought you were *different*. But you're exactly the same.'

Her heart felt an uninvited pang for him. Part of her wanted to hug him and apologise and take away the hurt that drove lines through his forehead and seemed to scar his very soul.

But who was he, really? Did he even have a soul? Or did he have to log into some software to activate that too? She took a step towards him, still feeling compelled to ease his suffering, even though she didn't have a clue why she should.

He put up a hand to halt her. 'And if you want to fling accusations about people not being who they say they are, I'm wondering if *Josie* being a trespassing impostor on a pumpkin farm because she wasn't the real interviewee for the job bears any resemblance to you. And there I'd been, wondering why a wild retreat expert didn't know a damned thing about living in the country and couldn't swim for toffee. Now it all makes sense.'

Rosie's mouth dropped open. Yes, she *had* still been harbouring a few secrets. But they paled into insignificance compared to him tricking her in love.

'Yes, there was a misunderstanding about my interview, but I am still the same person. The person who gets a lot of stuff wrong but does her best anyway. The person who perpetually struggles to write a decent love story, because until recently, she had no inkling how love felt. And the person who *always* chooses the wrong guy. Did you know that every relationship I've had has turned out to be a sham? I've had boyfriends who were secretly lollipop-wielding criminals, or who were only fake-engaged to me, or who were furtively *in flagrante* with actual flipping robots. I've been too ashamed to tell you, but seeing as we're laying our cards bare, this is me. A big, dumb loser in life *and* love. And stupidly, I thought you were different too. I just didn't realise exactly *how* different.'

His jaw clenched. 'Get out.' His voice was low. She didn't feel threatened, though she did know he meant it.

'Just for the record, I don't usually pry into people's stuff. I was just tidying up. You looked through mine too.' It was a valid point.

'The door to your hut was ajar. I thought Steve had pushed his way in. And then I saw what you'd been working on.' He nodded at the manuscript in his hand. 'I was interested. I care.' He shook his head. 'Scrap that. I *did* care.'

'Steve did come back, by the way.' She flapped her hand towards the table, under which the three-legged cat was now hiding. 'He disturbed your papers when he was bouncing about. And yes, I started to read them – even though I wouldn't usually. Though I'm *so* glad I did.'

But she'd lost Zain's attention. He thrust her manuscript at her and dropped to his knees, crawling towards Steve and making reassuring noises. She was surprised he didn't need a script for that too.

'I'll leave you to it,' she said, pulling her typed papers to her chest and striding to the door. His bizarre, hermit-in-a-hut life suited him. She had no clue why she'd ever tried to interfere.

40

Rosie arrived back at her hut to find the door still open. Maybe she *had* left it ajar when she'd rushed out to look for Steve, or maybe Zain had just barged in to nosy through the manuscript he'd seen her working on. She had no idea what the truth was anymore, and she was past caring. She was done with pinning her hopes and dreams on a fantasy.

How had she managed to kid herself that she'd found real love? Much like swoony heroes in romance novels, the man she thought she'd fallen for didn't even exist. Their love had been *scripted*.

Had she somehow become her own ridiculous version of a hermit in a hut at Autumn Meadows? She'd been hiding from her long list of problems. For a time, being out here had felt special and magical, like something from a fairy story.

But people didn't live in fairy tales.

How did she expect to live her life masquerading as a stranger called Rachel, pretending that someone had simply misremembered her name? She couldn't keep dodging the truth and hoping her ludicrous lies didn't come to light – or she'd be no better than Zain.

In fact, she couldn't do *any* of this anymore. She wasn't a pumpkin farm retreat expert, or a wild swimmer, or even a writer who could come up with inspiration for her own stories without the clandestine interference of a chatbot. Once again, she wasn't playing the starring role in her own damned life. She was the understudy. Rosie had let her wild writer imagination get carried away.

Worse still, Zain now knew everything. That she had a humiliating back catalogue of sham relationships, that she could barely write a love story without him as a muse, and that she'd been fooling Agnes all along because she was *not* the person who was meant to take this job.

How long would it be before he stormed to the farmhouse to tell their boss? He hadn't blabbed about her being a rubbish swimmer, because he'd said grassing on people wasn't his thing. But this was bigger. And she didn't dare stick around to find out.

She rushed around the hut grabbing her things and stuffing them into her holdall, including the pages of her doomed manuscript. One day she'd find a shredder and gleefully annihilate it.

Rosie chose to ignore the gnawing guilt that tomorrow was the launch party and auction night. Zain and Agnes would just have to manage, like they'd always done. If Rosie was forced to spend any more time near Zain, or panicking about which of her secrets he might spill, she might explode.

All packed, she took one last glance around. There was a pull in her heart about missing her little writing nook and that typewriter. The peace, the lake, the fields . . .

That was probably nonsense too.

'There are fields everywhere.' She yanked the holdall strap further up her shoulder in case it was having weird ideas about jumping off her body and staying behind. 'And I could buy my own typewriter.' She shook her head. Not that she'd be doing any more writing. There'd been enough rejection for one lifetime. She'd get a quiet job in a library, where she could enjoy other people's books.

Rosie bowed out of the little wooden hut, which had never really been hers, and marched past the lake, keeping her head down in case its still waters tried to mesmerise her. She ploughed onwards through the ever-greying semi-darkness, past Zain's hut, through the wooden gate, and cut the quickest path through the pumpkin patches until she reached Agnes's house. Something made her stop for a moment, even though she couldn't bear to look up. Could she leave here without saying goodbye? Without explaining herself? Was it time to be honest with Agnes that she hadn't arrived here to have a job interview, but had been stranded and a bit desperate, and had allowed herself to settle into a life that had been meant for someone else?

That's what any decent person would do. And Rosie knew she was a decent person, even if she'd lost sight of things in the confusing web of white lies and wonky truths. But could she face that today? All parts of her felt like they'd been dragged backwards on a rollercoaster and thrust off into a broken heap. And though her heart hurt to run off like this, she didn't have the words to explain herself. Maybe Zain would blurt out the truth for her anyway.

So her feet made the decision to keep on walking. Clomp, clomp, her borrowed wellies striding towards the dirt path that was the long, winding exit from the farm. The first place where she'd ever lain eyes on Zain, and if she had her way, the last time and place she would ever think of him. She was leaving this fantasy behind.

'Rosie!'

The voice came from behind her, somewhere in the distance. She could tell it belonged to Agnes. Urgh. Had she seen her? Was it too late to scarper?

'Rosie, please help. I don't know what to do.'

Rosie stopped and took a deep breath. Agnes sounded like she was in trouble, and Rosie couldn't bring herself to dash away and ignore a flustered plea. She would help the woman quickly and then get out of there. It was the least she could do.

As Rosie turned back towards the house, she saw Agnes flying towards her, stray animals skipping and flapping around her in an almighty commotion. Her eyes were full of panic.

'It's the house.' Agnes jabbed a pointed finger towards it. 'Part of the roof has fallen in. It's devastation in there. Tiles and debris. And so much dust. What am I going to do? I've got all the animals out, but it isn't safe to go back in there.'

Rosie looked upwards, straining her eyes to see in the semi-darkness. Wow, Agnes was right. It looked as if someone had swung a great wrecking ball at the top of Agnes's house. Rosie's stomach dropped.

'Right. Erm, it's OK,' said Rosie, thinking on her feet. 'You can stay in my hut tonight. It's probably too late to find you anywhere, with the animals too.'

Agnes's eyes darted to Rosie's holdall, which was sliding from her shoulder under the weight. 'Were you going somewhere?'

'No.' Well, that was a lie. 'I mean, yes. I had a falling-out with Zain, and everything's a mess, and . . .'

'You were just going to *leave me*?' Agnes frowned and put her head to one side, her mouth open like Rosie had just declared her undying love and then dumped her for Julia Roberts.

Her dog Onions did the same, his furry little face even more heartbreaking than his owner's. Damn, they were good.

'You don't need me,' Rosie reassured her. 'You'll be fine.'

'Fine?' Agnes's voice was almost a squawk. 'Do I look like everything's going to be hunky bloody dory? My house is falling down around my ears. I've got flocks of needy animals that won't live on fresh air. I'm a poor, elderly, helpless lady. And you promised to help me. *You* were my last hope.'

Rosie sighed. Agnes was laying it on thick again, with the helpless old lady thing. Rosie was pretty sure nobody viewed the determined, slightly scary woman like that, even if she was well into pensionable age.

'I need this new roof sooner than ever, Rosie. This big do and the auction tomorrow night can't come fast enough. It *has to* go smoothly and bring in some decent funds, otherwise where will we all live? What will become of us?' Agnes's hand was clutching at her own heart now, and Rosie was sure at least three of the dogs were whimpering. 'You're the brains and the fighting spirit behind everything. There isn't a hope in hell of me being able to take over at such short notice. And if you're hoping to leave Zain in charge of hosting and schmoozing, then we might as well call in the bulldozers now. We'll all be goners.'

Rosie let her holdall slip to the ground and screwed her eyes tight shut, because she couldn't believe she was about to say this. Again.

'Just one night. Or maybe two. And then I'm out of here. I mean it this time.'

Rosie could never live with her conscience if she didn't see this auction night through and try her best to raise the money Agnes needed. Rosie had to prove to herself that she could do this, and that the white lies she had told had been for the greater good. And Zain had better keep his bloody mouth shut, because he'd told enough lies of his own.

'Thank you, love,' Agnes said earnestly. 'And I'm sure you and Zain will make it up.'

Rosie's eyes popped open. 'That is not going to happen. If I'm going to stick around briefly to help with this, Zain *whatever-his-name-is* needs to stay out of my way.'

Agnes scratched his head. 'I think he's . . .'

'And I do not want to talk about him.' Rosie tugged her bag back onto her shoulder, hoping her tone was firm enough.

So it looked like Rosie would be spending the night avoiding her scoundrel of a neighbour whilst she topped and tailed in a small wooden hut, with an eccentric woman called Agnes. And approximately seventy billion cats, dogs, and for all Rosie knew, probably a flock of hens for good measure.

This surreal nightmare was getting worse by the moment. It couldn't be over soon enough.

41

'It's Kookaburra, isn't it?' Agnes stood at Rosie's side, scratching her head.

They were outside the log cabin that had once been Rosie's home but, after that night's launch party and auction was over, wouldn't be. Their guests would be arriving soon. The scene before her ought to have filled Rosie with joy. Day was slowly fading into night, the sky becoming dusky. String lights encircled the lake, throwing golden reflections. A rainbow fleet of wooden boats bobbed on the lake's surface, tables of pumpkin fizz were lined up, and jack-o'-lanterns and makeshift firepits were already burning brightly.

But far from feeling happy, Rosie's stomach was a tight ball of stress. She'd spent the previous night squashed into the cabin with Agnes and her menagerie of animals, and *none of this* could continue. After a frantic day of party organising, catastrophising about whether Zain would tell Agnes she was a con artist, and trying to keep her distance from him in case she went down for hot-blooded murder, her head was spinning.

'I'm sorry, what?'

'Or is it Kinnyburger? No, Kimberkoo. That's it! Though I always call him Zain K, because it's easier.' Agnes clapped her hands like she was pleased she'd remembered, even though they'd started that conversation the previous night.

Rosie exhaled the world's longest breath. Well, she must have assumed Agnes was calling him Zain Kay, as in the surname, rather than using an initial. Though right then, she couldn't care less if his name was Zain King-of-the-Sodding-Cucurbitaceae. Just because he hadn't actively lied about his name, it didn't change the fact he hadn't been honest about it. Or that he'd used a chatbot to trick her into falling in love.

'I said I didn't want to talk about him,' Rosie said to Agnes, who was now putting a tartan coat on Onions so he could help his owner on gate duty, notwithstanding that he'd be the least scary guard dog ever.

'That was yesterday,' Agnes replied, straightening herself and pulling on her Tweed jacket, which smelled a bit like mothballs.

'It still stands.'

'Funny how we sometimes get confused about names, isn't it? Remember that time Farmer Wilbur thought you were called Rachel?'

Rosie felt herself bristle. At least she'd told Agnes that wasn't her name, even though there was still *a bit* of a mix-up.

'We'll see Wilbur later. I'm sure he'll want to catch up with you.'

Bloody. Brilliant. Rosie just had to get through that night, raise enough money to replace Agnes's collapsing roof, and get out of there. No head-to-heads, no heart-to-hearts, and absolutely no fireworks. Was that too much to ask?

'I'll be too busy for socialising.'

Rosie knew her tone was clipped, but she couldn't help it.

Tonight would be tense enough, with the uncertainty of whether the final auction would be enough to save Autumn Meadows. Even if Rosie wasn't sticking around, she couldn't bear to think of it being concreted over to build a factory, otherwise the last few weeks had been for precisely nothing.

At least Agnes's back kitchen hadn't been damaged in the roof-tumbling tragedy, so their chef could still use it. And luckily, Agnes had been able to rope in Zain and some locals to cover the exposed parts of her roof earlier that day, so it was temporarily waterproof.

'You'll be fine, love.' Agnes gave Rosie an awkward pat on the back, even though comforting people really wasn't her thing. 'I'm proud of you.'

Onions barked in agreement and Rosie had to blink back a tear. She'd miss this funny lot. Well, *some* of them.

Warning Agnes to come back later to help with the auction so she didn't have to get within screaming distance of Zain, they said their *good lucks* and got moving.

Fresh from hayrides around the pumpkin patches and campsite with Zain, visitors soon began piling into the field around the lake, their excitement tangible. Guests were dressed in swishy skirts and casual trousers, paired with wellies and warm shawls, using big umbrellas like walking sticks, ready to celebrate, come mud or rain.

The sight made Rosie's spirits lift a little. She'd worked hard for this night, and she ought to enjoy some of it, even if it was tinged with an undeniable *end of adventure* sadness.

'Rosie! What a beautiful job you've done.'

Rosie spun around to see her swim friends bouncing over. She fought to swallow back the lump in her throat. She would miss being here with them too.

Mags had brought along her newly formed hurdy-gurdy

band, as encouraged by Luna and Ellen. Those two were behind, their arms draped protectively around Bonnie. Bonnie had already declared she'd be *looking for a hot gent* tonight, so Rosie guessed Luna would have to loosen her clutches on her mum, now that she was thriving.

They pulled in for their usual group hug, congratulating each other on how well they scrubbed up. Rosie had opted for a floor-length floaty dress that made her feel like an autumnal flower fairy, and a fluffy cardi that her sister had once told her looked like a pile of moss.

'I'm so glad you're here.' Rosie wasn't sure how she'd get through it without them, now she and Zain were warring, and he knew enough of her secrets to bring the whole night crashing down, if he was outrageous enough. She hadn't told them about their fall-out, because well-meant matchmaking could end in disaster.

'Luna, Ellen and I are donating ourselves as waitresses,' said Bonnie, plucking three pumpkin-patterned aprons from her bag.

'Oh wow, you don't need to do that,' said Rosie. 'I want you to enjoy yourselves.'

'Nonsense,' said Bonnie, pulling the apron over her ashy-grey mohawk, which she'd decorated with orange and gold bows. 'Many hands make light work.' She lowered her voice. 'And if I want to nab a hottie, I'll need to mingle.'

'Take it easy, Mother,' Luna breathed, as if she knew her words were futile.

'It's an exciting night for you, Rosie. Are you feeling OK?' asked Mags.

It looked like she'd already got her hands on some of the chocolates Rosie and Zain had made, that day in the kitchen.

She shook away a memory of him licking chocolate from her finger in a way that had made her soul dance.

Rosie lifted her chin. 'Yes, I will be.' *As soon as this is all over*, she silently added. Her holdall was already packed.

When her friends had dispersed, Rosie rushed off to begin hosting duties. She hadn't yet spotted Zain – *not* that she was looking for him. They'd kept a suitably standoffish distance all day, though it was clear they were both still steaming. She hoped her particularly angry stares had warned him not to dare tell Agnes she was an impostor, because he needed this night to be a success more than Rosie did.

Hearing a splash and some yelping from the lake, Rosie's head shot up.

The Three Tuxedos. She ought to have been furious at the sight of the three conspicuous men clambering into a wobbling boat, even if their squealing and shoving was farcical. They must have paid a small fortune for a *romantic dining* experience. With the tickets having been auctioned off to the highest bidders, many using discreet profile names, Rosie wasn't quite sure who would turn up. A fact that was adding to her nerves.

She tried not to wince as she noticed the boat they were climbing into was the one Zain had painted *Rosie and Him*, for their first real date.

Correction. No doubt his chatbot puppet master had come up with that too. She huffed. Perhaps it was fitting that the annoying bottoms of her Cyber Purrz nemeses would spend the evening wriggling around and probably breaking wind inside it. She couldn't help a wry smile when she saw a stony-faced Zain forced to help them. He deserved to be stuck with those donkeys.

Could her night get worse from here? She shook away the mental image of fending off a clowder of robotic cats whilst serving pumpkin fizz to her ex-boyfriend and his sexbot, Zoe. Because *surely* things wouldn't get that bad.

Right then, her question was partly answered by two more unexpected faces in the distance. *Oh God.* What had she done to deserve this? A huge part of her wanted to go and hide in a nice, autumnal bush. But if she was learning anything, it was that problems spread less when you nipped them in the bud. And tonight was about seeing through her commitments with her head held high. So she took a deep breath and marched over.

'Mum. Flick.'

Rosie held her breath, unsure what reaction to expect from them, after not keeping them in the loop. She'd been hoping that when she finally saw them again, she'd be the new, improved version of herself, rather than the one who chose rubbish boyfriends or lived in a naive dream. That hadn't quite worked out.

'Oh darling. So this is where you've been,' said Rosie's mother, Farrah, who looked as glamorous as ever in a fitted fuchsia shift dress and matching jacket.

'Rosie Featherstone! As if you would throw the county's most talked about party and not invite us. Good job we're on top of social news,' her sister, Flick, added.

Rosie guessed there was only so long you could evade the formidable force-ten gale that was the Featherstones, and sometimes a girl needed a whip of wind to strengthen her sails.

'You look . . . *different*.' Her mother cocked her head. She seemed more wobbly than usual, but that was probably because sky-scraping heels didn't work on muddy grass. At least Rosie had learned something about suitable footwear.

Her sister did a similar head-cocking thing, and Rosie tried not to dwell on how they both looked like they were fresh from a swanky salon.

Flick reached out and touched Rosie's hair, her manicured fingernails inspecting the ribboned braids. Rosie braced herself for a comment about hippies or needing a hairbrush.

'Totally different,' Flick concluded. 'It suits you.'

'You look wonderful,' her mother agreed, scooping Rosie into a hug. 'We've missed you. I'm so happy you're safe and well.'

'Oh!' The words of approval took her by surprise.

'You did all of this?' her sister asked, when she'd given Rosie an equally squishy hug.

'Well, I had help from some friends, and . . .' Rosie had been about to say Zain. As if he deserved her praise, when his ideas had been plotted by a chatbot.

'It's amazing,' said Flick, sounding more sincere than Rosie could ever remember. 'Honestly. I've been following on social media, before realising you were behind it. I'm ridiculously impressed.'

Rosie felt herself blush. 'Thanks.'

'She's a Featherstone. Of course she can throw a party. Rosie always could create anything she put her mind to,' said her mother, pulling Rosie in for another squeeze, even though there was serious danger of her jacket getting creased. 'My beautiful, clever girl.'

Flick nodded in agreement. Rosie brushed herself down and took a few deep breaths. Had they always been this nice? Rosie wondered if her memory too often clung to the put-downs and didn't give enough weight to the kind things they said.

It was just a shame she'd have to tell them she'd messed up again, and this time there was no option but to come home. At least they still had the final auction, and Rosie could hopefully go out with a bang. She just prayed it was a positive one.

'Oh *helloooooo*,' said Rosie's mum, recognising someone from one of the glossy magazines. 'We're the Featherstones.'

Rosie felt her stomach take a dive as the words 'cover' and 'blown' bounced into her head. She'd managed not to bump into Farmer Wilbur so far, but if Agnes realised Rosie was related to *the* Featherstones, of local schmoozing fame, she'd be looking less like one of Farmer Wilbur's friends by the minute.

'Erm, just these two!' said Rosie, dodging a camera lens and whispering to her sister that she was on an undercover mission.

Then she gave her mum and sister a quick farewell hug, because she had work to do.

It was nearly time for the auction, and if it didn't bring in enough cash to match the numbers Rosie had scribbled in her notebook, then the three men in the rowing boat would be home, dry, and sending in the diggers.

42

'Remind me again why we decided to leave the fate of the farm, Agnes's roof, and approximately eleven squillion helpless cats and dogs to an *auction*?' Rosie stood at a safe distance from the intermittently working microphone, rearranging her paperwork and giving her somersaulting stomach a rub. She had what Agnes would call *the collywobbles*. 'Auction basically means huge, terrifying gamble, doesn't it? Like when you put your best designer coat on eBay, and it only sells for a pound.'

Luna took the papers from her and put them down gently. 'If you shuffle those any more, people will think you're a magician.'

'Maybe I'll need to be.'

And where on earth was Agnes? She'd promised to help Rosie to run the auction, in place of Zain. If Rosie was forced to be in the same square hectometre as him, she would not be held responsible for the ensuing devastation.

'You have some great auction lots though,' said Luna. 'I mean, who wouldn't want a year's supply of wonky parsnips?'

Rosie couldn't help the chuckle that escaped her. Sometimes

laughter was the only medicine. 'You're right. I'll fight you for those.'

The opening event had brought a string of surprises, but so far Rosie had been dealing with them. It was surely a good sign that the night sky was dry, and the stars were twinkling. Lukas Knight's Michelin-star-worthy pumpkin-inspired menu had been served to countless guests in small bobbing boats and on picnic blankets around the lake. Most of the carved jack-o'-lanterns were still glowing, and nobody had caught their dress alight on a campfire. If Rosie could just get through this auction and raise the funds Agnes and her animals needed, she could bow out of there with grace.

She was ignoring the occasional tug on her heartstrings that reminded her of everything she was leaving behind. Her heart had already been crushed like a Ritz cracker, so there would be no getting swept away on a wisp of nostalgia or mistaking pumpkin fizz merriment for actual life.

In real news, Luna was right. They did have some excellent auction lots. With everyone helping to spread the word online, they'd had donations from not just local businesses, but pumpkin enthusiasts, cat and dog lovers and kind benefactors from all over the place. Lexie, who'd helped with the blogging, and her partner Ben had donated a weekend stay on their huge Tewkesbury estate, complete with slightly scary peacocks.

The mysterious Farmer Wilbur had donated a date in a cherry picker, even though Rosie had precisely no idea what that was all about. There were gift hampers and meals, mini breaks and artwork, event tickets and some particularly interesting services. They'd even had online bids in advance.

'Ooh, it's the waiter from the boats,' Rosie heard her sister, Flick, stage-whisper. 'Hotness alert.'

Every internal part of Rosie sank as she turned to see Zain

approaching. He was *not* meant to be part of this – Rosie had given strict instructions to Agnes on that point. Though Agnes was a law unto herself.

'Hotness is ridiculously over-rated,' Rosie hissed back.

Zain walked towards them with less confidence than usual, apparently not in his element in the presence of so many living things that weren't vine fruit or cats. Rosie chose to have no sympathy. She vaguely registered that he was wearing the same navy suit and tight-across-the-chest white shirt he'd worn on their own floating date. He'd probably consulted some software on the prescribed amount of shirt buttons to leave undone to make seventy-four per cent of women want to caress his pumpkins. Well, it wasn't working on her.

Rosie heard her sister let out an impromptu whimper, even though Flick wasn't the whimpering sort. 'If he's your colleague, no wonder you've been keeping this place to yourself. Your life is *sooooo* on the up.'

Rosie could only guess that her sister hadn't yet had the pleasure of using the compost toilets or being duped by Zain.

'What are you doing here?' Rosie hissed at him. 'And where's Agnes?'

'Busy on the gate.' He shrugged, still keeping a distance in case Rosie swung at him. 'She told me to come and help you. Not my idea.'

Rosie's lips pressed together like two cross sausages. She knew full well that the gates would be closed by this point. Agnes was meddling.

'I don't need you,' Rosie replied. 'I have . . .' She looked around, but her friends and family seemed to have dispersed. 'I'll be fine.'

'I'm sure you've got it under control,' Zain replied. His voice aggravatingly genuine – though it was probably an act. 'I'll just pass the auction lots and keep notes. I need this to go well too.' He pulled some notepaper out of his pocket.

She barked out a disbelieving laugh. 'Sure that's not your script?'

His face tightened, a small jaw muscle twitching. 'It's Agnes's list of auction items. I haven't consulted the chatbot in a long time, in case you hadn't noticed.'

'No, I hadn't. I have literally no idea which bits are you and which bits are from the cunning computer mind of Kimberkoo Chat.'

He huffed and grabbed the first auction piece, stepping in and thrusting it towards her. 'You seemed to know which bits were me when you described my throbbing penis and put the ins and outs of our sex life into your novel.'

The intermittent microphone chose that moment to transmit Zain's voice, at full blast, to the gawping audience. Rosie could have died at the looks on people's faces as they kicked off the auction with the words *penis* and *sex life*.

'Well, that got their attention!' Agnes clapped with glee from somewhere in the middle of the crowd, before bobbing out of view.

Rosie had known the woman wasn't busy on *gate duty*.

Even though things got off to a painful start, Rosie couldn't help getting pulled along with the excitement as the night's bidding progressed. Zain dutifully passed her items, giving her the occasional strange jolt when their fingers touched. That was probably the dodgy electrics, or the fact he'd had his soul replaced by a microchip.

As things moved on, Rosie was amazed to note she was feeling proud of herself. When it came to parties, she was usually the first to hide behind a plant or scurry off to the kitchen. But tonight, despite its odd curve balls and the passive-aggressive jibes between her and Zain, she was enjoying this role. Being the slightly precarious heroine of her own story felt good, even if it was only for one night.

And the auction itself was blowing Rosie's mind. Arms had been waving as bid prices escalated. Rosie had brought her notebook of figures, and as she recorded each total, she could see they were edging towards being able to fund Agnes's roof repairs and keep the land safe, even if there was still a good way to go.

'I can't believe how much that lady paid for Gretel from the village to recreate her house in gingerbread,' Rosie said to Zain, before remembering they weren't on speaking terms, and pretending she was thinking out loud.

They were taking a short break for Bonnie and the gang to refill glasses, which Rosie noticed had a favourable effect on bidders' enthusiasm for even the quirkiest of auction lots. And it *was* all in a good cause.

Mags had become the proud owner of one of Agnes's stray cats, Orangeade, after donating a princely sum. Agnes had refused to auction animals, but she knew Mags had already met and loved this little one. Mags was now carrying Orangeade in a thrown-together papoose like a teeny cat baby.

'And my biggest Prizewinner pumpkin went for a crazy price,' Zain replied, even though he wasn't meant to be talking to her either.

Rosie was still surprised he'd put it into the auction, but he was probably trying to make himself look good.

Rosie double-checked her notes. There was one last auction lot, and it needed to perform better than gold dust. There was still a big chunk of money to make.

'What's in the last box?' Rosie pointed to it.

Most of the donated auction items had arrived well in advance, ready to be catalogued and placed online for early bids. But Rosie hadn't seen this plain cardboard box before, and she certainly hadn't had time to open it.

'Not sure.' Zain shrugged. 'I'll look.'

'Come on. What else have you got for us?' someone shouted from the crowd.

'We're ready to shop!'

Rosie lifted her head to the sea of people, noticing that glasses were full, and the audience was clamouring to bid. It was time for the final auction lot. She took a deep breath and grabbed the box from Zain. Then with clammy palms and a racing heart, because this was their final money-making hope, she began to open it.

43

Rosie hadn't meant to scream.

Nor to topple backwards off the already rickety stage, taking the microphone tumbling with her like she was wrestling with a snake on a stick.

'Is it . . . *dead*?' She was rambling about the thing in the final auction lot box, which had been furry but stiff and cold, with frozen eyeballs that had caught the moonlight and glared at her. 'Who would send that?'

Zain was pulling Rosie to her feet, even though she was trying to bat him away. Disembodied voices asked if she was OK and shouted orders to put the stage back together, and to steady the mic and lights.

'It's . . . erm . . . *robotic*.'

Rosie allowed Zain's words to land as she straightened herself and reclaimed her place in front of the crowd. She wasn't sure if the microphone was back on, but suddenly she didn't care.

'It's what?!' She extracted the lifeless grey thing from the box, jumping again when it made a tinny mewing noise and tried to swipe her with its fake fur paw. Rosie did her best not to drop it, even though its sentience was more unlikely than Zain's.

She pulled the tag that stuck out from its ear. 'Cyber Purrz.' It was one of their robot cats. And from the strange noises it was making, which were not unlike Cassius's sexy robot now she came to think of it, she wouldn't mind betting it was a defective one. Any moment, it would probably start clawing her eyes out or plotting to take over the world.

Rosie's heart sank. As if her final hope to raise enough money to hit their target and save the farm balanced on *this*. 'I am not auctioning this dreadful *thing*. It's broken, it's terrifying and they can bloody well take it back.'

Her eyes scanned the crowd for the three men in question – but they were already hurtling towards her in arrow formation. The tallest one reached her first.

'You're not meant to have this. It's state-of-the-art and it's not for sale at your absurd auction. It's worth a fortune. We're not here to bail you out of your pit.'

'Why did you bring it?' the medium-sized man hissed to the small one.

'Thought it would be funny. She's going to lose anyway,' the small one scoffed back.

Rosie took a deep breath and stood taller, keen not to let this descend into a slanging match, with the eyes of the Cotswolds and so many media cameras ready to click. *Stay classy*.

'We're not in a pit, thank you.'

Though right then, Rosie could see no possible way of winning. Even if she had tried to auction the not-a-cat, it could never reach the sum they still needed.

Her soul was deflating, but she had to bring this catastrophe to a close. Perhaps, like most things she'd encountered here, it wasn't meant to be. She cleared her throat and leaned into the microphone. 'That will conclude tonight's auction. We seem to have run out of lots.'

'Did you reach the target?' a voice yelled from the crowd.

'Will you have enough to do the roof, so my cats and dogs don't drown?' shouted Agnes.

Rosie winced.

'Have you saved it from the threat of that robotic cat factory, because it would break our hearts to see this farm dug up and ruined.'

'Hear, hear.'

'Erm. I'm sure everything will be fine.' Rosie tried a bright smile, even though her face and fighting spirit were cracking.

And then Rosie heard the whispers begin. *They haven't raised enough. Has it been an enormous waste of time? What will become of the place?*

Rosie dared to look at Zain, whose brain seemed to be ticking under his creased forehead.

He grabbed the microphone. 'We have one more lot.'

Did they?

But before Rosie could work out what was going on, Zain was offering places on an Autumn Meadows Farm writing retreat, which would be run by none other than her, as their *expert writer in residence.* Which she was *not*. She let out a yelp and tried to yank the microphone from him. After tonight, she wouldn't even be living here. And she may have devoured many writing books and been on a few courses in her time, but she wasn't ready to run actual writing retreats. Here. In just two weeks' time. *Was she?*

Yet every time Rosie darted towards him, he dodged her. She

was acutely aware that it looked like she was chasing him, which she absolutely wasn't. Though it was too late, because he was on a roll. People were already bidding wild prices, and he was gleefully accepting offers.

'What are you playing at?' she hissed.

'Helping you to raise money. And it was what you wanted, wasn't it? To run writing retreats?'

Rosie thought her head might explode. 'I don't need you to save me. And you have no idea what I want.' She kept her voice low, but it wasn't any less loaded. He was infuriating. Dangling the carrot of the thing she'd once dreamed of, before things had gone so horribly wrong.

Though like a steam train, she couldn't stop him. And the farm did need the money, so she'd have to put up with his nonsense and work out a plan later on.

And if she couldn't beat him, she was damned well going to join him. When he'd finished selling her services without permission, she reciprocated the *favour*.

'And for our next fantastic offer, who would like day tickets to come and pick your own pumpkins with our resident pumpkin farmer, Zain, on his Prizewinner pumpkin patch – complete with hayrides and a chance to help with the October harvest? He'll even show you his speciality pumpkins. Happening here, from next week. Shall we start the bidding?'

As he gave her an incredulous, wide-mouthed '*what*?!' she winked at him.

'Well, you did say you needed help with the harvest, and that you knew your farming efforts were pointless if your pumpkins went to rot. Don't worry, if you get stuck for words, your chatbot can script something.'

As the audience seemed to sense the *all hands on deck* situation, something even more unexpected happened. People from the audience began filling their previously emptied auction table with extra things to sell.

By the time tickets for Zain's pumpkin patch experiences had been snapped up, Rosie's mum had placed down her latest designer watch. Mags brought up her hurdy-gurdy, insisting she had a collection at home. Then Bonnie offered herself out on a wine and dine date, the lucky bidder thankfully being the sweetly behaved man she'd been chatting to.

When Rosie's beige peacoat finally sold for twice as much as she'd paid for the thing, she looked at the total in her notebook and let out an embarrassing squeak.

'We've done it!'

With the additional auction lots, they'd reached their target, and more.

She heard Zain yell in joy at her side, and without thinking, she threw her arms around him. By some magnetic, uninvited force, their lips pulled together in a kiss.

Beyond the rush of blood to her head and the pounding in her heart, Rosie was vaguely aware of the crowd cheering, the bright stage light still on them. She could sense cameras snapping and phone screens flashing, and she quickly pulled away.

They both mumbled their apologies and darted off in different directions, Rosie's lips definitely not still burning with the imprint of his kiss.

'That's exciting,' said Agnes, appearing from who knew where.

'What?' said Rosie, her hands flying to her now colouring cheeks.

'That thing about your writing retreats, of course. I had no idea you could write as well as paint. And if you don't want to do any more *sex life* with Zain, you can always stay with me in the big house. The ground floor is safe now, so I'll sleep there tonight. And we'll soon have a brand-new roof. You could have your own space, now you're our *writer in residence*. We'll talk about it tomorrow, over a nice cup of tea.'

Rosie smiled and gave a non-committal *hmm*, then busied herself with packing away.

44

Would it be rash of her to rush off that night? Everything was peaceful again now they'd cleared away after the launch party. Most of the guests had gone, it was late, and Rosie was exhausted. And she *had* promised herself she would stay just one more night – or maybe two. If she slept in her cabin now, that would make it two, which wouldn't be breaking any promises.

There was also a small, nagging part of her that wanted to consider her options, before making any more wild decisions. Agnes's suggestion to stay had been tempting, and if Zain was planning to rat on her, he'd surely have done it by now. If she lived at the farmhouse and ran her own writing retreats, she'd barely have to see Zain. And perhaps she could even explain the awkward *Rachel* mistake to Agnes, now she'd proved she could do the job.

If nothing else, she should chat it through with her boss tomorrow, over that nice cup of tea. That would be the polite, sensible thing to do.

Rosie climbed the steps to her cabin, clutching the collection of ominous orange envelopes her sister had brought to the party, which Rosie was in no rush to deal with. At least she wouldn't have to share her hut with Agnes and her cats and dogs that evening, now part of the house was safe. The woman mumbled in her sleep, which was nearly as bad as the various snoring cats and her flatulent dog. Though maybe Agnes was still grabbing her stuff, as the light was on inside.

'Agnes?' Rosie called, as she pushed through the door. 'Whoa!' She dropped the collection of bright orange envelopes. They scattered to the floor. 'Who on earth are you?'

'I might ask you the same thing,' replied the older man. He was short and stout, with a ruddy face under his straw hat – and he was surely *not* meant to be in there. Though he was brandishing Agnes's toothbrush like it was a particularly scary weapon. Was he about to scrub Rosie to death?

'What business is it of yours?' Rosie stepped inside and put her hands on her hips, kicking the bothersome envelopes out of her way.

'Well, you're no more Rachel than I am a pumpkin sandwich.'

Rosie winced. This must be Farmer Wilbur – and she'd been terrified at the thought of him even before he'd made threats with a small brush.

'Erm. I can sort of explain.' Rosie edged her way around him. At least she'd be in snatching distance of the Colgate, if she had to bite back.

'Explain how you've been stringing along my dear friend for weeks? She'll be livid when I tell her. She doesn't like being played for a fool, our Agnes. I've been away on my holidays, and it turns out that flighty Rachel took a better-paid job and didn't mention it. Can't trust anyone these days. So what's your game, Missy?' He put the toothbrush in his not-so-clean-looking overall pocket. He must be there to collect Agnes's things. 'Are you trying to get money out of Agnes? Or steal her land?'

'No! Why would I do that? I love being here.' Rosie scratched her head. 'I mean, I did love being here. I worked hard for Agnes, and I helped to raise a whole lot of funds to save the farm tonight. Even if I didn't clear up the mistake about not being Rachel, surely I've proved my worth?'

He cocked his head. 'All that money. Planning to run off with it, were you? I see your bag's already packed.' He pointed to her holdall, which was still ready to go since she'd last started to flee.

'I am not that sort of person,' Rosie half-yelled.

There was a knock on the open door of the cabin. They both spun their heads to it.

'Are you Rosie?' The voice belonged to a blonde woman, who was a bit younger than Rosie and looked vaguely familiar. 'Oh, you did get my letters.' The woman pointed to the floor, where the orange envelopes were strewn. Rosie realised instantly that the woman was linked to yet another inconvenient truth that she'd been dodging. Her name was Bianca, and she was apparently her ex-fiancé James's other fiancée. Because why propose to one sucker when you could have two? 'It's just that you've got my late fiancé's stuff. I've been asking you to give it back for weeks, but you keep avoiding me. Why are you holding it hostage? Is it money you want?'

Rosie's shoulders dropped. Worst. Timing. Ever.

'So this doesn't look *great*.' Rosie put her hand on her forehead. Where did she start? Could she even be bothered? She checked her watch. It was nearly one a.m., and she was dog-tired. Tired of juggling fibs. Tired of having to prove herself. And bloody desperate to bury her head and sleep, quite frankly, with no one to disturb her. No awkward questions. No skeletons coming out of closets, or farmers waving toothbrushes, or women her late ex had been shagging turning up and demanding his stuff. Which she didn't even have, because it was still at her other ex-bloke's flat. The ex who preferred to have his end away with kinky hardware, rather than the one who used software to woo her. Just to be clear.

Rosie looked through the window, at the thought of him. And as if by annoying magic, there Zain was. Standing on the porch of his cabin with something under his arm. It looked a lot like his secret laptop. *I haven't consulted the chatbot in a long time.* Well, it didn't look like that was true.

If she stuck around, all Rosie could foresee was a night of unpicking lies and getting yelled at by Agnes. Maybe she'd want to sue her for trespassing. Were there laws against impersonating a person called Rachel? There ought to be.

That, or she'd have to fight off Wilbur with her toothpaste and try to hail a taxi with Bianca, who'd probably pull out more photos of the son James had apparently fathered, presumably while he was *working late*, but at some point before he was squashed by a cactus. She could have just about endured all that, if it wasn't for the complete shambles with Zain.

It was simply too much.

So she grabbed her holdall for the umpteenth time that autumn, together with a small torch that she'd probably get accused of pilfering, and hotfooted it out of there.

Zain seemed to have disappeared, which was just as well, because she had no energy for another slanging match. She legged it through the field, out of its gate and towards the farm's exit, with nobody likely to chase after her and beg her to stay. Not Agnes, not Zain. Not even Onions the dog, and he'd chase his own bottom for a bit of sport. Rosie Featherstone was leaving Autumn Meadows Farm, once and for all – and nobody cared enough to stop her. She knew she only had herself to blame.

'Even the rain can't be bothered with a decent send-off,' Rosie muttered, as she reached the end of the dirt track on her not so grand exodus.

In all the best novels, the weather came out in full force when a heroine dramatically fled. There would be great snows or storms. Thunder, lightning, hurricanes. All the clouds could muster for her was a bit of that spitty rain that made your hair frizzy.

Stop dreaming, Rosie, she chided. Even when she'd seen the chaos her wild imagination got her into, she was still doing it. When would she ever learn?

45

Going back to stay in the luxury of her family's Cheltenham townhouse ought to have been heavenly, compared to freezing outdoor showers and compost toilets where a spider might crawl across your backside. Yet, somehow, Rosie felt like she was festering in her own personal hell.

She spread out across the huge bed, feeling rubbish that she wasn't more grateful. Her mother had been lovely, and – with the help of staff – had made sure her old room was comfy, and that the kitchen was stocked with her favourite snacks. On paper, Rosie had more than a person could wish for. So why did her entire world feel dark, like a colony of bats was living on her head? She'd spent days here, sobbing to herself and scribbling angry doodles in her notebook. Doodles would have to do, now she'd resolved never to write again. The grim realisation that she could barely create a story without a chatbot having plotted it hit her again.

Rosie grabbed the box of tissues.

She hadn't heard from Agnes or Zain, although they didn't know where her parents lived, and neither of them had ever needed to know her phone number. She'd barely switched on her mobile at the farm, and she'd been living among them anyway.

But now, she wasn't. And she couldn't shake the feeling that living at Autumn Meadows and having *less* had felt like so much *more*.

She knew she would need to stop wallowing and get in touch with Agnes. Her phone was still hiding in a drawer. But the pumpkin farm retreats were starting in just a few days, not to mention the writing retreat weekend that Zain had single-handedly signed her up for. Agnes deserved fair notice to find a replacement. At least her old boss had the funds to fix the house and keep her animals safe, so Rosie wasn't leaving her completely in the lurch.

'Urgh.'

Her body felt heavy, knowing she was causing Agnes extra hassle. Rosie knew she should have got in touch before, but – like Farmer Wilbur had warned – Agnes would be 'livid' about Rosie misleading her for weeks, which Wilbur would surely have now divulged. Rosie had pretended to be a recommended expert, when she'd been no more than a woman on the run.

She pulled out her phone for the umpteenth time, toyed with it, and then threw it back in the drawer. It all felt too much.

And then there was Zain. She wanted to hate him, to feel outraged by his secret chatbotting and the mystery of his real surname, and to slam-dunk him into the cesspit of lying ex-boyfriends. Yet despite everything, she couldn't stop thinking about him – and she had no idea what to do about that.

The knock at her bedroom door made her flinch.

'Honestly, peeps. What are we going to do with Rosie Featherstone? Talk about wallowing in heartache. Shall we see if we can sort out her *#lifeproblems*?'

It was her sister Flick pushing through the door, her phone in front of her face.

'She's sad about this really hot guy she used to work with. Some of you might have seen pics of their *#PumpkinFarmKiss* that almost blew up the internet last weekend. Didn't they look cute together?'

'If you're livestreaming to your Insta fans, you can bugger off,' said Rosie, hiding her head behind a pillow and gulping at the thought of their impromptu launch-party kiss being ogled on social media. It had been an accident, for goodness' sake – even if the touch of his lips against hers had given her goosebumps.

'My followers care about you.' Flick pouted at her phone. She was in full show mode.

'They don't know me.'

'I've been telling them all about you. How great you are at writing. How you're the one with all the beauty and loveliness and talent.'

'Not true,' huffed Rosie.

'And how you never give yourself enough credit.'

Rosie sighed again.

'And how you hide from things,' said Flick, trying to snatch away the pillow.

'I do not.' Although obviously this wasn't the best example. Somehow being back at her parents' house and being stuck with her much younger half-sister had reduced her to her childish, teenage self.

Rosie sensed her sister moving away from the bed, towards the window. She knew how to find the best light.

'Ooh, lots of love in the comments for the pics of Autumn Meadows Farm. People are booking up for those retreats like they're on fire. Some are talking about your writing retreats too.'

'Well, I won't be running them,' Rosie muttered. 'I don't work there, and I don't write anymore.'

'Nooooo. Did you hear that? She's throwing away her talents because of a guy.'

'Am not,' Rosie bit back. Was she? 'Anyway, I told you to get lost. My life's not a bloody melodrama.'

'Look, she doesn't want to talk right now,' Flick told her adoring viewers. 'And we'll respect her privacy, right? But let me share one thing with you. Never hide from the truth, even if it scares you. Seek it out. Run after it. It might not always be what you expect, but it *will* be the thing you need. Let the truth set you free.'

Flick drummed up more likes and comments from her audience, before ending the livestream. She flung her phone onto the bed and flopped down next to Rosie.

'Let the truth set you free?' said Rosie, putting down the pillow and rolling her eyes. 'Seriously? I'm sure you sound more like an Instagram quote by the day.'

'What do you mean?' Flick replied, defensively. 'It's a thing. Anyway, I meant what I said about you not realising your talents. It wasn't just for the livestream hearts.'

'Whatever.'

'Stop being such a stroppy child and listen to good advice. For the intelligent one, you can be such a doofus.'

'Why, thanks.'

'Girl, you've been hiding in this bedroom for days – and quite frankly, it smells like a rotten farm. It's time for some tough love. When life gives you pumpkins, make pumpkin pie.'

'I'm sorry. What?'

'Rosie, you were in your element at Autumn Meadows – even when life was testing you. You were making things happen, rather than ducking behind the foliage. You were full of ideas;

you were finding yourself.' Flick was counting off reasons on her fingers and she was on a roll. 'You were writing your best ever novel. People are talking about you running writing retreats. Oh, and you and that Zain guy had the *hottest* chemistry. You two were ablaze.'

'Once.' Rosie sniffed. A lot had changed.

'And you're going to throw that away over a misunderstanding? Yes, what you told me about the Kimberkoo Chat stuff sounded tricky. But what if there's a simple explanation?'

Rosie pondered it – again. 'He was mad at me too, for snooping through his stuff and not being honest with him. Things are just too broken.'

'For God's sake, Sis. Words don't just belong in books. Sometimes it's OK to say things out loud. Now you've both had chance to cool off, maybe you should talk.'

Rosie shrugged and rolled over, her back to her sister. 'I'm tired. Can you give me a break?'

Flick jumped off the bed. 'I'll leave you alone, on one condition. I want you to write something. *Anything.* Because I know writing helps you to make sense of the world.' Flick was already setting up Rosie's laptop at the bureau by the window. 'It breaks my heart to see you throwing it all away. Don't let the chatbots win.'

Rosie sniffed. Perhaps her sister had a point, even if it did sound kooky.

Feeling a slight spark of something, Rosie moved to the laptop. 'Fine. But only because I want you to go away.'

'Understood,' said Flick, trying not to look smug. 'And if you're writing another novel, please cast me as the really awesome half-sister who saves the day.'

'I'm *not* writing another novel,' said Rosie. 'Just for the record.'

'Whatever.' Flick held up her hands and backed out of the room.

Rosie had no idea what she was about to write, but somehow her fingers were twitching again. Whether she wanted to hear it or not, it seemed her creative soul had something to say.

46

It was growing dark in Rosie's room. She'd been sitting at her laptop and hammering its keys for so long that her bum was undoubtably seat-shaped. She hadn't stopped to put on a light or take a break and her poor stomach was growling. But she didn't care. At last, she was deep inside a flow of words, and she had no intention of letting them disappear.

Although her heart felt heavy and the room filled with the melody of her sporadic sighs, as she typed, a world of revelations was opening – each one making her lighter.

If she'd once thought she could only write like magic in the peace and quiet of the pumpkin farm, that was no longer true. Even with her sister bounding up and down the stairs, her mum constantly nagging, the gardener mowing and the cleaner trying to polish every surface including her head, the words had kept on appearing. Like her whole body was under a spell, ideas fizzed and crackled, then shot through her tingling arms until they danced to life on the screen.

She didn't need candles or fairy lights, or an old-fashioned typewriter, or even a dark and handsome muse across the lake.

She was the creator. And from the romantic tale she'd begun to weave, she didn't need to steal ideas from her own love life either.

Rosie hadn't planned to start writing another novel. When she'd told herself *'never again'* she'd meant it. The number of years she'd been failing to write a suitably swoon-worthy story was too large to admit. *'Have you ever even been in love?'* incredulous publishers had asked. When she'd started falling for Zain, everything had felt different – like a new gateway had been unlocked. Then discovering that her best-ever manuscript had been unwittingly orchestrated by her nemesis Kimberkoo Chat had seemed like the death of everything.

Clearly her mind had other ideas.

She wasn't sure who these characters were, but they wouldn't stop speaking to her. They were filling her ears and spilling onto the page like they already knew the master plan. And surely *this* was what being a real writer was all about. *This* was the thing that couldn't be recreated by any AI chatbot. Because love stories came from real, beating hearts – not software.

Though somewhere deep in her subconscious, she felt the whisper of something else coming to life. When she wrote, it helped her to escape her troubles – and when her head wasn't obsessing, answers came.

'Oh my *gourd*. That's what I need to do.'

Rosie clicked open a fresh document and began to type. At last, the knot of problems was untangling itself. She had no idea if she could fix everything, or what others would say or do, or how they would feel. But the truth was finally rushing in.

Rosie had her own dreams to fight for. She didn't want to be *just* Rachel's stand-in or *just* Agnes's pumpkin retreat saviour, as much as she'd enjoyed those roles. Her soul was destined to write. And the opportunity that Zain had flung at her, which on the auction night had felt like throwing her under a bus, could be the stuff of dreams, if she dared. Something else was taking over her mind too.

She still had feelings for Zain.

Huge, ginormous ones that had grown arms and legs that had wrapped themselves around her and were threatening to squeeze the air from her lungs. Of course, there was no way she would let this be another Cassius or James situation, where she mentally hoovered up all traces of odd behaviour in the hope of a 'happy ever after'. Though her instinct screamed that she needed to do *something*.

Because like a Magic Eye picture that you couldn't unsee, Rosie couldn't *unfeel* this thing that had been growing inside her.

You deserve your own starring role, Rosie Featherstone, she'd typed on her screen. *Now GET OUT THERE. Face the awkward bits. Be honest. Embrace real life, exist outside the pages of a book... and don't be afraid to create your own, gloriously messy story – with or without pumpkins.*

Tears were falling as she read. The typed words were probably a jumble of things she'd subconsciously known – but they'd needed to spin dry in her mind before they came together, like neatly paired socks. Her thoughts were right. The best bookish protagonists got out there and faced things. They scaled walls or galloped off on horses or marched fearlessly across stormy moors. They allowed their lives to get wild and untamed, in pursuit of what they felt in their hearts.

Whatever the outcome, she was ready to try.

'Chicken noodles with cheese?' Her sister popped her head around the door, holding a bowl of something particularly smelly.

Flick barged in anyway, placing the bowl next to Rosie's

laptop and sinking into an armchair. As was customary, she was already pulling out her phone.

'Before you have a go at me and remind me to wash, I *am* going to do something about my *#lifeproblems*. I have a plan. Want to hear it?'

'Want to hear it? I want to be in it!' Flick sat up straight. 'Spill the news.'

Rosie's brow creased, imagining her sister begging to livestream Rosie's plight. She would be vetoing that – but there were a few things she needed help with.

As Rosie shared her game plan, her sister prodded her phone.

'You're not posting about this on your socials,' Rosie warned.

'Obviously,' said Flick, apparently tapping onto Instagram anyway. 'Promise I won't, but . . . wow. There are a lot of people sending you love and luck after my livestream earlier. Some of them seem to know you.'

Rosie snatched the phone from her sister. 'Let me see.'

As she scrolled, Rosie saw reams of supportive messages – many from total strangers, but some from friends past and present. Bonnie, Luna and the swim ladies begged her to get in touch. Even some of her old colleagues from KJ Marketing said the new chatbot software didn't write about tooth decay nearly as well as she did, nor did it buy tasty cakes.

Rosie had already decided she was ready to step up and stop hiding – but even superheroines needed a boost.

Then her eyes landed on the most recent comment. It was from a brand-new user, with no profile picture. *Zain K.* Just seeing his name sent her insides swirling. And when Rosie read his suggestion to talk, she knew it was time to get moving – whatever the outcome.

'Give me twenty minutes, then phase one of this plan is kicking off.'

Flick jumped up and gave a little hip wiggle. 'You know, you once laughed at me for having a 4x4, even though I would never get it muddy. But let me tell you, it's pretty spacious. I could fit several inanimate bodies in the back of that thing.'

'Good to know,' said Rosie. 'But we'll be leaving the deadlegs behind.'

47

The look on Cassius's face when he opened the door to the flat Rosie used to share with him in Cybourne Road was priceless. Of course, she could have used her old key card or even her Boots points card to waltz straight in. But no part of her wanted to witness a naked man getting jiggy with a robot, ever again.

'You're live on Instagram, so please do not swear. And I really hope you're not shagging androids this time, you big, geeky perv.' Flick's head popped up over Rosie's shoulder, her phone camera trained on Cassius's face.

Flick was absolutely not recording, but Rosie didn't care what he thought. They were simply there to get the rest of her stuff – a task she'd been hiding from for far too long. Among her things, there were personal items belonging to her late sort-of fiancé James. Those things needed a new home now too.

'What in the world . . . ?' Cassius held up his hand like he was avoiding the paparazzi.

'Which is pretty much what I said about your sexbot Zoe.' Rosie laughed, because she was past caring what her extremely ex-ex got up to. 'Don't worry, just grabbing what's mine. We won't ruin your love-in.' She could just imagine him cosying up with his synthetic girlfriend collection, showing them his boring tech magazines and pretending to feed them prawn crackers.

'There's no love-in, Rosie.' He reached over and batted away Flick's camera phone. 'Actually, I've missed you. I made a huge mistake with Zoe. She's no fun at all and I can't have an intelligent conversation with her.'

'Save the sob story,' said Flick, giving Rosie a gentle shove so that they both tumbled into the flat's hallway.

Cassius's eyes searched Rosie's face. They were wide and sad, and in times gone by, she might have felt sorry for him and agreed to hear him out. But Rosie two-point-zero wasn't giving him her time.

In fact, this swoop symbolised a great big, two-fingered salute to all of the past boyfriends who had less than measured up to what Rosie now knew she deserved. Dingo Dave and his collection of knicker-stuffed plush toys. That guy who'd been on *Crimewatch*. And of course, James, who she'd kept on a pedestal for far too long, even though she'd suspected for years that he'd been a two-timing dirtbag.

'Serena, do me a favour,' said Rosie, to Cassius's voice-activated virtual helper. 'Play Kelly Clarkson's "Since U Been Gone". I want to enjoy this.'

For once, AI Serena didn't even argue, or get her name wrong, accidentally-on-purpose. 'Sure, Rosie. We've missed you.'

As Kelly belted out song lyrics to the clamour of drums, Rosie swept around the flat with Flick, throwing things into their collection of bags.

They yelled along to the *so moving ons* and the *yeah, yeahs*, until they were having a lot more fun than Rosie would have thought was possible, for such a dire assignment.

In all honesty, Rosie didn't even like half of the things she was packing. She wasn't sure how the next stage of her life would look, but she hadn't missed her hair straighteners or other pointless gadgets.

'I'll send a van over for the rest,' she told Cassius, who was looking sorrowful in the corner. Rosie had had her moment of triumph, and she was keen to make one more house call, so she could start the next day feeling fresh.

'You don't have to leave me,' Cassius tried again, as though staying with someone who'd recently traded her in for a kinky sexbot was such a great option. 'You're welcome to stay.'

'Thanks, but no thanks, Cassius. I'd rather eat my own toenails.'

48

'I wish I'd been recording that. His face!'

Rosie and her sister were still laughing as they pushed the last of the bags into the back of Flick's Range Rover and flopped into the front seats, Operation Cassius conquered.

'Even he deserves his privacy,' Rosie replied. She was done with being unnecessarily nice to people who treated her badly, but what happened between a consenting adult and their rubber girlfriend was their business.

The next leg of their journey would be less fist-bumpingly triumphant, but it felt good to finally be confronting it – like a weight was already lifting. Rosie gave her sister the address, torn from the edge of the latest letter.

'Is this to do with those smelly orange envelopes that kept arriving for you?' Flick asked.

Rosie nodded. 'Yep.' She hadn't yet told her family the story, but as the wild woman on the pumpkin farm, she'd come to care so much less about being judged. And quite frankly, she had nothing to be ashamed of. 'Remember James?'

'The smarmy fiancé who kept dumping you and never gave

you a ring. Died in that freak cactus accident in Tucson, when he was meant to be at a business conference in Telford?'

'That's the guy.' Her sister had a nifty way of boiling things down to the size of an Instagram-worthy caption.

'Turns out that he was also engaged to another woman called Bianca. She was pregnant with his son when he died. I'd always suspected something but stupidly ignored it.'

Rosie explained about the watch James had suddenly acquired close to Father's Day, inscribed '*To Daddy*', which Bianca now said she'd bought for James as a present from their unborn son. When Rosie had noticed the inscription, James had made an unlikely excuse. As usual, Rosie had accepted it and had pretended everything was fine.

'I knew he was a dick,' Flick huffed.

'He wasn't always.' Rosie had the urge to put that small word in for him, seeing as he wasn't around to stick up for himself. Though that was all the praise she could muster.

Soon enough, they arrived outside the small newbuild where Bianca lived. It was gone nine p.m. She hadn't told Bianca she was coming in case she hadn't been able to get James's watch and small bag of belongings from Cassius – and quite honestly, Rosie didn't want to make a *thing* of it.

The handover was simple enough. Rosie apologised for how long it had taken her – because it had been hard to face the truth until she'd seen pictures of Bianca's son, looking just like James. And she *did* remember suspecting he was up to something, and then seeing pregnant Bianca at James's funeral, smelling like the perfume that had often strangely lingered on James's skin. The funeral had been organised by James's family, James having dumped Rosie *again* about a month before, and with-child Bianca still being a secret. And nobody knew who he might have been visiting in Tucson.

Bianca explained she hadn't known about Rosie either, until the later stages. She apologised for bursting in on Rosie after the launch party to ask for James's things. Her son now wanted them, and she hadn't known how else to get to Rosie. Despite everything, Rosie wished them both well.

Between the truths Rosie had perhaps always suspected and the way she'd come to feel about Zain, any attachment to James had long gone. He had never given her the kind of love she deserved.

But there was one man who had.

The following day, it would be time to find him.

49

Rosie gave her sister a hug and jumped out of the car. This was something she needed to face alone.

It had rained all morning, though Rosie had decided it was *not* a sign that the sky was spraying a hosepipe on her plans. It was simply a reminder to wear wellies. Or perhaps that it was time for rainbows.

As she paced down the dirt track towards Agnes's farmhouse, she could have sworn she saw a trace of one, hovering over the scaffolding around Agnes's roof, as though it ended right here at Autumn Meadows Farm. Unless that was its beginning. Rosie had no clue, but she was about to find out. It was time to put an end to her hiding, and the cobweb of half-truths she'd inadvertently woven. She'd let her own and other people's wings get caught up in them, and that didn't feel good.

Rosie passed the spot where she'd seen Zain on that first day, carrying a gigantic pumpkin on his back. One look from his woody brown eyes had made her want to write the best-ever love story, but all that had gone wrong somewhere. She hoped she'd have the chance to tell him he was so much more than a muse.

'Rosie.' Agnes's face was a mix of things when she opened the door.

Surprise. Confusion. Was Rosie about to get the rollicking of her life?

'Where the dickens have you been?'

Rosie gulped and followed Agnes's insistent beckoning inside. She paced behind her into the kitchen, where everything looked much the same, other than Agnes's dusty old computer, which was now in the corner. She guessed Agnes had been checking on retreat bookings since Rosie hadn't been there.

The usual welcome committee of cats wove themselves around Rosie's legs. Dogs barked and a hen clucked across the kitchen. It reminded her of that first surreal day when she'd arrived like another waif and stray for the collection – only this time she wasn't going to pretend to be someone she wasn't.

'Firstly, I came to apologise,' said Rosie, before she could bottle it. She was pretty sure Wilbur would have filled her in, but Agnes deserved a proper explanation, and the chance to reprimand her. 'For not being Rachel.'

Agnes had been busy putting a kettle of water on the stove, as if she knew this was time for hot, sweet tea. Rosie held her breath, wondering whether Agnes would put out one mug, or two.

Instead, Agnes turned and scratched her head, her brow creasing.

'When I arrived here that day, I had no clue about any interview, and I certainly wasn't a retreat expert. I was looking for a phone because my car had broken down. I'd just lost my job to a chatbot and my boyfriend to a sexbot, and I didn't have a place to call home. But somehow the more I saw of this farm, the more difficult it became to extricate myself from the misunderstanding. I'm so sorry that I lied to you for so long.'

'You strange girl.' Agnes shook her head.

Rosie exhaled, trying not to take it personally. Perhaps it was fair enough. But she was determined to continue.

'Secondly, you may think this is cheeky. Feel free to say no, or to ring the police to escort me off the premises. But I would really, really love to work here again and to try running those writing retreats, as well as all things pumpkin, if I'm allowed near them. I can't remember a time when I've been happier than when I was here.' Rosie stopped to read Agnes's expression. 'You still think I'm strange, don't you?'

'Well, yes,' said Agnes, matter-of-factly. 'I mean, firstly, why would I want you to be Rachel? God knows who she was, but she certainly wasn't the sort of person who turned up to job interviews. There's no way she could ever have had a patch on you, you big nitwit.'

'R...really?'

Agnes pulled two chipped mugs from a cupboard and clonked them onto the worktop next to her collection of knobbly pumpkins, before putting her hands on her hips like she wasn't taking any crap.

'Rosie, you saved me and these animals from a fate worse than vagabondage. You raised enough money so we can stay in our home, and so I don't need to sell off the farm to those three buffoons in suits. We've even got enough spare cash to make the place more of a rescue sanctuary. I've got two abandoned pygmy goats and a llama arriving next week.'

Rosie felt her eyes getting heavy with the threat of tears, even if she wasn't quite sure where Agnes would keep a llama.

'And ruddy Nora,' Agnes continued. 'You've done a brilliant job of helping turn the place into a pumpkin retreat paradise. Spaces are being snapped up like Ed Sheeran tickets, and folk are already demanding more dates for writing retreats – with *you*. So yes, you'd better have your job back. I'll be bloody miffed if you don't.'

Rosie gulped back the emotion that was rising. Her heart belonged here, writing, hosting, coming up with new retreat plans for every season. Starry nights and pumpkin fields. Friendship, laughter, love . . . So much love.

'But first, I need to clear things with Zain.' Things wouldn't feel right if he didn't want her around. As homely as Agnes's house would be when the roof was fixed, Rosie longed to be back in her hut near the lake. Near *him*.

Agnes pushed aside Rosie's mug and poured her tea into a Thermos flask. Some parts of this visit were feeling like a déjà vu – although Rosie had no idea of the ending. 'Then it's time to go. Chop chop. Not a moment to waste.'

With that, Agnes was thrusting the flask into Rosie's hand and bustling her out of the back door. Only this time, Rosie was going alone.

50

'You know, when I first saw those things lined up in there, I thought you were living with a bunch of gnomes.'

Zain put his hammer down and looked up, shielding his eyes against the late-morning sun. He was sitting on the decking outside his cabin, surrounded by a new batch of partly built bat boxes. When he managed to focus on Rosie, he jumped up and took a step towards her, then cleared his throat and stepped back again.

'Erm, hi.' He wiped his forehead with the back of his hand, in a way she would *definitely* have pinched for her romance novel, just a week or so previously.

'Hot work, making gnome houses?' she teased, putting down her flask of tea.

'They're not . . .' He waved his hand, seeming stuck for words.

Rosie smiled. 'I know.'

'You see why I'm better with a script?'

She noticed his slight wince, as though he wasn't sure that was a thing to joke about. But the truth was, she *loved* him like this. His vulnerability was the sweetest contrast against his rugged exterior, and she didn't want him to ever have to pretend to be anything different. In fact, his exterior was looking particularly fetching, in a tight white T-shirt that did everything to remind her of the firm torso she'd once lain her head on. Though she wasn't here to ogle or take notes.

'Not that I've consulted the chatbot for a long time,' he said quickly. 'I only experimented with it in the early days of liking you, when I had no idea how to be around you. I even sold my laptop that night, just after the auction, to raise more funds.'

So that's where he'd been going with it after the party.

'You don't need a script, Zain. You never did.'

He took a moment to think about it, then sighed. 'You see, the real me only has two settings. There's gruff pumpkin farmer mode, which is handy when I want people to leave me alone. Then there's the version who turns weird when he likes someone and starts rambling on about bats or the key characteristics of a Baby Boo pumpkin.'

Rosie thought back to the time she'd bumped into him in a meadow, not long after she'd arrived, when he'd got overly animated on pumpkin facts, before looking mortified. And their impromptu bat-spotting night, when he'd admonished himself for being a nature geek, even though she'd adored every moment. She instinctively *knew* all of that was from his heart, not a laptop screen.

'You have no idea how much I love that side of you,' she said, hoping her eyes conveyed how much she meant it.

'Really? I mean, it's not very macho, is it? Not the kind of thing any romance lover would go weak at the knees for.'

'Oh, I'm pretty sure you can do macho without a script.' Her lips were twitching into a smile. 'Unless you somehow orchestrated that time I walked in on you naked in the outdoor shower?'

'No! No way. I mean, you can check through my emails, or the printouts, or anything . . .' He pointed to a pile of logs, which had been dumped like they were ready to burn, wadges of paper stuffed among them.

'I mean, if that was acting, you deserve an Oscar.'

The way his neck was flushing red was definitely genuine.

'You don't need a chatbot to make you interesting or lovable, Zain. I fell for you long before the so-called "perfect" dates. And my favourite parts were always when you seemed off-guard, or you stumbled over your words or what to do. Now I know those parts were *you*, without instructions.'

He pushed a hand through his long black hair, which was sort of tied back in a knot but mostly flopping everywhere – just how she liked it. 'You preferred the messy bits?'

'Always. That's how life is meant to be, isn't it? Kind of untamed.'

'Huh. I guess. It's just . . .' He looked upwards and exhaled, before fixing his gaze on hers. Those deep, woody eyes had become her place. 'Nobody's ever wanted or accepted either of those versions of me. Not the gruff one, and definitely not the nature freak. Not that I let that one out much. I don't want to go on about my earlier years, but you know how that went. I rarely found a family who wanted me to stick around. Not even the ones who were related to me. And the occasional time I did . . .' He pinched the bridge of his nose and shook his head.

She wanted to close the gap between them and hold him. She longed to tell him that everything would be OK, and that she was here to love him always. But he still had some explaining to do, and so did she. She wasn't going to pretend everything was OK, just to keep him, because she was no longer *that* person.

'Zain, what's the connection between you and the chatbot

that *you know* lost me my job?' She'd since googled Kimberkoo, and it was not a popular surname.

'*Urgh.* Stupidly, I didn't even know Kimberkoo Chat was a thing, until you'd mentioned it. Us hermits don't tend to keep up with the news.'

Rosie could tell the light humour was to deflect his nerves.

'But back when I was a lonely kid in care, it wasn't just nature I was geeky about. The nature bit came later, with Pru and Dennis. Before that, I was a . . . *tech nerd.*' He winced. 'It feels like a different life. With a whole lot of lonely hours in my bedroom, I came up with an early, pretty crappy version of a chatbot, just for something to talk to. I mean, I was clearly no good at making human friends.'

'You? You created Kimberkoo Chat?' Rosie's face sank, almost as quickly as her heart.

'No, no.' He stepped forward and placed his hand on her arm. 'Not the version you know now, with all the bells and whistles. I had no idea it would end up writing novels and planning dates for losers.' He gave her an awkward smile. 'And though I'm sure it does worthwhile things too, I wasn't responsible for letting it loose on the world. I had no idea that had happened. That was my estranged father, all the way across the other side of the world.'

'I thought you barely knew him?'

'I didn't, much.' His face crumpled. 'I should have explained, but it's a raw subject. I hadn't known him as a kid. I'd always had dumb dreams of the father–son long-lost reunion thing, and getting to know my roots. So when I was eighteen, I flew to Montana to track him down. I found the rest of his family first. His brothers, sisters, my grandmother. They were good people, and they ran a pumpkin farm, with real history. They welcomed me in. That's where I got the rare seeds from, and that's when I began to fall for their way of life. To feel connected to something.' He'd begun smiling, but it faded. 'When I did find my father, he didn't have much to do with his farming family anymore, and he didn't show much interest in me – until I mentioned this clunky software thing I'd invented. I was trying to sound cool and get his approval. I wanted him to like me, to think I was worthy of his attention . . .' He rubbed a hand over his face. 'Pretty needy, hey?'

'No,' said Rosie, firmly. 'Please don't think that.' She gestured him to go on.

'Well, it did get his interest. More than I did, it seems. He pretended like he didn't believe me, so that I was quickly laying out the tech and trying to prove myself. Anyway, we had a big argument, which he probably engineered. It worked. I fled, leaving everything I'd created. I was more interested in working on the land by then, anyway.' He shrugged. 'This was years ago. I guess he's been improving what I left him with. I had no idea he'd unleashed it onto the world, until you said the name. It's true that I'd barely used tech since then. Until this.' He waved an arm towards the would-be bonfire. 'And look where that got me. Rosie, I'm so sorry.'

His eyes locked with hers. 'I'd only meant to check out this chatbot and see what he'd made of it. I was curious. So I bought an old laptop and found a pub with Wi-Fi. I didn't intend for the thing to plan our dates. It started as a *what-if*. Then suddenly, the software seemed more interesting than me. I just wanted to sweep you off your feet, like you deserve to be. I never *ever* meant for you to feel tricked. I clung to those stupid instructions at first, because I was out of my depth. But the way I feel about you was never scripted. *I love you*. I'll never need a script for those words.'

Her once sinking heart soared.

'And your love was *always* enough. You are enough, Zain Kimberkoo. Exactly as you are.' Rosie stepped towards him and took his face in her hands. 'And I'm so sorry for all the things I wasn't truthful about. I was going to tell you I wasn't the real interviewee for this job – it just never seemed like a good time.'

'Hey, if Agnes doesn't mind.' He shrugged.

'And I shouldn't have turned our relationship into a romantic story. I didn't plan to. I just started typing and couldn't stop. I would *never* have shown it to anyone without your say-so. Anyway, you can have it for your bonfire. You're right that I should create my own stories, not copy our chatbot-inspired dates. I'm writing something new.'

'Don't you dare burn it – it was incredible. Well, the bits I saw of it, before I realised naked Cain was me, and got self-conscious. I over-reacted, and I'm sorry. Thanks for the generous description, by the way.' He gave her a shy nod, his hair flopping across his face. It was both hot and adorable.

'Oh God, I should have thought more about your privacy. It's almost like painting you in the nude without asking.' Rosie hid her own face behind her hand. 'Though I would have edited those bits out.'

Zain gently removed her hand and held it in his. 'No more hiding.'

Rosie nodded. He was right about that.

'And I honestly don't mind if you want to use me in your work, now I'm used to the idea. I'm pretty honoured you find me interesting enough.'

'Oh, you made a fascinating muse.'

'Tell me more.'

Zain squeezed her hand and guided her away from his cabin, towards the lake. The sunlight shimmered across its water, giving it the magnetic pull she'd come to know and love. The day was warming up, and Rosie couldn't help thinking about stripping off to jump into it, preferably with a certain pumpkin farmer. But they had talking to do.

'I'm not sure what a muse does,' Zain said, as they walked across the grass. 'But I know being with you has brought me back to life. Before you came here, I'd given up on people. I was hanging out with a hairless cat, obsessing over the ultimate knobbly fruit and shutting out every chance of being happy. I was just *existing*. Usually, quite grumpily.'

Rosie laughed.

'You didn't look like you belonged here one bit,' he continued. 'With your fancy beige coat and those heeled boots that slid around in the mud. Steve and I had a bet on, and I gave it two days, max, before you'd be calling a taxi. But I guess I didn't know what you were made of. You climbed on roofs and made bug houses. You forged ever more ridiculous plans. And you didn't let anything faze you. Before I knew it, you'd set up a damned treehouse in my heart.'

They reached the edge of the lake, and he turned to look at her, his eyes heavy with the weight of everything he was trying to say.

'You showed me that people *can* be good, Rosie. I need more of you in my life.'

He held her face and tilted it tenderly towards his. The touch of his skin against hers, the intensity of his gaze, the pull of her heart as it dragged her towards him. It was the stuff of a million romantic novels, and it didn't need a script.

A light autumn breeze swept around them, bringing birdsong and a few damp leaves, and the sweet smell of harvest. Rosie felt as if she could belong here forever, with this man. She felt almost complete. The only thing missing was his smile.

'You made a bet . . . *with a cat*?' Rosie could barely keep the giggle from her voice.

And finally, he beamed back at her, with a richness that reached his eyes and seemed to set them alight. 'I pour my heart out – which was completely unscripted, by the way. And the main thing you take from that is my bet with Steve? Yes, OK. My best friend used to be a cat. I told you I was different.'

They stood grinning at each other, like being different was the best thing ever.

At last, their lips met, somewhere in the middle, and Rosie felt so light she could almost float. His kiss was soft and warm, laced with the promise of all that would come. It was the perfect welcome home, as though she'd always belonged with him, and everything before had been a journey to be right here. Held and loved. Safe in his arms and giving him shelter too. Nothing could have made her happier.

51

'Woo hooooo! Rosie Featherstone is *back*.'

When Rosie had thought she couldn't be happier, she'd clearly forgotten the love and effervescing joy of her new friends. And suddenly, they were making it their business to remind her.

The first voice had been Luna's. She was legging it across the grass towards Rosie and Zain, who'd been lost in the depths of the best-ever kiss. Behind Luna was her girlfriend Ellen, who was laughing gleefully and pushing a wheelbarrow containing goodness knew what.

Bonnie wasn't far behind them, her long boho skirts billowing, her arm waving what looked like a bottle of pumpkin fizz, which would now be considerably fizzier. And at the back were Mags and Agnes. Mags was carrying her new ginger cat in a sling, and Agnes was marching in her frog-eyed wellies, Onions the dog barking around her. Rosie had no idea what they were doing, or how Agnes had become part of the ensemble.

'Sorry to interrupt the hot action.' Luna panted as she arrived next to them, pink hair and piercings glinting in the sun. She gave them a wink.

'Blame me,' said Mags, as the rest of the group gathered. 'I put Agnes on strict instructions to let us know the second you arrived back.'

'Because we knew you would,' said Bonnie, giving Rosie a squeeze.

'I sent them a message on Instagram,' said Agnes, looking pleased with herself. 'I've been following that sister of yours, and her livestream whatchamacallits. *#LetTheTruthSetYouFree!*' She clapped her hands.

So that's what the computer in Agnes's kitchen was all about.

'I'm more of a *#PumpkinFarmKiss* fan myself,' said Luna. 'And we just got front-row seats to the live-action show.' She gave a celebratory, arm-wavy dance, in the carefree way Rosie had come to love her for. Ellen too, judging by the way she bounced over and sprang a kiss on Luna's cheek.

'Honestly, it's so great to see you all.' Rosie hadn't realised just how much she'd missed them, until she'd seen them careering across the grass. 'But what are you doing here?'

'Making sure you don't escape again.' Luna shrugged as though it was perfectly obvious.

'You're free to make your own choices, love,' Bonnie clarified.

'But if you're staying, Bonnie's brought the fizz,' said Mags.

'I've got the glasses.' Agnes clonked the box down so firmly, Rosie prayed they were shatterproof. 'And I didn't lug them all this way for nothing.'

Rosie looked at Zain, who was smiling at her friends' antics in a way that told her he did quite like people. The possibility that they could continue to grow these friendships, with Zain too, made her heart swell. Although maybe she should check that.

'What are your thoughts about me coming back?' Rosie asked Zain. 'I mean, you were here first, and maybe you don't want me living here again so soon, or perhaps we should talk about this in private...'

Zain stepped in and put a playful finger to her lips. 'As much as I love your voice, I'm not letting you talk yourself into leaving. Of course I want you back here. I want nothing more than to see you striding around the place, leaving wildflowers in the toilet hut and decorating the meadows with leaf-shaped bunting, like trees don't have enough foliage.' He grinned. 'Towels folded into the shape of winter squash, pumpkin-spiced everything, your quirky family of friends.' He gave them a wink. 'I'd be made up if you'd stay.'

'Even if I was running writing retreats too?'

'Knew you'd be hot for the idea.' He winked at her. 'I'm your resident muse.'

Bonnie cheered and popped open her bottle, most of it spraying everywhere.

'Talking of writing retreats,' said Ellen, stepping forward with her wheelbarrow, which Rosie now saw was filled with old-fashioned typewriters. They'd been carefully cushioned with dustsheets, and the sight of them filled Rosie with joy. 'Can you make use of these?'

'Yes!' said Rosie, crouching down to touch them. 'They're beautiful.'

'Looks like I'll need to heft some logs over and start making writing desks,' said Zain.

Rosie was loving the sound of this already. 'Now I'll need to round up more guests.'

'I've made a waiting list,' said Agnes, who clearly never took no for an answer. 'I knew you'd see sense. Frogs only jump forwards.' She gave her frog-eyed boots a nod. 'Not backwards. And you, Rosie F, belong perfectly here.'

She would raise her glass to that.

For the next couple of hours, they sat around chatting, Rosie fetching picnic blankets, Zain bringing pumpkin bread and whatever he could find in his fridge. Bonnie emptied out her basket, which always harboured a selection of treats.

Ellen had brought a copy of the local paper, which had run a story about the Cyber Purrz directors having a fall-out. There was word of the robot cat company dissolving. Rosie didn't want to wish bad luck on The Three Tuxedos, but she kind of hoped it was true.

Mags shared that she was going to help Agnes with her new, improved animal sanctuary. In the meantime, Agnes was going ahead with the best quote for the building work and no doubt had a hard hat so she could keep the builders in check. And both Agnes and Mags had been reading up on llamas.

Bonnie had been on her wine and dine date with Theodore, who'd been the highest bidder at the pumpkin farm's opening party auction, to Bonnie's delight. They'd had the best time and were planning to meet again, this time without Luna spying on them from the next table in case Theo was an axe-wielding outlaw.

'We should keep ourselves busy too, Luna,' said Ellen. 'Maybe we could start a family.'

Luna's eyes bulged. 'Erm . . .'

'A fur baby, I mean.' Ellen leaned over and gave Mags's kitten Orangeade a fuss. 'Obviously. Ever fancied a rescue cat?'

Luna exhaled a slow breath. 'I'm more of a dog person. But yeah, I'm up for a pet. As long as you don't want one of those robotic things.'

They all pulled faces at that.

Rosie could already tell she was going to relish watching her new friends taking charge of their next chapters and being a part of hers too.

When the others were busy talking, Zain had something else to confide. After Rosie had fled, he'd got in touch with his father about Kimberkoo Chat.

'I couldn't believe it when the stingy git offered me money for my early input with the chatbot. I told him to get stuffed if he was hoping for a big reunion, to boost his PR. But I did accept a payout, in lieu of me suing his arse. I got him to send it to Agnes, for the farm and retreats. Those treehouses will need better heating for the winter, and I could expand my speciality pumpkin patches, and maybe throw up a shack for people to buy produce.' He shrugged. 'I guess money isn't always bad news.'

'Wow,' said Rosie. 'Great ideas. Would you have sued him?'

'Nah. Too much hassle, and what would I need with even more cash? Everything I want is right here.' He squeezed her hand, his touch setting off a million fireworks.

And then it was time for her to explain what she'd been doing since she last saw him. They laughed about her triumphant raid on Cassius's place, and when it came to the tale of James's stuff he was surprisingly understanding, to say she'd once sort-of compared Zain to James in the manuscript Zain had found. They agreed that all of that was history.

Soon enough, their friends began leaving, and it was back to being just her and Zain, taking a stroll around the pumpkin fields, exactly as she'd been dreaming of. She hadn't been sure how her heart-to-heart with Zain would go. She hadn't tried to write it in her head, and she knew he would never again be scripting his part. But it had turned out just perfectly – as life often did when you let it.

As the sun went down, casting a kaleidoscope of colours across the sky, they curled their bodies together on a blanket among the vines, next to the warmth of a camping heater, by the light of a pumpkin lantern that had been carved with a smile.

Their lips met, moving lazily in another kiss that Rosie wished would last forever. They knew they would have peace here now. No guests were due for another few days, and Agnes would be back at the house. They had the Prizewinner pumpkin patch to themselves.

She'd already shared her deepest pumpkin field fantasies with him. But right then, all she wanted was to lie next to him, wrapped in his arms. Flesh touching, bodies snuggled under a pile of discarded clothes, feeling the warmth of his breath, the rise and fall of his intricately patterned chest. Running her fingers across the map of him.

Rosie had always been an autumn girl at heart. Pumpkin-spiced lattes, cosy blankets, writing by candlelight. But she knew now that she'd never experienced the true joy of it until she'd found this place and this incredible, multilayered man, who had set her world alight. He'd shown her what true, head-over-heels love felt like. She never wanted this real-life fantasy to end.

52

Rosie finished the chapter she was typing and gave a happy sigh. She was back in the writing nook inside her log cabin at Autumn Meadows, and everything felt glorious. She'd spent the night in Zain's cabin, as she often had in the week since she'd returned. With her words written and her pumpkin-spiced hot chocolate finished, it was time for some fresh air. Her mind and body needed it, especially with her first writing retreat weekend starting in just a few days.

She stood up and stretched herself.

Working on her latest story was a joy, and she knew this one had something special. It was flowing with all the same magic as before, but this time the plot and characters were from her own imagination. Much like with real life, she didn't know exactly how the story would end. Perhaps that was part of the enchantment. There would be ups and downs, and bumps in the road. Her characters would change and grow and become so much stronger. And she knew that hand in hand, they would reach their happy ever after. Everyone deserved a chance at that.

Tap, tap, tap.

'Rosie.'

It was Zain's voice at the door. She wasn't sure if she'd ever stop smiling to be back in his world, and to have him back in hers. He lit her up.

'Can you, erm, come out here? I have a surprise.'

He sounded nervous, as he did at times, when something was important to him, or he didn't quite have the words. She loved that about him.

'Of course,' she replied.

She grabbed a coat, the late October temperatures growing cooler now. Soon enough it would be weather for mittens and bobble hats and blowing clouds of foggy breath. She had a feeling she would embrace and find happiness in every season here.

Rosie opened the door, expecting to see Zain. Instead, she found a large Cinderella pumpkin with a note attached. It was handwritten, in Zain's writing. Her heart always filled when she saw his words. She read it:

Follow the trail. We're going on a date. (Promise I made this one up myself. Might not be that good.) Zain. X

Rosie laughed, knowing that everything they did together was good – even the mundane bits, like sorting out the compost toilet. Though she hoped their date wasn't that.

She looked up to see a trail of small pumpkins, leading out of the field and beyond. Well, it looked like she'd be off on an adventure. She'd better bring her wellies.

As Zain's note had instructed, Rosie followed the line of miniature pumpkins, the names and stats of which she was coming to know. Zain's quirky passions fascinated her. She greeted them like old friends as she walked. Jack be Little, the smallest of the bunch. Munchkin, looks cute in a decorative basket. Baby Bear, tastes delicious in a pie.

Once she'd passed the orange glow of the pumpkin patches, she was at the dirt-track exit from Autumn Meadows Farm. Following the last tiny gourd, she rounded the corner to find Zain. He was sitting in the cab of the tractor that he now used for hayrides, though it wasn't hooked up to the trailer of hay. The cab was decorated with the leaf bunting Rosie had made for retreats, and bunches of autumn wildflowers. He'd taught her the names of some of those too.

Hearing her surprised laugh, Zain turned to look at her, and then jumped down, running a nervous hand through his hair before putting both in his pockets and then taking them out again, as if he'd forgotten what appendages were for.

'Fancy a date?' He swept an arm towards the tractor. 'Nothing elaborate this time. No starry picnics on the lake, or whatever. Just a normal, let's go on a date, kind of date. Thought I should prove I can manage that, without a chatbot.' He winked at her, then looked unsure whether he should have mentioned the 'c' word.

'Just a normal date?' Rosie teased, nodding at the tractor.

Zain shrugged. 'Well, a normal date for a gruff pumpkin farmer.'

'Where are we going?'

He scratched the back of his neck. 'This is where it gets a bit sketchy. I don't get out of my pumpkin patches much, other than for farming stuff. Maybe a country pub? Pie, chips, one of those log fires that crackles and spits out dangerous red sparks that burn the carpet.'

'You had me at pumpkin patch.' If she'd been describing

herself like a character from one of her novels right then, she'd say her eyes were twinkling.

He breathed a sigh of relief, stepping towards her. 'I'll even shout you pudding. They do a mean apple crumble.'

She bounced towards him, putting her arms around his neck and kissing the tip of his nose. 'Perfect. And when we get back, will you show me your Prizewinners?' She raised an innocent eyebrow.

'Always.'

Then he kissed her.

Slowly and softly, as though trying to show just how much he meant it. And she knew that like all good stories, theirs may have ups and downs too. Bumps in the road. Changing, growing, getting stronger. But now they had each other – and together, they would keep stepping. Because everyone deserved their chance of a happy ever after.

~ The End ~

A LETTER FROM ANITA FAULKNER

Dear Wonderful Reader

I'm right here doing happy star jumps that you chose to read *You Had Me at Pumpkin Patch*. I had SO much fun playing with these characters (and throwing lots of pumpkin-themed trouble at them!) I hope some of that joy and well-meant mischief comes through on the page.

The setting was inspired by various places I love in the Cotswolds, brought together in a glorious mishmash (with added speciality squash!) Autumn will always be my favourite season, and I had the best time basking in its glow.

In the name of research, I dipped (precariously) in cold lakes and stroked many pumpkins. Unfortunately, I did not have the chance to burst in on any naked men in outdoor showers. (Let me know if you see Zain on your travels.) You may spot quirky bits of me in Rosie, and I hope I grow up to be half as bolshie as Agnes.

If you've read my previous romcoms (*A Colourful Country Escape* and *The Gingerbread Café*) you may have noticed familiar names popping up in this novel. I put those in as an extra treat, especially for you. Thank you for staying with me on this wild and fantastic journey.

It's a joy when lovely readers like you take a moment to leave a review. Writing novels can be a little lonely (apart from all the imaginary friends!) So knowing that our stories are being read and enjoyed means the world. We need your kind words.

When I'm not hanging out with my characters and dreaming up happy ever afters, I love getting to know more bookish people like you. If you're a reader, author, budding writer (whoop!) or a generally lovely human, please do come and find me. I'm excited to meet you...

Love

Anita. Xxs

Here are my favourite places to share good fun and gossip with you. Jump in!

My Facebook group, Chick Lit and Prosecco:
https://www.facebook.com/groups/chicklitandprosecco/
My author mailing list:
https://bit.ly/anitafaulknerhotnews
My Instagram:
https://www.instagram.com/anita_faulkner_writer/

ACKNOWLEDGMENTS

Where do I begin?!

OK, I'll start with a little secret. Writing the acknowledgements is the scariest part! That's because there are so many people to thank for their hard work, loveliness and never-ending support – and I don't want to miss out a single person. You ALL deserve some sparkle!

If you're reading this and you've taken time to cosy up with *You Had Me at Pumpkin Patch* – THANK YOU. I have absolutely loved writing this story and I'm so grateful that you're right here, embracing the autumn antics.

Big thanks to my brilliant and patient agent, Kate Nash. Without you, this story wouldn't have its fabulous pumpkin theme. Your inspired thought brought this tale to life! I'm so grateful for your bright ideas and generosity with your time.

I'm also super grateful to my incredible editor Georgina Green for believing in this story and sharing the perfect ideas to make it pop. You're a joy to work with and I'm hugely indebted to you and the teams at HQ Digital and Harper Collins. You all work tirelessly to bring authors' dreams to life and we can't thank you enough.

Thank you to copy editor Helena Newton for your eagle eye and fantastic feedback too!

I couldn't do any of this without my own hot hero and husband, Neil. Thank you for inspiring me, keeping me alive and smiling, and being THE person of my happy ever afters.

There will never be enough words to describe how grateful I am to have found you and 'put a ring on it'.

A big shout out to my small person, Luca. Thank you for handing out the biscuits at my book launches (and for not stealing *all* of them). And thank you for putting up with a mum who lives in a dream world. You're brilliant and creative, and I know we'll see your stories on bookshelves one day too.

Thank you to my mum for bringing me up with the sense of belief that anything is possible. And thanks for shouting about my books to your friends at tai chi and the garden centre, and for traipsing around after me through *allllll* the book events! You're my one-woman entourage.

Huge thanks to my friends and family for always being ready with your pompoms to cheer me on, rock up at my book signings, and for so graciously eating the bookish cupcakes! It would take too long to name you all, but you know who you are. (Sneaky shout out to Carrie, who insists everyone must check out my books – and then hovers menacingly over their shoulders until they've bought them!)

To my online book friends – thank you for lighting the way. Your kindness, cheerleading, reviews and quirky book photos are *everything*. Extra thanks to all of the gorgeous Facebook groups, especially my soul people in Chick Lit and Prosecco. (If you're reading this and you haven't joined us yet, come and find us!) I also love the support in The Friendly Book Community, Jenny Colgan and More Great Books, Riveting Reads and Vintage Vibes...and so many more.

An extra *yaaaay* to the authors and budding authors in my fiction writers' membership, Writers' Dream House. It's wonderful to have your daily support and accountability, and to help you to bloom and grow too. If you're not yet published, you will be! And I can't wait to celebrate with you.

Massive thanks to the bookshops and libraries that support authors and stock our books. A special wave to Gloucestershire Libraries, Waterstones Gloucester, The Cleeve Bookshop in Cheltenham, Alison's Bookshop in Tewkesbury and Rossiter Books in Cheltenham. People who celebrate books are my kind of people.

Bonus joy and sparkles for the world of book bloggers – who are like bookish royalty! And enormous thanks to the people who show up daily on social media to support authors, for the sheer love of stories. (Meena Kumari, Grace Power and Sue Baker – to name a few!)

Sending a lovely shout-out to Christina and Gloucester Book Club – you're all fabulous!

Thank you to the Romantic Novelists' Association and their New Writers' Scheme, for being the springboard for my writing career. (If you write love stories or you aspire to, please check them out.)

To my author friends – just wow. Thank you for inspiring me with your page-turning stories, kind words, positive reviews and boundless beautiful energy. There's not enough ink to shout out all of you! But I can honestly say there's no better place to be than the land of authors, books and stories. And if you've read this far, thank you again.

Do come and join us in the Chick Lit and Prosecco Facebook group for readers and writers – where more fun and friendship awaits...

https://www.facebook.com/groups/chicklitandprosecco/

Dear Reader,

We hope you enjoyed reading this book. If you did, we'd be so appreciative if you left a review. It really helps us and the author to bring more books like this to you.

Here at HQ Digital we are dedicated to publishing fiction that will keep you turning the pages into the early hours. Don't want to miss a thing? To find out more about our books, promotions, discover exclusive content and enter competitions you can keep in touch in the following ways:

JOIN OUR COMMUNITY:

Sign up to our new email newsletter: http://smarturl.it/SignUpHQ

Read our new blog www.hqstories.co.uk

X: https://twitter.com/HQStories

Facebook: www.facebook.com/HQStories

BUDDING WRITER?

We're also looking for authors to join the HQ Digital family! Find out more here:

https://www.hqstories.co.uk/want-to-write-for-us/

Thanks for reading, from the HQ Digital team